FAIRYTALE RIOT

The Clarion Call, Vol. 4
An Agorist Writers Workshop Anthology

Edited by:
Jon Garett & Genesis Mickel

With stories by:
Marie Anderson
Allen Baird
Andrew Bundy
Alexandra Faye Carcich
Christine Cassello
Christa Conklin
Jackie Ferris
Justin Fowler
Lynne Lumsden Green
Justine Johnston Hemmestad
Blake Jessop
Keturah Lamb
G. R. Lyons
Lela Markham
Skian McGuire
DonnaRae Menard
Cameron Metrejean
Genesis Mickel
Jakob Morris
John M. Olsen
Karen Over
Robina Rader
Cara Schulz
Billie Holladay Skelley
Ronel Janse van Vuuren
N. B. Williams
Patricia Worth

The Clarion Call, Vol. 4: FairyTale Riot
The Agorist Writers' Workshop

Published by
Very Good Books
www.vegobo.com

Cover design by Matthew Lewis
& Genesis Mickel

This volume is an official release and copy of The Clarion Call, Vol 4: FairyTale Riot, by the Agorist Writers' Workshop, published by Very Good Books. All proceeds from the original sale of this volume go to support the Agorist Writers' Workshop, Very Good Books, and the contributing authors.

Anarchical Copyright © 2018 Very Good Books &
Agorist Writers' Workshop
First Edition

Violence-enforced rights are not reserved on this work by either Very Good Books or
The Agorist Writers' Workshop.
After all, why should guns and government have anything to do with literature and ideas?
Individual contributors retain all other rights to their respective works.
However, fraudulent distribution of "Official" copies of this volume will be addressed under appropriate voluntaryist and non-aggression principle processes.

ISBN: 1725158639
ISBN-978-1725158634

YOU AND I WHO STILL ENJOY FAIRY TALES
HAVE LESS REASON TO WISH ACTUAL
CHILDHOOD BACK. WE HAVE KEPT ITS
PLEASURES AND ADDED SOME GROWN-UP
ONES AS WELL.

-C. S. LEWIS

CONTENTS

Editor's Note	i

STORIES

The Gingerbread House by Karen Over	1
The Emperor's New Contract by Allen Baird	17
Ashley by Lynne Lumsden Green	23
All That Glitters by Robina Rader	35
Fait Accompli by NB Williams	37
The Piper's Last Song by Keturah Lamb	57
The Bremen Town Musicians by John M. Olsen	69
Tears on the Sword by Catulle Mendès (Patricia Worth, Trans.)	83
Meadowland by Justine Johnston Hemmestad	87
Kat, The Jailer, and Jack by Christa Conklin	93
Necromancer: Deal With the Dark Gods by Jakob Morris	103
Jehovah ♥ Gaia by Skian McGuire	107
The Road by Christine Cassello	129
The Crowning Temptation by Justin Fowler	131
An Investment Returns by Lela Markham	157
The Katydid and the Katydidn't by Genesis Mickel	175
The Fairy Mothers by DonnaRae Menard	179
A Tale of Two Boots by Jackie Ferris	185

Frogs by Marie Anderson	205
The Big Bad Elephant by Andrew Bundy	211
Artie the Millennial by Alexandra Faye Carcich	219
Prince Perfect by Keturah Lamb	229
The Turtle and the Rabbit by Cameron Metrejean	241
The Inn by Ronel Janse van Vuuren	243
Sonic Sam of Boston by Billie Holladay Skelley	261
The Red Shoes by Cara Schulz	269
Godiva by Blake Jessop	277
Vision In Action by G. R. Lyons	285
About the Contributors	299

Note From the Editors

An anthology of fable, folklore, and fairytale retellings has been the seed of an idea since the founding of The Agorist Writers' Workshop. Forming as we did to entertain while telling stories of liberty in our own voices, it seems inevitable that we would instantly and firstly think of these three forms:

Fairytales. The first stories one hears as a child.

Fables. The tales that guide and teach both children and adults alike.

Folklore. The narrative of who we are and how we got here, specific to each own's time and place in the world.

Together, this collective mythology is the basis of so much of humanity's knowledge, world view, and culture. Who wouldn't want to gather and share these timeless and universal tales set within the stage of our modern understanding?

Others more erudite than we have already thoroughly discussed the universality of themes and story structure in mythology, and we happily admit to lacking in any meaningful contribution to this scholarly discussion, even while celebrating that we are a test case for this broad appeal.

From very small and local beginnings four years ago, we have been surprised with each successive volume at the growth, reach, interest, and support our little project has received, from our open-call Vol. 1: Anarchy Rising, to historical fiction Vol. 2: Echoes of Liberty, to fantasy-themed Vol. 3: Unbound. But nothing could have prepared us to the response that this year's theme received. We received submissions from five continents and dozens of countries. The authors were of all ages and backgrounds, each one sharing a tale close to their hearts and enlivened with their unique voice. All of this global knowledge flowing into our humble Minnesota headquarters. We received recognizable stories with local and personal flavor added to make them new again. We received stories previously unknown to us that still resonated and spoke to our hearts and funny bones.

Our authors deftly and artistically reimagined beloved classics such as Snow White, Rumpelstiltskin, Princess and the Frog, The Emperor's New Clothes, Jack and Jill, Cinderella, The Pied Piper, and so many more. They join the legacy of story tellers and weavers from the beginning of oral tradition, to the printed word, to the silver screen, and onward to the digital realm.

It seems there truly is a universal drive to have one's voice heard in the collective mythology: to mold and reprocess ancient themes in new and stirring ways. With gratitude, we share a small selection of that with you. The 28 stories included in Vol. 4: Fairytale Riot tickled us, thrilled us, moved us, and spoke also with a voice of liberty and voluntary action. We hope that they remind you of the fables, folklore, and fairy tales of your own past and entertain and guide you anew.

We would end this note with thanks to our past and present judges and helpers. To Trent Sehnert, Tanner Schake, two faithful judges working behind the scenes with us, year after year. To Richard Walsh with his Twitter savvy and incisive project guidance. To Matthew Lewis for rescuing us with a tricky cover design, trumping all previous covers by far. To Justin Fowler for his sharp-eyed reality-checks down the line. To our newest members of the AWW production team, Bokerah Brumley and Heather Biedermann, who supported this volume in ways too numerous to mention. And lastly, to our current and past contributors, and to you, our reader. Thank you.

Jon Garett and Genesis Mickel
August 2018

THE GINGERBREAD HOUSE
BY
KAREN OVER

Evening shadows came creeping into the cottage at the edge of the village. A young girl and her little brother sat at the scrubbed wooden table, feet dangling, stomachs growling with hunger. Their chores finished at last, both gazed with longing eyes at the glazed jug their mother, Magda, had placed on the windowsill during their meager breakfast.

"This is for supper, but only if the chores are done properly!"

It seemed they only pleased Magda by giving her ample opportunity to torment them. If one of them didn't measure up, the other would be punished. Greta was routinely pronounced "impossible," leaving Hans, the most defenseless, to bear the brunt of Magda's temper. Their mother's eyes would light with an ugly gleam as she carefully chose a birch rod. She would smile as she took little Hans by the ear, dragging him to the smokehouse at the very edge of the barren garden. Greta would cower in the twilight shadows beneath the kitchen table, shoving her fists into her ears while each stroke of the rod upon Hans's flesh left a scar upon Greta's soul.

None of that was going to happen again. Greta had a glimmer of a plan, shared with Hans in whispers during the dark of night. It was time to put an end to their mother's vile games.

Fists and face clenched with rebellious determination, Hans slid off his chair, tugging it toward the window. The screech of wood against the flagstones made both the children freeze, frightened eyes swiveling quickly to the tall door across one chimney corner.

Only snores emerged from behind it. Magda's husband Fritz had been drinking away her screaming tirade while the children worked. As the snoring continued, Greta helped Hans move the chair. Before she could stop him, the smaller boy had scrambled up, reaching for the glazed crockery. It was much heavier than it looked, and the glaze made it slippery. His small hands never had a chance to gain control.

Time and the children froze together as the milk jug, contents flying, tumbled to shattering ruin on the merciless floor. Clotted cream clung to the rough stones of the wall while the milk ran down and across the worn flagstones at their feet. Their ragged, scrawny forms slumping in dismayed silence, they watched their supper seep away through the cracks, leaving behind only the sweet, tormenting smell. The largest of the broken shards was still vibrating on the floor when the snoring from the chimney cupboard ceased. The door slammed open, allowing a haggard man to come tumbling into the gloomy kitchen. A reek of sweat and stale wine swept away the fresh scent of cream.

"Look at this mess! You know what she'll do when she sees this! Get out! Out! I swear, this time I really will leave you in the woods. I'll dump you right at the witch's front door!"

She keeps a fancy gingerbread house, gleaming white through the dark of the woods because the trees won't grow near it. She steals naughty children who stray into the woods, lured by the sight of her house. She works them to death, taking care of her house and her garden of flesh-eating plants. They are never seen again.

That was the story their mother told them, if they dared say they were tired or hungry. If they dared say anything at all. Tonight, if they played it right, old drunk Fritz really would take them to the witch.

Now, small and trembling, Hans stood firmly upon the chair, eye to eye with this man who lived with their mother. It was Greta who faded into the shadows, cowering as usual beneath the kitchen table.

The drunken man, however, would not let her hide. As his hand fastened in Greta's hair, she got a firm grip on his wrist, pulling herself out from under the table. Better to let him think he was in control. That he could make good on his threats. He

The Gingerbread House

was angry enough, but what if he stopped to think about how Magda would vent her mad rages, once the children weren't around? Or worse, what if he was so drunk he left them in the woods without finding the gingerbread house? She and Hans might wander until they died.

Sometimes Greta heard the older village children frightening the youngest ones with tales of the evil hag who spent all day with the men at the village tavern, and all night in her strange, dark smokehouse. That if you didn't watch out Mad Magda would catch you, beating you with a birch rod until you were tender, and hanging you in there with her strange meats. She would smoke you and eat you for dinner on All Hallows' Eve. When they always pointed to her mother's cottage, Greta was not surprised. In all her listening, though, she never heard them tell scary stories about the witch in the woods.

Needing information, she had coaxed Hans into sneaking out with her. Hans fit right in with the trembling little ones, shakily asking the dam-breaking question, bringing the answers Greta sought.

"But what about the witch in the woods? Aren't you afraid of her?"

A boy not much older than Greta spoke up.

"Old Myrta? She's a white witch. My granmam took me there once when I had the fever, and Myrta made me well. My granmam's from the other side of the woods. That's how Granmam knew how to find her. Granmam says Magda stole something from Myrta, and they cursed each other till the village ran both of them off. Mad Magda came here to live, and Myrta went into the woods."

Greta's gaze couldn't penetrate the forest deeps. Her mind, however, saw an escape route, at the end of the boy's pointing finger.

"She's in there, in her gingerbread house."

Then all the children laughed, running away from Hans and Greta, back to their own homes. A house made of gingerbread? Maybe they were making fun, but Greta had a memory of the fever, so maybe the gingerbread house was true, too. If Old Fritz knew where it was, didn't it have to be true?

Greta knew the poor drunkard would get rid of them if he could pretend that by leaving them in the woods he was punishing them, doing what Magda wanted. She knew this by the misery in his eyes whenever Magda screamed at him, the pain whenever he saw the bruises on Hans.

The sun was already low in the sky, and darkness would come quickly under the trees. Gulping down half a bottle of wine, Fritz made them put on their warmest clothes, even though the year had barely turned. Exchanging glances, Hans and Greta remained silent, following the stumbling man into the woods.

The tiny lights of the village and the smell of wood smoke faded behind them. Through deepening shadows, they trudged, damp leaves smothering their footsteps but not the eerie night sounds. Greta kept her eyes fixed firmly on the lantern swinging from the drunkard's hand, clinging tightly to little Hans as he stumbled along beside her. She could faintly smell pine, with the hint of another clean scent that somehow lightened her heart. She felt Hans tighten his fingers around her hand.

"I smell bread, Greta. And savory stew."

The drunk stopped short, swaying slightly as he turned to them. Suddenly, Greta realized she hadn't fooled this man at all.

"Yes, you'll be well cared for, just as long as you never set foot in our village again. You know what Magda will do if you should ever try to come back, so don't do it. Stay with the lady in white. And if you can, someday, forgive me."

It was the longest, and the kindest speech he had ever given them. Pointing to a faint glimmer of light in what might have been a clearing far ahead and to their left, he turned away. Taking the lantern with him, he stumbled back the way they'd come, leaving them in darkness.

Hans began whimpering. He was tired, and it was growing cold beneath the trees, standing in the damp undergrowth. Greta put her arms around him, for her own comfort as much as for his.

"There's the light he showed us, Hans, see it? And I can smell the food too. We'll just follow our stomachs, and we'll find the gingerbread house. Don't be scared."

The witch met them halfway, coming through the trees with a lantern on a pole. Dressed in white, to their frightened sight she seemed to be floating toward them, her shape shifting as the lantern swayed above her.

"I saw his lantern. I heard him running away. I felt your fear.

The Gingerbread House

Come now, darlings, come into the house. No need for you to be cold and hungry. I have been expecting you for some time now. I am so glad to have you safely back at last."

Hans held Greta's hand so tightly she thought her fingers might break off. As they reached the clearing, approaching the gleaming snowflake of a house in the midst of it, Hans planted his little feet. Tugging at her, he sobbed in her ear.

"Does she have a switch? Is she going to hurt us?"

"I won't let her."

The White Lady turned to Greta. Placing a gentle hand beneath Greta's chin, she lifted her face, gazing into her defiant eyes.

"Good girl. You are on the right path, but I still have much to teach you. I am Myrta, and this is my house. Bring the little one inside."

Just before the lady shut the door, closing out the night, Greta saw her turn once more. She was gazing back through the woods, along the path taken by the defeated man.

"Darling Fritz. The life you now lead has become your punishment. But since you found courage enough to redeem our children, I can forgive you."

Greta looked into Myrta's eyes as she turned back toward the children, seeing there a joy clouded by sadness and mystery. Curiosity overcame Greta's caution.

"Do you know him?"

Myrta smiled, the joy fading somewhat from her eyes.

"I thought I did. I know his story. You will learn it yourself, in time, for it is also part of your own story."

Greta felt the truth of Myrta's words opening her eyes to Magda's falseness. As if she had just stepped from total darkness into brilliant sunshine, she was still unable to see clearly. Yet she was somehow content. There would be time to match answers to questions.

Hans was dozing off at the table, and Myrta scooped him up before his face went into to the bowl of hot stew. Greta followed, finding a neat bedroom with two beds. Myrta laid Hans on one of them.

"Come, Greta, start getting him undressed while I find you each a nightshirt."

Greta had only succeeded in getting Hans's shoes and

trousers off by the time Myrta returned. Hans whimpered and pulled away when she reached for his hand, which was still clutching a chunk of brown bread.

"There now, Hans, just put that down for a moment. You can have it back once you're ready for bed."

Myrta gently coaxed the mostly sleeping boy out of his worn shirt, frowning at the bruises. With a sigh, she slipped the nightshirt over Hans's head, placed the bread back in his questing hand, and tucked him under the covers. Hans was quietly asleep in seconds.

"Now then, Greta, would you like to finish your supper?"

"I'll stay with Hans, thank you."

"Of course. There's a nightshirt for you on the other bed. I know you can take care of yourself, but I'll be close by if you should need any help."

Greta nodded, watching Myrta smooth Hans's unruly hair out of his eyes. Once she was out of the room, Greta swiftly checked on her brother. He seemed to be sleeping peacefully, but he wouldn't let go of the chunk of bread. Greta gave up trying and let him sleep, finally getting herself ready and climbing into the other bed.

It seemed she had no sooner closed her eyes than she heard Hans screaming. Bright sunshine filled the room. They had overslept, and their mother must have taken Hans out for a beating. But Hans was jumping on top of her, yelling.

"She's trying to cook me! Greta, make her stop!"

Myrta stood in the doorway, sleeves rolled up. Her face was amused, her skirts splotched with water. Greta pushed Hans away and got out of bed, eyeing the woman blocking the door. Myrta smiled gently, standing aside. Greta took Hans by the shoulders until he looked her sheepishly in the eye.

"Show me, Hans."

Leading his sister into a large, tiled room, Hans pointed mutely to the tub of steaming water. Greta tentatively stuck a finger into it, then her whole hand.

"It's just bathwater, Hans, and if you don't want a hot bath, I certainly do."

"No! Me first, me first!"

Hans quickly stripped off his nightshirt and threw it on the floor. Climbing into the tub, he was soon playful as an otter.

The Gingerbread House

Eventually, he allowed Myrta to wash him thoroughly, and after toweling him off, to apply a pungent salve to the bruises on his back. Then there was a set of new clothes, and a pair of shoes that didn't have any holes in them.

"Now you, Greta."

The process was repeated, with subtle variations. When she had put on the new clothes Myrta gave her, they sat together by the kitchen fire. Greta had rarely had her hair properly washed and combed out, but Myrta helped her. After brushing her hair until it was floating about her shoulders, Myrta gave Greta a mirror. They looked in it together, their faces side by side, giving Greta the first of her answers.

After breakfast they cleaned the house. Greta found the work pleasant, because Myrta told them about everything they saw, answering all their curious questions. Before they knew it, they were again sitting round the table, having lunch.

In the cool of the early evening, they worked in the large, neat garden, and the children got a better look at the outside of the house. They had never seen a house built of wood, only stone cottages or brick buildings. Myrta explained to them that the silvery-white color was a lime wash, and the intricate, lacy trim work was called gingerbread.

"The man who built this house was a very talented wood wright, and he loved making beautiful things. But we have taken divergent paths, he and I. A darkness came between us, and he no longer makes use of his gifts. But come now, our chores are done so it's time for food and rest and fun. Yes, Hans, fun! Unless you eat so much brown bread that you can't frolic on the lawn by the light of the moon!"

The days grew shorter. They harvested the garden, making preserves and drying herbs against the winter. People came to the gingerbread house from the village on the other side of the wood, and in exchange for remedies prepared from the garden's herbs and other woodland plants, they stocked Myrta's pantry with smoked meats and fish. Sometimes they chopped firewood and made repairs for her. Sometimes, in the mornings, the children would find small, carved wooden toys on their window ledge.

Hans and Greta learned many things from Myrta, most importantly what they saw when they all three looked into the mirror. Greta sometimes wondered if Hans ever saw what she did. Myrta's honey-brown hair, the same on Greta, and on Hans, darkening from wheat gold as he grew older. Fritz's eyes, staring back at Greta from her own face, from Hans. Who was the hateful woman in the dirty stone cottage, the one called Mad Magda, and why had their father taken them from Myrta and gone to live there? Greta knew, looking at them all in the mirror, why they were constantly warned never to go back.

Greta came to hope that one day she would become the White Lady, roaming the woods in search of the plants and roots for her healing remedies. Hans eventually discovered Fritz's woodworking tools in a forlorn old shed. He spent many days diligently trying to copy the intricate gingerbread designs. Soon the time came when he went to Myrta's old village, as an apprentice to the master wood wright there.

With Hans no longer around to question her, Greta eluded Myrta on the long summer evenings, slipping through the trees by the faintest sliver of moon. Returning to the dirty stone cottage to see what had become of their father.

Hans, also, spent his apprenticeship learning more than cabinetry and woodcarving. The master here had also trained Hans's father, and had been much saddened when Fritz gave up his vocation. Always the master asked any traveler, passing through both of the villages, if they had seen or heard of his former pupil.

Most had seen an old drunk, outside a soot-stained cottage said to be owned by the village hag. Sometimes he whittled, making nothing more than tinder for the fire. There was always a fire, always greasy black smoke from a smokehouse, but no sign of any meats. It was a place to be avoided.

The old master would sigh, and point whatever tool he had in hand, shaking it at Hans for emphasis.

"And you, Hans, when you are a journeyman, don't you journey there! There is a curse upon that village. Fine young men are setting out, but never are they arriving. Of course, they blame it on poor Myrta, the witch in the woods they call her, those ignorant louts with their ugly stone houses. If anyone has cursed that place it was Magda, not Myrta."

Then the master would fall silent as if he had said too much, but for Hans he had said just enough. He knew without having

The Gingerbread House

to ask that Magda was the woman who had beaten him so savagely and turned his father into a drunken fool. Magda was the woman who, by stealing Myrta's husband and children, had cursed herself.

Greta, slipping through the trees, saw the fires; saw the old man sitting outside in all weather, drinking and whittling, and drinking some more. Inside the fires burned as well, for pretty boys and smiling young men newly arrived to take their place in the life of the village. They first took their place in Magda's kitchen, paying over their journey money for the bunk in the cupboard by the hearth.

Greta watched Magda warm them with wine, follow them into the tiny cupboard. While her father slept rough beneath the eaves, the young ones slept warm in his place. In the dingy light before the dawn, Magda would shake the old drunk awake before going off to the village alone. Greta no longer cared where the hag spent her days. She was more interested in what her father was being forced to do.

He would sit at the scrubbed wooden table, drinking. Then he would open the hearth-corner cupboard, pulling out the stumbling lad who had sheltered there. Before the sun could rise or people could see, he would drag him across the weed-choked garden, locking him, dazed and mumbling, into the smokehouse. Then he would scrub the inside of the cottage before falling asleep by the hearth for a few blissful hours.

Magda had not given up playing her cruel games. Like a spreading cancer, her evil had grown through the years, ignored, unchecked. Greta shoved her fists in her ears, just as she had done when Hans had been whipped with the birch rod. While Greta's father slowly starved, drinking himself to death, Magda gloated over the money taken from her victims. Greta watched her filling her pillow with it, sleeping with a greedy smile on her face.

Greta couldn't save them. She'd been lucky to save herself and her brother. Weeping with frustration, Greta fled back into the woods, falling through the door of the gingerbread house and into her own bed, exhausted with grief.

She tossed and turned in feverish nightmares, finally awakening with Myrta at her bedside, placing a cooling cloth on her brow.

"You've been on a dark journey, maid-child. One for which you were not yet prepared."

"But she's killing them. She's killing Fritz. He's dying right in front of our eyes. She's a monster."

"Your father walked into the trap knowing exactly what it was, pretending the lie was truth. Pretending she loved him for himself. Once she'd gotten all of you, you meant nothing. Magda only desires everything she isn't meant to have. Now she seeks darker amusements, and she will be stopped."

"But you said I'm not ready."

"Not alone. Hans will prepare the way for you."

"NO! You can't let him go back there! She'll kill him!"

"Hans must face her on his own, Greta, in his own way, just as you must face the reality of Magda. Why do you shove your fists in your ears, Greta? Are the screams from the smokehouse so disturbing, or do you find you enjoy the sound of them too much?"

Without realizing what she was doing, Greta hurled herself out of the bed and on top of where Myrta was sitting. Myrta, however, wasn't there.

"You must face the monster within yourself, Greta. The only way to keep it in check is to know it for what it is."

Again, Greta launched herself at the damning voice, her own voice raised in a bloodcurdling howl, screaming to shut out the truth, but only bringing it thudding home in her boiling brain, even as her body was thudding against the wall. Again, Myrta was standing somewhere else, her voice undaunted.

"Confront the beast, Greta. Acknowledge it. Becoming one with it, you'll gain its strength, and can use it to bring good to the world."

Greta slid down the wall, curling into a ball upon the floor, twitching. Myrta approached her slowly, as if approaching a wild, wounded animal. Greta wanted to lash out, to smash everything around her, to shut out the gentle words making such impossible sense.

Myrta guided her gently back to bed, back to sleep. Back to dreams in which Greta was no longer the White Lady in Myrta's place. She was a stalking figure cloaked in gray, moving amongst the shadows, waiting, watching, until the time was right for dark justice. Myrta couldn't do this job. She was the

The Gingerbread House

white witch. She had banished all darkness from herself, just as her sister Magda had banished all that was light. When Greta awoke in the morning, her mind was clear. She didn't know what was coming, but she knew what had to be done.

When Hans came back to the gingerbread house, Greta hardly recognized him. Gone was the fearful, underfed little boy, now grown into a strapping, confident youth. Once, Greta had taken him by the hand to follow the man they didn't know was their father back to the mother they had been stolen from. Now, Hans took his older sister's hand, ready to lead her back to the place that had shaped their destiny.

"You've always watched over me, Greta. Now you must watch over me as never before. And promise me one thing."

"Hans, I can't keep any promises when I don't know what's going to happen."

"Just promise me you won't act until it's time. I want her to know who it is that's bringing her down, Greta. I want her to know that we're taking our father away from her."

"Is that what we're doing, Hans? Bringing her down? Taking back what's ours?"

Hans's eyes, their father's eyes, locked with hers.

"We're calling her to account, Greta. There's a balance to be restored. Now one more thing, one last thing while we're still not quite grown up."

"What's that?"

"Frolic on the lawn with me."

Greta let him lead her out, running about on the summer-dry grass where a fallen leaf or three signaled a change to come. Oddly enough, running in circles, tumbling like puppies, spinning like wild maple seeds on a rising wind until they were giddy-mad, it all quieted the rage in her heart.

The beast became still, and Greta, falling through the moonlight and feeling the earth whirling beneath her, also became still. She and the monster within knew they were one. Chaotic rage cooled into controlled resolve.

They were Greta, the Lady in the Twilight. The watcher in the shadows, seeing all things bright and dark. Weighing them against the counter of justice and restoring the balance with ruthless efficiency.

"Hans?"

"What."
"I promise."
"I know."

At the edge of the wood, a grimy smokehouse stood at the back of a ruined garden. Soot smudged the back wall of an old stone cottage, where a bright young man with honey-brown hair stood, clearing a thick tangle of vines from the windows, and opening the shutters. Looking out across the garden to the edge of the woods, just as the sun was setting, he saw the swirl of gray, and smiled.

If Hans could see Greta, she could see him.

Indeed, she could see from her old vantage points that Magda was less than pleased about the open windows. Magda didn't like the clear view. Hans quickly changed her mood by handing over his journey money, and praising not only the tiny hearth cupboard, but the greasy stew served up for supper.

Greta, however, noticed he was careful not to eat any of it. Instead, he had brought fresh bread and other treats from the village shops, sharing them round, giving most to their father. Greta was alarmed by the old man's appearance, so thin and worn he was almost transparent. As if he wished not to be noticed but passed by and left alone.

Hans poured wine while paying compliments to Magda, giving most of his attention to his father. Magda purred like a cat in cream, basking in the warmth of her latest acquisition. Greta's lips pulled back from her teeth as she watched, knowing Magda was paying attention only to Hans's empty words, not to what he was doing.

Laughing silently as she watched through the window, Greta appreciated how Hans extracted payment from Magda. When the supper was finished, and their father was nodding in his cup, Hans refilled it once more. Taking it in one hand, he slipped his other arm round his father's waist, and with the old man feather light, lifted him right into Magda's bed, his head pillowed on Magda's hoarded wealth, his wine cup to hand on the night stand.

"Now then, Madame, what form shall our evening entertainment take? Will you have a song, a dance, an epic recitation?"

Magda clenched her teeth in something trying to be a smile but failing miserably. Greta could see that she badly wanted to

The Gingerbread House

take a birch rod to this impertinent whelp. Her eyes flew about the room, lighting on all the places she'd used to keep them hanging. The direction her eye went to most often, however, was the smokehouse.

"I wonder if you might help me with one last chore. I must tend to my smokehouse. I must make certain there is enough wood, and that the firebox is burning slow and hot enough to smoke through tonight."

"Oh yes, Madame. I noticed your smokehouse. You must have some very savory meats in there."

Magda's eyes went cold and hard, her body stiff.

"Why do you say that?"

Hans's fetching smile beguiled, as Magda's smile had once beguiled their father.

"Why, you have such a monstrous padlock on it. The other villagers must be very jealous of your delicacies."

Magda's eyes took on an ugly gleam, sweeping Hans from head to toe.

"Oh yes. Very jealous. There's many a goodwife wishes she'd had even the smallest taste of what's been hung in my smokehouse."

Greta remembered shoving her fists into her ears to shut out the cries of pain, and rage stirred within her. But she had made a promise, and it was not yet time.

Hans made quite a show of splitting enough kindling for both the firebox and the kitchen hearth. Greta noted the careful placement of the ax, and Magda's fingers twitching toward it.

"Darling boy, would you help me with the heavy lock? Then we'll check the firebox."

Magda groped for the ax while Hans flipped open the smokehouse door. The ax was not where Magda had seen it. Smoke roiled out through the door, opened at just the angle to send it right into her face. Eyes suddenly stinging, she lost her prey.

"Miserable brat! You did that on purpose! Where have you gotten to?"

"A thousand pardons, Madame. Do you require my assistance inside?"

"Of course, I require assistance! I can't see, you wretched fool! Help me rinse the soot from my eyes!"

Magda groped again for the ax, choking as a second wave of

smoke crossed her path. She had been following the sound of the boy's voice, and she screeched in pain and outrage as her hand came into contact with the scalding firebox. She had wandered blindly into the smokehouse.

"Where are you? And where is my ax?"

"Here."

The voice, behind Magda, was not the boy's voice.

Time. Greta struck with the flat of the blade.

Fanning the smoke from Magda's face, Greta leaned in close. She was old enough now for the resemblance to her mother to be most disconcerting.

"Remember me?"

Magda's screech was cut short by Greta's boot in her ribcage.

"But I don't really have to stifle you, do I, Magda. No one ever hears the cries coming from this place. No one ever heard poor little Hans. Even his sister shut her ears against his peril. Only his father loved him enough to destroy himself for his children. Did he ever really love you, or was that just a wicked woman's common magic? The greed of a woman who only wants what isn't hers, and when she gets it, doesn't want it anymore. Like a spoiled child with too many toys, the only thing that amuses you is to break them."

"Myrta..."

"No, Magda. Not Myrta. Greta. Greta, come to save my little brother, and to take my father home."

"You always were a monstrous little bitch, just like your mother! Take that sorry excuse for a man and leave me alone. Get out of here and never come back!"

"Hans and Fritz are already gone. I will follow them in a moment, but you, murdering hag, will remain. The lost souls bound to this spot by tortured, untimely deaths have some unfinished business with you. I don't think they'll grudge remaining a few more days, since this is a matter of restitution. What will it take, I wonder, to make a toughened hag tender? But you're the expert, Magda. I'm sure you can give them a few tips to speed the process along."

At the edge of the village, the street faded into a footpath, winding its way up toward the dark woods, the dark cottage, and the darker smokehouse behind it. A figure in twilight gray fixed the heavy padlock to the smokehouse door, before fading away

The Gingerbread House

on the eerie, howling wind. The villagers, sniffing at the foul air, prayed for the wind to change. They did not pray for the honey-haired journeyman who never returned to his job.

A few days later old Mad Magda's smokehouse fell in with a bang, letting loose a huge cloud of black, greasy, stinking smoke. An old granpap or two gave comfortless thoughts to old Fritz, Mad Magda's drunken companion. When the smoke and stench had cleared somewhat, some of the men went up the footpath to see what had happened. It wasn't very long before they came back down, moving much more swiftly. The whispers swirled with the smoke on the wind, hovering.

"Poor old Fritz is disappeared, and Mad Magda's been cooked in her own smokehouse."

They pulled down the cottage stone by stone, piling them up over the still cooling wreckage. They burned the noisome garden, the stones of its wall added to the cairn over the smokehouse. Snow took it all come winter, burying the memory, unless a wolf came howling. Then the villagers would shudder, each locked within the prison of their own conscience, and finding it grim.

With the dead of winter came fever, threatening to take their children. The few elders left urged the youngers to go to the White Lady in the wood for remedy.

"Go to the witch? Like as not she's brought this on, along with the business up yonder."

Heads would nod toward the footpath, which no one ever walked. Despairing, they were caught in their own web. They had been lying to themselves so long they no longer knew the truth.

She came to them with healing. A Lady in the Twilight, cloaked in gray, walking down the footpath. A young man walked beside her, laden with a heavy basket. Silently they moved from cottage to cottage, bringing hope and relief from dread and sickness. They were gone before the villagers really knew them, fading back into the woods where none dared follow.

When spring came again, the children ran wild along with all of nature. At the top of the footpath there grew a glorious tangle, a wild garden bursting with life and sweet fragrance where there once had been nothing but the stench of death. Memories of lurking evil disappeared, banished by the laughter of children, and if there were pricks of thorny rose or scratches of berry brambles, these were kissed away by parents who counted themselves most fortunate.

But if ever a hand or voice was raised in anger, the parent might see a gray figure in the shadows, might hear a beast howling in the dark of night. They would remember the evil, thriving for years on their carefully cultivated ignorance. Then, if they were lucky, they would know their own monsters.

THE EMPEROR'S NEW CONTRACT
BY
ALLEN BAIRD

Once upon a time there was an Emperor who loved to feel needed. More than anything else in the world, he enjoyed it when his subjects came to him and said, "Emperor, we need you to build roads for us," or "Emperor, we need you to water trees for us". Then the Emperor would smile and sort things out in the way that only an Emperor with a massive army could do.

In fact, the Emperor had such a love of feeling needed that he made it his birthday present! On the first day of April every year, the Emperor asked for lots of new tasks to do and spent the whole day making others to do them. Then he gave himself a special medal, and his subjects clapped their hands and shouted in unison, "Three cheers for the Emperor!" as if their lives depended on it, which they did. That was better than any other present to the Emperor, far better than foreign wars or raised taxes. Well, almost.

Or, at least, that's how it used to be. The Emperor found that less and less of his subjects came to him for help than when he was first crowned, many years ago. For hours at a time, the Emperor would sit on his throne and wait for his subjects to ask for his protection or intervention, but no one came. This made the Emperor sad, since he felt he wasn't needed anymore, and he loved to feel needed and hear his name cheered, more than anything else in the world.

"What's the point of an Emperor who isn't needed?" said the Emperor to himself. "Why, an Emperor who isn't needed is like a glazier in a world where no windows ever get broken! No, this can't continue. I know what I'll do. I'll disguise myself like one of my ordinary subjects and see why it is they don't seem to need me anymore."

So, the Emperor put on a fake beard (complete with fresh cake crumbs), dirty coalminer's clothes, and a cord cap instead of a crown, so he would look like one of his peasants. And, for the first time in many years, he left the safely of his palace, Velvet Glove Towers, and walked out into the streets, with no tall bodyguards or armoured stagecoaches or anything else that an Emperor usually has when he travels among his loyal, beloved subjects in his peaceful empire.

The Emperor spent a day walking around New Iron Fist, the capital of his empire, to see what he could see. And what he saw surprised him greatly. It seemed to him, in some strange and preposterous way, that his subjects were surviving quite well without him. Surviving? Why, some of them almost looked as if they were happy! And none of them were dressed in the dirty, silly clothes that he was.

Well, I thought my subjects were too weak or daft to visit me, or that some evil enemy was holding them back, said the Emperor to himself. *But what I see is the opposite of that. Everywhere I look, people are buying and selling, talking and reading, living and loving. They're getting on with their own business very well without me. It's almost like they don't need me at all!*

And with this, the Emperor's heart turned very glum. Instead of feeling grateful that his subjects were living in peace and prosperity, the Emperor couldn't help but think of himself. After all, he was the Emperor, the most important person in an empire! He walked slowly back to his castle and became so sad that he stopped wearing his crown and sitting on his throne, but no one noticed. Then the Emperor locked himself in his bedroom and wouldn't come out, even for milk and cookies.

One week later, two strangers arrived at the Emperor's palace. One had an oven crest on his chest, and the other was dressed entirely in red. They had to bang on the Emperor's bedroom door for a full fifteen minutes before he opened it.

"Your Majesty, we can make you the most beloved and needed Emperor in the whole world so that everyone will want to ask you for help," said Mr Hob, bowing low to the Emperor.

The Emperor's New Contract

Ah, this is all that I've ever wished for, thought the Emperor. *To have things so that my people need me again, need me forever, so that they can't imagine living without me, for their own common good, of course.*

"And how will you do this?" asked the Emperor.

"Magic," said Mr Ruddy. "We will make you a magic contract on a magical piece of paper. You'll hold a marvellous parade at which you'll make everyone eat cake, and you'll get all your subjects to sign it. And, once they've signed it, they'll never be able to do anything again without you giving them permission."

"What, nothing at all?" said the Emperor in surprise, with eyes as large as his expense account.

"No, nothing, from selling lemonade to owning a dog, from driving a coach to drinking water,"

said Mr Hob. "They'll need your help for every little thing."

"Then you shall make me this contract immediately!" ordered the Emperor.

"It will have to be a very long and a very large contract, to fit all the names of your subjects and all their activities on it," said Mr Ruddy.

"I don't care," said the Emperor. "Whatever the cost, whatever the sacrifice, whatever the loss, I want it, I want it, I want it!"

The two strangers smiled, bowed to the floor, and left the Emperor's bedroom.

For weeks and weeks and weeks and weeks the strangers worked on the contract and wouldn't let anybody see what they were doing.

But the Emperor grew impatient. He wanted to see the magic contract now! So, one day, he marched in to the stately pleasure-dome where the strangers were working and demanded to see it.

Mr Hob stood up from the large table and pointed to what was on it. "Here it is, Your Majesty!" he said.

At first, the Emperor couldn't see anything on the table. Then he came closer, closer, and still couldn't see anything. Finally, in frustration, he walked all around the table, from one end to the other. But no matter how hard he looked, how much he strained and squinted, he could not see his new contact anywhere.

"Where is the new contract I paid you so handsomely to make!" demanded the Emperor. "My taxpayers demand value for my money!"

"But it's right here, Your Majesty," said Mr Ruddy, pointing at the table. "What do you think? Isn't it made of the most pleasing parchment, the most incredible inks, the most legendary letters?"

The Emperor looked around, confused. He still couldn't see anything!

"I can't see any contract at all," the Emperor said.

"Is Your Majesty quite sure about that?" Mr Hob asked. "This contract is so special and rare that only the cleverest people can see it. It is too fine and philosophical to be seen by stupid people. That is the magic of this amazing new contract!"

"Oh, of course, of course," said the Emperor quickly, for he had always considered himself by far the smartest person in the empire and told himself so frequently. "It is amazing, astounding! It is just what I've always needed! I'm sure my new contract will be greatly admired by all my councillors and subjects. Can I show it to them?"

"Well," said Mr Ruddy. "As you can see, it's not quite finished yet. But if you could pay us a bit more, by which I mean a lot more, I'm sure we could have it ready in time for the big parade."

The Emperor promised to pay the strangers anything they wanted if they would have the new contract ready on time. He wanted everybody in the empire to see it!

The day before the day of the big parade came, and the two strangers presented the Emperor with his new contract.

"Everyone will admire you, Your Majesty. Your new contract will be the talk of the seven empires. All the other emperors will turn green with *ressentiment*," said Mr Ruddy, in his strange accent.

The Emperor didn't know exactly what this meant, but he was still very excited, because green was his favourite colour. He called for his special team of councillors to come and admire the new contract. They too were dressed in green, with the sacred sign of the empire's coinage upon their chests.

By this time, word had magically got out that this new contract was so special it could only be seen by clever people and, not wanting to appear ridiculous or retarded or rural, all the Emperor's councillors complimented the new contract when he showed it to them.

"How sophisticated! How stylish! What depth! What metro-

The Emperor's New Contract

politanism! Your new contract is magnificent, Your Majesty!"

Oh dear, thought the Emperor. *All my councillors can see my new contract, but I can't. Does this mean I'm stupid and ignorant and not fit to be Emperor? I will just have to continue to pretend I can see it so that nobody thinks I'm stupid. No one can know the truth!*

The next day, when it was time for the big parade, the Emperor laid out his new contract on the back of a silver cart, and shouted "Come to me, come and see," to his subjects, who were gathered around in the street, eating bread and watching circuses, both of which were very exorbitantly priced, but free at the point of need.

Crowds of people lined the road and watched the Emperor and the big parade. There were knights on horseback, huge elephants with jewels and smartly-dressed soldiers parading along the street. But the star attraction of the big parade was the Emperor's new contract! The crowds had all heard that only clever people could see the Emperor's new contract and, not wanting to appear stupid or ignorant, they all shouted out the correct words as it went past.

"What a superb scroll!"

"What a dazzling document!"

"What a perfect parchment!"

"What a marvelous manuscript!"

The Emperor was very pleased that everyone was admiring his new contract, even if he couldn't quite see it himself!

Suddenly, a single, little boy shouted out from the herd.

"Hang on! There's nothing on the cart! The Emperor's cart is as naked as the day he was born!"

A hushed silence fell over the crowd and the big parade stopped.

Then, everyone burst out screeching!

"This stupid little boy is mocking us, and the contract, and the Emperor," they shouted. "How dare he say there's no contract! Only a peasant of low breeding, little education and less loyalty would dare to mock the poor Emperor thus! We only feel ashamed that we have not signed the new contract already!"

The Emperor blushed a bright crimson. They were right. They should have signed his new contract long before now. The fact that they hadn't was further proof of how much they needed him, so that he could make them sign the contract, which said how much they needed him. It all made such perfect sense.

"Pass me the new pen that came with my new contract," he ordered one of his councilors. "I must insist that you all form a long, long line (may it be the first of many!) and sign my new contract at once! I should never have trusted you to live in my empire without signing it first!"

"That won't be necessary," said the strangers. "This contract is so magical that the names of all your citizens appeared on it the moment they were born. As also did the names of all their forefathers and all their descendants. Everyone in your empire has signed it implicitly, for now until the end of time!"

"I'm so glad to hear that," said the Emperor, "for, as I always say, man is born in chains, yet everywhere he pretends to be free." The Emperor has never said that before, but now it seemed to him that he should have said it, and if he should have said it, then he did say it, because that's how things would work now, going forward.

From that day on, the Emperor gave the two strangers, Mr Hob and Mr Ruddy, the most important jobs in his palace because they were the only ones that had made him necessary. And, whenever the Emperor needed advice on how to feel more needed, he would always ask the strangers first. For example, they had invented, for the Emperor, magical paper money that was as valuable as gold, and boxes into which his subjects placed their wishes every four years that always magically matched the Emperor's own wishes for the empire.

As for the little boy, he also enjoyed the special attentions of Mr Hob and Mr Roddy. For, shortly after that day, darkly bricked, wondrously-sized workhouses appeared all over the empire. Into these cheerfully-named Corrective Labour Camps – for who doesn't like camping? – the little boy, and others like him, were steered and shown how to see the Emperor's new contract, along with many other magical things.

And, if they still couldn't see it, there they would stay, staring at the tables in front of them, hoping that one glorious day, their eyes would behold what others saw, so that they too could live happily ever after.

ASHLEY
BY
LYNNE LUMSDEN GREEN

"They just won't do. They don't go with my dress!"

By this time, Eda and Dana had run to see what the fuss was about. Both were still in corsets and petticoats, as they were helping each other get ready.

"Oh, Ash. No one will mind except you," said Eda.

"You can't stay home. Simply everyone will be there," added Dana.

Ashley was unconvinced. "I won't go. Not with mismatched shoes," she said, determined. Then she saw the faces of her sisters, and said, "But you three can still go and have fun."

Her family knew there was no use arguing once Ashley had made up her mind. One might as well argue with the wind, for all the good it would do.

Mrs Peabody shooed the two younger girls out of the room and turned back to Ashley. "Would you like me to stay home with you? We could make toast and tea and have a pleasant time, just by ourselves. Eda and Dana can chaperone each other."

"No. No. You've been so generous with your time and with your dresses. It would be a shame for you to miss out on the free food and entertainment," said Ashley. "And it will give me a chance to give the house a good going over with no one else in the house to disturb me."

"Well, if you change your mind, just let me know."

Mrs Peabody bustled off to finish dressing, but she glanced back at Ashley as she exited the room. Her heart went out to the girl. If only Ashley wasn't so obsessed with everything being perfect.

So, off went Mrs Peabody and her two youngest daughters to

the Royal Ball, and not without some regretful thought towards Ashley.

Ashley changed into her workaday clothes and made her way down to the kitchen, to make herself a light supper before starting on her cleaning plans.

The kitchen, like the rest of the house, was almost brutally clean and tidy. Everything had its place, and Ashley made sure everything was put back as soon as it was used and cleaned. There were no dust bunnies, mice, cockroaches, moths, silverfish, weevils, or ants to be found anywhere in the kitchen ... which meant there were no spiders or lizards as well. You could have eaten your dinner off the floor, if Ashley would have let you.

Ashley was just finishing up washing and drying her supper dishes when there was a knock at the kitchen door. It was her Fairy Godmother and mental therapist, a small redheaded woman who often used her magic wand as a cattle prod when irritated.

"I rushed right over when I heard you weren't going to the Ball," she said, as way of greeting as she strode into the kitchen, and poking Ashley with her wand. "Why in the world would you miss out on an opportunity like this! You might meet a wealthy man to marry. Isn't that what you want?"

Ashley sighed. "Of course it is. But I really don't like my dress and I don't have any matching shoes. And I wanted everything to be just right for my first ball."

"What have I told you about unrealistic expectations? You have to learn to be more flexible, my girl," scolded her Fairy Godmother. "But we don't have time to discuss this now. We have to get you ready to go to the Ball."

"But my dress! And my shoes! And I don't have any way to get there."

"Tsk. Fetch me that dress and a pumpkin from the garden. I don't suppose you have any pets?"

"Ugh, NO! Fur and feathers all over the place? No, thank you!"

It was the Fairy Godmother's turn to sigh. "We will just have to make do somehow. Now scoot."

By the time Ashley had made it back with the pumpkin and the dress, her godmother had rustled up a cage of white mice and a little black poodle with one eye. "I've borrowed these from the children next door, so you must return them safely. Now pop on that dress."

Ashley slipped on her homemade ball gown.

"Oh, it is lovely," exclaimed her godmother. "Whatever is wrong with it?"

"It makes me look washed out. I wanted a stronger colour, a darker blue, to make my hair look more golden and my skin creamier. And none of my shoes will do *at all*."

"I can soon fix all that."

The Fairy Godmother pushed up her metaphysical sleeves and got to work. She transformed Ashley's dress into a delicious sapphire blue silk, trimmed with gold embroidery and studded with golden beadwork, with dancing slippers to match. Her hair twisted itself into a chignon, and a dainty tiara with sapphires popped into existence, with matching earrings and necklace. Ashes of roses wafted from her dress and hair. The animals and pumpkin were transformed into a coach with snow white horses and a coachman/footman dressed in elegant black, with an eyepatch.

Ashley smiled for the first time in hours, as she examined her outfit and her transportation. "Oh, how wonderful. How ever can I thank you?"

"Be home before midnight, no ifs, buts or maybes. My magic evaporates at the last stroke of midnight. And don't lose or injure the mice or the puppy."

The Royal Ball was being held in the main suite of rooms in the palace, which opened out into one of the five rose gardens that were part of the palace grounds. No expense had been spared in lighting the rooms and gardens, with the ballroom a dazzling display of crystal chandeliers and strategic mirrors to reflect the light. The buffet in one of the side rooms was designed to tantalize even the most fatigued tastebuds; the centrepiece was a 21-tiered birthday cake in honour of the Prince's big day. Dancing music wafted down from the musicians' balcony. Rumours whispered in corners promised fireworks and other entertainments as the evening progressed.

Eda and Dana found the spectacle both fascinating and overwhelming, as they trailed after Mrs Peabody while she did her first circuit of the rooms. No party they had ever previously attended was even a tenth as large as this event. However, Mrs Peabody was undaunted as she inspected each room and noted its details to report back to Ashley, because she was concentrating too hard to have time to be awed.

Around them strolled the largest collection of girls in the kingdom. There were rich girls wearing stylish dresses from international fashion houses, and poor girls wearing their Sunday best. There were plenty of short and medium-sized girls, but few of the girls were as tall as Ashley or had her golden hair. The little family didn't stand out, which was both a comfort and something of an annoyance (at least for Dana).

The Prince had yet to put in an appearance.

They had been at the ball an hour when they heard Ashley being announced.

"Oh, she must have changed her mind about coming," said Mrs Peabody, surprised and pleased. "How extraordinary. Quick girls, we should make our way to the front door, since she will be looking for us."

Ashley wasn't looking for them; it hadn't even entered her head to join her family. She just wanted to get seen in her magical outfit and gauge its impact on the crowd.

†††

If she heard her stepmother and her sisters calling out to her, she ignored them, and swept solo into the ballroom. A satisfactory hush fell over the crowd and for a heady moment Ashley thought it was meant for her. Then she saw the Prince was making his way down a staircase, with some of the court trailing behind him.

The Prince was not a tall man, but he was trim and his bronze-coloured suit was tailored to perfection. Ashley was taken by the strong planes of his face; the high cheekbones, the broad nose, the square chin, his dark copper skin and his curly black hair. He commanded the attention of the room without demanding it.

In turn, Ashley was framed by the doorway, which was all to her advantage. The chandelier lights reflected highlights off her hair, her jewellery, the beads on her dress, surrounding her in a glittering halo. As she had hoped, the blue of her dress made her hair glow flaxen by comparison. Her height meant she rose well above the heads of the women around her. Her face floated above all others; the one swan in a flock of geese.

The Prince didn't slow down once he was on the dance floor, and he strode straight to Ashley's side. He caught up her hand and bowed low over it. Ashley curtsied in return, while he retained hold of her hand. They were exactly the same height, lip to lip and hip to hip.

"Would you honour me with a dance?" he asked.

"Of course, Your Highness."

The rest of the Peabody women arrived at the ballroom just in time to see the Prince escort Ashley to the centre of the room, and signal for a waltz.

"Oh my!" gasped Mrs Peabody. "Where did Ashley find that dress? And is that the Prince she is dancing with?"

Eda and Dana clutched each other's arms and jumped up and down while laughing. Their sister was dancing with the Prince! And she was smiling, a carefree smile they nearly didn't recognise.

Ashley was oblivious to anything but the Prince, all she could feel was the warmth of his arms holding her. Her heart spun like a moon around the tidal pull of his smile. It was like they had practiced dancing together all their lives, as they waltzed without a single misstep. She never wanted the dance to end.

Of course, the dance ended. It was someone else's turn to dance with the Prince. And yet, the Prince did not release her. Indeed, he leant closer and whispered in her ear.

"I don't suppose you'd like to partner me for the next dance? And maybe the one after that?"

Would she?

Of course, Mrs Peabody and her daughters were filled with delight at Ashley's obvious happiness. Her family watched on as the Prince danced every dance with her. He took her into supper and served her with his own hands. The besotted couple took a gentle walk around the rose garden, chatting quietly, while the rest of the party attendees envied Ashley, or loathed her, and the rumours abounded.

Everyone was taken by surprise when Ashley suddenly glanced at a clock, went a faint shade of green, hitched up her skirts, and ran from the palace. The Prince hotfooted it after her, calling after her, "My darling! What is it? Was it something I said?"

Ashley was an excellent runner, particularly after she kicked off her shoes. She managed to grab one, but the other disappeared into the shrubbery. For a moment, she was tempted to try and hunt for it; after all, what is a dress without matching shoes? Then she remembered that everything was going to evaporate at Midnight or revert to their original form and abandoned the idea.

She managed to hide in a clump of trees just as the final stroke of midnight was struck. Her sparkling dress turned back into her homemade gown, while her jewellery melted away like mist, and her hair reverted to its original bun. Even if the Prince were to stumble onto her hiding place, it was unlikely he would recognise her. She bit back her tears.

Instead, she went to hunt down the black poodle and the white mice, and then find her family's carriage to wait for her stepmother and her sisters.

She didn't have to wait for long. After witnessing Ashley's dash for freedom, they had been quick to make their excuses and leave. Mrs Peabody was relieved to see her eldest child waiting for her, all safe, even if she was uncharacteristically tending to some sweet little animals. It wasn't until they were on the way home that Mrs Peabody asked, "What just happened tonight?"

Ashley explained all about the visit from the Fairy Godmother, and why she had left the ball so abruptly.

Dana looked up from where she was petting the little poodle. "Your Fairy Godmother? Normally she just gives you advice. How come she hasn't helped you in this sort of manner before now?"

"That is an excellent question, but I don't have an answer," said Ashley.

Mrs Peabody frowned and bit her lower lip, and said, "The Good Folk aren't people you can rely upon. It's usually best to let them decide what help they will give a mortal." She fanned herself as she spoke, as if she could fan away any back luck her words might bring upon her. Being a fair-minded woman, she added, "Though that dress she conjured up was lovely on you, Ashley."

"Yes, but like fairy gold, it didn't last," said Eda, who was caring for the white mice in an old straw hat. "If that's something she designed, she should give up godmothering and become a dressmaker."

"We would never be able to afford one," remarked Dana. The poodle had decided Dana was his best friend and was trying to lick her mouth. She had to hold her chin up to prevent his enthusiastic, unhygienic kissing.

"I wouldn't fret about it," said Ashley. "It is unlikely I will ever get another chance to socialise with the Prince." Her expression was as bleak as a tundra in winter.

†††

The next day, proclamations were announced all over the country, requesting anyone to come forward who knew the identity or location of the 'mystery woman' from the ball. The Prince refused to marry anyone but the woman with one blue shoe. There was a delegation from the court who was going from house to house, looking for this woman.

Ashley didn't want to come forward, to the surprise of her family. Instead, knowing the delegation was coming, she cleaned the house from top to bottom, while her family tried to understand her behaviour.

"Isn't this your dream come true?" asked Eda. "The Prince is young, rich, and handsome, and he wants to marry you. Why won't you step forward?"

"Don't you understand? He is looking for an expensive dress and jewellery, and not for me. And I feel too strongly enough about him to prefer not to disappoint him."

"Are you in love?"

"I don't know. I've never been in love before."

"You're prepared to sacrifice your happiness for his. In any romance book I've ever read, that sounds like love."

"That sounds completely stupid," snapped Ashley, but Eda found the sting was taken out of her sister's words by noticing the glitter of tears caught in Ashley's eyelashes.

"You should risk it. For your own sake," insisted Eda.

Ashley shook her head and knuckled the tears out of her eyes. She said, "I'm not a risk taker, you know that. I like everything in my life to be ordered and orderly. And what do I know about being a princess?"

"Plenty! You know how to budget. You certainly know plenty about cooking and cleaning. The palace needs to be kept clean and have someone sort out the food and things."

"It still sounds scary. I don't know courtly manners. I don't know how to order servants about."

"Manners can be learnt. And you're pretty good at ordering Mother and Dana and me around, when the mood takes you." Eda was nervous about how Ashley would react to that last sentence, even though it was meant as a joke.

She didn't even notice. Instead, she just picked up her broom and went off to sweep the front hall, shoulders slumped.

Eda watched her sister with thoughtful eyes.

†††

The very next day, the delegation from the palace arrived on their doorstep. It was a group of eight people: The Prince, his father's secretary, a couple of courtiers, a couple of ladies-in-waiting, and a brace of guards wearing the colours of the King's Guard. While her mother and sisters went into a frenzy of dressing, Ashley went and opened the door. They walked straight past Ashley, relegating her to 'maid' rather than a daughter of the house.

She tried not to mind, but her eyes kept straying to the Prince and she had to suppress the urge to run into his arms. How awful it felt, knowing that he didn't recognise her. He had barely even looked at her.

Mrs Peabody met the delegation in the parlour. She was wearing her gown from the ball, as it was still the very best dress she owned. As she settled the Prince and his entourage, she managed to take Ashley aside and tell her to go change out of her cleaning pinafore and into a tea gown.

Eda and Dana met her on the stairs, and promptly dragged her up into her room.

"Whatever are you doing?" asked Ashley.

"You'll see," said Eda.

She helped Ashley into one of her prettier dresses, while Dana sorted through their small supply of cosmetics, perfumes and jewellery. Both her younger sisters donated something of their own to her outfit, in the way of lace shawls, earrings, and brooches. Then they dressed her hair using her string of pearls as an ornament. Their kindness eased her aching heart and made her smile. When she looked into the mirror, she saw a different Ashley, a woman with softer features than she usually wore.

One of the courtiers was impatiently calling up the stairs by the time they were finished. He said, "This isn't the only house we want to visit today. Either come downstairs or we will have to leave."

"We're on our way down," answered Dana, her voice high with excitement. She went down the stairs first, followed by Eda, and Ashley came last, and that was the order in which they entered the parlour.

Mrs Peabody watched the Prince's face as her daughters entered the room. His disappointment was clear as he caught sight of Dana and then Eda.

Ashley hesitated about entering the room. This was the moment when either her heart was broken, or her life would change. Both prospects scared her. Then she shook herself, straightened her back, and walked through the door.

Her eyes met with the Prince's gaze. He stared at her, a small wrinkle between his eyes as he studied her face. Then his face cleared. "My darling! It is you."

He rushed over to her and threw himself on her feet. "I apologise if I offended you in any way," he said. "I'll spend the rest of my life making it up to you if I have to. Please, don't run away from me again. I want to marry you."

Ashley stood frozen as he made his declaration. Then she reached down and pulled him to his feet. "Are we allowed to talk in private?" she asked him.

"Of course."

"Would everyone please leave the room?" asked Ashley.

"But, sire," began the secretary, but the Prince cut him short with a gesture.

"Everyone," he said, pointing to his entourage. "Out!"

Mrs Peabody and Ashley's sisters led the way to the dining room. Mrs Peabody said in a sprightly voice, "I'll put on the kettle, shall I?"

Ashley sat down on the settee and patted the spot beside her.

The Prince sat down, looking hopeful, but with a tinge of concern flickering in his eyes. He was both reassured and encouraged by Ashley's smile.

"What is it you want to discuss?" he asked.

"Let's get one thing straight from the start – I do want to marry you, and not because you are the prince and will one day be king. But we hardly know each other. I don't want to get married in a rush."

"Of course. Whatever you want, my darling." He caught up her hands and held them to his heart. His love had agreed to marry him, and he was nearly drunk with delight.

"And I don't want you to announce our engagement. I want to learn about court procedure and manners before I have to start making public appearances. I dare not appear anything than your perfect princess, or people will gossip behind your back. That's the last thing you need or I want."

The Prince kissed her hands and said, "You have asked for nothing I can't give you. But I can give you so much more. What about clothes, a carriage, servants, jewellery?"

Ashley shook her head at him, but her smile was still in evidence. "You can give me all that when I come to live with you. However, you might give my family some of those things before the wedding, so that they can come in style. And if you insist on giving me a present, I could certainly do with a new mop."

The Prince laughed. "You will let me give you at least one servant, and make sure your family has everything they need."

"Just so that servant is a cook. I prefer to do my own cleaning. Even when I'm living in the palace, I want to spend a part of each day cleaning. It comforts me."

"I don't know how the court is going to cope with a princess who prefers to be usefully engaged," said the Prince. "With luck, you'll start a new fashion." He kissed her fingertips, and Ashley felt a deeper affection for the Prince.

"Is there anything you want to ask of me in return?"

The Prince laughed again. Ashley was pleased that he laughed so easily. He said, "You've already given me the answer I wanted to hear. Better yet, the more we talk, the more certain I am that you are my perfect princess."

"No one is perfect."

"No. I have to disagree. Who is the perfect wife for a

mysophobe? I would say that would be someone obsessed with order and cleanliness."

"A mysophobe?"

"Yes. I have a terrible fear of dirt and germs and have since I was a child. Travelling is a terrible ordeal to me, as I have to see so much rubbish and muck and endure becoming grimy. As soon as I walked into this house, my anxiety dropped to manageable levels. Everything looks and smells so clean." The Prince dropped another kiss onto her hands. "I felt comfortable."

"Oh. Oh!" exclaimed Ashley, as she came to understand exactly what he was saying. Here was a man who wouldn't leave things untidy and wouldn't complain about her cleaning habit. Here was a man who knew exactly how she felt without needing an explanation. He was her true love-match.

So, everybody was happy. Ash and the Prince married, and her little family were moved into the palace. Mrs Peabody and the girls were relieved of the constant worry of keeping everything clean to keep Ashley happy. Even the maids were happy, because the new princess understood the effort than went into cleaning, and so made sure that no one had unreasonable demands made upon them.

Everyone remained happy right up until the first royal grandchild was born. His nickname was 'The Pigpen Prince'...

ALL THAT GLITTERS
BY
ROBINA RADER

"Let's go, Blondie. Move it. We ain't got all day, you know. "

"Sorry," she said, blowing her nose again. "It's being locked in that room full of straw. Really made my hay fever flare up. Can we stop soon?"

"Just down this path. We can get to my brother's house before dark. But we need to talk. Figure out what you're gonna do next. Then I'm out. Except for what you promised, of course. I'm not helping you out of the goodness of my heart, you know."

"So," he said, after they reached the house, "how'd you get in this fix in the first place? What made the king think you could spin straw into gold? I'm the only one can do that. It's a gift. Unique, you know? And the king never heard of me or my gift. Why you?"

"Oh, my dad was at the tavern one day, going on about his beautiful daughter with hair as yellow as straw. And when I sit in the sun, spinning, it turns to gold. He meant my hair, not the straw, but some flunky just heard 'straw... spin... gold', and the next thing you know, I'm 'invited' to the palace and told to spin straw into gold or die. I don't know what I would have done if you hadn't showed up, Mr. Stiltskin. I guess I'd be dead by now."

"But I did show up, and you could have been the next queen. The king was planning to marry you after that last batch of gold, right? Why leave that cushy crib, girl?"

"And do what the next time he wanted more gold? If you weren't around? And the politics in that palace? Everyone jockeying for position and power, wanting favors? I'd never be able to trust anybody again. Besides, I'm engaged to Peter the shoemaker. I have enough gold in my pocket for us to relocate to Swanovia. He has relatives there and we'll be able to live happily ever after. You can come by every week for a pie, like I promised."

The next morning, she started out for the shoemaker's shop. "Goodbye, Mr. Stiltskin! Thanks for everything."

"Yeah, well, good luck with that happy-ever-after thing, Blondie, and don't waste any time moving on. The king'll be looking for you, you know. Good idea if you'd dye your hair." He turned and disappeared into the woods, whistling merrily. Oh, wouldn't a lot of people be surprised next week when the gold turned back into straw!

FAIT ACCOMPLI
BY
NB WILLIAMS

"*I am NOT a fairy godmother!*" Clotho, the Fate Who Spins the Yarn of Life, stepped away from her spinning wheel, her hands clenched in fists. Every inch of her slender body quivered with anger. Even her jet-black curls writhed around her angular face, a dark halo of indignation. Lachesis the Weaver eyed the golden roving piled at her sister's feet, ready to be spun.

"Patience, sister. It doesn't matter what they call us, we know the true magnitude of our profession." She picked up one of Clotho's hands and stroked it, gently massaging the fingers until they relaxed. She upended the hand, cupping it in her own and *tsking* at the bloody half-moons Clotho's nails had made in her palms. "Let not humanity's silliness trouble you to self-harm," she admonished. "Your hands are a precious gift and you must keep them safe.

Clotho shrugged and skewed her mouth into a sulky moue. "Really, Lachesis, I don't know how you put up with such disrespect. We Fates don't just sit in judgement over humans, but also *gods*. All are bound by the strictures of our terminal threads." A deep sigh pushed through her parted lips. "You'd think they'd be more . . .," she waved her hand in the air, searching for the appropriate word.

"*Reverent?*" Atropos the Cutter strode into the room in a swirl of gauzy black silk. The color did nothing for her pale complexion and the fabric bunched in awkward clots, draping poorly over her angular figure. The oldest and most grounded of the three Fates, she shouldered the burden of keeping her siblings focused on their tasks.

Stepping carefully over a pile of spun thread on the floor she settled into her chair in the corner, moving aside the sharp shears that hung from her silver girdle so they didn't tear her skirts.

"Time progresses, sisters, and obscures our craft from the eyes of mortals. Gone are the days when men knew our names and cried to us for mercy." She paused for emphasis. "While we don't have the pleasure of quitting the tasks we are created to fulfill, we need not be relegated to the realm of faeries and sprites and other silly fantasies. We must teach humanity that *mythology* is not to be confused with nursery rhymes and foolish doggerel." She pressed her lips so hard their color faded, her mouth a horizontal slash.

Lachesis, still holding Clotho's hand, shrugged. "Why bother? It doesn't matter what we're called in the world of men. We are what we are."

Atropos' dark eyes narrowed. "It matters." She gestured to Clotho, whose cheeks still flushed with anger. "Your sister determines which soul's time has come to be made flesh. She alone holds the key to life, the beginning, the genesis of all. We can't have her making poor decisions. Imagine the world that would bring into being – a world of strife and repression for the masses rather than the destiny of freedom she so often weaves." She gestured at the large spinning wheel, sitting still and silent. "Now, tell me, Clotho, what has vexed you?"

Clotho, the youngest and most animated of the three, fell to her knees at Atropos' feet in a dramatic half-swoon, resting her head and slender arms on her sister's knees. "Oh, where to begin?" She looked up, large brown eyes brimming with unshed tears. "There are tales circulating in the human world. Tales of destiny and chance, birth and death. In them, people's fates are controlled by plump, giggling creatures that men call 'fairy godmothers.' These ridiculous, roly-poly sprites are assigned to stand watch over the humans' destinies." As Clotho spoke, her words came faster and louder and the red flush spread down her neck to spatter the top of her chest with blotchy patches.

"And mothers tell these tales to children, who imagine us to be fey creatures, public servants if you will, able to be bound by a litany of words on paper they call spells, instead of creators, individuals — creatures deserving of adoration and sacrifice," added Lachesis, getting swept up in the emotion of the moment.

Atropos stroked the silver shears that hung perpetually at her side. "Alright, calm down. Who creates these stories?"

"The Grimm Brothers, nasty German men who seek to undermine our very existence!" Clotho bunched her sister's skirts in her hands, wringing them in her fury. Atropos removed the cloth from Clotho's fingers and smoothed it, a slight wrinkle forming between her brows.

"Germans?" she asked.

Clotho nodded and clambered to her feet. "Yes! Those vile, forest-dwelling barbarians!"

Atropos smiled—a thin, humorless stretch of her lips. "It is indeed surprising they'd tell such gentle tales, my dear, since they are known for cruelty and violence. How is it these tales have become so trivialized?"

"It's modern days, now, sister. People don't believe in gods, goddesses, Fates, or Furies." Lachesis sighed heavily, dismayed by the current conditions in the world. "They've made the tales into children's entertainment and instead of moral lessons, they tell of lovemaking and happy endings." She cocked her head to the side, adding, "Not that I disagree with some happiness every once in a while, you know."

Atropos nodded, considering. "It seems we would do well to get back to basics. Perhaps if we step back in time and rework a tale or two, we can effect a change." She shifted on her seat and her eyes rolled into her head as she was taken by trance. Clotho wrapped her arms around Lachesis and rested her head on her shoulder, letting herself be drawn into her sibling's comforting embrace while their sister disengaged from reality. The whites of Atropos' eyes glistened like peeled eggs as her pupils focused inward.

When a light moan signaled the ending of her trance-state and her eyes returned to normal, she addressed them with a confident voice. "The Grimms were not the first to corrupt these tales. One began as the legend of Cupid and Psyche, then, Lucius Apuleius Madaurensi reworked it in the 2nd century A.D., and later it was known as "The Pig King," an Italian fairytale published by Giovanni Francesco Straparola. It obviously fascinates, so we should fashion our own version. Let's give humans a taste of true power. Faeries, indeed!"

Clotho clapped. "When do we begin? What do we do?"

Lachesis, always practical, asked, "What is the name of the tale now?"

Atropos smiled. "Modern humans know it as *Beauty and the Beast*."

"Ohhh! That sounds wonderful!" said Clotho, settling into her place at the large spinning wheel and grabbing a hank of roving. "How should I begin? Which soul should I choose to be our heroine?"

Atropos stroked her sister's curls. "That's your decision, Clotho. You choose the soul and the time of its birth. Let your yarn give life to these players! Lachesis, as is your duty and design, you'll plot the destiny of all, measuring out the strands and weaving them as you will," She stopped for a moment to glide one fingertip over the sharp edge of her shears, then met her sisters' eyes. She lifted her chin, "And I," she said, "I shall have the pleasure of determining when their story ends."

†††

Rose Edith Kelly wadded the handkerchief in her hands. Damn her father! When she was but a girl, he'd married her to an affluent man, sixteen years her senior, cementing a loathsome union that left her shattered inside and out. Now, he was marrying her off again, widowhood notwithstanding.

He'd told her that was the way of things and she'd best get used to it. "Each according to his ability," he'd intone. "Each according to his need." Her ability, apparently, was to fill the family coffers by marrying "correctly." But what about her need?

First, her father had laughed when she asked him that question. Then his dark eyes had narrowed to shards of dark, glittering jet. "Your need," he pronounced through clenched teeth, "should be to fulfill your filial duty, *according to your ability*."

She pondered her fate with growing dismay. At least she'd only suffered the frequent beatings for two years before her first husband, a hideous old libertine possessed of foul breath and even fouler temper, drank himself to death. Who knows how long the next dubious spouse would persist?

She shuddered. Being the favorite child of the curate for the Parish of St. Giles was no easy task. She had a sister, Eleanor, and a brother, Gerald, but neither of them drew her father's eye. She was, unfortunately, the target of all his scheming and machinations. *A questionable honor*, she thought as she peered into the looking-glass on her dressing table.

She'd piled her thick auburn hair into a luxurious mass on her head and powdered her pale skin till it gleamed like white velvet. Dark eyes under the protection of delicately winged brows sparkled like stars at midnight, and her lips were neither too thick nor too thin. When she chose, they curled into a perfect Cupid's bow of a smile. In short, she was beautiful.

She toyed with the chain at her neck. Being beautiful was a curse, or so she felt. Her father's newest choice of suitor — a decrepit merchant old enough to have a child her own age — was persistent in his attentions and her father encouraged the wealthy old roué. In the language of the day, 'favorite daughter' translated to 'most marketable' and Frederic Kelly meant to gain the best deal he could from his most attractive spawn.

But Rose was determined not to be so easily chained by her father's beliefs.

Her brother and sister had dutifully gone on to perform the tasks society — and their father — had prescribed for them. Gerald shuffled interminable papers as a clerk for a solicitor. His "abilities" apparently determined that he'd never rise higher, even though his candle burned long after midnight each night as he labored over anatomical studies he claimed would revolutionize the success of modern-day surgery. But no one would heed the rantings of a mere clerk, and his genius would be lost to time.

Her sister Evelyn was a talented writer, but to Father she was another pawn in the marriage game, and he'd betrothed her to some crusty old judge. Now her days were spent managing his children and her nights wrapped in his elderly embrace, her flow of prose atrophied by the ennui of harsh reality and the strictures of a society that suppressed all but the chosen, influential and affluent few.

Rose pinched her cheeks for color and steered her thoughts away from her gloomy future. This evening she'd received a bouquet of highly-scented blood-red roses from her mysterious admirer, one with whom she'd been exchanging furtive missives for more than a month.

She buried her nose in the center of one overblown bloom and inhaled, relishing the rich scent. Her affair with her unknown worshipper had begun with a note tucked in her hymnal at mass, a thick, cream-colored sheet filled with lines written in a fast, sharp hand and coupled with a single pressed rose petal the color of freshly-spilled blood. It read:

Long I've watched you through the needle's eye
Hoping you'd fain meet with me
I'm doomed to love you ere I die
My lovely Rosa Mundi.

At home, she'd clasped the letter to her heart in a swoon more appropriate to maiden than widow. *Rosa Mundi* he'd called her. Rose of the World. She was unused to being courted by someone not of her father's choosing, and the idea titillated her. Intoxicated by the possibilities, she'd tucked an answer along with her address into the same hymnal on the following Sunday. That very night, a box bearing rose-flavored chocolates was delivered to her family's home with her name upon it in delicate gold letters.

Her father's eyebrows had risen at the idea of a strange man sending presents to his daughter, but he turned a blind eye. Women had no say so in their own destinies in Victorian England. She'd be married before the month was out. The paperwork had been completed, the banns read and published. There was no escaping the inexorable turning of a society built on status quo.

But that was where Frederic Kelly was wrong.

A new thread was being woven between his daughter and her prince of roses, one that would bind them tighter than a miser's purse strings and would shake the very foundations of his generation's code of conduct.

✝✝✝

Rose's steamer trunk was packed and ready when the carriage arrived. Aleister (for that was her beloved's name) had arranged for their elopement to occur on a Sunday. She was to feign illness and lay abed while her family went on to church. A carriage would carry her to the docks and to Aleister, who would escort her aboard the ship that would take them to Cairo, Egypt. As a terrifying — but exciting — fist in the face of conventional society, they'd chosen not to marry, but to live as partners — united by common ideals and passions.

There would be no banns, no paperwork, no publication of their intent. She would not become his wife, but his helpmeet. She loved all things history, and Aleister had promised she could pursue her love of knowledge to the ends of the earth — and beyond.

Dockside, Rose pulled her wrap tighter. Even though it was August, the day was overcast, and she was chilled despite the closeness of the summer air. She kept her eyes open for a man who could be Aleister, as she had never before seen him in the flesh. Theirs was a romance of paper and ink, blooms and candies. He'd observed her, but she'd never laid eyes on him. Instead, she'd fallen in love with the man behind whatever flesh he wore—his words, his thoughts, and his philosophies.

He'd whispered sweet freedom in her ear, told her they could begin their own society in a far-off land with like-minded souls — a collection of intellectuals who thought ideals like freedom and liberty were meant for everyone — not just men, and not just those with the money or power.

These ideas sparked a passion she thought long buried. Long ago, she'd secretly applied to University. Rather than tell her no, the school required such reams of papers and permissions, including one from her then-husband, that the task was impossible. She'd given up and remained the dutiful wife and daughter, her burgeoning individuality hidden behind primly-starched skirts.

And now? She shivered as she considered what she was doing — running off with a virtual stranger and setting sail for a country leagues away from stolid British soil. What was she thinking?

As the ship's signal blared across the crowded dock, she shook off her morbid thoughts. This wasn't something to fear. It was magical, wonderful, and best of all, it meant the stifling shackles of society would fall away and she could focus on discovering her true abilities.

A light touch drew her out of her reverie and she turned to see the most wonderful pair of dark brown eyes staring at her from under a handsome brow. The gentleman was dressed for travel in a natty topcoat with a dark cravat tied at his throat and a single crimson rose pinned to the lapel. In one hand he held a cane, the other he held out toward her.

"My dear Rose. It's Aleister. Aleister Crowley."

Her cheeks flushed as she took the hand he offered. Two servants hoisted her steamer trunk to follow the couple aboard. Aleister, with a sleight of hand, tucked an errant wisp of her hair behind her ear and drew forth a blood-red rose, handing it to her.

"Rosa Mundi," he said with a wink.

Rose blushed again and held the rose to her nostrils, breathing in the heady scent. Her lashes brushed the tops of her cheeks as she whispered shyly, "Aleister."

†††

Aleister was an accomplished traveler, having spent his life in such far-flung cities as Hong Kong, Ceylon, Calcutta, and Rangoon studying traditions of ancient cultures and religions. This vast experience gave him a confidence that allayed Rose's fears on her first voyage away from home.

During the days they spent en route, Rose found her handsome husband had many interests and came from an eccentric and esoteric family. He had a Greek aunt who'd taught his mother classical mythology and the rudiments of the Greek language. He studied ancient languages and performed yoga each morning for mental and spiritual clarity. His poetry, both profound and profane in nature, was prolific. He championed freedom of speech and thinking outside the norm and told Rose of the Order he hoped to found in Egypt — a society of freethinkers designed to challenge society's very origins. As a high-level freemason, he believed in the art of Alchemy, but also in the study of Science and performed experiments in each as the mood struck. These he detailed to Rose over glasses of Möet and delicacies of every kind so that she felt seated at a never-ending feast for the senses and mind. Her love for him blossomed into something rich, heady, and seemingly everlasting.

Upon arrival in Egypt, Aleister registered them at the Hotel Shepheard in Cairo as a prince and princess, against Rose's protests. She thought the ruse flimsy and feared they'd end up embarrassed, or worse, cast out upon the street.

With his unique mixture of philosophy and overweening confidence, Aleister explained true royalty was in the quality of the mind, not in social status or bank accounts. Since they were both possessed of superior intellects, they were royal in a way most of the aristocracy could never be. Whatever the case, his misrepresentation was not discovered. In fact, his prodigious charm and perceived status procured them special permission to spend the night under the triadic shadow of the Great Pyramid itself.

Beneath the pyramid's hulking shell, she reclined on a camp cot made comfortable with quilts and pillows of brightly-colored silk from the bazaar. In her hand, a libretto of Wagner's *Tannhauser*, and on the table at her side, a bouquet of the ever-present dark roses Aleister favored.

Called *Sang de la Bête,* or 'blood of the beast,' they were a cultivar produced by his own dabblings in hybridization, or so he claimed, and he kept them at hand everywhere they went. A large steamer trunk full of rooted cuttings travelled with them, although how he managed to have them always in bloom was a mystery to Rose.

She was caught between imagining the musical nuances in the libretto and contemplating the stifling scent of the roses when a whisper struck her ear. A garbled rasping, like a phonograph played too quickly, hissed through the room, echoing off the rock walls until it faded to silence.

She sat up and the fringed shawl fell from her shoulders, exposing her white skin to the candlelight.

"Aleister?" she said in a soft voice, as if fearful of being heard.

Silence met her. She gathered the folds of her dressing gown and took a candle from the table. Perhaps Aleister was at work in the temple room. She tiptoed into the adjoining chamber, holding the candle to the hieroglyph-covered walls. Inside, Aleister was on his knees beneath a lamp-lit stone plinth, his head grazing the rug he'd laid there for comfort.

She touched his shoulder. Her touch elicited no movement, but his rich voice rumbled from beneath his bowed back. "What is it, Rose? Why do you disturb my meditations?"

His voice was strident and stern, a tone she'd never heard from him. Her heart skipped a beat and for a moment she was catapulted back in time to where she waited for the hard hand of a husband to rain blows upon her for her insolence.

"I, um," she said, her tongue tripping over her words in her nervousness. "I heard a noise."

Aleister's shoulders slumped and he sighed into the carpet's colorful weave. With irritation, he climbed to his feet and brushed the wrinkles from his suit.

Her eyes were wide and doe-like in the candlelight, the flame dancing like fireflies in the dark midnight of her pupils. Her skin was luminous, and her lips parted as she breathed through her mouth like stressed creatures often do.

Aleister's face softened at the sight of her delicate features pulled taut by anxiety and he passed the back of his hand across her cheek. "Fear not, my beauty. This temple has many souls afloat in its bosom, but none would seek to harm you." He let his lips graze the line of her jaw. "If you did indeed hear a voice, my love, then it was a kind one, I am sure. I have warded protection about us, and nothing evil may pass."

Rose pondered his words with growing unease. *Was he a magician, then? Or worse yet, an occultist?* She shivered and drew her gown tight to her body, glad for its meager warmth as he led her back to their makeshift boudoir.

He settled her back into the pillows on the cot and wrapped her in warm quilts. "Enough of the champagne, my dear. What you need is some old-fashioned tea to lift your spirits. Perhaps with rose hips, for good measure?" Aleister smiled indulgently as he tucked the silks around her legs. When he reached for her glass, however, the smile slipped from his face like rain from a cloud.

"What happened here?"

She followed his gaze to the crystal bowl of roses. One stem had wilted, the bud of the flower dangling forlorn from its browning stem and its petals shriveled and blackened. Other petals had fallen, forming a black puddle on the table's top. The other roses, while lively, were less vibrant than earlier, an air of slow decay about them.

"Rose." He grasped her shoulders, his fingers pressing into her tender flesh. "What happened?"

Rose, disoriented by his change of demeanor, shook her head, large eyes filling with tears.

"I-I don't know, Aleister. They were fine a moment ago." She sat up as a thought struck her. "Perhaps they need water?"

He cut her an annoyed glance. "The bowl is full. Anyway, why would one wilt and not the others?"

Rose kept quiet in the face of his dismay. He'd always been confident, bold, and indulgent. Here was a side she'd not seen: petulant, irritable, and — *conventional*. It must have something to do with their disquieting surroundings. The pyramid, she knew, was no more than an ancient tomb. That would unnerve anyone — it certainly unnerved her. She moved deeper under the covers, wishing for the night to be over.

†††

Aleister snugged the quilts around her, hoping to still her unease and redeem himself by showing compassion. As he pulled away, his nails caught on the delicate silk, snagging the fabric. He thrust his hands deep in his pockets. No sense in upsetting her with signs of his affliction when, hopefully, by morning all will have returned to normal.

†††

At sunrise, they returned to Shepheard's Hotel to find not one, but two vases full of *Sang de la Bête* roses in their room, the heady perfume wafting through the suite. Rose, who had once found their scent intoxicating, gasped at the cloying sweetness and opened a window to let the breeze sweep it away. Aleister frowned but said nothing. Instead, he plunged into his paperwork. The British press had denounced his beloved Order of freethinkers and he was in a frenzy to cultivate their acceptance. He filled out forms, scribbled letters to influential men in Parliament, and thought up new ways to gain access to the cognoscenti of high society, until Rose interrupted his mania.

"Are we to have no breakfast this morning, dear?" Her glance moved pointedly between him and the pile of correspondence.

A flash of anger danced in his eyes. "Forgive me for not thinking of your needs, *darling*," he growled, "I'll escort you to dine *tout de suite*." He gave a sarcastic bow and stomped into the next room to change for breakfast, slamming the door.

Tears filled Rose's eyes and she dabbed at them with a handkerchief, determined not to smear her maquillage. She was out of her element in this strange land which, she thought, was causing her to make a mess of things. She'd just gotten angry over a bowl of roses — how absurd. That's no way for a free-thinking mistress of her own destiny to behave.

She smoothed her skirts and threw her shoulders back in an effort to be the logical, erudite companion Aleister deserved. By the time he returned, coiffed and ready, she had regained her composure. *Poor man*, she thought as she watched him tuck his pocket watch into his vest pocket. *He has his studies to attend to while trying to entertain me.*

Determined to turn the day to her advantage, she gave him a beaming smile and looped her arm through his. From the corner of her eye, she saw his lips curve. Amicably, he placed his hand on hers and gave it a squeeze as they walked downstairs to the dining room.

At table, she gazed at him with rapt attention as he rambled on about the god Horus and how he'd decided his Order's motto should be "Do What Thou Wilt." She thought it strange that someone who claimed to be a nonconformist was energized by the need for his revolutionary mindset to be accepted by the current beau monde.

He was so engrossed in recounting his passions that she could study him unnoticed. His face seemed broader — had they been eating too indulgently? And his hair — she'd not noticed a slight gray streak winding through the dark hair of his left temple before. At one point, as he recounted a night out in Paris with the sculptor Rodin, he burst out laughing. She caught sight of his canine teeth, which seemed longer and sharper than usual.

He finally caught her studying him and his face lost its animated vivacity. "What?" he said tersely.

Rose smiled. "Nothing, dear. I was just marveling at that bit of gray in your hair. I never noticed it before, and it caught my attention in the sunlight." She motioned to the window against which their table was set.

Aleister put his fingers to his hair as if to feel the color. "Gray hair?" he said. "I have no gray hair, woman."

Rose, shocked at his tone and language, bristled. "I am looking at it, Aleister," she said.

"Then your eyes are deceiving you, which is not entirely

unexpected," he replied through gritted teeth.

Rose's face flushed, her positivity draining away like water through a downspout. *How dare he speak to me as if I were some young housemaid!* She would not play the simpering, abused wife. *Never again!* she thought angrily. She balled up her linen napkin and placed it on her plate, covering the still-warm breakfast she'd barely touched. With haughty dignity, she excused herself.

"Since you seem to be displeased with anything I have to contribute this morning, I'll take my leave for a stroll in the gardens. And," she added tartly, "you may want to start the day with a fresh boutonniere. That one seems a bit unbefitting. Good day, sir." With a sweep of amethyst skirts, she fled the dining room for the peace and quiet of the conservatory, leaving Aleister staring at the crimson rose wilting against the rough weave of his coat.

†††

Aleister returned upstairs, leaving breakfast untouched. *What,* he wondered, *was up with Rose?* Why was she suddenly so intractable? He fiddled with the faded bloom on his lapel, noting his lengthened nails. His aggravation heightened, and his lips curled into a snarl, revealing those pointed canines. Her unloving behavior was having an unfortunate effect on his countenance, just as his mother said his long-dead aunt predicted.

As he swung open the doors to their rooms, his nose was assailed by the pungent smell of sulfur. He found his vases of roses wilted, their petals dropping like rain. His eyes grew large. "No!" he cried and tore at the sides of his face with his nails, which, fortunately, he'd blunted last evening so there was nary a mark upon his cheeks, despite their length. *The process was accelerating.*

Wasting no time, he ran from the room, taking the stairs two at a time and running through the dining hall to the distress of the waitstaff. He burst into the conservatory, yelling *"Rose!"* at the top of his lungs.

There were a few couples inside along with a young man writing in a journal, but he saw no sign of Rose. The writer looked up. "Are you looking for a lovely young lady with auburn hair and a violet dress?" he asked.

Aleister nodded, eyes searching the room for a glimpse of her bright face.

"She went into the gardens, sir," the young man said. "I —,"

"Thank you," said Aleister, and he was off through the back doors and into the hotel's extensive garden.

He caught up with Rose at the entrance to the hedge maze where an enormous tree with lilac blossoms spread its showy branches over her in a protective embrace. She leaned against the trunk with a bloom to her cheek, staring wistfully.

"Rose!" Aleister fell to his knees at her feet. Rose, startled, jumped away, then looked around with embarrassment.

"Aleister. Do please get up, you're causing a scene," she said with icy dignity.

He pulled at her hand in desperation, covering it in kisses. "I will not," he mumbled through the kisses, "not until you forgive me for being an absolute bear!" He growled into her hand.

She tried to remain cross, but his beard stubble tickled, and she couldn't help but giggle at the sight of him groveling in the middle of the garden.

"Oh, get up, silly goose!" she said, rapping him playfully on the head with her knuckles.

He stood and crushed her in a strong embrace. "My dear *Rosa Mundi*, I am so sorry to have displeased you. I had no right to speak to you like that. Forgive me?"

Her heart expanded at his loving words. This was the man she'd risked home and reputation for—the man she'd crossed oceans to be with. She rubbed her face against the rough wool of his jacket, where a sharp thorn stuck her cheek.

"Oh!" she said, and stepped back, looking for the offending object and finding a beautifully formed *Sang de la Bête* rosebud in his lapel. She smiled, "I see you took my advice and changed your boutonniere, sweetheart," she smiled. Aleister, distracted by the bead of blood staining her cheek, looked down at his suit.

"Oh, yes — in the room. I mean I changed it in the room after breakfast." He gathered her into his arms, carefully angling her face away from the flower. "Thank you for telling me, darling." Relieved, he ushered her out of the garden.

He had not changed the rose.

†††

Days turned into weeks and the two settled into a comfortable rhythm. Aleister worked on his experiments, journals, and paperwork in the morning whilst Rose studied her own interests or walked in the garden. But the longer they remained, the more Aleister moved from spontaneity to rote repetition, working endless hours on papers, papers, papers.

Apparently, governments must be petitioned so he could access libraries and artwork, and that entailed copious legal papers, requests, passports, and payoffs. He had to know the right people, carry the right cards, and jump through the proper hoops, all of which gave Rose a headache. She'd thought his philosophy was to move counter to their restrictive society, but here he was, courting it.

Most evenings, Aleister met with fellow intellectuals to discuss science, philosophy, and alchemy. But sometimes, he and Rose visited one of the many museums of antiquities where Aleister imparted tidbits from his vast catalogue of knowledge.

One day as they strolled through the Museum of Cairo, they happened upon a display of ancient Greek pottery. One vase, a beautiful water jar of terra-cotta and bronze, caught Rose's eye. It had a wide body, with a handle to either side and a spout for pouring. On its side, an image of three women was worked in sharp detail. The sign below read: *Mycenaean Vase.*

"Look, Aleister! This vase is beautiful. The women seem almost real, they're so finely drawn." She leaned closer, ignoring his sharp tug on her sleeve. The dark figures on the vase were in motion, one portioning out a strand of yarn, another weaving, and a third holding shears ready to cut loose ends.

"Darling, they're goddesses!" she said, delighted. "And one of them resembles the head on the ring your aunt gave you, you know, your Greek relation?" She looked up at her husband, who was still trying to pull her away from the display. "What was her name, dear? I know you've told me but I've forgotten." She laughed. "All this knowledge you're putting in my brain and I've no time to organize it all." She patted his hand. "Now, let me see. It was a funny name. Like something edible. Teas? Cheese?"

Aleister scowled. "Lachesis."

"Yes, that's it, Lachesis. Odd name, that, but then your family is so far-flung it's not exactly surprising, is it?"

He shook his head, distracted. "Can we go now?"

Rose hesitated. Normally Aleister loved to expound on some dusty artifact and that love was only matched by his passion for talking about his family and how interesting they were.

"Certainly, dear. But remind me, when did she give you that ring again?"

Aleister sighed. "She didn't give it to me. She gave it to my mother just before she died — when I was born, Rose. To remember her." He took her hand and began walking further down the aisle of vases and pottery. "Not to be rude, but I don't want to talk about her. It makes me sad." He glanced at the case of pottery. "And they're not goddesses, either, just minor mythological figures."

Roses pursed her lips in concern. "Poor Ally. I won't say another word."

Just then, a cheery soprano voice cut through the musty atmosphere like a knife through cloth.

"Aleister! Fancy seeing you out in broad daylight!"

A slender blonde woman propelled herself through the crowd like some marvelous figurehead splicing the waves of a violent sea. Rose was shocked at the woman's masculine manner and her forward speech, but she wasn't prepared for what happened next.

The woman embraced Aleister. Not just a social how-do kiss that one made in mid-air betwixt cheek and neck. No, she threw her arms around him, placed her voluptuous red lips upon his and engaged in a deep and meaningful caress.

Aleister dropped Rose's hand to cup the woman's waist. When the woman was done vampirizing her husband, she turned her aquamarine gaze to Rose.

"So very pleased to meet you, dear," she said, her eyelashes in a sultry half-mast over those glittering turquoise eyes. "Aleister has told us so much about you."

The hidden meaning of this sentence fairly dripped off the woman's tongue. *Is this what — no — who Aleister had been up to all those nights when he claimed to be "doing paperwork"?*

Rose's neck flushed with anger and her dark eyes flashed. "Good evening, Madame," she said simply, then added, "Aleister," and calmly exited the museum. She ran all the way

Fait Accompli

to the Shepheard's Hotel without once looking to see if her husband followed.

†††

When Aleister arrived at their rooms, Rose had packed her trunk and was checking drawers for overlooked items.

"Rose, listen," he said.

Rose whirled on him, a vision of fury. "Listen to what? Silly stories about how Horus talks to you and your family comes from a line that begat mythological characters? Or how you're going to start a new world order, when all you're doing is what everyone does, kowtowing to the establishment to win a place amongst their sanctioned illuminati? What will you fill my head with next, Aleister? Hmmm?" She threw a bangle in her reticule and pulled the strings tight.

"Please, Rose, hear me out." She whirled and began opening drawers, checking for bits and bobs.

Aleister wrung his hands in earnest terror. He felt the ache in his nail beds as they lengthened and thickened, and every pore tingled with affliction. The rose in his lapel was more than dead — it was nearly dust. He must act.

"I need you, my love," he pleaded. "Don't leave me — let me explain."

Rose slammed another drawer, sending a vase of *Sang de la Bête* crashing to the floor. As spun as the dirty water which stained her silk skirts.

"No, Aleister. No more fairy tales of freedom and individuality. Your Order is just another "members only" society like those at home. I should know — I've been bound my whole life by intricate social rituals and oceans of useless ceremony. Nearly buried by the mountains of legal documents that declare me — nay, all of us — slaves to our betters.

"I can no more exercise freedom to discover my God-given abilities now than when I was under the auspices of my father or my first husband. You said you and I would open a door to free thought and freedom of action. You, who brought me chocolates and roses and promised I would be an individual, my mind and talents cherished. Well—," she kicked at the dead roses at her feet, "I hate your flimsy promises, your smelly roses, and—"

"No! Rose, please! Look what you're doing to me."

His teeth hung heavy over his bottom lip, making speech difficult. The gray in his hair had multiplied and begun to cover his face, sprouting from all the flat planes —forehead, cheeks, chin — while his nose lengthened and turned black.

He hunched, struggling to speak, but each word was forced like gravel through his changing throat.

"Rose, I—I love. You. Can stop. This."

Her mouth opened to say the words he wanted to hear, but as his body twisted, a gold locket slipped from his pocket, rolling to her feet. The weak clasp opened on impact, displaying the face of the woman from the museum.

Rose's eyes iced over and her heart hardened.

He had never loved her, only kept her feelings for him alive to stave off this curse of his. She'd defied her father for the freedom to love who she would, to travel where she would, to choose her own circle of friends, and cultivate her own interests. Instead she'd traded masters. Hands akimbo, she glared down at the beast clinging to the last vestiges of its humanity.

"I hate you," she said quietly.

With those words, humanity fled.

†††

Clotho clapped her hands in glee. "Oh, sister! What a wonderful story, and delightfully wicked, too!

Lachesis laughed and spun in a circle, her skirts swirling. "Did you see his face when he saw our vase in the museum? That was classic."

Atropos nodded as she poured wine from an amphora decidedly like the one in question.

"You know," Lachesis added, "I might have had mercy on him if he'd not called us 'minor mythological figures.' That sealed his fate, as it were." She cackled at the pun.

Atropos, sensible as always, smoothed her black skirts. "Now, sisters, we've had our fun, but we've made a statement, metaphorical though it may be. Aleister Crowley's story will be told and retold until our original weaving is in tatters, just as *Beauty and the Beast* ends up a story to send children to dreamland. The difference is ours will stand the test of time. No matter how he is reshaped by human imagination, Aleister Crowley will go down in history as The Great Beast.

She sipped her wine and poured a cup for each of her sisters, handing them round for a toast. "My dears, we have done what we set out to do — prove to ourselves that no matter what names humans bestow upon us: fairy godmothers, witches, or worse, we remain, and will always be, Fates."

She ran a finger along the edge of her shears, testing their sharpness. "And I have not yet decided how to end the lives in question, if at all."

"What do you mean, sister — *'If at all'*?"

Atropos smiled, her grim countenance unimproved by the expression. "Aleister Crowley will be quite infamous. He may serve us best by remaining extant, in one form or another, to keep the silliness at bay." She turned to Clotho. "Can you think of another tale we can subvert using his, er, enigmatic charm?"

The sisters, who could scan millennia in a moment, thought carefully. Finally, Clotho proffered, "Anastasia?"

Atropos' smile expanded. "Excellent choice, sister. And who better to play the part of the villain Rasputin than our friend Aleister? When the high and mighty Romanovs snatch the right of freedom from the masses," her smile grew, "Aleister will be the chink in their armor — ironic, no? The man who championed free-thinking yet sold out to the bureaucracy for the sake of fame will become famous for championing freedom." She paused, "And being deviant and evil, of course. Some things never change."

Lachesis and Atropos exchanged glances as Clotho produced striking gold threads for each of the Romanovs, handing them to Lachesis to gather to her loom. With shuttle poised, she waited for Atropos to relinquish the blood-red strand that represented Aleister Crowley, weaving it deftly into the cloth with such skill that, when finished, the cloth resembled a column of richest gold divided by a river of blood.

They held up the finished piece to admire it and, once again, the Fates smiled.

THE PIPER'S LAST SONG
BY
KETURAH LAMB

In a little German village encircled by hills, there lived a kindly Piper.

He played harmless ditties for all passersby, and all he asked for in return was a smile and maybe a few coins.

He played his shiny brass pipe, eyes laughing, lips floating, his feet dancing. So enchanting was he to all that heard him sing, saw him dance.

His clothes were pied; colors of red, of yellow, of blue. His hat also boasted the same, matching in its colorful way. On top of the hat of many colors poked a proud, stiff feather.

The Pied Piper sang his songs, danced his dances, and all around him the people nodded with pleasure.

As long as the Piper danced, all was well for the little German town.

His cheery melodies chased away any grudges, every displeasure, all anger.

The happiness in his songs united the people.

One day the King's army came over the hills. Through the valleys they galloped, into town to the people therein. Sent from the Pope, they brought ill will that spoke of danger. A danger that not even the Piper's music could withstand.

But the Piper played for them as he would anyone. He danced. He raised the pipe to his lips, capturing a tune, then sang this innocent rhyme, stopping every once in a while to let his pipe sing also.

Keturah Lamb

I found a silver farthing,
a silver farthing,
a silver farthing.
I found a silver farthing,
A shiny silver farthing,
On this beautiful morning.

I found it upon the ground,
upon the ground,
upon the ground.
I found it upon the ground
A shiny silver farthing,
On this beautiful morning.

Now, you ask how I found,
how I found,
how I found.
Now, you ask how I found,
My shiny silver farthing,
On this beautiful morning.

My eyes saw a dirty mound,
a dirty mound,
a dirty mound.
My eyes saw a dirty mound,
Where lay a silver farthing,
On this beautiful morning.

The Piper drew the pipe to his lips and repeated the silly tune, then skipped in wide circles around the bemused soldiers. The small instrument sang rapturously.

The soldiers hollered, hoorayed, and hailed the Piper. "Sing us more, Pied Piper. Another song to ease our tired ears!"

The Piper smiled and continued to play.

†††

The commoners of the little town were servants of the King of Germany, and of the Pope — who thought he was king of the whole world.

The Piper's Last Song

These people as one paid their taxes, said their prayers, and worshiped one God without freedom. Though the people had small arguments and feuds, they were like-minded — by threat of punishment and banishment. It was a hard time, but few realized this.

Except the Poor of Lombardy, followers of Peter Waldo.

They were different. They chose another life, another way. They wanted to follow God, not man, and follow their consciences and beliefs. They chose evident hardships over a safe pretense.

They begged the Pope to grant them this freedom, to let them study the Good Book for themselves.

But those in high places were angered by their words. Soon, these people were known as blasphemers, as traitors to God and country.

The Pope and the King wanted all to be one. All to serve the same king and the same God, to eat the same bread, and to drink the same wine, to be one everywhere.

The Waldensians refused. They practiced the true faith, hiding from the Pope. They lived simple, sincere lives, working hard in satisfaction and forsaking all frivolity.

The Piper thought them odd. He saw them as an uncanny people and wondered at their ways.

Could not all men follow God and Pope and King? Must one differ? Could not all live as happy and carefree as he? Who were these people that chose rags over riches, death over life?

The mere name of them made the Piper shudder with questions. Unanswerable questions. Questions he had no will to search out. For who would want to give up the joy of life for rebellion? They were not a pleasant subject to discuss.

And the King's men. All knew why they had come. To root out and exterminate every last one of these people.

Beware, Poor of Lombardy! Your time is drawing near. The end is now. The whole place seemed to say, in a warning, yet taunting sort of way. *The King's men, the Pope's army — they are here to serve justice.*

The Piper found his smile once more. Dark thoughts were not for him. These people were of no concern of his. He put his pipe back to his lips. He would be joyful — play his music! This was life! He would live.

He skipped, jovially running through each street. His coat

Keturah Lamb

flashed brightly, and his pipe sang once again, glistening in the daylight.

If you could make a rhyme
And add a pinch of thyme,
If you could make a rhyme
That tasted like a lime.
You'd be an expert cook,
It'd be printed in a book.
If you could make a rhyme,
If you could make it chime.

The people laughed and cheered. The rhyme did indeed chime in all their ears. The people danced and threw their payments — bits of food, silver, gold, and trinkets of no great value — at his feet.

The Piper bowed. He waved his hands and pipe around. Then he played and played and played. Every once in a while, he'd drop his pipe and open his mouth, uttering beautiful words, sad words, funny words.

People laughed, cried, and cheered at his music.

They are the King's men —
Have you heard?

They wear their armor
In fashion and style.
They'll rob our larder
And treat us all vile.

They are here again —
Have you h-

The Piper stopped short. His face burned red. His feet were still and would not dance, for before him stood ten of the King's men!

"Uh... Ach... " He stammered and shifted nervously. "Good day, good men." His voice squeaked in an unmusical sort of way.

Uneasily, he started another tune — this one not about the soldiers. The music held no voice — only fear. His hands sweated and trembled and the pipe slipped around inside of his mouth.

The soldiers watched him, purposely making him tremble with their authoritative stares. But now they started to mock the Piper. "A stupid fool, the dunce has no sense." They walked away laughing.

The Piper sighed in relief and danced with joy once again.

†††

The village gates opened. The soldiers, astride black stallions, marched out toward the caves in the hills. Their swords gleamed. The spears were sharpened. Armor and shield were polished.

All knew their mission. Death.

"Death to those who dare defy. Death to those heathens, those heretics, the Waldensians!" shouted soldier and common folk alike.

Away they sped, trot increasing to canter over bridge, vale and hill; through creek, wood, and field. On went the King's men on their horses.

The people stopped their work. The Piper's pipe was silent. No child went to school that day, no store sold goods, no fire was stoked, nor garden plowed. For off in the distance a massacre was in occurrence, and people were killed.

Though every man had just screamed for the Waldensians' death, each man felt something close to sympathy in his soul. These were neighbors, friends, relatives. Heretics, yes, but still...

Voices — screaming, wailing. All could be heard over the hills. The Piper put his hands to his ears. No music ever sounded like this!

Men and maiden, old and young, all were slaughtered alike, torn limb from limb.

The day was almost spent. The sun dropped low and shone red against the horizon. Its bloody light spilled over the hills into the town, symbolic of all the death below.

And then it was over. The sounds stopped. The soldiers returned slowly, laughing and talking of their wicked deeds with shameful pride, finding pleasure in their evil.

Amidst them walked the only survivors, nearly a hundred

and fifty small children. A quiet anxious murmur of wailing rose from them as they were antagonized by the soldiers' cruel words and kicks.

One lame child lagged far behind and received most of the soldiers' brutality though he struggled to keep up.

Sobs and cries were stifled by a boot's quick kick or a spear's sharp point.

The people of the town dispersed, frightened and ashamed. Unsure of what was right, what was wrong, trying not to think traitorous thoughts against Pope and King.

"Served them right," they said to each other. "They had it coming." Yet, inside, all were horrified, and hid away from the children.

The Piper, too, hid behind a house, and watched the soldiers with eyes wide and scared. More forbidden questions arose. All his life he had been taught what was right or wrong. But how could this be good? Dare he even question this? Better to just ignore it. How could he bear what these people suffered?

How would he and his people live? For others, God, and truth? Or as cowards?

His heart longed to know, yet it wanted everything to go back as it had been yesterday. Peaceful, loving, joyful. Simple, without any dangerous questions or choices.

A soldier spotted the Piper and called out to him. "You, come here! Make haste, you coward!" He laughed at the Piper's walk—so slow, unsteady, and fearful.

"Play us a tune, Pied Piper. Hush these filthy rats. Give us joy after our long work!"

He withdrew his pipe and started a tune from his heart. Its sad beauty surprised even his artful fingers. The music seemed to say:

Little Children, stay your fears:
Rest and hear,
And do not cry, little dears,
Day is near.
All of the flowers still grow,
Sky is blue,
And all the creatures still show
God loves you.

The Piper's Last Song

The melody was soft, the tune comforting. The children dried their eyes. They remembered this promise and believed that life could be good again with all their might. Momentarily they had hope. And for a few short seconds, they were able to forget everything bad and evil, even the deaths of their families.

The soldiers, too, were touched by the beautiful tune, but in a moment, evilness returned to their words and eyes.

They prodded the children forward and called them horrid names.

They led the children down the street called Bungelosenstrasse. At the end was a church. The soldiers forced all the children inside. The lame child entered last, as fast as he could go, which was very slow indeed. Then the soldiers bolted the door from the outside.

"Ha, now sleep well! Just remember, it's your last night. At daylight the building will be burned to the ground as an example to all those considering joining false religions."

Laughing, the soldiers left the children to their misery. Off they went to drink and celebrate, leaving one man to guard the Waldensian children.

The Piper, too, lingered close, not able to leave the children. He wanted to sort through the forbidden questions, dangerously curious. He found a dark alley nearby and sat just to watch.

It was almost midnight and still the Piper could not sleep. The moon was high. The stars sprinkled across the night sky, and their light danced as if singing. Their voice grew louder, yet it was soft — like a child's.

Wait! It was indeed a child's voice, and no star. The Piper stood and searched for the voice. It was coming from the church, floating out, speaking sounds of fear and loneliness.

The day is dark, the day is gone,
Still I see your face.
And, even though I'm far from home,
I feel your good grace.

The Piper drew even closer. He listened to the sad voice, the beauty and depth giving him pleasure. What a sweet sound!

The enemy has found me out.

They have me in chains.
Oh, Father! Let me ne'er shout
Or surrender through pains.

Something glistened in the Piper's eyes. Tears of pity? Could this carefree Piper feel for others? His ditties and silliness seemed so vain just at that moment. So purposeless. They stood for nothing.

And though I never see the light,
I'll stay to what's true.
I'll remember to do what's right —
Hold me close to you!

The Piper looked into a window at the side of the church, the prison of the faceless singer; a death chamber for children. He soon saw the child, close by the wall. His eyes were looking to the sky through another window, praying silently. It was the lame child.

It was then that the Piper fully realized what he wanted, what he needed — that he even needed anything at all. He yearned for peace — true peace, like this child possessed.

Looking up to the same sky as the lame boy, he gave up his heart and soul. And on that night, he found peace.

†††

What? The crowing of a rooster?

The Piper opened his eyes to dim daylight. Dawn was drawing nigh. He had fallen asleep.

The Piper lifted his head from off the ground and smiled. He knew what he must do. Pipe to mouth, agile feet poised to dance, the Piper made his way around the church, a soon-to-be-tomb.

"What's this? The Pied Piper!" The lone guard bid him to play.

And so he did. His eyes just hinted at his mischievous and secretive plan.

The tune — haunting, eerie, wonderful — enchanted the guard. His eyes became heavy, and soon closed in slumber. He slept unaware as a child.

The Piper's tune grew louder; his feet danced faster. He went up the stone steps and the doors opened before him as his music beckoned. Many said the spirit of the pipe worked in magical ways that day. A few said that God was for the children and performed miraculous wonders. Even fewer, more skeptical than the rest, said that the lame child opened the door and hit the guard with a large club. But these people forgot that the doors were locked from the outside. Turning, the Piper skipped down the cracked steps and through the alley.

None of the children had slept. They were distraught over witnessing the horrors of the day before and waiting for the ones to yet happen. Once the door opened, they crept toward it, cautious, yet hopeful. One, two, then three. More followed until all were dancing with the Piper.

The Piper danced amidst them, brass pipe ringing with melody. He led them to the city gates. Once there, the children ran for the hills. Far, far, far away. The music led them on. Toward mountains, through creeks, to some secret place.

The Piper stayed inside the gates. He watched the lame boy with worry. He was still behind, far from the other children. The Piper played harder, and his music seemed to give the lame child more strength. The Piper watched him disappear.

The lame boy had vanished from sight when a shout arose from the people. They had seen the children vanish.

"Have the mountains consumed them?"

"Did the river swallow them?"

"The trees, did they take them?"

The soldiers ran out of inns and taverns. They found the church building empty and the guard still sleeping. They screamed and cursed.

"Who did this? Who let them go?"

The Piper laughed without fear now that the children were safe. Once his pipe left his lips the others began to regain their senses and notice him.

"It was he! The Pied Piper! He put me to sleep and took the children!" said the soldier.

"He's a magician!"

"He's a wizard!"

"One of the heretics!"

The Piper smiled and looked to the hills. He was not afraid. He repositioned his pipe and played a tune both sad and sweet, a melody continuing to encourage the children, and mock the King's men.

"Kill him! Kill him!" the people said. Though the day before the people had given him silver and laughed at his silly ways, now they acted as if afraid of him. Riled with stress, fear, and guilt from the last couple of days, they forgot how they had once loved the Pied Piper, of how he was simple and never portrayed any maliciousness.

The soldiers surrounded the Piper and his pipe. He spun in a wild dance, his colorful clothes blurring proudly in the street.

"Fall to your knees and repent!"

But the Piper danced.

A soldier sent a blow towards the Piper, his sword knocking the Piper to the ground.

"Repent! And give up the Waldensian brats."

Still, the Piper played his pipe.

The soldiers enclosed around the Piper. The people threw rocks. Some bounced off the Piper and hit nearby soldiers. But the soldiers seemed not to care. They were too focused on the Piper. The soldiers gave the Piper one more demanded chance, but he kept his pipe at his lips.

The soldiers beat and stabbed the Piper. They kicked him and cursed him. They commanded him to repent to the King and the Pope, and to confess what he had done with the children, all the while striking him with their swords and spears.

The people kept their stones and their irrational curses aimed toward the Piper, fear and guilt replaced with heated hatred.

Finally, the brass pipe fell to the ground. Never would it feel the Piper's lips again. The Pied Piper's blood stained the cracked stone of the street. His bones had been broken, his body crushed and mangled, yet he had never made a sound or groan. Just music.

The Piper lay in his own blood, breathless, but a smile was on his face. Even in death he had won. The people and the soldiers were amazed and fearful all at once. His melody continued to echo through the hills in children's voices.

And all were afraid, fainting and dropping in fear to the ground.

"The Piper's dead," the children said.

The Piper's Last Song

"Yet, his song still lingers.
He hath found death, yet we saith,
They can't stay his fingers.

"Over a hill, another still,
Is how we all escaped.
The Piper's life was filled with rife,
Yet, he died not ashamed."

THE BREMEN TOWN MUSICIANS
BY
JOHN M. OLSEN

The old bus station smelled of lost dreams and diesel fuel as they all had over the last year. A free travel pass was the best I could get as a retirement gift from my employer when my eyesight got too bad to drive my big rig. As if I hadn't already driven the length and breadth of the United States for decades, my old boss said, "Travel and see the sights. Oh, that's right. You're going blind."

My old boss was a jerk, but I'd taken him up on the pass, anyway. I used that pass almost every day to catch a bus or train, often overnight to save myself a hotel stay. At each stop I hung out, looked around, and talked to complete strangers. I met a lot of cool people wandering the country like that.

I left the station and crossed the street to a small park in the outskirts of Atlanta to get my bearings. Traffic lurched to life on the streets as everyone tried to get home, so it was a relief to find a nice tree to lean up against to watch people wander past. That's when I heard "Love Me Tender" riding on the air from across the park.

I wasn't old enough to be an original Elvis fan, but who was anymore? As a long-haul trucker I knew the words to nearly every song played on the radio for the past thirty or forty years, plus most of the oldies. Whoever the singer was, he knew his stuff, so I strolled over to listen in.

A thrill ran through me as I saw his guitar, a Gibson Ebony Dove with white banding and a mother-of-pearl inlay that spelled out "Elvis Presley" in its rosewood fret board. The original sat in a museum somewhere. This had to be a replica, but it looked just like the one Elvis had played for so many years, even down to the kenpo karate decal on the body. I'd never learned to play more than a handful of strummed chords, but I knew enough to recognize and appreciate the instruments played by some of the greats. A few months back I'd gone out of my way to hear someone play a Stradivarius violin. Over the years I'd gained an appreciation for old things since I was an old thing now.

The guitar player didn't have a hat out for donations, so I sat down nearby and filled in some tenor harmony on the chorus. He smiled and nodded, so we eased into a duet and finished the song to scattered clapping from nearby folks who had stopped to listen to the improv in the park.

I held out my hand. "I'm Jack Packer. You have quite a guitar there."

"Thank you very much. You can call me Hound Dog." He took my hand and gave it a firm shake.

"You're an Elvis impersonator? I don't see many outside of Vegas these days. Don't even see them there much anymore." I'd been through Vegas a few times over the past year and caught a few shows.

He gave a knowing nod. "I used to spend a lot of time there. Not much call for an old, gray fan of the King these days. I couldn't find any work near Memphis either, so I came east to relax. I have family nearby."

The sun ducked behind the magnolia trees at the edge of the park as heavy traffic made its way past. We ran through a couple more songs before I said, "Say, it's about supper time. You interested in getting a bite to eat? My treat."

I didn't know if he was down on his luck or just drifting, so I figured I'd make the offer in a way he could easily refuse. Some people don't want a handout even when they need one. Since he hadn't been collecting money in the park, I figured he could afford a meal, but our duet had raised my spirits and I felt generous for a change. It felt good.

Hound Dog said, "I'd be happy to join you, but there's nothing near the park here that's any good. There's a burger grill by the name of Gary's a mile up the road if you're okay for a little hike.

The Bremen Town Musicians

I think you might like it."

I'd sat in a bus seat all day, and a walk sounded great. We traded stories along the way and talked about music. Hound Dog let the guitar ride on his back with the strap over his shoulder as we strolled. Talk turned to a good-natured bragging contest as we approached the burger place.

"I never got paid to sing like you have, but I know the top forty from the seventies to now. 'Course I prefer the older stuff to the new pop."

Hound Dog took that as a personal challenge and fired off one song title after another from the sixties, with me singing the opening line of each. Then he rattled through the current top hits and I nailed all but one rap song I'd somehow missed.

A car door slammed in the parking lot across the street at an elderly care facility as we approached Gary's Broadway Grill. Hound Dog's left arm came up to block me from moving forward while his right went to his hip where a pistol holster would have been if he were wearing one. A guy in a dark sweatshirt and jeans gave us a startled look, then headed into the building.

Hound Dog relaxed. "Sorry, old habits. It's not as bad as the flashbacks some friends get from our time in Viet Nam, but loud noises still make me jumpy."

Savory smells of grilled meat wafted out of the burger joint as we entered. The clink of silverware on ceramic plates was its own kind of music. My stomach grumbled, encouraging me to hurry to the menu posted on the wall so I could pick something. Luckily, the wall's menu was made up of two-inch-tall letters, so it only took a little squinting to read. The dark wooden banisters set up to guide patrons felt almost warm to the touch as Hound Dog followed behind, absorbing the ambiance with a deep, appreciative sniff.

He said, "The food's good here. Sometimes I point at the menu with my eyes closed just for variety, but the mushroom burger is great if you're into that sort of thing."

We ordered two mushroom burgers with fries and tall glasses of iced tea, then moved over to the pickup area. Several tables were free, so I didn't feel the need to reserve a space while we waited. The sound system played old Broadway hits, and "Oh What a Beautiful Morning" came up in the playlist. A clear soprano voice carried the tune flawlessly, other than having a particularly strong vibrato. I didn't recognize the recording.

Hound Dog froze, then turned. "Katie?" Then he smiled and shouted, "Katie Ringer?"

The voice I thought was a part of the recording stopped and a lady of African descent with almost white hair waved with both hands from a corner table, inviting us over. Generous smile wrinkles at the corners of her eyes appeared as she stood to greet Hound Dog. She seemed overdressed for a burger joint with her sequined red dress and obvious stage presence.

Hound Dog ran over as I picked up our order and followed at a more careful pace. He did introductions while I set the tray down and moved our plates to the table. "Jack Packer, meet my old friend Katie Ringer. Katie, my new friend Jack."

She held out a hand, not for a firm business handshake, but more like a Victorian lady greeting a member of the royal court. I gave a bow and touched my lips to her knuckles. "My pleasure, Katie." Her infectious smile set the mood for the table as she moved a knitting bag to the floor to make room for us.

She picked up a fork from beside her salad and turned to Hound Dog. "I haven't seen you since my last tour near ten years ago." Her smile faltered for a moment. "Ten long years. Time flies, doesn't it?"

Hound Dog went into brag mode on her behalf as he spoke to me. "Seated before you is a queen of Broadway. She's been on more casts than I can count, and she's done tours all across the nation. Some in Europe, too, if I remember right."

To make conversation, I asked, "What brings you here to Gary's Broadway Grill, Katie?"

She glanced down and melancholy invaded her smile. "Home." She nodded toward the street. "My kids signed me up for the care facility across the street. I never should have signed all those papers from my kids' lawyer without reading them. It's easy to be bitter about it since they took over my living trust, but they figured I'd get better care here. They might be right. The place has good security, so I expect they'll discover I'm not in my room soon and come over to get me." Her deep brown eyes twinkled with mischief.

I gave her a nod and a smile. "I'm sure we can substitute as your security detail until they arrive. It's a real pleasure to meet you." Hound Dog sat with his back to the wall where he could

The Bremen Town Musicians

scan the whole room for trouble. I don't know whether I'd call it paranoia or preparedness, but he made you feel safe to just be near him. These were good people. The best I'd come across in my last year of wandering.

Hound Dog turned toward the order counter and his eyes narrowed. I turned in time to watch as a twenty-something said, "Hey, Buck Buck Bob, tell me the weather forecast for tomorrow. You were always wrong, so I'll know what not to plan for."

A skinny man somewhere past his fifties turned, trying to ignore his heckler. The gal at the cash register stared, eyes darting between her customer and his tormenter. She had to be new since she seemed so unsure of how to handle the problem. So many kids these days had no training to deal with confrontation.

My chair and Hound Dog's slid back in unison. At his querying glance, I told Katie, "We'll be right back. Save our seats."

At the counter, the loudmouth dug himself in deeper. "Local TV got a lot better when they fired you."

I took the left side and Hound Dog took the right as we strode up behind him. Hound Dog said, "Don't be cruel."

The loudmouth turned, then got quiet as he found himself flanked by the two of us, arms folded but showing off more than enough muscle to handle him. I don't know what exercise routines Hound Dog kept up, but after my forced retirement I worked out in every hotel weight room I could find.

I said, "You should find a different place for supper. I'm sure it will work out a lot better for everyone if you make use of that exit right over there." I inclined my head toward the main door and flexed my biceps.

He glanced between me and Hound Dog, then at Buck Buck Bob, whoever he was. It took only a moment for him to decide it wasn't worth a fight. He stormed out, glaring at us over his shoulder, hands jammed into his pockets.

I leaned against the counter near the cash register. "Sorry about scaring your customer away, but he seemed to be causing trouble."

She looked behind her to a young man rushing forward from the back of the food prep area. The manager. He nodded and gave us a thumbs up. With relief plain in her voice, she said, "Thanks. Here's your order, Bob. Thanks for coming." She was back on her script.

Hound Dog asked, "Care to join us in the corner? We have an open spot at our table."

Bob pushed his glasses up and nodded. "I'd like that."

He sat and introduced himself. "I'm Morning Bob. Now just Bob Pullet, retired local weatherman and brunt of endless jokes. Some self-inflicted, others not so much."

Katie lit up. "I loved your morning show. It was always a joy to watch as you swooped in with your chicken jokes during the weather report. Your retirement left a big hole in the local station, and the news isn't the same now."

Bob grinned and dropped a sizeable ring of keys beside his tray. "Swoop. I see what you did there. Thanks for inviting me to sit with you. I hate eating alone, but it's better than trying to cook for myself. I got out of practice after years of TV schedules. I'm not sure what set that young man off." He shook his head.

Introductions went all around as before.

With a start, Hound Dog held his hands out for silence, then swung his guitar up and into position. The opening notes of "All Shook Up" wafted over us from the overhead speakers. It was from a movie with Elvis, not the Broadway production.

Hound Dog sang the melody as Katie and I picked up harmonies. Morning Bob pulled out his phone and thumbed a recorder to life and held it up as he tapped his foot along in time.

When the song ended, Bob turned off the recorder. "That was great. How often do you guys perform together?"

Katie spoke up first. "You have our one and only performance on your phone now."

The keychain beside Bob's tray looked too big to fit in a pocket. It was no wonder he'd set it on the table. It gave me an easy topic to keep the conversation going, so I chimed in. "We just met today, same as with meeting you. What's with all the keys? I don't recognize half that stuff."

Bob itemized his gadgets. "Thumb drive, car key, WiFi locator, house key, pliers. I really should get rid of the old pager. I haven't used it for years, but I keep it charged because I might have a use for it someday. I have a thing for gadgets, old and new. Once I had to rewire the microphone system at the station five minutes before we went live."

I'd driven a lot of vehicles over the years and the logo on his car key was one I'd known for ages. "How do you like your Benz?"

The Bremen Town Musicians

Bob paused with thinned lips, then said, "I don't drive anymore. The grandkids were right to take the car with my slowing reflexes, but I keep the key for old times' sake. They drive me around on errands, and I take public transportation a lot."

I held up my glass. "Here's to children and grandchildren who love us enough to take things from us. And to us for doing what we want to do, anyway."

We clinked our glasses together in a toast.

All that remained of our meals was dirty plates and empty trays. We sat around talking for an hour after the food was gone. I'd forgotten how much fun it was to sit and talk with friends, even if they were all newly met.

Katie's smile faded as she glanced at her watch, a sparkling thing on a loose bracelet. Twilight had arrived. "It's about time I got back. They'll be in a panic soon and send out runners to hunt me down. It's been wonderful to meet you all."

Bob pulled his phone from the inside pocket of his jacket. "I'd love to get together again some time." We traded contact information, plugging it into our own phones as well. We made our slow way to empty our trays, then gathered again outside the door for goodbyes.

The unmistakable sound of a semiautomatic pistol being racked froze my blood.

"Not so tough now, are you?" Bob's bully stepped out from the shadows. "Keys, wallets, phones, jewelry. And that guitar, too. Put them on the ground."

Hound Dog reflexively patted his side where his fingers curled. If he'd been armed, the bully would have found himself suddenly dead. There was no mistaking the look of restrained wrath in Hound Dog's eyes.

Katie fingered the knitting needles she'd poked through her ball of yarn. I gave her a subtle shake of the head and said, "Okay. No need to get jumpy." I pulled out my wallet and phone, setting them on the ground.

I prayed that Hound Dog had the sense to avoid anything brave or stupid as Katie and Bob dropped things onto the pile from pockets and purses. Bob's keys made an impressive pile by themselves as they clanked to the ground. Finally, Hound Dog put his own phone and wallet on the stack and set his black guitar beside the pile even as he glared daggers at the thief.

"Now get back." The thug waved his gun as we eased away from the pile of loot. He tossed everything but Bob's keys into a bag, slung the guitar over a shoulder, and stood. He held the Mercedes Benz key up. "Where's the car?"

Bob shrugged. "I don't drive it anymore."

"Four of you, and no car? What a bunch of old losers!" He turned and ran around a corner. An engine revved in the distance and faded away. The mugger had a car of his own already. Probably stolen.

Tears welled up in Katie's eyes as Hound Dog fumed.

I said, "Well, that's a problem. No phone, no credit cards, and no cash."

Bob raised his eyebrows as he pulled his phone from his jacket pocket with a flourish. "Our mugger friend didn't count how many phones he got. My pager must have tricked him. I bet the young punk's never seen one before."

I threw my hands in the air. "Great. At least we can call and report the robbery, but we're still out all our stuff. We'll never get it back." The trucking company would drag their feet replacing my travel pass. It would be a nightmare.

Katie gripped her knitting needles like a dagger. "That watch was a gift from my Broadway agent, God rest his soul. It's not worth a lot, but I loved that watch as the last thing he ever gave me. I should have jabbed his eyes out."

Bob said, "Don't worry. We have more than just my phone." He poked at his phone and brought up an app.

Hound Dog's face lit up with a grin. "You gave him the WiFi tracker on your keyring. But how to we follow it?"

Bob rolled his eyes. "Please. There's a tech answer for almost everything. I'll call a ride for us. Who needs a credit card these days? That is, if you're serious about wanting your stuff back."

Hound Dog said, "We should at least find where he took our stuff. If we report it to the cops from there, we have a chance of getting everything back. Who knows, we might be able to put the hurt on the punk and take care of it ourselves. I might have to curb stomp him if he's scratched the guitar."

Hound Dog might have talked about calling the police, but I knew it wasn't part of his real plan. From what I knew of him, it wasn't his style to stand back and let others do the work.

A half-hour later in a rundown part of town closer to Atlanta

The Bremen Town Musicians

proper, we got out of an Uber van. Bob waved to the driver. "Thanks! We might see you later."

The neighborhood didn't look terribly safe, but Katie insisted on coming along. Between us I figured we could keep her safe. Mostly. Except that we hadn't kept her safe when the mugger surprised us at the burger place. I came to terms with the idea that I had no control over the situation. Life was like that sometimes.

The whole evening was a mess now, and it kept getting worse. If I left them, they'd continue on without me and be in more danger with less protection. I wouldn't do that to new friends any more than I would do it to family. Fate thrust us together, so we would face this as a team.

Bob peeked at his phone, then pointed. "That bungalow over there." The brick façade and concrete front porch resembled most of the neighboring houses, all built near the same time in the fifties. Tall trees lined the street, so we gathered on the far side of a tree away from the porch.

"The locator shows my keys just inside. We can call the cops as soon as we—"

Hound Dog held up a hand as the front door opened. A quick peek showed our favorite mugger carrying a big trash bag as he headed for the street. We eased around the tree to stay out of his view on the opposite side as he moved.

I whispered, "I have an idea, Katie. Hit a high C, full vibrato, and *fortissimo*. Just a half-second should do. On my signal."

Hound Dog's mouth hung open in a silent "oh" as Katie grinned and took a deep breath. Bob's eyebrows bunched together in curiosity, but he didn't interrupt.

As the mugger opened the lid on his garbage bin, I gave Katie the signal. It's interesting how a singer with strong lungs and the right coaching can sound like the warbling of a police siren. Katie nailed it.

The mugger dropped his garbage can lid and sprinted across the street where he jumped a fence. What we hadn't counted on were the two others who bolted out through the front door of the house, jumping bushes like Olympic hurdlers as they fled. The door stood open and inviting.

I stayed quiet until we entered the living room and had the door closed, then I chuckled as Hound Dog and Katie busted out laughing.

Bob said, "Pretty quick thinking there, Jack." He pointed at a card table. "There's our stuff."

It wasn't just our stuff. These bad boys had been busy. A dozen phones, small piles of cash, and collections of keys decorated the table. Except Bob's keys weren't there. Bob pulled out his phone. "He must still have my keys. They're a few houses away. Wait, he's coming back."

Hound Dog searched the room with a piercing gaze. "They must have taken the weapons with them."

Bob said, "We've got to call the cops now. This is getting too serious for me."

Hound Dog nodded, but said, "Standard response time won't cut it here. We need to delay these punks for a few minutes or scare them off."

I killed the interior lights and squinted through a large window, watching for movement. "I've got the front. Bob, keep an eye out back while you guide the police in. We'll want them here even if they can't make it before the punks come back. Katie, these walls are solid. Over there in the corner will be safer."

She glared at me and pulled the knitting needles from her yarn. "How about I cover this other window instead?" It was clear she wasn't asking for permission. "I raised boys when that meant it involved dirt, pocket knives, and a moral compass. I'm not a delicate little flower."

I wasn't going to be the one to tell her what she could and couldn't do. She'd kept her cool as well as any of us through the whole situation.

Hound Dog opened the front door and left it ajar. A single exterior light shed dim illumination on the concrete porch and the yard beyond, filled with dry brown grass.

Bob whispered from the back hall, "He stopped a couple houses away to the left."

Katie slipped along the wall to stand next to the door. "If they're slow enough, the cops will arrive first." I glanced through the window and saw no rescuers. We'd been lucky so far, but someone could be hurt if anything went wrong. Luck was fickle. I hadn't won my million-miler driving awards by relying on luck.

Bob let out the breath he'd been holding and spoke up. "He's leaving. Three houses away. Now four. Good riddance to the

The Bremen Town Musicians

little punk."

The door burst the rest of the way open and one accomplice charged in and fired his gun into the dark toward the empty table where we'd stood earlier. The sound echoed through the enclosed living room with a deafening roar. Aside from the muzzle flash, the only light in the room spilled in from the front porch through the windows and the rebounding door. Katie's reflexes kicked in and she hit his blind side, a knitting needle in each of her fists. The man screamed and dropped his gun as one needle punctured his shooting arm and the other went through an ear. Katie didn't fight fair. The man backed into Hound Dog with his arms out and the two of them slammed into a wall. Hound Dog got ahold of the man's good arm and bit down on his hand.

Hound Dog pushed him toward the door as the man howled in pain. I got a run at him jumped with both feet out and kicked him. The door had sprung closed in the excitement. It made no difference when the guy flew into it. He went straight through in a shower of wooden splinters as the old panel door disintegrated.

Adrenaline makes you do stupid things. I realized my mistake on the way to the ground where I landed with a resounding thump. I hit with heels, butt, arms, and head all at once. Outside, I heard banshee shrieks mixed with profanity and panicked words sounding something like SWAT team, ambush, and body armor. The shrieks faded into the distance.

I hadn't pulled a move like that in years, and now I remembered why as I lay on the floor gasping for breath. Forty extra pounds and a calcium deficiency came to mind as I lay on my back. I wasn't going anywhere while I caught my breath. With luck, nothing had broken.

Less than a minute later, red and blue lights flashed through the windows as police arrived. Their sirens died out as they stopped and piled out of their cars. The police made better time than I'd assumed. This would get messy.

Bob's voice rose above the confusion in the front yard. "Thank goodness you're here. The men from this house all ran off that way." From the dark interior I watched Bob point down the street.

"Well, they're gone now." The officer didn't sound like he was in any hurry to leave on a wild goose chase in a sketchy

John M. Olsen

neighborhood.

Bob's good-natured smile turned into a wolfish grin. "If you install this tracker app on your smart phone, you can chase them to the ends of the world. They have my keys."

We sat inside while Bob worked his magic. "They'll never know you're coming. See, they're three streets over on the map here. It looks like they're in a car." Somehow, he'd borrowed the officer's phone through his smooth talking. A few button presses later, he handed the phone back. "Now you can track them anywhere. Taking down a serial mugger and his crime ring will look fantastic on your report."

The officer said, "Stay here. Backup is on the way to secure the site." He got on his radio and called directions as he put his patrol car in gear and took off.

Bob strolled in through the destroyed door, cheerful as usual. "It's a good thing I did the occasional stint monitoring police radio for news when I was the weatherman. Based on the radio traffic, we have about two minutes. Anyone want a ride before they get here? Our children might not be amused at what we've been up to."

Katie laughed. "Maybe it will teach them not to mess with me. I say we wait."

Bob said, "Right you are. The police would figure it out before long and wonder why we ran. They will want to chew us out for taking them on ourselves to make sure we don't try anything so stupid in the future."

Hound Dog hummed "Jailhouse Rock" as we talked.

None of us had anything to hide, so far as I knew. Hound Dog had a mysterious side, but he had a good heart until you got him truly riled up.

We made our official statements when the backup arrived, then the officers gave us tongue lashings and rides to our homes or hotels. I don't know if they bent any rules letting us keep everything that had been stolen from us rather than putting it into evidence. Plenty of other stolen goods sat in the house with the broken front door, so they may not have needed anything more to put the thugs away for a long time.

They didn't need us to testify, but they did want Hound Dog to take a medical test or two because of the bite marks they found on one of the thugs later that night. Hound Dog conceded

The Bremen Town Musicians

the bite marks might be his but wouldn't take any tests. The thug's rabies injections would be painful. I think that was Hound Dog's plan all along.

The following night we gathered back at Gary's Broadway Burger to share supper and to plan. The children, those who were local, were not amused, as I'd suspected. They watched from a nearby table as kids (grown adults, actually) from three families got to know each other. I gave them phone numbers, so they could conference call with my kids to make it a full set of frowns and disapproving glares. Everyone got what they wanted.

†††

Bob gave us a hand-signal as he finally cut our microphones. The sold-out charity concert came to a close with Katie, Hound Dog, and me on stage, with Bob handling the electronics and sound mixing. His wizardry had done wonders, and he'd recorded the whole thing for later, something about podcasting.

The audience looked like none I'd ever seen, including an eclectic mix of ex-hippies, long-haul truckers, opera and Broadway fans, and a table filled with black leather BACA jackets. The BACA guests had helped pick out a children's charity for the concert proceeds. Then there were Bob's fans, often more interested in the electronic gear than the music. All were welcome.

Sure, we were still old. We still had issues to work out with families, and my ex-boss was still a jerk. The aches and pains of age plagued us every day, but we'd created something, and our new mutual friendship grew stronger. We discovered the power of synergy, of working for something bigger than any of us could accomplish on our own. I'd found meaning in a life I thought I'd lost when I began my bus tour of the country the year before.

We had our limits, both financial and physical. That became part of the challenge to overcome as a team. Venues in nearby Atlanta cost too much for volunteer work, so we'd contracted with a music hall in a small town to the west called Bremen that catered to an interesting mix of musicians on tour. We rocked the hall and gave the audience what they wanted. The name probably wouldn't stick, but for the night we were the Bremen Town Musicians.

TEARS ON THE SWORD

BY
CATULLE MENDÈS
TRANSLATED BY PATRICIA WORTH

I

Once when the valiant knight Roland was returning from fighting the Moriscos, he was letting his horse catch its breath in a Pyrenean pass when he heard a shepherd tell of an enchanter, not far from there, who was making himself odious to the whole country by his tyranny and cruelty. At this tale the horse pricked its ear, shook its mane and made ready to gallop away, for it was aware that its master usually put little time between being informed of such crimes and punishing the guilty parties. But the righter of wrongs, patient that day, questioned the mountain shepherd at length. He learnt of some very strange things. The evil magician who lived in a castle by the sea did not limit himself to robbing travelers, laying the countryside to waste, setting villages on fire, ravishing young girls and bashing old men; he was also victorious over all the noble men who came to challenge him with the intention of putting an end to so much barbarity. The most worthy of them bit the dust; even by fleeing, they could not evade death. The castle keep was lashed on one side by a furious sea, and on the other there were enormous heaps of bones gnawed by animals and bleached by rain; and there was always a flock of ravens hovering in the sky, unfurling like a black banner at the top of the tower. Good Roland could not help laughing! How could he believe that an evil sorcerer had defeated paladins clad in iron, their swords drawn or lances couched? The storyteller did not know what he was saying, or else those who had defied the lord of the keep were cowards unworthy of the name of knight, little pages who had put on battle dress for play.

"Good master," said the shepherd, "it is not out of bravery that the enchanter brings harm to all his enemies. He has invented, with his infernal science, a weapon unknown until this day, that kills from a distance with no danger to the one who kills."

"What?" said Roland, much surprised and feeling a bad taste rise to his lips as though he had swallowed rotten meat.

The shepherd continued: "He is careful not to go down onto the plain to face the combatants, for he well knows that if he offered his breast, even covered in bronze, it would quickly be pierced. He stays crouched behind his fortifications or behind the bone heap. Then from his hiding place comes a sharp sound, a flame suddenly bursts out, and with no time to say an Our Father, the knight who had been confidently advancing falls to the ground, a red wound in his neck or forehead."

"In the name of Jesus, conqueror of Tervagant!" cried Charlemagne's nephew. "I've never heard of such cowardly behaviour! It's truly very fortunate that I stopped in this wild place to let my horse catch its breath, for I think that before the day is out, if the saints will lend me their assistance and if his dwelling is not too far off, I will have punished the treacherous man whose life is an offense to God. But, speak frankly, do you know how, and of what, this diabolical weapon is made?"

"It is said to be composed of a rather long tube, in which a bit of saltpeter is lit at one end, and from the other end comes a metal ball which shoots through the air, goes straight to the target, and strikes with lightning speed."

Roland asked nothing more. He gathered up the reins, squeezed the horse with his knees, the metal clanking, and with its mane flying, the horse galloped shoreward. But the gallant knight hung his head sadly during the ride. He was loath to soil his sword with the blood of a coward. It was the first time he was going into battle without pleasure.

II

The clouds of the sunset were red over the sea when the castle came into view. One might have thought the horizon was drenched in blood from all the crimes committed before these stones. Roland stopped. He looked at the horrible abode up to which rose, under a sky black with cawing birds, a pale staircase of skeletons! He sought a path amid the dry bones; he saw there was none, for the human remains were numerous, pressed down and heaped up; there was no possibility of reaching the keep without walking over death.

Ah! You generous combatants who came from every corner of the world to confront the perfidious enchanter, you whom an invisible adversary had foully struck from a distance, how Roland pitied you and honored you in his heart! How he would suffer to hear your tombless bones cracking beneath his horse's hoofs! Yet, he was overcome by a terrible anger, and the duty to avenge you prevailed over the instinct to respect you.

He spurred his horse on, his sword Durandal in his hand. Then, from among the castle stones came a sparking flash in a harsh boom that rolled from echo to echo; something whistled past the knight's ear. The sorcerer was using his treacherous invention. But he did not have the liberty to use it a second time. Roland had dismounted and thrust open a gate that squealed, groaned, creaked and yawned amid collapsing stones, and the enchanter, seized by the throat, strangled, spitting out his soul with a blasphemy, fell onto the flagstones beside his useless weapon, while the valiant knight, barely out of breath, was smiling, pleased with himself. Meanwhile the ravens were flying away from the turret that was lit with the glow of the sun's farewell, as though an oriflamme of light and gold were replacing the black banner. But Roland soon stopped smiling. After kicking away the corpse, he bent down, picked up the weapon and long examined it, handling it with disgust. To be sure, it was composed of a tube with two openings; through one, death went in, it came out through the other. The knight mused forlornly.

III

When night closed in, he walked toward the water. There he found a barque. He boarded it and broke the mooring, and with his strong arms rowed out to the open sea. The steel of his armor, in the toing and froing of his body, gleamed beneath the stars. Where was he going? What journey tempted him in the darkness? Weary with battle fatigue, had he devised a plan to take his rest on one of the miraculous islands where the light hands of beautiful fairies caress sleepy knights and fan them with large green leaves? Or else, informed of some injustice under far distant skies, had he decided, faithful to his mission, to go to that place amid lies and betrayals, and flash the sharp-edged righteousness of the sword? No, he wanted to complete his work for that day, as yet unfinished. The enchanter lay lifeless, the ransacked castle stood like the enormous and glorious sepulcher of so many knights defeated by treachery. This was good; but it was not enough! The cowardly weapon with which one can strike from afar must disappear forever, must never be found again. At first, he had thought of breaking it, but an evil man could have picked up the pieces, could have made another weapon like it by bringing together the broken remains. Hide it underground? Who knew whether someone, one day, by chance, would not dig it up? The surest way was to throw it into the briny deep at night, far from the shore; this is why he was rowing out to the open sea. When he was far, very far, from the water's edge, when he was certain he could no longer be seen, when he himself could no longer see anything except the immensity of the waters and the boundless sky, he rose, took the diabolical weapon in his right hand, spat on it and hurled it into the sea, where it very quickly sank. He stood pensive, his lofty stature paled by the stars, rocking slowly with the swell. He did not feel at all peaceful in spite of what he had done. He told himself that there would come a day, in a near or distant future, when someone would perhaps have the mind to invent a device similar to the one he had cast into the waves. He, the valiant knight, he who reveled in lances broken during palfrey skirmishes, in the bright clash of broadswords, in chests colliding with chests, in blood-red wounds close to the arms that inflicted them, he had the somber vision of a strange war in which men hated one another from afar, in which those who strike cannot see those they are striking, in which the most cowardly can kill the most brave, in which traitorous chance, amid smoke and noise, alone determines destinies. Then, gazing upon Durandal as it shone under the stars, Roland wept and wept a long time; and his tears fell one by one on the loyal steel of the Sword.

MEADOWLAND
BY
JUSTINE JOHNSTON HEMMESTAD

Persephone took a bare-legged step into the tall grass meadow amidst a morning shaded by clouds and dashed with colorful birds in flight. She was daughter of Demeter, Goddess of the Harvest, and she had not strolled the earthen land for more than fifteen years. Her short linen gown flowed upon her body like the glow around the moon; her long golden hair streamed over her arms and down her back like a fierce wave that gave life to the ocean body. To her gentle touch, the blades of grass were like sharpened threads of silk from the furthest reaches of eastern lands, through which western men had not yet ventured. But the golden flower that she pinched from the stem possessed the feeling of even more, a sense of what was to come – reflecting the nightfall.

She cast her gaze upon a lone, bright red pomegranate hanging low on the branch of a tree on the edge of the meadow. She could easily step toward it and reach out to take the fruit without leaving the safety of the meadow, but even more, she wanted to taste the sweetness of the rebellion in her step. Placing the pointed toes of one foot carefully ahead of the other, she approached it. She imagined it before grasping it – the juicy fruit, tantalizing her tongue and flowing through her mouth in a gush of flavor – she wanted it more than her own safety, like she longed to taste life more than she wanted to remain hidden by the will of her mother. Her fingers delicately conformed to it as she tugged it off the branch.

"Persephone – let go of that!" snapped Artemis. Persephone turned and met her protector's vibrant blue gaze amidst a torrent of long auburn hair as treacherous as her voice. "Your mother concealed you in this meadow for your own good; do not partake of *anything*. Others will know you are here if you do."

"I know," Persephone answered. "I am never allowed to touch anything in the meadow – I cannot even move! I can never see anyone but you and Athena; I can never imagine the One I will fall in love with. I must always be alone here with two goddesses to control me on behalf of my mother. I am more restricted than a fish caught in a net. My 'own good' is a fate worse than death, for I believe my mother has forgotten me."

The clouds loomed overhead as though to show nature who *really* ruled. But she took a deep breath, for she knew that she and Artemis were very much alike – they both pushed the boundaries to see how far they could go without causing harm to each other. The arrows of Artemis' bow were affixed to her back within a cylinder leather pouch as she clutched her bow tightly in one hand, but it was the arrow of her gaze that pierced Persephone's heart; she felt her mother had left her in the meadow only to be rid of her. She believed that her mother was so concerned with herself and her own willful rule that she abandoned her daughter. Persephone had begun to doubt that her mother cared for her safety at all.

"Listen to Artemis," said Athena, appearing from the other side of the tree, tilting her radiant face toward their leaves with her hand outstretched as though to touch their moistened veins. In the other hand she clutched a spear, the blade sharp enough to stab a distant doe with the slightest force. Her shining light brown tresses were slightly unkempt and hung in a clump over one shoulder. She sighed as though *she* controlled the wind, and asked with great command, "Where is your mother? She wants to keep an eye upon you, especially since she just refused Hermes and Apollo marriage with you." Athena's gaze drifted to the mature pomegranate of Persephone's temptation, still within her curious clutch.

"Apollo wanted me?" Persephone asked, intrigued to be free of her mother and the confines of a single meadow.

"Of course, he does, you are beautiful," Athena said. "But your mother does not want him for you, nor does she want his brother

Hermes for you."

"Who *will* she want for me? It is as if she will never allow me to taste a god," Persephone said with pursed lips that slightly cracked in their dryness. "I must wait until darkness comes upon the land and the pomegranates lose their seeds before I can marry and leave my mother! I need the subtlety of love now – I must have it!" She stomped one of her feet down in the meadow like a defiant child.

"Gods are fiends of power – they do not care for your welfare. Your mother does not want you to marry a god – *this, I know*. She will not allow it. She wishes you to marry a hero, a man."

"I have never seen a hero, and I *want* to marry a god – I want to marry someone as powerful as my mother, someone she cannot gain control over."

Athena tilted her head forward, her eyes slanted as though she longed to keep an innocent girl from falling into earthly trappings. "You want to marry a god?" Athena's gaze was plagued by the confusion that turned her blue eyes gray. "Do you not want to marry a *mortal* man – a hero? You may watch mortal men any time you wish. You may choose at your own will."

"No! That is why *I* am here," Artemis said, "to protect you. No god or man will force his hand upon you as long as I am here. It is your mother's will and you must do as she wants."

"And I speak wisdom to you," Athena said, "so that you become enlightened to what you need to know. Demeter is a just goddess and mother."

"You can withstand anything, Athena, for you are goddess of wisdom and war." Persephone sighed as she glared into the angry clouds that seemed to mirror her mood. Birds struggled against the wind to leave what they sensed would soon be a stormy area. "And you, Artemis, are goddess of the hunt, you can ward off any threat. I want to be open to something new, I want to be open to *love*." Spitefully and not entirely aware of her actions, she brought the pomegranate up to her lips and took a small bite. The thought of running away from her protectors was defiant and pleasing to her.

Her eyebrows narrowed as a strange feeling suddenly shot through her toes. The vibration rose from the ground, gentle at first and absorbed by her feet – but the gentleness quickly grew stronger. She tried to stand still, her lips quivering, her brow furrowed, and her hands drawn to her sides and clenched at her gown's skirt. Her gaze darted to Artemis, whose hair lifted into the same destructive wind that methodically tore up the meadow. The clouds swirled violently in the sky, thundered, and became even darker and lower to the ground. Persephone bit her lip, but as the ground shook and her own golden hair whipped beside her face, she did not know where to turn for safety.

Athena screamed, "Persephone – come with me! I will call upon your mother to save us!" Persephone struggled, her feet drudging up the earth as she tried to move. "Persephone!" Athena screamed again, and Persephone lost balance just as she saw Artemis raise her bow and shoot an arrow into the ground. She had seen something Persephone could not.

The vibration in her bare legs, as she tried to stand upon them again, grew more intense; even her gown appeared as though it were spilling milk. The ground shifted beneath her. Her tightly clenched fists were growing numb. Then she smelled the rotten-egg stench of sulfur, and she peered downward. The ground became warmer, almost hot against her skin, and took on a glowing, reddish hue.

A low roar droned through the wind, though another sound penetrated through it. Persephone heard the stomping, clapping sound of horse hooves upon dirt – a thunder beneath the earth, from somewhere unseen. She tried to turn toward the sound, but she shook, crying, and could not move. Her eyes filled with horror and disbelief.

She was pushed back by the rising mound of earth at her feet. Her limbs stumbling and awkward, she was unable to keep her balance and was thrown against the tree on the edge of the field. She stared to the breathing, cracking mound, stunned. "Persephone!" Athena screamed as though afraid for her life, but she did not know what to do; Athena's voice terrified her more than the deafening noise of moving earth and unseen horses. Before her eyes, a hair's breadth away from her feet, the ground fully split apart, and the red glow overcame the meadow.

Out of the earth emerged a horse's hoof, then another, followed by the powerful head of a beast, starkly black and dull. A rustic silver chariot followed out of the earth, so deeply silver that it seemed tinged with black. She squinted, for riding upon it, clutching the leather reins in his dark fists, was a lithe man with long legs, his arm muscles bulging, his thigh muscles protruding beneath his short black chiton. His hair streamed past his shoulders and was midnight black, and the hands that clutched his leather reins were wide with strength, as long black fingernails struck out from the bend of his hand. He wanted her to go with him.

Persephone wondered what her mother would do, for her mother's rule did not extend into the bowels of Earth. What would Demeter do now that Hades wanted her? Hades, in his possessive rapture, his utter dominion. She looked over both shoulders, but her mother was nowhere to be seen, even on the furthest reaches of the field. Once again, her mother was helping another mortal whilst forcing her own daughter to be subjugated. Persephone was alone in her sorrow, for her mother always left her alone. She would most certainly be abducted by Hades, and all she could do was hold onto life.

She whirled around, distress tightening her brow. The man came further out of the dirt toward her – there was nowhere for her to run even if she wanted. It was as though he were a forceful shadow and his horses breathed fire; darkness cloaked his eyes and the strong outline of his body echoed in mystery. The thunder of the splitting field was deafening; rocks, falling from the crust of the earth toward the unseen center, smashed upon one another with numbing crashes. Uprooted meadowland shot into the air; shifting soil turned with the torrent of a typhoon. The dark man's horses seemed infused to the earth itself, for as the mound had split, so too erupted the violence of the steeds. Persephone panicked, for the fear of what was unknown to her seized her heart. "Mother!" she screamed, her hands pressing against her face and tears streaming down her cheeks. But she knew her plea would not matter. She was left alone with the god of the Underworld.

Persephone's heart skipped a beat as she saw a glint of red beneath the hood of his cloak, for she sensed the power that was his alone. Faint white smoke arose from his body into the sky, for he was so tall that he may have touched the clouds. Her skin tingled. She felt powerfully drawn to him as though he had tied a rope around her. His shoulders were wide and powerful, his chest broader than any other. Her knees trembled, for she anticipated him; she had been awaiting a savior. Truly, she had never felt so filled with intrigue, which flowed from her fingertips and the ends of her hair. An ocean of purpose emboldened her uncertainty.

She felt the hot wind of his horses' huffing; out of the corner of her eye she saw Hades' long, sharp, darkened blood-fingertips curl toward her, beckoning her. Though his head and face were shadowed by a black cloak, his beauty was clear to her in his pronounced and subtle movement. He was anonymous, and yet she was fully wrapped in his attention. She was called, more by the force of her own heart rather than by any supernatural power of his, to accompany him into the depths of his lair. Just as he reached toward her and clutched her bare ankle, his grasp firm yet seductive, his fingers long and black, there was no escaping nor turning back, she finally heard her distant mother shriek: "Persephone! Hades – leave my child alone!"

"Do not listen," Hades said, his voice rumbling and shattering Persephone's soul. "She does not love you like I do. She cannot take you where I can. Come with me, and you will be my wife and rule the Underworld with *me*. You will be my goddess."

Persephone could not reject the rebellion that the sound of her mother's voice stirred within her. The great Goddess of the Harvest had failed to save her own daughter from impending abduction though she had saved many, many mortals who screamed and struggled for her. Hades pulled Persephone by the ankle toward himself, dragging her into the chariot upon which he stood...or she stepped on willingly. The mystery that awaited her, the dark, sunless kingdom she would rule, was too tempting to withstand in favor of a mother whose love had no depth, a mother who had chosen mortals as her benefactors, a mother who did not allow her to choose her own fate.

Persephone clamped onto Hades' taut waist as he whipped the horses forth, deep into the earth. She withstood the heat as flames licked her skin, for she was free, living without the dominion of her mother. Persephone would rule the Underworld alongside her powerful husband, and never would she emerge to the surface again.

KAT, THE JAILER, AND JACK
BY
CHRISTA CONKLIN

"But, we're cousins," Kat pleads.

"This is my first week on the job," I say, turning to pace the other way in front of her cell. "Why can't I get five days under my belt before take-my-family-to-work day?"

The rubber soles of my shoes make a dissatisfying thud against the concrete with every step. A sturdy pair of pumps would give me a more authoritative gait. Dumb uniform.

"Trust me," she says, "I will do you more good outside of this cell than in here."

"I trust you as far as I can throw you."

"You callin' me fat?"

I make another pacing turn.

"Oh, c'mon," she says. "You always laugh when Aunt Mary says that."

"She's my mom, Kat. She says it almost every day. If I've laughed in mixed company, it's out of respect for her, not amusement at her worn-out joke."

"Mixed company?" She overdoes a pout. "But we're cousins. It's not like I'm Jack."

"Is that some sort of jab at his being adopted?" I ask. "You're adopted!"

Kat covers her heart with her hands and takes a few drunken steps backward.

"You decide to tell me that now?" she asks. "Kicking me while I'm down, trapped, and unable to search for my birth family?"

I stop in front of her cell. My bangs blow into my eyes as a breeze kicks up in the twilight. A few raindrops hit my face. The cells are outside to punish inmates with exposure to the elements. Our prisoners are small-time offenders and don't stay long, but we want to discourage them from ever coming back. However, it seems that I am the most afflicted by the weather. I weave my arms through the bars and interlace my fingers.

"Enough, Kat. You were adopted when you were twelve, by your grandmother. Your mom lives next door to you."

Kat belches.

"Wow," I say, resuming my steady walk. "You really know how to convince someone to help you."

"I knew my charm would win you over."

"I'm not letting you out. You are my only prisoner. My first week, Kat. I can't screw this up."

"Listen," Kat says, trying to sound sober. "There's a good reason why I lost it."

"Yes, I know. It's called alcoholism."

Kat reaches through the bars, grabs my arm, and pulls me toward her. I could use her breath as hand sanitizer.

"Grandma is sick," she says.

"Your grandmother has had chronic stuff going on for 40 years. She'll outlive us all."

"No, this is different."

She lets go of my arm.

"If you let me out," she says, "I'll go directly to rehab."

"Kat, this is not my decision to make."

"You have the keys; therefore, you decide when to use them."

"It doesn't work like that," I say. "I have the keys because I am trusted to make the right decisions. Freeing prisoners because they beg to be released is not the right choice."

I begin pacing again. The motion of my legs keeps my brain on a determined path.

"I promise," she says. "I'll get help. I won't let this hurt you or our family. I'll even twist your wrist and punch you in the eye so it looks like I lured you close and wrestled the keys from you."

"Wow, Kat. Thoughtful."

"I'm ready to change. I can't live like this anymore. I need to help Grandma, and I can only do that by first helping myself."

I stop and face my cousin. We both feel my determination

Kat, The Jailer, and Jack

wavering.

"I know I haven't earned your trust," she says, "but I need to take out a loan until I can."

"I lent you money before, Kat," I say, reaching for my keys. "I expect this debt will also be defaulted."

Kat's eyes are wide with anticipation.

"You can take me straight to rehab," she says.

I turn the key, and she is free.

Kat leaves the cell and stands before me.

"My sweet cousin," she says as she touches my face.

Her left hook is swift and direct. I am on the ground before the pain in my eye has time to throb. For a drunk, she runs a fairly straight line. I cradle my face in my hands.

I regret my decision. A drunk woman brandishing a broken bottle because the bartender cut her off for the night just needs to sober up in a safe place, and this is it. If she'd stayed a bit longer and slept off the booze, she might have realized that her circumstances were not as dire as her intoxicated mind imagined.

She is sure to escape our low-security prison. I had ONE job! I thought it was ridiculous when Amy told me that I would start off guarding a single prisoner. I hate proving demeaning methods right. I look up. Kat is out of sight.

I stand up. Nursing my eye, I set out. I pass the hall to the visitor's entrance and exit through the main prison gate. There is no trace of Kat or any sign that her escape was noticed. I walk along the road that leads to town.

I reach into my pocket for my phone and turn it on. There's a voicemail from an unknown number, but I am sure I will know the voice. I listen:

"I'm starting over. I'm getting out of here. This place, the weird grandmother/mother thing, it's not good for me. Do you really want to work at Jailhouse Al Fresco? If you want a new beginning, call my cell - a friend is holding it for me - and I will tell you where to meet me. If not, I hope the black eye gets you out of trouble."

I stop in the middle of the poorly-lit sidewalk and wonder if Kat is the clear-thinker, and my mind is clouded by some sort of intoxication. If I stay here, I am likely to lose my job and need an entirely different career track. Trusting Kat with my future

Christa Conklin

doesn't seem like a wise choice, either.

I need counsel.

I stop at Calf-A Au Lei for caffeine and a dry place to sit and think.

I open the door, which is purposely over-oiled so that it slams into the wall and sets off the odd collection of hula dancing figurines.

"Aloha," Charlie says, with no hint of enthusiasm.

"Hey, Charlie," I say. "Have you seen Kat?"

"I serve coffee, not gin."

He still hasn't looked up from the espresso portafilter he is cleaning.

"Harsh, man," I say.

Over his pineapple-print reading glasses, Charlie looks up at me briefly, without lifting his head, and then returns to his task.

"No, I haven't seen her, but I wish she'd sober up. No one sucks down coffee like a recovering alcoholic."

"I'm glad you have her best interests in mind."

"Besides this pleasant repartee, what do you want? The yoozh?"

"Please."

Charlie puts his machine part down with a little slam and a big sigh, as if my asking for coffee in his shop is an inconvenience.

I sit down and wait for him to serve me.

He delivers my cup and asks, "I guess you want half-and-half?"

"Don't I always?"

"Yeah."

"So, wouldn't that be part of my 'yoozh'?"

He looks at me steadily, as if he may punish my backtalk by taking my cup.

I grab it and take a sip.

He smiles slightly, knowing I hate black coffee. I can't contain my grimace.

Charlie goes in the back and returns with half-and-half and two packets of unrefined sugar.

"Charlie," I say, "I think you frustrate your customers with unnecessary questions so that you have something to be angry about."

Kat, The Jailer, and Jack

"Hey," he says, "you're lucky I stock that ridiculous giant-grained, never-dissolving sugar. I don't get why you like it."

I fix my coffee, stirring long and slow to give my giant grains the best chance to melt into my drink.

"I have a question for you," I say. "Kat's run off. She has a plan to start fresh. She suggested I join her. Would you do it?"

"Did she give you that black eye?"

"Yes, but with the best intentions."

Charlie gives me another look over his glasses.

"Does she want you to meet her at some as-of-yet undisclosed location?"

"Yeah, she does."

Charlie displays a rare grin.

"Go ahead, kid," Charlie says. "If it were me, I'd meet up with her. I'm fed up with this place. I'm a cattle rancher who lost two-thirds of my land to eminent domain. I'm trying to make ends meet by filling cups, but I'm still such a patriot that I can't get myself to import coffee beans when my own country produces the stuff. I think I've created a niche market that will end in bankruptcy. The best intentions will likely be the end of me, too. Go meet your future, kid. At least I'll be able to cut that ridiculous sugar out of my budget."

"Thanks," I say. "I think."

I slide a $20 bill in front of Charlie.

"I'll be right back with your change."

I leave as soon as he disappears into the back.

Thankfully, the rain has stopped. As I walk deeper into town, I hear a ringing bell approaching behind me. It's Sarah and her rickshaw.

"Need a lift?" she asks.

She's frowning even though her fanny pack is bulging. Unexpected precipitation is good for business, but it doesn't make her job easy.

"I'm not sure where I'm going," I respond.

"Sounds like easy money," she says. "Hop in."

I climb in the covered cart. It's not as comfortable as her taxi was, but I hand her a $20 bill, and she begins to pedal.

"Have you seen Kat?" I ask.

"Nope," she says.

"She's taking off to begin a new life, and I'm invited," I say.

"Charlie thinks she's going to kill me, and that I should let her."

"Charlie's seen some hard times," she says. "He and I, we're no spring chickens. Instead of looking toward retirement and leisure, we've both been put out to pasture. But, we can only graze what we cultivate, and we're locked in a sandlot."

"Why don't you open your own taxi service?" I ask.

"Can't afford the taxes and insurance. Plus, now there are bigger fish in the sea that are a click away for the transportation-needy. I can't blame them for being smart. I just can't get myself to do the old 'if you can't beat'm, join'm' routine. So, here I am."

"I prefer the rickshaw," I say, sincerely. It may not be the most comfortable ride, but it is more fun than a car.

Sarah smiles back at me and says, "Thanks to a lack of parking, the theater, and a few new restaurants in town, I won't starve, but I won't grow fat and happy, either. I don't know what Kat has in mind. But, it can't be worse than this place. Give it a go."

"Thanks," I say.

Sarah stops and says, "Look, there's Janie. She's all over town. Maybe she's seen Kat."

I slip out of the cart, shake Sarah's hand, and walk toward Janie. She's wearing rubber gloves, holding a trash bag, and collecting cigarette butts from the sidewalk.

"Hey, Janie. Have you seen Kat?"

"I have a lot of butts in my bag, but no broken gin bottles, so no, not even a trace," Janie says.

"Wow, word gets around," I say.

"Jailbreak?" she asks.

"Yeah," I say. "It's complicated."

"It always is."

"She's planning to make a run for it, and she's waiting somewhere for me," I say.

"Are you sure you want to find her?" she asks, pointing at my black eye.

"I think so. This was actually a favor," I say, wincing as I touch it.

"That *is* complicated," she says.

"What are your thoughts?" I ask.

"Well, I suspect you are going to be unemployed if you stay. I

Kat, The Jailer, and Jack

also have my suspicions about Kat, and her intentions. But I spend my life keeping a clean city for townspeople who think their discarded trash magically disappears from the ground. I'm stuck in an inescapable Catch-22 of garbage and entitlement. I say go, see what a drunk can do to get you out of your predicament."

"Um, thanks," I say.

I begin walking, take a tissue from my pocket, blow my nose, and throw my trash in the nearest bin.

I look back at Janie who gives me an unenthusiastic thumbs-up, shakes her head, and gets back to her work.

I turn a corner and almost run into Jack.

"Hey," he says. "Shouldn't you be at work?"

"I'm on patrol," I say.

"Whoah, what happened to your eye?"

"Kat."

"Did you lose her already?"

"I can find her if I want to," I say. "I'm just trying to make a decision."

"Need some help?"

I explain everything to Jack.

"How about we go find Kat," he says.

"Have you seen her?" I ask.

"Who's the upholder of the law here?" he asks. "Isn't the rule of thumb to return to the scene of the crime?"

"I guess it can't hurt," I say.

We walk past the bar where she accosted the bartender.

"Why aren't we stopping," I ask.

"I wasn't referring to that crime scene," Jack says.

We continue walking until we get to Jack's car. He opens the passenger door for me, and I get in. He gets in next to me and starts to drive.

"I'm still confused," Jack says. "Explain to me again why you let her out."

"She's our cousin, Jack. She said she was ready to change and would go to rehab. I believed her."

"And, the black eye," Jack says. "I still don't get how that was a good thing."

I don't like this line of questioning. This had all happened so fast with Kat. Analyzing it was revealing cracks in the comforting thought that everything had happened for a reason.

"She wanted to protect me," I say, the words getting quieter as the preposterous sentence comes to an end.

"Still puzzled," Jack says. "You said she was intoxicated, yet came to a sudden, purifying, life-altering decision, and then punched you. I'm just not clear on this one."

I hold my head in my hands. I'm an idiot. This can't be fixed.

We pull up to the prison gate. I hand Jack my card, the bar goes up, and we drive in and park the car.

"Show me your beat," Jack says.

I lead him to the cellblock where Kat had been held.

The door to her cell is still open. I stand in the doorway and see Kat sleeping, handcuffed to the bench.

I look at Jack, who is jingling the keys at me.

"She never left the jail," Jack says. "I was coming to check on both of you. Your runaway stopped at the prison phone to make her one call before vacating the premises."

"She headed to the visitor's entrance?" I asked. It was a strange thing on which to focus, but if I had just turned right instead of heading straight to the main gate when I left, I would have had a cousin pile-up instead of a stroll around town.

"Wait a minute," I say. "Where did you get keys?"

I pat myself down for my set.

"That's right, Sherlock," Jack says. "You dropped them right in front of the cell when you went down. Lucky for you, I saw them before Amy did."

"Amy knows?!"

"Nah," Jack says. "You can thank your cunning cousin for that, too."

Jack waits, grinning and rhythmically nodding his head.

"I'll hold onto my gratitude until I know exactly what you did."

"Alrighty. Amy rounded the corner and saw me and Kat at the phone. She looked confused and unhappy. Before she could ask questions, I told her how I was visiting, and you and I were bringing Kat to make her phone call when you were suddenly ill. She wasn't happy that you didn't follow proper protocol, and that Kat wasn't restrained, so she cuffed her. She and I brought Kat back to her cell. I walked ahead and snatched up the keys before she noticed."

"Kat stayed quiet?" I ask.

"When Amy locked the handcuff, I watched the last glimmer of hope leave Kat's eyes," Jack says. "I think she decided to just give up. Now I'm even more scared for her."

"Ugh, what a mess," I say. "Thanks, though. You covered for me, and got rid of Amy, but I don't want to know how."

"It involves dinner plans this weekend. I'm a master of distraction."

Jack pushes me hard and I lunge forward, falling onto the floor of the cell. He slams the door shut.

"What are you doing?" I ask him. I'm sore all over. I'd cry if I weren't afraid that my eye would hurt even more.

"I think I was adopted into this family to put an end to the inherited inclination toward killing yourselves or each other," Jack says. "You, of all people, should understand why things are now not much different than they were a few hours ago."

"I need to receive the justice I deserve," I say.

"More than that," Jack says. "But, I am glad to hear you say that you deserve consequences for your part in this. It gives me hope that one member of our family can stop playing the blame game."

"Personal accountability."

"Precisely."

"When she wakes up," I say, "she's going to be unhappy."

"I'm not leaving," Jack says. "I just did something I have no right to do. I won't let it bring you any harm. Then I will stand by your side, shoring up that soft spot you have for Kat, while you do your job and get her the help she needs to sober up. Once she's in rehab, you can put your family hat back on, and you and I will support her through this."

"Thanks, Jack."

"Really? I just locked you in a cage with a sleeping wild Kat and you're thanking me?"

"Thank you for being clear-thinking," I say. "I am more at peace right now than I have been all day. I may be locked up and hurt, but I can now see a future that is much better than the way things were."

NECROMANCER: DEAL WITH THE DARK GODS
BY
JAKOB MORRIS

It was another night at the job. In between tailing cheating spouses and talking to dead grandmothers, you don't find a lot of gigs that really spice things up. Something like the Cyber-Sec conspiracy was something I would have rather avoided, but it just so happens I found something even worse.

Alcibiades was one of the city Councilors. You wouldn't think that would be the career path he followed considering his early life. He was a model and let's say "Actor" and leave it at that. He was never good with money until a few years ago when he made a killing in stocks. With money and looks he was a shoo-in for a seat in the Council. It was just over a year after his election that he came to me in hood, sunglasses, the works. Sitting across my desk was one of the most powerful men in the city and I just know I'm not going to like what he's going to say.

"Interesting look. Would have gone for a mask myself."

"I'm not looking for the Necro-lifestyle, Gregor. That's going to attract attention, and that's the last thing I need right now."

"Attention from who? The Hobs? Cyber-Sec?"

"I've paid those guys off long ago. No, it's some kind of Sorc thing. Some guy who called himself 'Kaz Tulliman,' offered me whatever I wanted for a set amount of time after which he would come back to claim my soul. I thought it was just a sick joke at the time, but I took him up on his offer because 'why not?' I figured since you're a Necro you would know whether this soul business was real or not."

I stood up from my seat and opened a drawer in my desk. In it was a file that I had stuffed to the brim. "Top-Hat-Kaz." I laid the file open for its content to be seen.

"That's him right there." Alcibiades pointed to a photo.

"He's been connected to a number of disappearances, but nobody in Cyber-Sec or the underworld has been able to pin him. Arcanet chatter suspects he's a Warlock."

"So, he's a Sorc?"

"Practically, yes, but he gets his power from one of the Dark Gods. Signs point to his patron being Ka-Tu'il, lord of knowledge and chaos. Explains why he's so slippery."

"Look, I don't know what any of this means. Can you help me or not?"

"I wouldn't know. Necro policy is not get involved with the Dark Gods in the first place. If I'm going to get you out of this, then I'll have to consult someone who knows more than I do."

†††

Sitting on a bench and reading a newspaper in one of the only public parks that wasn't covered in trash was what you might mistake for a homeless man. He was, but he was a little more than that. His name was Albern, and he was a part of the Druidic Order. As a druid, he lived an ascetic life and preached about the sagas and the meaning of virtue to any passersby that came his way.

Albern saw me and huffed. "Gregor, you've returned."

"I need some help. Let's skip the lecture about the 'leftmost path of necromancy,' and get to what I need to know. Warlocks."

"Does your hunger for power know no ends that you would even consort with the Gods of Destruction, Necromancer?"

"Not interested. This is for a case. This Warlock's been kidnapping people after giving them boons. I need to know if there's a way I can keep somebody safe from him."

Albern shook his head "I've heard of these kinds of things before. Both in the sagas, and in person. The only way I've seen someone get out of this is to join the Orders in the Isle of Skara

Brae. The Warlock would not wish to traverse its hallowed lands."

"So, all he needs to do is give up all his worldly possessions and travel thousands of miles in the badlands to safety? I'll pass on the message."

"I might know some people who could help with that. Were you around for the parade today?"

"That explains the noise. Couldn't get a lot of sleep in before tonight."

"Well the guests of that parade made it in today's newspaper."

†††

The Green Knights. They're one of the Knightly Orders of Skara Brae. See, in Skara Brae they have some of the most talented sorcerers in the known world, so they don't have much use for technology like we do in the city. They don't have a formal government either. Closest thing is the Tuatha of Druids who help with interpersonal disputes and a king whose only duty is to protect the land and its people. The knightly orders go around helping people and keeping the peace while holding to a code of virtues. The Green Knights take it upon themselves to test others and themselves of their virtue. Sometimes these knights travel from the Isle to places like here. I took the liberty of calling these visiting knights to Alcibiades's office.

"What is this?" Alcibiades sat at his chair tapping his pen to his desk.

I introduced the three knights. "This is Sir Bors, Sir Hans, and Sir Henry. They'll be taking you to safety."

Sir Bors, their captain, spoke "That is correct. We are willing to escort you to Skara Brae if you are willing to take an oath upon the virtues."

"So, all I have to do is abandon everything I worked for and traipse off to who knows where? No."

"Look," I stepped forward. "This business with the Warlock is serious. This is the best option we have if you don't want your soul to be a play thing for a Dark God."

Alcibiades got up from his chair and turned to look at the window. It was there he saw a reflection of the man he didn't want to see, Top-Hat-Kaz.

Kaz grinned ear to ear. "I see you got yourself a little party. Well, I hate to be the one to spoil it."

Bors placed his hand on the hilt of his sword. "You were not invited, and this man will not fall prey to the machinations of your lord."

"Well I'd hate to bring these festivities down. How about a party game? One of you will take a chance to chop off my head. Then, I'll take my turn to do the same. Any takers?"

The room was silent for a moment until Alcibiades stepped out from behind his desk. I put out a hand to stop him.

"Al, you don't have to do this."

"This is my best chance to get rid of this psycho. Nobody has to be afraid of him again, and I get to keep my job."

Bors slowly drew his sword and held it out. Alcibiades respectfully took the sword and approached Kaz. The warlock bowed over and presented his neck. Alcibiades lined the blade up, raised it high, and chopped down. It was a clean cut all the way through, but the body did not fall. No, its hand grabbed the lopped head and hat that had fallen off and placed it back in its original position.

"Now that was a nice, clean cut." Kaz grabbed Alcibiades by the collar and the two of them quickly flew backwards out of the door and into the dark hallways. Me and the knights gave chase. When we entered the hall, it was not as it was before. No, the hall was twisted around like a corkscrew as if the powers of the Dark Gods had warped the physical space. We ran through the twisted hall until we got to the stairs. We were on the top floor, but the stairs went from bottom to top from where we stood. There was a clanging sound as Bors's sword fell down this stairwell to the bottom where we stood. We ran up these stairs hoping to catch up, but when we reached the end, we ended up at the entrance of the tower where there was no sign of either of them. Alcibiades had gambled at gaining power and prestige and lost. Top-Hat-Kaz and his master had their next victim to do with as they pleased.

JEHOVAH ♥ GAIA
BY
SKIAN MCGUIRE

Jehovah fell for Gaia the instant He laid eyes on Her, fell like a megaton of dense matter down a gravity well. The only thing that kept Him from hurtling through space/time like some lust-crazed waterfowl was Her age: She was just so young. So misty blue-green, fresh as the dew. Virginal, even. It only whet His appetite, but He made Himself wait. From across the galaxy, He gazed, enchanted, while She dabbled in the primordial ooze, cooking up life forms, building mountains out of Her tectonic blocks. He watched while She played with Her dinosaurs, eon after eon, until He grew bored and, at last, impatient.

When the asteroid came out of nowhere, She was shattered. All Her lovelies – the big gentle brontosaurs with their graceful necks, the growling tyrannosaurs, the silly, plate-studded stegosaurs – shivered and died in the howling chaos. Shrouded in the storm clouds of Her grief, She pulled up coverlets of ice, inconsolable. For a moment or two, Jehovah wondered if He had gone too far, then He put His doubts aside. He had waited long enough.

Faster than 186,000,000 miles per second, He raced to Her. He would dry Her tears. Sweep Her off Her feet. He would be Her big palooka, She would beat Her fists against His brawny chest, and when He kissed Her, She would swoon into His arms. He would possess Her completely. He would ravish Her. He could hardly wait.

How could She could resist Him? He drew back the curtains of dust and let light shine upon the deep. When all the creeping, crawling things, all the birds and the furry creatures She'd nearly forgotten came out to sun themselves, He let Her think they were His gifts to Her. She smiled, and they were fruitful and multiplied. He took Her tiny hand in His and led Her through the teeming savannas, the clamorous rain forests, the bright tropical gardens. Together, they wondered at the sabertooths and the dodos. He made the dolphins laugh and teased the monkeys in the trees to delight Her with their antics, but Her attention had begun to wander.

"Look!" He snatched up a handful of clay. With deft movements, He fashioned a monkey of His own and breathed it to life. It shook its hairless self and teetered about on its hind legs. Her laughter burbled like a sparkling mountain stream.

"Silly," She giggled, "you forgot the tail!"

Frowning, He reached out and righted the tottering thing. It beamed up at Him. "Goo, goo," it started to speak, "ga, gah, gahh...duh!" It landed on its tailless bottom with a thud, grinning extravagantly.

She burst into peals of laughter. "Ooohhhh!" She could barely speak. "It looks just like you!"

Jehovah scowled. The foolish creature was struggling to its feet and tumbling back down of a purpose now, making a spectacle of itself. Sheer slapstick. He wanted to smite it, but She was watching.

"Gahh?" It repeated. "Gah? Da? Da? Da-da?"

She laughed until tears flowed, gasping, "What will you call it, the precious? Awww!"

"Oh, what a damn..."

"A-dam...," She repeated, crooning to it, "Adam. You sweet, sweet wittul thing!"

Jehovah rolled His eyes. In the distance, thunder rumbled.

"Please," Gaia cajoled, "make another! Pretty please?"

There was nothing for it but to humor Her. Muttering to Himself, He shaped another lump of clay into an ape-thing much like the first, but female, this time.

"She shall be just for Me," Gaia declared, "and I shall call her Lilith!"

Jehovah forced Himself to smile.

Together, They built a garden for the creatures, filling it with all manner of things good to eat, so that they hardly had to stir to be sleek and well-fed and absolutely full of themselves. It was sickening, how She doted on them. The dinosaurs all over again, Jehovah realized, gritting His teeth. It was time to have a little talk with that creature, what was his name?

"Adso," Jehovah called quietly. She was on the other side of the globe, separating land masses. No need to bother Her.

No answer. They'd been spending most of their time coupling like bunnies; probably the little dunderheads were at it again. He tried again, louder.

"Addle?" Silence. Jehovah fumed. He made the stupid things, He could unmake them if they couldn't show Him a little respect. What did She call the damn...ahh.

"Adam!" Jehovah commanded.

"Here I am!" Adam came crashing through the rhododendrons. "Here I am, Pops!"

"What did you call Me?" The sky darkened and flashed with the lightning of Jehovah's displeasure, and the little beast cowered from it.

"P-pops?" Adam whispered, "She said You were my father." Thunder crashed, but Adam did not run away, though he shook like a quasar flipping polarities. "Aren't You?"

Jehovah's brow cleared. Sunlight peeked through the breaking clouds. "Gaia said I was your Father?" It had been a geologic age He'd been courting Her and nothing more to show for it than a peck on the cheek. Maybe now, She was ready to settle down.

"Gaia?" Adam bit his lip. "You mean Mama?"

Was He about to get lucky? He should know things like that. He knew everything.

"It wasn't Her. It was Lilith told me." Adam beamed. "She knows everything."

Adam ran howling from a flight of hail as big as dodo eggs. Jehovah threw in a few frogs for good measure, then looked guiltily over His shoulder. She hated it when He wasted things. Never mind that She was as profligate as salmon. He might hurt one of Her *toys*. Jehovah salved His wounded pride with a quick plague of locusts and went off to bide His time.

He had to wait until She was off playing with finches in the Pacific one afternoon, as if there weren't enough of the little brown jobs already. At least it wasn't more of those blasted beetles. Anyway, He had the garden to Himself. Now that the Know-Nothings had started reproducing, chances to get Adam alone were few and far between. Gaia could hardly leave the things alone, giving one snotty mewling lump a few more inches of height, giving another a bigger braincase. Jehovah cleared His throat.

"Adam?"

"Yeah, Pops?" He was leading one squealing naked little man-thing by its tiny sticky hand. Jehovah quelled His disgust and chucked it under the chin. It screamed.

"Sorry, Pops," the man said, handing the baby off to the woman. The horrific wailing faded into the distance as she disappeared back into the garden with it. If the nasty little creature was going to make such a fuss, Jehovah thought, He'd give it something to cry about. Snip a bit off its little wanker, that would be just the thing. The thought cheered Him. He was only trying to be friendly, for Cosmos' sake.

"Uh, Pops?"

Jehovah snapped out of His reverie. "Don't call me Pops!"

"Gee," Adam said, "sorry, Po...uh, Mr. God?"

Jehovah frowned. They called *Her* Mama.

"We needn't be so formal," He said, pasting what He thought was a genial smile on His countenance. Adam grew pale. Still, he found his voice.

"What...what's Your name?"

That would never do. "That's a secret," He retorted automatically. Have them calling on Him by name, umpteen times a day, day and night, all however many billions of them there would someday be? It didn't take omniscience to see it coming. Just look at the cockroaches.

He considered. Adam was, after all, almost a son to Him. She had merely supplied the clay.

"You could call me Father, I suppose." Didn't She say Adam was the spitting image of Him? "Or," Jehovah said, warming to the idea, "you might call me Lord."

"Lord. Lord God." Adam beamed. "Okay, Po...I mean, Father."

"That's very good," He said, in as fatherly a tone as He could muster, "son." He stretched His face into a grin. Adam shot a worried glance at the sky and put his arms up protectively over his head. That wouldn't do.

"Harumph." Jehovah said, "Now, listen here...son. There are

a few things we need to talk...."

"Adam? Honeybunch?" There was a crashing through the underbrush. "Oh, Adam!" The feminine voice grew nearer. "Sweetie, I need you!"

The fronds parted, and Lilith emerged, a large snake twined around her neck and shoulders. In her arms, one of the more recent sprats was cradled, its head completely engulfed in the snake's mouth. She peered into the creatures unblinking eyes, her brow wrinkled with concern. "Poor snake! Punkin' was playing with Brother Snake and got stuck, didn't hims, hmmm? Brother Snake doesn't want to swallow baby, does he, now? Nooooo." She turned to her mate. "Could you just take this end, and I'll try to pry the poor thing's jaws open a bit?" She handed the bare bottom half of her offspring to Adam, which chose that moment to squirt.

"Aw, Lil...." Adam said, brushing the sprinkle off his chest as he curled his elbow around the infant's squirming torso.

Lilith glanced up. "Oh, hi, Dad!" She flashed Him a quick smile and returned to the task at hand. "Now hold tight while I..."

His rage was extraordinary, even for Him. In the end, He put in a security guard at the gate, with a flaming sword to keep the bitch out. Lilith was out of there, her and her disgusting progeny, too. Good riddance.

He thought that would be the end of it, and everything would have been hunky-dory except for that big cry-baby Adam. He was lonely, he said. He missed his helpmate. Hah, Jehovah knew what *that* was about: he just misses his cozy cooze. Since Jehovah himself still hadn't gotten any since the beginning of time, He had very little sympathy for the creature. Didn't He give the lout opposable thumbs? But then, what if She got wind of it? She still hadn't noticed that Lilith was gone.

"Oh, all right, all right," Jehovah muttered. "I'll make you a new female. How's that sound?"

That perked Adam right up. *Oh, it had been true love all right,* Jehovah thought bitterly, *and all cats are gray in the dark.* "No, no," He told Adam, "put away the clay. I'm going to do it differently this time. Just lay down, will you?" Adam just stood there. "Go to sleep!" Jehovah commanded, irritated.

Adam did. When he woke up in the afternoon light, it seemed

like a whole day had passed, or maybe even three, he couldn't tell. All he knew was that, boy, did he have to pee. And his side felt weird. He probed it tentatively with one hand while he felt his skull for bumps with the other. Had he gotten beaned by a coconut again and just didn't remember it? Then a slight motion across the clearing caught his attention.

The naked woman with the exquisitely formed mammary glands was pushing herself to her feet. Her hair was the color of ripe wheat, another one of Pops' presents. Adam had to admit she was every bit as beautiful as...as...as what's-her-name had been.

"Hubba hubba," Adam said.

†††

There was only so much of that putting-bodies-together stuff they could do. What's-her-name said that's what made the babies happen, but Adam was not so sure. Shouldn't there be like, a gazillion of them by now? At any rate, Eve didn't want to do it as much as he did, and he couldn't do it all that many times in a day, himself, anyway. He finished naming everything ages ago, and he suspected it was just busy work, anyway. The lion was always taking naps with that stupid lamb and nobody wanted to play chase-me. What did they have to do but explore?

†††

Finally! She put the finishing touches on – a little iridescence, some crazy colors, those big multi-lens eyes – and it was done. She sent it off to do its thing and was rewarded with a little loop-the-loop; She clapped Her hands in glee. It really could fly backwards! That had been one of the tricky ones. She'd go ahead and let it mate with the previous versions and see if the design changes held. She dusted off Her hands and wondered what to work on next. Maybe that thing with the armor that could get a baby underway and then hold off giving birth until it had juuuuusssst the right time and place? She really ought to give it a little more brain. Someday something would come along that could just crush that armor like an egg. It was inevitable. Gaia was happy to let Her creations multiply on their own; She wasn't a control freak like Jay. He really needed to loosen up some.

She wondered what He was up to? She'd hardly seen Him ever since He'd taken over that little reserve of His between the ear-shaped chunk of land and the big hat; Eden was what the Man decided to call it. Lilith said so, anyway. She liked talking to Lilith, and it had kind of bothered Her that He had just thrown her out and replaced her with a bimbo. Really, there was no other way to put it. Eve was just not very bright, but she certainly had boobs. And what an appetite for mating! It was obvious that Eve had been Jehovah's handiwork, not Hers. She liked to give the females a break and not be pestered about mating unless the hormone clock said it was time, but not Him. Males: so predictable. Still, She probably ought to check in again. He came all this way to see Her, and after those first few lovely walks together, She'd hardly given Him the time of day.

She had to admit, He made Her a little uncomfortable. He was just so...intense. She told Him She needed space, and He'd gotten all huffy and hurt-looking. She had actually started to worry that She'd been unfair, when She began to notice little things out of place – that big mountain, was that a little closer to the sea than She thought She'd left it? And the footsteps that had filled with water -- She wasn't stupid. She hadn't put lakes there. She knew what they were. He was sneaking around, watching Her. But then...

Of course, He was lonely. There weren't any other Gods to talk to, and He was the chatty type. Maybe She could invite some of Her relatives to visit.

†††

"Yoo-hoo!"

He was sitting on that hill He liked, just beyond the Garden, and He almost jumped up to run to Her. He caught Himself in time. It wouldn't do to seem too interested, too eager. Too much like He'd missed Her. If She thought He actually needed Her, She'd have Him by the balls forever. He smoothed His robe and waited.

"Oh, I'm so glad I found You! I've been having so much fun! You should see all the new creatures I've been making...." She trailed off. "Are You okay?"

Skian McGuire

"I'm fine."

She waited for Him to say a little more. Something. Anything.

"Are You...mad at Me?" Honestly, it was like pulling teeth.

"Mad? Why would I be mad at You? Of course not. I've just been watching over things here. The humans, you know. If they didn't have Me looking out for them, they'd surely be a banged-up mess by now. Not a lick of sense."

"Ohhh..." She gave a little relieved laugh. At least He was talking. "What have they been up to, the silly things?"

"Well, Adam – that's the male, you know—"

She had forgotten the creature's name and blushed a little. She hoped He didn't notice – She hated to admit that She'd been so wrapped up in Her own projects that She'd put the Garden humans right out of mind.

"Adam keeps trying to do things he's not built for. He climbs up trees and jumps off, flapping his arms as if they were wings."

"Oh, no! Did you have to make a new one?" She knew He'd tweaked the rules so that there was no death in His little resort, because He hated having to do the same job twice. Not like Her; She could keep working on improvements forever.

"No." He looked down, sheepishly. "I just did some quick hurling of matter and got a big pile of poop from those big hairy things of yours, the ones with the long nose and the tusks? Soft landing."

"How lucky for him you were watching!"

"Well, that time. The next time, he actually broke his back, stupid thing. I let him drag himself around by the elbows for a while before I fixed him, but he still did it again."

She was a little horrified; was He really that mean? She shook Her head. No, it was just His way. He wasn't very patient. She wouldn't make an issue of it. "See?" She said instead. "This is why pain is a good idea, Jay. It teaches them not to do things like that."

He got all stiff and quiet. Uh-oh, She thought. Stuck Her foot in it. What did She say?

"My name," He told Her, "is Jehovah. You know, I don't share that with just anyone."

"Oh, I'm so sorry." She felt awful. "I didn't mean to offend you. I just...well, we've known each other for ages, now. I just thought..."

"Well, You know..." Now He was the one to look embarrassed. "You don't come around very often... we aren't... we haven't had all that much chance to, um, get to know each other."

She felt bad. She resisted the urge to hug Him – He could be so formal!

"Well," She said, blowing a strand of loose hair out of Her face. "Let's do that then!"

He looked up at Her, so full of hope! Her heart melted. Somewhere in the hot jungles of the other ear-shaped land mass, a thousand new species of frogs sprung spontaneously into existence and started singing their little hearts out. She took His Hand.

They'd have a real day out and leave the Garden to His staff for the day. He hadn't taken a break since Adam had started pulling those stupid stunts of his, probably just trying to impress the woman, not that she needed any persuasion. Later, He would look back on it as His happiest day ever. It would be a bitter memory; He knew that already. He knew everything, but He didn't care. They'd have a holiday! He could use the rest.

†††

"What do you see up there, honey? Sweetie?"

He didn't answer. Eve could be so annoying. If she wanted to see, she could climb up here herself. Scaredy-pants.

"Honey?"

He thought, at first glance, they'd come up on another gate. That had been a surprise, the first time. He hadn't realized that this wasn't the whole world. Of course, he wanted to go out and see what else there was. That must have been where what's-her-name went, her and the brats. Life certainly was easier without *them*, he had to say. But then there was one of those servants who wouldn't let them pass and brandished that hot yellow-and-orange flickering thing at them. It would have made a mess of him and he'd have had to wait while Eve got Pops to fix him; what a freaking nightmare. So they turned around.

But it wasn't a gate, this time.

Eve started yanking on one of the lower branches. "Honey?" He was just trying to shinny up one more little branch and had to grab on tight.

"Hey! Stop that!"

It was...something else. What? He dropped from branch to branch like those monkeys that used to hang around with what's-her-name. He hadn't seen any since she'd left, and for a moment he wondered what happened to them. But now there was something really interesting to check out!

"Come on!" He headed off toward it, whatever it was. She stood there like a post. "Come *on*!" He turned back and grabbed her hand. Why did she have to be so slow?

It didn't take long. The trees thinned out. There was a little babbling brook and mossy rocks and a little wall of stone circled around the most beautiful tree he'd ever seen. It was just drooping with fruit. Beautiful, juicy-looking fruit. He got so tired of the same-old same-old, the apples and pears and breadfruit and bananas. Tasty, yes, but boring. That was one of Eve's favorite words. Boooorrrrr-innng.

He took a step up on the wall.

Boom! There was that servant again, waving the pointy hot thing around.

"Watch it!" Adam yelled, jumping out of the way just in time to avoid a swipe across the gut. "You almost got me with that! What's your freaking problem?"

The servant just rippled its shimmery wing-things and didn't answer. He'd never heard one speak, but usually you knew they were around because they were always singing this stupid, la-la-la "isn't the Lord just wonderful" crap until you wanted to ram bugs in your ears. Not this time, the tricky creep.

Then He was there.

"Child," the Lord God said, "that tree isn't for you."

"Uh, hi."

Eve had sidled up and was hiding behind him, the coward. Why did he always have to be the one to stick his neck out? "I don't get it. Didn't You put all this stuff here for us?"

"Not that one. You can eat everything else. Isn't that enough?"

Adam was confused. He couldn't leave, he couldn't eat this, he wasn't supposed to fly, what else was he being kept from doing and he didn't even know it yet? He summoned up his courage. Pops could be a real stinker, sometimes, but He was looking pretty relaxed today. Maybe Him and Moms...no, he didn't want to think about that. Yeeeesh.

"Why not?" Adam asked.

"Because I say so," Jehovah answered.

Adam blinked. "But…" he began.

That's when the storm clouds filled the sky and enormous cold drops of rain pelted down at them. They ran, slipping and flailing in the sudden slick mud, Eve screaming her silly head off. They didn't stop to catch their breath until they got to the little cave they'd found the day before, when the noon shower was about to start, and Eve was wearing that new flower-thing she'd made for her head. The rain just kept coming down. They had nothing better to do so they did that body-putting-together thing. It was fun, but afterward, he wished they'd brought in something to eat. Boy, that fruit had looked good, but he knew very well that it would be better not to mess with it. Pops really could be a stinker.

†††

It had been a really lovely time. She liked Him a lot, yes. But there were … issues. He could be very rigid and boy, did He have a temper. She didn't think He would make a particularly good parent – too impatient. And full of Himself.

He did love to talk, though. And He loved to show off how much He knew. As They strolled, He kept a running total of all kinds of silly things – the grains of sand they stepped on, the hairs on the tails of every squirrel, the distance in cubits they'd covered. He was a little compulsive about it, frankly. Or maybe He was just trying to impress Her. It was a little weird, She had to admit, that He seemed so prudish. All the other Gods She knew had been randy to the extreme, always cheating on their wives and knocking up random nymphs and dryads whenever they got the chance. Not Him, and She almost wondered if maybe She just wasn't attractive enough. Not that she really wanted to get it on with Him. She had so much to do! And, well. He had issues.

He was lonely – She could tell, but He swore He liked being alone. And when She very hesitatingly suggested that maybe She could invite some of her relatives for a visit, He was not at all pleased.

"Like who?" He wasn't smiling now. "Not that Chronos guy."

"My brother? You know Him?"

"Not really. I've seen Him around. We're just about totally different things."

"Ooooh-kay," She said. She thought for a minute; She wasn't sure She wanted to invite any of Her sisters to meet Him, though She wasn't sure why. She didn't think She had to worry about Him hitting on them, but He was a guy, and She hadn't liked how obsessive He'd been, following Her around and all. Maybe She thought her sisters wouldn't like Him, and She didn't want to deal with that.

"How about my cousin Mummu? I think you'd like Him."

His eyes narrowed. "How close a cousin?"

"Not very," She answered. "I haven't seen Him in eons. He's very cute, though, and a lot of fun to be around. He likes making things, too. And he's very conversational."

Now He was glowering. There was no other way to describe it.

"How well do you know Him?"

Whoa, She thought. Is He jealous?

"Not *that* well."

They were sitting on the big rock just where the oceans met. After a long silence, He said, "Thank you. But I really don't need any company."

They wandered around for a while after that, but it felt to Her like the mood was gone. She was *very* glad She hadn't invited any of Her family as a surprise. He really wasn't Her type, and that made Her sad. To be honest, She was a little afraid of Him. She didn't think He could hurt Her, but Her lovely creatures...She'd seen Him throw things around when He was angry. It would be better to let Him down gently. She hoped they could be friends. It really had been a lovely day, and She wanted to kick Herself for ruining it. Oh, well. Maybe it was for the best.

†††

She wasn't there when he woke up. He didn't think anything of it, at first. She liked to bathe in that pretty little pool they'd found, with the goldfish. She fed them bits of stuff she'd saved, and she laughed when they tickled her. He got himself out of the grass and moss they'd made for their bed and rummaged around

Jehovah ♥ Gaia

for something to eat. When she hadn't come back by noon, he started to worry that maybe she'd decided to try to fly, and maybe she had broken something? He went to look.

He found her by the tree. That tree. The one he hadn't been given to name, and Pops hadn't said what it was, either. He was furious.

"You know we're not allowed to eat that stuff. What were you thinking?"

"I just wanted to look. I didn't pick any. I didn't even get close. I just looked!"

"Well, you don't need to do that. Stay away from that tree. Pops said so, and you know how he gets."

She pushed out her lower lip and pouted, just like the brats used to do. Sometimes he really missed that other one. Lilith. That was her name. "I can do anything I want," she said. "You're not the boss of me."

He sighed. There was no reasoning with her. The best thing to do was give her something else to think about.

"Well, let's go play with the otters, then. You always have fun with them, right?"

"Okay." But she wasn't going to forget about the tree. Pops hadn't told *her* not to eat it, just Adam. Besides, she only wanted to look. And she wanted to talk to that Snake again. She hadn't told Adam about that; he never gave he a chance. He never listened to her, and she was tired of listening to him go on and on and on about himself, day in and day out. Sometimes all she wanted was somebody else to talk to.

She got her chance a few days later when Adam, the idiot, had stuck his head in a tree hollow to see if the bees had left some honey for him and got stuck. The bees were really angry! They buzzed so loud she could barely hear him yelling, and from what she could tell, they were probably getting in his ears and mouth and everything (she'd done the same thing once, only she wasn't stupid enough to get her head stuck). She tried to help, but his head was just too big, and he kept turning it funny. She yelled for Pops, and when the clouds parted, and the light streamed down, and all those stupid servants were singing their la-la song at the top of their lungs, she saw she had the perfect opportunity to slip away. Pops never just pulled Adam out of the mess; He had to give the idiot a nice long talk, too.

The tree was not very far. And the snake was there.

"How come you can talk?" None of the other animals in the Garden had ever talked, at least not to her. She didn't know they could.

"Lilith taught me," the Snake said.

"Who's Lilith?"

"She was Adam's first mate. Did you never hear of her?"

"Where is she? I've never seen another woman here."

"Your Father threw her out of the Garden. That's why there's an angel guarding the gates with a flaming sword. To keep her from coming back."

Eve was thunderstruck. So much new stuff to think about! Angels. Swords. Talking snakes. She furrowed her brow.

"So how did she teach you to talk, if you're here and she's out there?"

"Oh, we animals can go back and forth. Mother insisted on that. Biodiversity, she called it. It's just you humans that can't."

Eve thought about that for a while.

"Okay," she said. She didn't like the idea that Adam had a woman before her. She didn't like it that nobody told her.

"Is Lilith pretty?" Adam was always telling her how beautiful she was, usually while he was trying to get her to do the putting-bodies-together thing. He wanted to do it a lot more than she did, even though he couldn't always get his dangly thing to work.

"I wouldn't know," the snake said.

Eve thought for a while. Her head was buzzing with questions like Adam's bees, except his were outside. She had a moment of panic, wondering how long she'd been there, maybe Adam had gotten loose by now? But no, there would be the lesson. She wished she'd brought something to eat.

To eat.

"Why doesn't Pops want us to eat that fruit? Is it puke-making?" Sometimes the things they tried to eat were not really meant for that, and the stuff came right back up. Adam named it puke. After it came back up, anyway.

"No," the snake answered. "There's nothing bad about it. It's perfectly good to eat, though not all that tasty. In here, all we snakes get to eat is fruit, so I know. Somewhat boring. It just looks pretty."

"Oh," said Eve. Taken aback. "Then why?"

Jehovah ♥ Gaia

"It's a power trip, sweetie. He just wants you to do what he tells you to do."

"Huh." She thought of the servant – the Angel – with the hot sharp thing – the sword. "Do we have a choice?" she asked.

"Good question," said the snake.

"Thank you," Eve said. "Do you know the answer?"

"Yes. There is only one way to find out if you have a choice, and that is to choose."

"Choose what?"

"Choose to obey the Lord or eat the fruit."

"But can I choose?"

"Can you?"

"I don't know!"

"You'll know if you eat the fruit."

So she did.

†††

He would have gone to look for her as soon as he'd gotten the bees out of his nose, but God made him wait while He fixed every one of them. It still would have been too late.

He found her sitting on the little stone wall, licking her fingers.

"Why did you do that?"

She looked him straight in the eye.

"I have free will, too, you know."

"Free will? What the..." He was bewildered. "What do you mean, free will?"

"If we can't disobey, we're just slaves."

"Slaves? What are slaves?" His eyes narrowed. "Somebody else has been here. You've been talking to somebody. Is it her? Did Lilith come back?" Oh, yes, he remembered her name now. He'd find her and...

"Oh, Lilith. Now you bring her up. When were you going to tell me you were married before?"

"Married? What? I was never...."

"Oh, you never married her, either?"

Adam was dumbstruck. He didn't even know what married was, but clearly, it was something he should have done with Eve.

"Well," she said, standing and brushing the bits of husk from her thighs, "We'd better pack." She tossed him a fruit.

He caught it automatically, then dropped it like a rock hot from the sun. "I don't want that!" She was going around the clearing, gathering up big leaves. He looked down at the fruit. Was he even allowed to touch it? Oh, boy, were they in trouble now.

"You might as well try some." She had laid out a bunch of the big leaves in a row and started pushing a strand of vine through holes in them.

"Pops said we aren't allowed!"

"I ate some. They were okay. If you don't eat any, you'll never know, and He's going to throw you out, too. Or maybe He'll just kill us."

"Kill? What?" He felt like the time he'd gotten in that place where the water goes crazy and he couldn't get out. "You were talking to her, I know it!" He started running around the clearing, peering into the trees. "Where is she? Lilith? Come out here!"

She sighed and held up the panel of big leaves to examine. "She isn't here. The Angel won't let her back in." She put the leaves down and sat to add another one. "Fat, fat, fat," she muttered.

"Who? What?" Adam sat down hard on the moss. "Why?" he wailed.

"It wuzza Snake," she told him around the end of vine in her mouth. "Animals can come and go, iss jus us." She spit out the vine and tied off the end. "He told me that this is the Tree of Knowledge." She stood up and put the skirt of leaves around her waist. "I wanted some," she said simply.

"Snakes don't talk."

"This one does. Lilith taught him."

'Lilith! I knew..."

"Oh, I know all about her, now, too. I can't wait to meet her." She walked back to the tree and tossed him another fruit. "Like I said, you might as well."

He did want to. He thought about when the tree broke him, and he laid there peeing himself while he waited for Pops to fix him. How was he supposed to know that bones were so breakable? Instead, he asked, "What are you doing?"

"The Snake said that outside, we'll have to wear coverings

over our skin. Bugs bite you and it feels bad, there, and the air gets a lot colder, and the sun turns your skin red and that feels really bad, too." She was gathering more leaves. "He said this is 'clothes.'" She pointed to the ones around her waist. "Skirt. I'll make you one, too."

He was staring, wide-eyed. Without even thinking about it, his hand rose to his mouth and he took a bite.

"Ecchhh!" He threw it down. "I didn't mean to do that!" He spit out dry bits of husk. It didn't even taste good, and now he was in so, so much trouble.

"Stand up," she said. "Give me that." With a deft motion she tore the husk and pulled out a dripping mess of gleaming red seeds. She took his hand and slid the juicy blob into it.

"It's better if you just suck the sweet part off and spit out the seeds."

He did so.

The string of big leaves was too long. She took one off and wrapped it around him, tying it the same way she'd tie her own. He had such a scrawny butt; maybe she should get another piece of vine and tie it on?

"Adam." The voice came from behind them, surprisingly soft. "Eve."

God came into the clearing, only man-size. It was, in its own way, scarier than when he was tall as the biggest pine and thundering.

"Why are you wearing skirts?"

Eve's bravado was gone. She hung her head.

Jehovah sighed. Later, after she had learned what Death was, Eve remembered that sound as the saddest thing in the universe.

†††

Lilith met them not too far from the gate. The Snake was with her, and so were a couple of dirty little ones and a very hairy little man. Adam thought he looked a lot like the monkeys they used to have in the Garden, before Lilith got thrown out. Several older ones, two girls and a boy, stood behind them, trying to hide, Adam thought, but peeking out with an eager curiosity, and he realized that they were the ones Lilith made from the putting-bodies-together with him. His children.

Within minutes, Eve and Lilith were chattering together like they'd always known each other. He tried to carry on a conversation with Jarabal, Lilith's husband — he still wasn't sure exactly what the word meant — but the little guy had such a weird accent, Adam wasn't sure if he understood one word in ten. The three that were his stood behind, listening; they didn't seem to know who he was, although he was sure Lilith must have told them. They weren't very old when she left.

Eve was showing off the new skin coats that Pops gave them as a going-away present. The idea was pretty gross, but He'd been pretty good about the whole thing, Pops had. Adam never guessed, with all the yelling He'd done about little stuff like when the lion tore his foot off by mistake. He was still pretty mean to the Snake, though. Eve said she didn't think the Snake had anything to worry about, because Pops didn't have any say out here, it was all Mama's. Adam wondered where Mama was, anyway? He hadn't seen Her in a long, long time.

†††

Yes, She was the first to admit: She could be a little forgetful. She hadn't paid much attention to those clever hairless creatures Jehovah had made for Her, and She felt bad. A little bad, anyway. She'd been having such fun with that gigantic kidney-shaped island in the big ocean. Mammals that laid eggs! All the gorgeous corals! And the fuzzy cuddly gray things — She was sure Lilith's family would love those, so She did give them a little help on the trip. But She should have done more. Jehovah was still hanging around. She thought that surely He was taking care of them; hadn't He told them they were His favorites? And She supposed that was part of the problem, to be honest: He just gave Her the creeps. She'd wanted to let Him down gently.

She felt bad for Adam, though. She should have gone back when they had that terrible thing with his sons. Poor Abel. She heard all about it from the Snake, but She'd been so busy working out how to get the land creatures back into the water again with legs switching over to be flippers and how to breathe and all that — She hadn't felt that She could spare the time. And She just didn't want to deal with Jehovah. Giving Him space seemed like the best thing to do.

†††

He knew it was hopeless, of course. He knew everything. Still, He couldn't let it go. He'd been so besotted. Such a fool. He never meant to grow so bitter.

It was all Lilith's fault; her and those knuckle-draggers she'd hooked up with after He booted her out of the Garden. Her and the other female, what did Adam call her? He made sure His creatures – His children! – never forgot whose fault it was. Adam's clan were *His*. *He'd* chosen them, *He'd* looked after them, and She'd gone ahead and brought Her lousy freeloading relatives over in spite of Him until He was forced to make an issue of it: *His* creatures were having none of that, or they'd have Him to answer to. He gave them rules, yes – rules were a good thing. Discipline. Self-restraint. Proper submission to authority. And of course, they knew He was right; for the ten He gave them, they went ahead and invented a thousand. They got so crazy with it, He actually went in there Himself to try to get them to chill out a little – boy, was that a mistake. He'd taught them too well. None of that "peace, love, and understanding" crap for *them*.

Even so, He just couldn't seem to forget Her. He was hurt. He was pissed. He told His creatures that the whole damn planet was theirs to do with as they pleased, knowing full well what greedy, messy little jerks they were. He made sure they bred like fruit flies. Her locusts were nothing compared to them.

He knew it bothered Her, but She was too much of a mealy-mouthed wimp to tell Him to His face. Fine. She sent that Yersinia bug; He nudged the Spaniards into burning all the Lilith-wannabe bitches they could find. Two could play that game.

†††

She'd let the whole thing go too far, and now it was too late. What could She do? For a little while it had looked like they were cleaning up their act; funny, She'd never expected that it would be the dying songbirds – songbirds, of all things! – that opened their eyes to the mess they were making. It didn't last long, but some of them tried. Some of them remembered Her. They were all mixed together now – Lilith's clan and the hominids, Adam's sons and Eve's daughters, even the big-headed gentle ones that buried their dead with flowers: all one species now, not that they would admit it. He never lifted a finger to keep them from slaughtering each other. Egged them on, in fact. She sighed again, for perhaps the 50-millionth time; She should have known what would happen to the gentle ones, after the thing with Cain. Her bad.

She wondered if She should have just let Him have what He wanted. Would it have satisfied Him? Would He have been a good Husband, if She'd given Him Her hand? To His credit, He *had* tried, once, to fix things, but it was too little, too late. And the way He'd done it – that poor girl. Mary, they called her. Did she really have a choice, either, any more than Eve had? Always playing coy, always making up stupid tests. Love was not enough for Him. It had to be worship.

All the damage His tribes had done, to the planet and to each other, and He never said boo. She was sick over it, literally sick. She felt a fever coming on, and She knew from past experience that few of Her creatures would be left after it broke. She'd have to start all over again. Maybe next time She'd see what She could do with otters – they knew how to have a good time without breaking things. Or maybe the dogs. All She wanted was to see what stories and art the new life-forms might come up with, if they only had the brain. Could dogs be poets? They were already good at jokes. Maybe if She started with dogs…

†††

He never meant to hurt Her. He never meant to let it get this bad. Oh, His stubborn, foolish, all-too-clever kids! They never really did grow up, and that was their blessing and their curse. They did learn to fly, after all, without having to jump out of trees. They even flew to the Moon. They split the atom and figured out how to kill just about every bug She invented to try to slow them down. Maybe, if He prodded them a little, they could all pull together, pick up after themselves – that mess of garbage in the big ocean would be a good place to start. But how?

Jehovah ♥ Gaia

Extravagant spectacles were out. Parting the Red Sea wouldn't cut it now that they knew about tsunamis. Subtlety didn't work, either; He'd get some to listen, and they'd just be branded nutjobs. Of course, they usually were nutjobs; nobody else would pay attention. He'd had some luck whispering in the ear of the one who just took over Peter's job, for what it was worth. He hated to admit it, but what they really needed were a few more Liliths. She knew how to get things done.

Gaia: She was older and wiser now, no longer the sweet innocent thing He'd spotted across a crowded cosmos but just as beautiful. More beautiful: the glory of Her forested mountainsides, the majesty of Her snow-covered peaks, was even more heartbreakingly precious now that He'd seen how His misguided children had stripped the mountaintops for coal. Her jewel-like oceans, once so full of life, were dying. Her great fecund, swarming jungles were slashed and burnt for the sake of burgers and fries. Every day, more and more of the living things She'd created were passing from the Earth, never to be seen again. He hadn't wept since he was Jesus. There was no denying: He loved Her still.

Was it too late? No. He knew it wasn't, and if He didn't, who would? He'd leave it up to Her, this time.

Maybe He should call Her.

THE ROAD
BY
CHRISTINE CASSELLO

The road was narrow and hilly,
just right for Billy and Milly.
With no kids in their way,
it was a great place to play.
They ran to the top
trying hard not to stop.
Then rolled themselves down
going right into town.

No one could pass,
not one small lass.
"Get out of the way!"
people would say.
Away they would rush,
falling into the brush.
They looked pretty silly,
thought Billy and Milly.

At the bottom of the hill,
waiting at the flour mill,
was a very angry crowd.
Shouts were getting really loud.
"You could have been hurt!"
"You're covered with dirt!"
the children's parents said.
"And the lass has hurt her head."

Christine Cassello

"You're banned from the road,
unless you've a load."
The mayor told Billy and Milly,
"You can't use it willy nilly."
The leaders made signs,
all threatening fines,
to any who roll down the hill.
And, the parents were given a bill.

THE CROWNING TEMPTATION
BY
JUSTIN FOWLER

"How ya doin', kiddo?" Hunter asked.

The landscape blended together into a rapid green blur as they sped past miles of rural Virginia forest on US-520. Bianca Snowden rhythmically tapped her fingers against the window every couple seconds. She stared into nowhere, her crystal blue eyes, rosy lips and wintry pale face a stark contrast to her midnight locks. The 18-year-old's comely appearance had already helped her to amass quite the following on social media. Which was also helped by the fact that some erroneously concluded that she was related to a certain Edward of the same last name.

The radio droned between bouts of static, "Russian oligarchs are soon to be held in question before the House Intelligence Committee..." before Hunter, her driver, turned it off.

A couple beats after his question, the finger knocking abruptly stopped and awkward silence ensued. Hunter turned briefly from the road to look over at her through his Ray-Bans.

"Kiddo?"

"Yeah."

"You doin' alright over there?" he said, with a nervous chuckle.

"Um, sure. Just bored," she replied, with a barely detectable quaver in her voice. To tell the truth, she was starting to get a bit apprehensive for some reason. "This sure seems like a long drive for some simple target practice." She'd had some wilderness training with him from time to time, but it had been awhile.

Still, she was unaccustomed to being this far out of range of contact with the rest of the world.

Hunter smirked. "Eh, I thought we could skip the practice and I could show you how to knock down a real, live moving target. A nice buck or somethin'."

Bianca snapped her face to him with raised brow, trying to read him. "Why didn't you just tell me that's what we were doing from the outset?"

He paused as if trying to gather his thoughts, clicked his lips, and when he finally spoke, it was in a more pensive tone. "Look, kiddo... I just thought you could do with being away from things for a while. Certain folks just — put some pressure on me to get you... out of the way for a bit. If that makes sense. Tensions aren't good for any work environment."

"What do you mean, 'make sense'?" Bianca retorted. Her voice rose nervously as her pallid cheeks began to flush bright red. "No, it doesn't make any sense in the world. Who's tense!? Oh, I get it now. My aunt? Well, everyone crosses her. How am I any different?" She scoffed, shaking her head. "Everyone but her would have to leave to make the work environment 'tension-free' — and even then..."

Hunter fixed his gaze straight ahead, acknowledging the point. A moment later he sighed, rubbing his head, and said, "But y'know, kiddo, a job's a job. After all, she is the Commander-in-Chief."

Bianca just flicked the window with a fingernail and said, "Rest stop, half a mile. I gotta piss."

†††

Hunter's eyes flicked to the blue entry sign as they pulled off the highway: *Rest Area [Unattended]*. As he pulled into a spot, he noted it was all but deserted, with weeds splitting the blacktop and not a car or truck in sight. He watched Bianca enter the facilities and leaned his head hard against the steering wheel, breathing heavily with his heart thumping in his throat. He just couldn't do it. Yet he had to. She'd have his head if he didn't finish the job. But he'd known Bianca since she was a little girl, and she'd grown on him a great deal. This wasn't like other jobs, cut and dry, swallow your inhibitions and just do it cold. No. But

The Crowning Temptation

he knew how ol' Evergreen worked. She had her ways... and he had to provide the required proof.

†††

Bianca pulled her belt buckle tight as she exited around the corner of the stucco walls, letting out the breath she was holding as she scowled at the putrid stench of the scarcely serviced restroom she was happily escaping.

"So, where are we headed after the expedition then, Captain?" she shouted towards their car as she approached, before gasping in horror. There was Hunter, his gun slid out of its holster and pointed up at her, looking like it was aimed right between her eyes. "What the--" she started, and, panicking, flounced around the side of the building and ran toward the outskirts of the woods behind it.

She scanned the edge for an opening, and finding a slight break between bushes, dove in. Losing her footing over the edge of a drop-off, she rolled a few times down to the edge of a brook. Leaping over it gracelessly, she tripped over a rock in her hurried rush and sprawled to the ground. Well-muscled arms gripped her shoulders and flipped her onto her back, Hunter's grimacing face flashing above her.

"STOP! Now just listen to me..." he shouted aggressively, before clamping his lips and looking side to side. He pulled her close and whispered with ragged breath, "Now just look here... yes, this was a direct order from the top. Your own Auntie. And how can I refuse and save my own skin?"

Bianca's eyes narrowed beneath her tousled hair, in furious shock, lips tight and defiant, nostrils flaring. She was not about to go down begging and pleading. If this was it, then *screw him!*

One heavy hand still upon her, he drew his gun again. She clenched her eyes tight just before hearing a loud BANG! that went all through her, surrounding her with the scent of gunpowder. But she hadn't been shot. Slowly opening her eyes, she saw his arm upraised to his right.

What happened next puzzled her even more. He took out his phone and yanked out his comms unit and threw it as far as he could.

"Look..." he said, under his breath, "I was thinking... she's sick in the head, y'know, she asked for proof — you've heard some of the rumors going around about her. Heck, you probably know better than I do, being family... but she asked for—for..."

Hunter was clearly floundering now. He didn't have the gall to end her life, clearly... "What?" Bianca demanded. "Just tell me. I'm already in a pile of shit here. Just tell me, dammit!"

He closed his eyes in exasperation, finally weakly breathing out the words, "She asked me to bring back your heart, Bianca..." and fully letting go, sat down heavily next to her.

"Unbelievable," responded Bianca, pulling herself up. "So, what's the plan now?"

"I'm—I think I might go on that little hunting trip myself, while you high-tail it to the nearest—well, to somewhere. I refuse to even guess. But I'll hunt a young doe, as their hearts are similar to humans, and I'll put it on ice..."

"And the DNA? It obviously won't match." Bianca shuddered, but knew she couldn't shrink from considering the worst contingencies.

"I highly doubt she'll go so far as to test it. She has no reason to doubt me. And you know she won't even think about using any part of it, or spend any time, on that. Marina... always insists on whole, fresh organs..."

At this, Bianca's muscles tightened, and her stomach began to churn. She knew exactly what that implied, as her imagination quickly painted a picture of chalk circles, candles, spattered blood, chantings — the scope was unmentionable... Eyes as big as saucers, she awkwardly crab-crawled backward away from the man, hand over hand.

Hunter winced at this and looked down, shielding his eyes from her view. After a moment, he cleared his throat and met her wide gaze once more. "Yeah... so you get what's going on here. My suggestion... for your sake and mine. Run, run like there's no tomorrow. Go completely off-grid. Trust no one, not even the people you think you know like the back of your hand. I've taught you some survival skills — use what you know. I know your chances may be slim, but I just — I can't do it, kiddo. This was a mile too far in my book. At least you've got a fighting chance. Remember: she's got her eyes and ears everywhere."

He threw something that landed by her right hand. It was a waterproof box of flint and steel wool. Then he unlatched his belt

The Crowning Temptation

holding his own hatchet, Gerber buck knife, and pistol, and tossed it over to her.

"It's fully loaded. Use the rounds sparingly. If you need to take someone out before they attack, sneak up on them with the knife or hatchet if you can. Now run. Find yourself a place hundreds of miles from civilization. GO!"

Bianca rapidly fastened the belt around her, fingers flying in near panic, as though there were an additional hit on her (for all she knew, there was) and secured the flint box. She threw her phone into the brook before turning around to sprint. She stopped, looked back momentarily and breathed, "Thank you."

Hunter's eyes gleamed above his grim frown, as he quickly nodded in acknowledgement before she turned to run again.

And that was it. *Your life can be drastically altered in that fraction of a second between heartbeats,* she thought. *Bianca Snowden. You've just hit adulthood and you are already a girl on the run.* One day a beloved social media figure well-loved for her beauty and finesse, connected to the most powerful politician in the world, the next... a fugitive? But she wasn't a felon or anything like that, she knew. She'd just been chosen, targeted, to be the next victim of that unholy monster who called herself her aunt, because she had been chosen, crowned by the powers that be, to be the next in succession over the most powerful nation on the globe. Her aunt had her own daughter, Bianca's older cousin, in mind for that role.

There was no returning to her former life now, at least not for the foreseeable future, she reflected, as the trees were once again a blur. She panted, lungs burning and chest aching with each pounding footfall. She'd just have to stake out a scant existence in the middle of nowhere and hope to God that her aunt would see justice someday. Even out of office she's a threat, Bianca reminded herself, as she mentally went over the rumors and conspiracy theories she'd seen on her Twitter feed, but had never fully taken seriously until now: the purported content of Wikileaks, the cause of Seth Rich's untimely death, and the trail of bodies lining the President's long path to the White House over the years, some of whom she'd been familiar with herself...

Hopefully her tyrannical ways could provoke some faction of the populace and government to rise up and impeach her, or she'd somehow croak... fat chance, but what other slim hope did she have left...?

†††

"Yes, tell Deripaska and Veselnitskaya I'll get back to them on congressional testimony. We need to be subtle. Trump will dearly wish he never quote-unquote *'colluded with the Russians'*." The Commander-in-Chief cackled for a good ten seconds at her own mocking wit before descending into yet another coughing fit. Contrived laughter came through on the other end of the phone.

Hunter waited, patiently clutching the styrofoam cooler next to the door of the soundproof, bug-free room. She glanced over in his direction and curtly nodded. "Well listen, I've got other business to take care of. We'll get into further detail later. Okay. Bye."

She clasped her burner phone shut and gestured her head at the cooler. "Well?" she queried, a morbid smile forming across her crackling face. "What do you have for me, Callahan?"

"Just what her majesty desired. A fresh, beating heart from the snowy white herself... well, except it's not so much beating anymore," he grinned at her evilly, as he opened the container for her inspection. He was glad he'd spotted a rare albino doe just a couple miles from where he'd left Bianca. Bald-faced lying to ol' Hilldog could prove... difficult for him to do.

The decrepit President clutched her chest and gasped melodramatically as she leaned back in feigned surprise. "For me? Oh, you shouldn't have... it isn't my birthday, is it? Why, I'll just have to treasure this in the best way possible." Her bulging eyes feasted on the delicate organ before her, as she savoringly drooled over it like a tasty morsel. She reached out to grasp it, only to stop as if she suddenly recalled that she'd have to be seen in the hallway again.

"Thank you, Callahan. A promotion may just be in the cards for you." She winked with that plastic smile of hers, as she covered the box and carried it toward the door. "I may even invite you to a private dinner gathering I've planned in celebration," she followed, with that weird, creepy glint in her eye.

The door shut and Hunter hunched over the table, bracing himself over what he'd just witnessed. Hardened, middle-aged man though he was, it was almost too much. Suddenly he shot up and strode quickly to the restroom, where from outside one could hear distinct sounds of retching.

†††

Thickets and crashing limbs tore at Bianca's clothing as she plunged further and further into the night-flung woods. Grabbing, poking, clawing at her. They could be anywhere, behind or beside or before her. Special ops agents, private hitmen, whomever. Faces emerged from the knots of wood and horrific presences seemed to lurk in the shadows between trunks. A hooting owl caught her off guard in the mostly quiet forest and shocked her system.

As night drew, Bianca thought she must be well into West Virginia at this point. Her path had been winding and unpredictable, but she yet feared that she could still be followed. Her heart thumped in her head and lungs ached in pain. She was a frequent runner, but she'd been at it all day with nothing but a couple of granola bars she'd brought for the original trip and some berries she'd found along the way and several quick draughts from fresh running brooks.

She slowed down to part some particularly dense brush concealing a bit of a downward slope with a cavernous entrance to the side. Blood was still pounding in her head, her lungs heaving, as she carefully stepped between the tangle. Suddenly an innumerable chorus of night shrieks erupted, and a flurry of leathery wings and bug-eyed faces came launching out at her forehead and swarming all about her as they flew past like a shrill mythological flock of demons.

Bianca screamed in shock and then ducked, hands on knees, letting them fly over her in what was seemingly a never-ending stream of hellspawn. The encounter had shocked her nerves beyond what she even thought possible. All she could do was gasp the crisp, cool night air before collapsing into a heap on the ground.

How could she last for years out here with her first night like this?

†††

"Start up Magic Mirror," President Hillary Clinton croaked, her leathery smile resting in a self-satisfied pose. Her iPhone lit up with a dark crystalline graphic display, surrounded by an elaborate Art Deco-like design forming patterns around the perimeter, like a frame. Finally, a theater mask emerged from the midst of the mirror graphic, fading in from black, its face bearing an expression that seemed an optical illusion that could be seen as either a frown or a smile.

"Magic Mirror 2.5, who's the noblest one alive?" chanted Hillary, as if she had practiced it through thousands of recitations.

"Your wish is my command, my queen." The mask spun around to indicate a loading process, as the app rhythmically chimed and pinged endless NSA servers through metadata searches and old information archives, as well as Google's latest AI development software — specifically featuring a program which calculated reams of user searches conducted over decades to ascertain the attributes of high-level constructs such as 'nobility' and 'fairness', as well as popular preferences for important figures.

Hillary was patient enough. She had been waiting for this final note of satisfaction for years... and she knew it was right at her doorstep. The last time she ran this query, a few days ago, it had come up with Bianca Snowden. *Wretch!* She was sure that in addition to calculating high social honor, polished presence, etiquette, methodical grace, and refined familiarity with power, it also threw in hoi polloi concepts such as even-handedness and self-sacrifice. *Ptah!* She'd then promptly spoken with Eric Schmidt about tweaking an algorithm here or there.

The mask stopped spinning, and the chimes took on a triumphant tone. An atmospheric light radiated from behind it as it announced in an honorific voice, "You of all, my President, are noblest amongst all Earth's residents."

"Now that," Clinton tapped her finger on the mask's nose, upon which it scattered into a million points of illumination, "is exactly what I like to hear..."

†††

Squirrel meat fell from the bone as Bianca greedily gnawed into its greasy flesh. As she ate, she cast her glance from side to

The Crowning Temptation

side at slight noises she thought she picked up in her environment, hand ready to dart for her hatchet. Quiet resumed, and she relaxed and dug in again. The fire was bright enough to light up a good swathe of ground, but the woods beyond the clearing were still impenetrably dark.

Out of the places she'd slept for the past few nights, it was one of the best spots she'd come across for homesteading. It was a barren, low spot obscured by dense trees in a medium-sized ravine, but it also looked like the creek bed might flood in the spring. She'd just have to strike out tomorrow again and keep looking. She wasn't lacking for time, after all...

The next day Bianca was walking along a lengthy stretch of meadow lined by trees on either side, when she swore she heard a cuckoo clock. She listened again to see if she wasn't just mistaking a bird call for an actual man-made object. Standing stock still, she listened intently only to hear it sound off again! It sounded like it was coming from her two o'clock. The clock position analogy struck her as welcome, though inadvertent, comic relief as soon as she thought of it.

She advanced toward a copse of evergreens from where the noise seemed to come. Parting branches, she saw, snuggled in amongst a clump of tightly encompassing trees, a quaint little cottage in the shade of this newfound grove. Something drew her to come closer. It had a strange magnetic quality to it. Walking along the stepping stones, she peered into the dim light of the doorway and stepped carefully through.

It was a rather simple dwelling, with a bit of an Old World design to it. It was also quite untidy and unkempt. Dishes lay out on the table, featuring half-eaten muffins, partial strips of bacon and bits of egg. Her stomach growled like an uneasy lion and began to rebel against her finer scruples. She didn't even care that they were partially eaten. It'd been days since she'd been able to fill her gut.

The food gave Bianca an unusual amount of energy, so after cleaning the dishes she went right on cleaning the table, counters, and indeed the whole cottage. That's when fatigue hit her, as immense weariness settled in and she wandered upstairs to the nearest bedroom.

She hadn't even taken stock of the fact that the amenities around the whole place were unusually small until she saw the

Justin Fowler

seven short beds arrayed side by side. *Doesn't matter*, she thought. Ten times better than sleeping on the forest floor. *I don't even care if I sleep forever and never wake up again.* So she stretched along several beds and dozed off as soon as her head hit the covers.

But she wasn't to sleep forever. Her next moment of consciousness was filled with a racket of banging cupboards, loud foot stomps on the stairs, banjo strings being plucked, and a handful of obnoxious shouts and chattering, including someone yelling, "Nope, our fine young woman's still sawin' logs awright." That didn't help her growing headache. She turned and blinked into the lamplight, asking, "What the hell's going on?"

"Ha! You can start by tellin' me," one of them shouted, with a somewhat mischievous grin, though he still preferred to look at her through the lens of his rifle sight.

"Whoa, whoa," Bianca said, backing up and raising her hands. "I'm not here to cause any trouble, I just–well, I..." She eyed her belt slung over a chair on the other side of the room. *Well, shit,* she thought. *I've gotta earn their trust anyway.*

"You thought you'd take advantage of our open doors and dee-fact-o hospitality, didja?" He was a somewhat stocky fellow on the short end of the scale, with a grizzly white beard and plain, homespun clothes. The others gathering around were about the same height as he, more or less, and had just as much of a down-home look to them.

"Hospitality? Where I'm from, we don't normally point guns at our guests!" *What are you saying, Bianca?* she rebuked herself, squinting her eyes. *Do you have a death wish or something? Granted, there's not much to live for anymore...*

Disarming laughter caught her off guard, as the little man relaxed his gun and rested it on the floor, descending into knee-slapping, bellyaching guffaws. The rest of those gathered around joined in, and before she knew it, Bianca caught the contagion herself.

"Hee hee... haw haw haw..." her former antagonist finished off, after about a minute straight of guffawing. Wiping tears away from his eyes, he noted, "You sure have a way about you, fine lady... it's been a mite too long since we've humored a visitor 'round these parts. How'dya do? My name is Jefferson Slink," and kissed her outstretched hand.

The Crowning Temptation

"That's very sweet of you, Jefferson... my name is Bianca. Bianca Snowden." A few of her listeners perked up their eyes and ears and turned the name over in their minds a few times, looking as if they were trying to place a song they'd just heard on the radio, before finally shrugging it off.

The rest of the little men introduced themselves in the same way as the first, one at a time.

John Jolly was a rotund little fellow, with rosy red cheeks and a reddish-brown beard, the most brightly dressed of the group.

Bubba Buckley was the most rugged of the bunch with grizzled chin, squinting eyes, and a cheek full of tobacco. He wore a cynical scowl disguising bucketloads of charm and good-naturedness.

Forrest Jackson had a rather orderly affectation about him, looking much like a well-kempt woodsman and farmer with a fastidiously groomed beard, a green plaid shirt and suspenders, leaning on a hoe with a hatchet on his belt. *If I didn't know better, I'd think he was a hipster,* she thought amusedly.

Huck Humblebee seemed a very casual type of guy, a white-haired fellow with loosely fitting clothes and a slack posture, still carrying his fishing pole from the day's endeavors.

Rufus Arkwright wore clothes covered in grease, and looked to be the silent type, preferring to spend most of his time under vehicles than otherwise.

Philmore Cowbell was the one who'd been playing the banjo, and as such seemed to be very musically inclined. His beard was styled very artistically, and he wore light clothing with a huge floral belt buckle in front.

"Very nice to meet you all," Bianca said finally, with a genuine grin. It'd been so long since she'd seen anyone's face, let alone such friendly ones, that she was so happy she could nearly cry. "So are you all midg—er... little people?"

"Hahaha," Jefferson chuckled good-naturedly, as the rest giggled and snickered around him. "You can be sure to let your hair down 'round here, lass. We don't give no mile for that po-litical correctitude in this house. You can just call us dwarves," he said with a sly wink. "But nevermind you us, just how did a lady of your class and finesse end up in such a godforsaken neighborhood as this? You owe us at least the story from the beginnin'."

Well, bumpkins such as these don't seem like they'd rat on me to my aunt, she thought. *So if they require a story of me, I'll give it to them...* And so, Bianca launched into her own personal life story, beginning with her connection to the Clinton family, the drama and controversies that had afflicted her leading up to the crucial climax of the past few days, ending in that exact explosive turn of events when her whole life went to pot.

They were very easy to entertain. They hung on her every word, gasping and shuddering and giving looks of disapproval at every turn of the narrative, and even laughing at the humorous moments she related. Even Bubba raised an eyebrow or two. At the end, they each sucked in a large breath and exhaled in wonderment.

"Why, that's a mighty tale to tell, and if half of it is to be believed," Jefferson finally said, "you've quite earned your rest with us, that I tells ya. Continue to touch up the place here and there and you've got your room and board, for as long as you like it. 'Fact, it'd be an honor, all said and done."

At this the other dwarves nodded vigorously in agreement and began speaking over each other in their own words of affirmation. "Charmed!" "D'be delighted!" "Place could use a motherly touch!" and as they all shuffled out, Jefferson added, "Now, you just rest here for the night, and we'll come getcha for breakfast in the morn. Don't you fret yourself over that. We'll find places to rest."

"Thank you, you're all too kind... I don't think I can keep my eyes open a moment longer, to be honest."

"That's right. Sweet dreams now, lass!"

†††

The pleasant aroma of sweet, sweet maple bacon snuck into Bianca's nostrils and practically lifted her off the bed by its own power of enchantment. She virtually floated down the staircase and right to the head of the table. The food was even more scrumptious freshly cooked, and this time she was less hurried in her savoring of it. The flavors mingled and melted into her mouth before creating a warm glow in the pit of her stomach.

Afterwards they all gathered on the back porch, where there was a bit of a clearing, and Philmore took up the banjo, John the fiddle, and Huck the washtub bass. Jefferson picked up his Win-

The Crowning Temptation

chester and began shooting tin cans set up twenty yards away, striking them down each time.

"Yeppp... them tyrants a bitch, ain't they?" he said, before knocking an empty can of green beans clean as a whistle off the wooden railing.

Bianca looked over at him, not sure what he was getting at. "Whatcha mean? My aunt is quite a horrific specimen, but--"

"No, no–think, think about it... bring it back a pace and take a gander at that forest in the mix of the whole damn trees. This ain't the product of one night's affair with dictatorship. People don't just wake up one day and spontaneously get an itch in their drawers to vote in a monster of epic pro-portions. Naw, they cede and cede it every day. Little by little, a tax here, a tax there, everywhere a tax tax, and next thing you know, they be outright givin' their kids up to the state and blowin' up goldurned craters halfway acrost the other side of the globe.

"Takes generations of creepin' growth, most usually. You gotcher James Garfields mixed in with your Teddy Roosevelts, but purty soon the deck is stacked more and more with FDR's and LBJ's rotating with vacillatin' fellers who get second thoughts like your Eisenhowers and as you go on, your Kennedys and Reagans who somehow slip in front of bullets soon's they get silly ideas in their funny little heads.

"Seem's though Trump woulda been one of 'em in that respect, though I don't know how far any reforms woulda gone. The State is sunk in deep, deep as the roots of time almost... but I guess time, she tells all." Gunpowder filled the air again as he let off another shot, this time at a squirrel playing peekaboo in the foliage, which promptly dropped to the ground like so much dead weight.

"Damn right," Bubba piped in, mouth full of chew. "Them rat bastards claw in and get real sunk in there. You ain't just got Hillary, it's a whole consortium of no-good weasels 'n sneaks 'n traitors. Folks who'd sell you out to the executioner's block for a bowl o' mess." At this, he, clearly disgusted, spit his wad into a nearby spitoon, which wobbled a bit upon impact.

"So did you folks vote...?" Bianca inquired, starting to grow a sense of despair over the seemingly hopeless picture being painted.

They all looked up at her with bemused smiles, Jefferson giving her a look of cherishing pity. "Nahh, darlin', we dwarves don't vote... wouldn't change much if we did." He sat on the porch and began studiously cleaning his gun. "Nope, it'll take a lot more doin' than a coupla dwarves fiddlin' around in the affairs of ordinary folks. Can't risk gettin' caught out in the line o' sight of the sergeants and commissars and whatnot, and 'sides..." and here he leaned in real close, "when the American public get real fed up, then we'll see fireworks. Nosiree, don't gotta wait four more years for that kinda show. The Good Lord is ever ready for a fight the moment people get serious, and he always helps out the humble in heart. Don't gotta wait for the comin' of the Sunna Man."

Here Bianca began to inexplicably get the distinct impression that these dwarves had some powerful connection to the land, and were supplying help to humankind in some other, intangible fashion that she couldn't quite put her finger on. In any case, it seemed almost as if they were of quite a different sort than "ordinary folks," and that politics somehow did not directly concern them. Almost as if they were magical—but no, she was not living in a fairy tale, she reflected, as she squeezed the thought out of her mind.

"No, 'fact, to tells ya the truth... this is all the result of the collective dream of mankind. Man can't handle his disputes with man, so he takes it up to the next highest bidder and makes the third man a god. When the god betrays his desires, as he always will, the gathered parties snuff him out and ask for a higher god yet. This rotten process repeats and pro-ceeds until you get a centralized bure-o-cratic institution of monumental proportions on high. 'Course, it takes different forms with each new i-teration, but point bein' that tyranny begins with the masses bottom up, not just some folk pushin' their ideas onto the rest. T'aint never as simple as all that. When good folk start wipin' the sleep outta their eyes, they learn right quick how to throw off the powers that be."

During this last part of his spiel he'd had his rifle trained on something in the distance. As soon as he was done speaking he fired off a shot and a raccoon fell out of the underbrush, a bullet hole between his eyes.

"But that's enough jawin' for now. Ya wanna take a gander at our mine?" She followed him as he collected the squirrel and raccoon by their tails and proceeded to an old step-side pickup truck, where he dropped them in the bed. Jefferson opened the passenger door for her. "Git in, lass!"

†††

"Yessiree, this here's our fountainhead of endless treasures," Jefferson beamed. He patted one of a countless succession of brightly lit machines in a large server farm nested in the gigantic cavern they'd entered. "This here's ol' Betsy. She calculates how much coin we've carved us out thus far."

"Betsy" was the only server she could see that actually had a screen, which featured a display with a long list of servers and, in the center, a giant dialog that read, "Total BTC: 576,893."

"So you're mining... Bitcoin?" Bianca observed, not without amusement.

"Well, what else would we be minin' here? This cave done dried up of joolery 'n precious metals long ago. I mean, we're lookin' to diversify a bit, but I imagine your surprise is that we're tapped into crypto. Well stuff your shock back down, because while we're downhome-type fellers, dudn't mean we don't know a ripe investment when's we see it. Got a right smart generator system to keep 'em all goin' too. Rufus maintains some of the technical mechanics hisself."

"Speakin' of, we might wanna replenish the cooling system," Rufus spoke up. "I'll get on orderin' some supplies right away." And with that, he scuttled over to an alcove in the cavern wall where a desktop machine was sitting and plopped himself down.

Bianca turned a slow circle to scan the cavern, which had a fantastical effect of multicolored lights reverberating off of every reflective surface in the area and created the sense of being inside an actual magical dwarven cave, just like in all the old childhood stories.

"So you do have access to the internet," Bianca mused.

"Yep, well we try to be careful on that thing. Got all kindsa backdoors 'n governmental spying and whatnot goin' on. We've got Linux runnin' to avoid backdoors and use an encrypted browser with proxy IP's. Can't take too many chances, 'specially these days. We certainly do not run amuck on Suckerbug's space, that's for right sure. The moment they make a connection point there's a chance our whole server system might light up and location be identified. Hard sayin' what capabilities some of them sorry creepsters have these days."

After a brief tour of the rest of the homestead, including some of the traditional mining spots that were used before the dwarves' income stream was diverted, they all clambered back into their pickup trucks and drove the few miles back to the cottage.

All the way back, Jefferson was giving an economics lesson on the Federal Reserve with its fiat currency, and resulting boom and bust cycles, to explain why they were investing so strongly in crypto. The discussion made Bianca's head spin, despite his explaining it mostly in layman's terms and his typical redneck lingo.

"The long and short of it is," he continued, "they do it all to control folks' paychecks and bank accounts and grab 'em by the kahunas 'till they say uncle. Folks think it's the fat cats got some magical pow'r to control world events and the guvmint isself-- when really it wouldn't amount to nothin' without prior constraint 'pon all market goin's-on via all that funny money you gotsta pay taxes with.

"But it all come crashin' down someday. You cain't feed horses with the promise of oats. It's a gigantic bubble that's gotta pop someday, and these glorified rats think they can slink away with their sorry hoard in fancy getaways before the rest of the world catches on while fallin' from riches to rags. But plenty of people're onto their ways." He emphasized this by spitting out the window. "And when everything and the kitchen sink come crashin' down, we got a way to kick the gears back into motion and point out who the real malcontents are."

Storm clouds began to brew as the wind rushed through fields of grain in such elaborate wave patterns that it was a divine sight to behold. "Y'see," Jefferson continued, "some folks try to control reality, but they can't harness which way the wind blows nor what time the cock crows.

"And if you ask me, I think it all comes down to brute jealousy. They know very well they could be livin' high as a hog makin' others happy through a little bit of spit-palmed hard work in the rough and tumble of a good ol' honest enterprise. But they're a mite too fragile and insecure for that — the only way they know to get ahead is to strangle the wealth and attention they so de-sire outta other folk and consume their very bein'. It's the crownin' temptation in all of creation.

"You might notta thought of this 'un, but I betcha all the hairs on my pasty white rear end that your poor ol' auntie considered you a threat to her own sense of self-importance. Chew on that one a bit and try your durndest to disprove my theory. Might be surprised what threads of thought it brings together."

Indeed, Bianca stayed awake well into the night considering this possibility. To think, the President of the United States envious of her! But it made just too much sense, the way her aunt had made snarky comments and her eyes would flare up in Bianca's personal moments of glory. Barring opportunities for growth and promotion and the list goes on. *She's quite petty for being the most powerful person in the world*, she thought. *But then maybe that's part of the whole point...*

✝✝✝

Six months passed, and Bianca was getting along swimmingly with the small dwarven community. She found they worked as a perfectly synced, harmonious whole, and she fit right into her own niche and flowed with the rest of them, keeping up the home, feeding the animals, and inventorying stock to free up Forrest for other tasks such as woodworking.

But still her old life gnawed at her, with so many loose threads found wanting. The idea that her old crone of an aunt successfully put the boot on her neck, and that her parasitical lifestyle enabled her to thrive at the very height of power, was a growing irritation. Bianca had lost everything, and yet there that witch was, dancing on top of the pile of dead bodies and the backs of "ordinary folks" she'd crushed beneath her feet.

She had to see what was going on in the wider world. Surely, she couldn't be surviving completely unchallenged. Perhaps a true revolt was taking place and gaining some steam. Or even if not, she had to know how deep the talons were sinking in. Something, some kind of clue. And what were her friends up to, and how did they feel about her apparent passing on? Was she even really missed?

It seemed as if her body moved of its own accord as her hand put the key in the ignition of the truck she used for checking the fields and her foot pressed on the gas. As she headed for the town library, Jefferson's words seemed to plague her thoughts:

"Envy does funny things to people, settin' them up in a conflict with other folk wherein each one acts just as much a fool as every other whilst thinkin' they're the worthiest out of the whole group. Or on the flip side that it's the other folk who inevitably hold all the glory and fame and they're just tryin' to make sure they can keep their grip on what little they got—when, really, they all amount to the same insofar as there's any rivalry at all. The eyes of love see through all the bull and know that we gots more in common than not."

In that moment, however, it seemed all a bunch of fluff. Hillary Clinton was a deranged megalomaniac, that much was clear. And she had to be stopped. How, she didn't know. But something had to be done. Little did she know that her very timing and method of approach was fueled by her personal vendetta, no matter how accurate her evaluation of her aunt was.

Bianca parked the truck and made her way inside the library. Finding a guest workstation, she settled in for a quick session. One sneak peek at her Twitter account couldn't hurt, could it?

Much to Bianca's shock, her hundreds of thousands of followers (many of whom has followed her because they'd assumed she was related to Edward) had been reduced by half. And she soon found why. It wasn't that she was considered dead, because apparently the public understanding was that she was merely missing. Of course. It would be too suspicious that Hillary's own niece, who lived in the White House, just turned up dead one day. Much better to leave her fate hanging in the air, at least for a good while. Her inbox was flooded with messages of concern and alarm, and apparently there were also search parties seeking her location.

This alone was a shock, though it allowed for a hopeful reemergence someday. But she also noticed in the midst of all of this were reports of mass bannings, which were the real source of her reduced follower base. Her feed additionally informed her of the takedown of alternative media sources via lawsuits and FCC crackdowns on spuriously identified hate speech and fake news. Several prominent leaders in that domain had been arrested, including Jack Posobiec, Scott Adams, and Ben Swann. They were currently being charged in court for criminal conspiracy to collude with foreign powers to undermine a national election. Julian Assange had finally been extradited, and Donald Trump as well as a number of his campaign staff were awaiting trial. Judging by active social media accounts, it seemed as if part of the public was in a state of resigned shock and the other part foaming at the mouth to see the apparent traitors in prison.

Police brutality had exponentially increased as BLM decried the white supremacist system, and all across universities, student mobs were holding campuses hostage and punching Nazis.

The world was a shitshow, and all seemed lost. She was almost glad that her wicked aunt had hunted her down and Hunter had given her cover. It may have been the best possible scenario in her case.

Having taken in her fill of news, she navigated to Google maps to pinpoint the exact location of the dwarves' cabin to see just how far away she was from any of this mess. *Right in the heart of Kentucky wilderness,* she thought. *That's good enough.*

Bianca deleted her history and closed the browser, but unbeknownst to her, logging in to Twitter had revealed her precise location at that computer station in the middle of nowhere, and based on her Google Maps search, the location of the Dwarves' enclave was now also known to the NSA. The two points of data were cross-referenced with each other, and the information was transferred to the CIA's seven major global intelligence computer databases: Doc, Dopey, Grumpy, Sleepy, Happy, Bashful and Sneezy. 1's and 0's carried Bianca's indelible mark upon the internet back and forth from server to server and database to database.

†††

Meanwhile, a smug Hillary Clinton reclined in her familiar chair in the White House and cued up her favorite app as she did every Friday evening.

"Magic Mirror, Magic Mirror 2.6, who's the most cunning of the mix?"

She grinned from ear to ear, just waiting to hear the inevitable affirmation of her interminable prowess and unfailing resolve. The mask only spun around a couple times before facing forward and formulating a rhymed response. Here it was!

"Of all the heroes of legendary feats,
Those who skillfully your wiles beat
Deserve a rightful place beside Odin
And that one is named Bianca Snowden."

Shock, disbelief, and furious rage brewed within Hillary's eyes as she mounted up a scream to compete with the likes of ancient harpies. Staff ran in as she flung glasses against the walls and lost complete control of her faculties. "Somebody... get her!!!"

†††

The next morning the reports were rolling out in CNN, MSNBC, ABC, NBC, and all the other major media outlets (practically the only ones left) that Bianca Snowden was a Russian collaborator on the run and was believed to be somewhere in the wilds of Kentucky. Tips on her whereabouts were encouraged, and a hefty reward was promised for anyone bringing her in. Talking heads everywhere were excitedly jabbering about how a close relative of the President's could actually be a foreign conspirator. It was just the gasoline on the mimetic fire of viral news narrative creation that was needed.

†††

Back home at the cabin, Bianca now felt like a new woman. It seemed as if a huge burden had lifted off of her shoulders, as she let her former life and world finally slip away from her. Though she could be worried about her old friends, it was questionable how accurate of a description "friend" was for many of them, and she was now all but dead to that whole world anyway. The last surge of longing for any kind of connection to it fell away like an old, rotten bridge. The simple life it was for her from here on out. She didn't even want to think about what might be happening in the outside world.

Humming as she hung up a long string of freshly-washed dwarven laundry, she sunk into the feeling of the warm sunshine caressing her face, as the songbirds seemed to serenade her personally. Forrest was out harvesting crops, Jefferson and Rufus were out at the mine, Bubba was hunting game, and Huck and Philmore were catching fish. John Jolly was headed out to town for a few necessities.

Presently, an elderly woman Bianca had never seen before happened to be wandering by and called out what wonderful weather they were having. There was something odd about this lady's sudden appearance, which provoked Bianca to ask what brought her this way, after agreeing that the day was quite nice.

"Oh, I take a long stroll to have supper with my son and his family every Friday evening. They live a ways over there, on the other side of the river," she said, as she pointed toward the southwest. "I started out a little earlier today, so I thought I'd try out a new path. Never fancied I'd run into someone this way, especially such a fine young woman as yourself."

Bianca blushed. The woman's demeanor seemed so delightful that she swallowed her initial suspicion, and they got to pleasantly chatting for a good thirty minutes. At one point the topic of technology came up, and the old lady pulled out her Apple iPhone. She asked for help with an app that had been irritating her, and Bianca expertly troubleshot it with finesse to spare.

"Why, how did you do that? You worked so fast I could hardly keep track!"

"Just comes naturally, I guess. Want me to show you again, slower this time?"

"Ohhh... no. You know what? This would probably be a better fit with you anyways. I just don't know what I'd do with this whatchahoozit. It seems more of a burden sometimes than a blessing. Here, just take it. You can have it."

"No, I couldn't. I'd feel like I'd be robbin' ya blind. Besides, I'm trying to take a clean break from society, and this would be too great of a temptation against that."

"Oh, don't kid yourself. You can just use it to play games or listen to music or somethin'. I don't need it. Don't feel an ounce bad about it. Just more deadweight in my purse is all. Here, consider it a gift from this elderly woman to a wonderful young woman such as yourself." And, so saying, she clasped Bianca's hands around the device.

"Awww, alright... if you insist," Bianca replied. To tell the truth, the itch to see what was going on was suddenly coming back. "I'll take it, then... as a gift."

"That's right. Now I must be on my way. I'm already running

late for dinner at my son's. You have a delightful rest of the day now, ya hear? If I'm ever in the area again I'll be sure to make a call. Been nice chattin' with ya."

"Thank you very much, it's indeed been a very lovely conversation. Seeya around."

Bianca took the phone back to the porch and began toying with it. Meanwhile, the elderly lady walked on until she found an enclosed grove out of view and shuffled another smartphone out of her purse. She hit an autodial number and said with quite a different voice than she'd been speaking with into the receiver, "Device is with target. Repeat, device is with target…"

†††

Jefferson, John, Huck, Philmore, and Forrest gathered around Bianca's body in the hospital, where they'd registered her as a Jane Doe. They knew they were putting themselves in a potentially vulnerable situation, but at this point they were ready to risk that kind of sacrifice. Bianca had really grown to be such a part of them that it was like losing a dear limb to see her go.

"Ahhh, lassie…" Jefferson began, sadly. "I warned ya not to cede your power. You were growin' to be such a healthy young sprout, and to see it all go to pot breaks my heart, God help me…" and the rugged old-timer burst into a flood of tears, as did the rest of the crew.

Bianca laid there motionless and still as eternity, her face more sickly pale than snowy white.

Philmore sniffled and whispered to Forrest, "Is Bubba and Rufus sealing up the mine?"

Forrest replied, "I think they about got it sealed before we left. They's probly jumpin' about in the bushes shootin' at the SWAT team fellers and givin' 'em a run for their money."

Philmore nodded, and they went back to bowed heads and folded hands.

Suddenly the door burst open behind them, as a young man in scrubs slammed it shut and ran up to the bedside. He looked up at the heart monitor and started disconnecting it. "No time to lose," he whispered hoarsely. "The feds could be here within minutes. Bianca's needed for some very important hearings."

The Crowning Temptation

The dwarves looked at each other for a moment in stunned surprise, but before Jefferson could ask about these new developments, the heart monitor sounded off two alert beeps just as the last electrode was being removed. It fell silent.

The newcomer checked her pulse, then, alarmed, got to work performing emergency CPR. "What did they do to her?" he demanded as he pumped.

The shocked dwarves stammered a bit, until Forrest spoke up, "They done shot her with a couple highly potent tranqs before we ran up and fired at 'em and gave 'em a right showdown. Little did they know we off-the-grid fellers have a right arsenal. Then we drove her straight to the hospital as fast as we could scramble. Unfortunately, her face is all over the news, so there was no hope for keepin' her back at home."

The dwarves' faces spelled out frowns at these words, though there were added notes of anxious hope for Bianca.

"Yeah, she isn't just known by the nightly news," the young man said. "We've been following breadcrumbs about her whereabouts on the Alternet for much longer than she's been a national scandal. It really threw up a red flag for us when Hunter Callahan sent out a cryptic tweet before he was recently disappeared. That's when we knew something was definitely rotten in Denmark and that Bianca would be integral to Hillary's trial. But we were able to finally track her down. A source that goes by AlbertJNockOnWould appeared and provided the clues that enabled us to start an actual rescue mission."

John Jolly gasped and looked at the other men. "Why, isn't that Rufus' screenname...? He's been scourin' a heap o' message boards lately on his workstation."

"Well that explains it, then!" the young man exclaimed between rescue breaths. "Name's Brenden, by the way....... I'm not actually in the medical field, but I have some basic emergency training....... I'm a legal intern from D.C. who just so happens to be here on vacation. We saw that....... I was the closest to get her. Things are changing in the swamp, but there's no time to explain right now."

Brenden felt her pulse, then took out the nearby defibrillator, charged it and shocked her, then went back to the chest compressions, much more forcefully this time. Her heart at last jumped beneath his hands and restored to a strong, steady rhythm. One final time he put his lips to hers and exhaled, to which Bianca awoke with a wide-eyed start, her head smacking back into the pillow. She stared up all dreamy-eyed and smiling and slurred, "Well, hello... am I awake or asleep...?"

"Quick, there's no time for that," Brenden replied. "Here, put on this," as he thrusted toward her a long-haired brunette wig pulled from his passenger bag, "and act cool. I'll have you out of here in a jiffy."

He held her up while they attempted to walk out of the room, as she stumblingly tried to keep up.

"There's been a delay in federal agent presence because we've been hacking systems to throw them off the trail. Video feed has been manipulated to make them think she's been taken to St. Anne's Hospital twenty miles in the other direction from your home. We probably have a handful of minutes left. I've also been in contact with a Secret Service agent who has a dispatch waiting several miles down the highway. They'll provide protection the rest of the way to D.C. You guys can meet us there," he nodded to the dwarves. "We'll have someone hang back if you don't catch up."

Bianca was still struggling, so finally he placed her in an unattended wheelchair and they were off to the races. But not before calling behind him, "Now you guys stay back a pace so it doesn't look suspicious. You'll all be reunited again, promise. We just gotta get her to safety."

Around the next corner Bianca's doctor was sauntering along, looking down at his clipboard. Engrossed in his notes, he didn't notice what was happening until they were passing him, at which point he noticed her unusually pale skin and wildly spun around, shouting after them. "Security!!" he bellowed.

But they were too quick for the chase. They flew around another corner and by the time security was running up, the elevator doors were already closing shut, hiding the two refugees inside.

Thankfully, they were only on the second floor and nearby the side entrance, and there was no time for staff to alert downstairs security to the imminent escape before they were out the door and Bianca was shuffled into the passenger seat of his Mustang. Brenden screeched out of the parking lot and was on the highway before you could say Jack Johnson.

The Crowning Temptation

Half an hour later, Bianca came fully to as they were flying along the freeway. "What are we doing? Where are we going? Who are you?" she asked, still somewhat in a fog.

"I just saved your life. You can thank me later. I found your location on the Alternet with the help of the 8chan brain trust."

"Alternet? Alternative... internet?"

"Yeah. In the wake of your aunt's censorship crackdown, patriots and freedom fighters got together to create an encrypted mesh network across the entire contiguous United States. It's essentially impenetrable and unstoppable. Our team broke into interagency comms and learned that you were being hunted down in this region."

Brenden quickly checked the rearview mirror before continuing, "Then they hacked cameras everywhere around here, including this hospital's CCTV footage and found you. Autists took note of the amenities, angle of sunlight at time of day, and a billion other details you never would've dreamed of to figure out exactly which hospital you were located at because God knows they weren't officially telling anybody. Probably because they knew someone like me would try to snatch you up."

Bianca's head rolled over to face Brenden. "Well, aren't you just a regular Prince Charming," she grinned widely. He had just that perfect complement of well-chiseled face and sensitive features all rolled into one. She could get used to this guy.

"Anyway, as for where we're going... don't freak, but I'm taking you straight to Washington D.C."

"What!?" Bianca reacted. Now she was awake. "That's the very LAST place I need to go!"

"Don't worry. You'll be delighted to know things are moving and the tide has turned. Public pressure has mounted: a large segment of the military has turned, white hats have pulled some strings, and reputable lawyers are making their cases now.

"Welcome to the second American Revolution."

†††

The warm, friendly sunlight gleamed in Bianca's eyes as she walked down the steps of the Capitol. The sights, sounds, and smells of simple, everyday realities — birdsong, hot dog vendors, casual conversations — had never felt richer and more satisfying.

"Wellll... don't it feel right good to get all that off yor chest?" Jefferson winked.

"Why yes it does, Jefferson, yes it sure does..." Bianca replied. "I never thought I could ever feel as good as I do right now." She breathed in the crisp, chill air, as she gazed upon the beautiful autumn trees all around.

"Them Congress critters sure were outright shocked at somma the things you had to say. It was a pretty funny sight to read their faces at certain key moments, if I do say so m'self. I have a feelin' Hitlery will be locked up for a good long while yet to come," he whistled shrilly. Laughter erupted from the rest of the boys at this. "Good thing too they got Hunter out of his coma to get his special take on things. And a mighty fine tribute to his security pals who got him out of danger's way before his testimony t'would be lost f'rever."

"Yes... I will be forever indebted to that man. And all of you. And you..." she turned to Brenden, whose arm was linked into hers. "I just might be able to keep you around for quite some time, if you considered that an ample enough reward."

Brenden stared deeply back into her eyes in open appreciation, smiling unreservedly, before gulping and glancing down for a moment. "Y'know... I just might be able to put up with that." They both laughed as they embraced and, at last, kissed.

"Okay, okay, alright! I reckin we've had a good helpin' eyeful already. What say you all we pick up some vittles somewheres? My stomach is startin' to turn inward and gnaw on itself. I think it has a hankerin' for some I-talian if I read it aright."

Everyone laughed as they headed toward their vehicles. And they all lived happily... ever... after...

AN INVESTMENT RETURNS
BY
LELA MARKHAM

The beds made and the carpets vacuumed, Mallory walked into the dining room of the Fox Creek Roadhouse for a short break before her next task. Except for a group of five Japanese couples eating breakfast near the large front windows, the long main room of the roadhouse was quiet this weekday morning. The city folk would pack out the pools come the weekend, intermingling with the Asians who were here for the yurts with see-through domes that allowed aurora watching.

Mallory poured herself a mug of coffee from the pot on the big wood stove near the kitchen and drifted toward the employees table.

"You up for an adventure today, Mallory?" her boss Paula asked. She'd been entering receipts into her laptop.

"Of course. What do you need?" Mallory sat down, back to the huge wood stove. When the sun came up, outdoor activity commenced.

"You know Webb Palmer up on Moose Creek?"

"Yeah, I like that old man."

"Webb's shipment came in this morning. How'd you feel about taking a snow machine out and delivering it?"

"Sure. I saw the DOT plowed out the turnout there at the top of his road the other day. Can I take a truck and trailer or ride out from here?"

"It's too cold to start here. I had Joel pack the shipment onto a fold-a-sled and you can take the Bronco. It's got a full tank.

Make sure you set the command start to turn on once an hour so it doesn't freeze up on you."

"It's only a half-hour into his place."

"Yeah, and then there's the invitation to dinner and the half-hour trip back. I swear I have more employees decide to spend the night there than not. Man's breakfast is legendary." Paula grinned to herself, her smoker's lips smoothing out and her faded blue eyes glowing with humor. "Might as well plan for it so I don't have to get a tow for the Bronco. And make sure you leave enough room to park there in case Justin Branaugh comes out to harass his boy."

Mallory had met Justin Branaugh last summer when she'd backed a skid loader into his F250. You'd have thought she ran over his dog. He'd raised a ruckus so that Mallory thought she'd spend the winter in jail. Paula had intervened, offered to pay the damages and even agreed to dock Mallory's pay when Justin had balked. In the end, the man had stomped off muttering how Mallory owed him.

"You thinking about that accident last year?"

"I do kind of owe him something."

"He dropped it after he thought about it a while. Thirty years of parking around this place, he knows to stay well back of the woodshed. And, besides, it was a tiny scratch. Bet the body shop laughed at him when he brought it in."

"How much did it cost? I should probably reimburse you now that I have some savings."

"He never sent me a bill. He's all rattle and no bite. Likes to act like he's king of the taiga, but then he gets over himself when he calms down. But, it would be a good thing to leave some parking room."

"Neighborly, right?"

Paula grinned that crazy smile again and Mallory finished her coffee before donning her cold weather gear to head out. A spray of aurora lit the black sky as Mallory paused to look at the Temperature Dogs thermometer outside the kitchen door. It had warmed up to 25 below. The sun would pop over the horizon in another hour, so the aurora was merely green with just a hint of pink around the edges. Last night the sky had been afire with color and Mallory had stayed up way too late to watch it. The outdoor hot springs pool made aurora viewing at these

An Investment Returns

temperatures tolerable. She must have drunk two gallons of water since going in last night.

Bundled within her parka, she crunched across the parking lot of the Fox Creek Hot Springs and Roadhouse toward where Scott Parsons waited. Even once the sun came up, with an inversion underway, it wouldn't warm up – at least not down here on the lows. Up in the hills around Webb's place, though ... you could hope.

Scott helped her hook up the trailer and strap down the snow machine. He'd picked a machine that almost classified as "tired iron", which meant it was reliable and slow with a lot of torque. She must have passed some sort of test with Scott that he allowed her to do everything inside the garage where the temperature hovered around freezing thanks to the barrel stove in the corner. Last winter, she'd learned the value of warmer socks and layers of gloves to guard against the warmth-sapping metal she was working with.

"You packed?" he asked while she buckled up. Scott and Paula were partners in several ways and he considered himself Mallory's outdoor boss. Neither of them ever treated their male and female employees differently. David and Blaine sometimes had to fluff pillows and vacuum carpets while Mallory hauled firewood, but Scott was more into oversight than Paula. Not, take a gun – are you carrying the gun right now?

Mallory patted her coat where the .357 rested in the shoulder harness. It was too early for bear, but you never knew what you might encounter in the woods. There were plenty of big hostile wildlife that you might need a gun for. Even bucolic moose could turn violent if they thought you were threatening their calves.

"Remember, I got twenty dollars that Conover's going to take gold in the half pipe."

"Yeah. That's a reason not to stay out at Webb's."

Laughing, Scott stepped away and she rolled up the window then slid the 4x4 SUV into gear. In the warmth of the cab, it was easy to think you didn't need your survival gear on your person, but people had died or lost fingers unable to reach their coat or gloves in the backseat after a crash. She looked both ways before turning left onto the highway too, just in case the one car an hour typical for this time of year would be coming by the roadhouse right now. If she'd looked around a little better when she was backing that skid-steer, she'd not have hit Justin Branaugh's truck.

†††

The light of dawn crept across the living room and woke Dan in the bedroom. The air on his nose felt cold. He breathed out. Not freezing yet, but the fire had been out for a while. He rolled out of bed, muttering at the cold wood floor under his unprotected feet. He'd overslept, tired from watching the aurora lights by an open fire in the yard. You could afford to sleep in when an automatic heating system kept you from freezing to death, but not here where a wood fire had to be tended every eight hours.

The walls of the old Earth Stove were still slightly warm, but the fire was all the way down to glowing ash. He hadn't needed to fully start a fire since he got here, so he'd neglected to ball up newspapers, though he had a ready supply of kindling. He scrunched several balls and shoveled them all into the firebox at once. The coals caught the newspaper while he was placing the kindling and smoke began to boil back into his face. He closed the door, hooking just one handle and reached up to open the chimney damper. The thin stream of smoke that had been leaking out the back of the stove stopped, and the chimney thermometer nudged from zero to 100. Dan eased open the door and watched the fire through a narrow slit that acted as a bellows to funnel air to the nascent fire made of piled up coals. The wadded newspaper turned black around the edges as flames rose to catch the black spruce branches he used as kindling. Sparks floated up the chimney, smoke boiling around them. Some smoke tried to escape the crack, but he adjusted its width until the chimney draft sucked it back into the growing fire. The spruce pitch in the kindling began to pop and crackle. The thermometer on the chimney climbed to 350 degrees. He cozied two spruce eighths on the kindling.

Outside the front window, he could see the brief February sun turning the snow into glistening blue diamonds, marked by black shadows of the taller white spruce to the south. Soon the snow would turn white and it would be a perfect day here in the mountains. The chimney temp had reached 450 and the spruce eighths had settled slightly, fire licking between them and

An Investment Returns

around their edges, so he closed the wood stove door and locked it down, then adjusted the air supply to a sustainable level. It wouldn't take long to heat the small cabin. He'd be ready for the day by then.

Hauling wood and melting snow for water were his main chores these days. You couldn't afford to take a day off out here. He made quick work of making his bed in the small bedroom, his bare toes curling against the cold floor. The hand-washed underwear made the pants and shirt tolerable, though he really thought he'd wash that shirt and another one tonight. He'd only brought three sets of clothing and he'd been here since – well, Thanksgiving and now it was February, so .... Maybe it was time to launder a pair of pants. He slid his feet into Alaskan moccasins before spending a few minutes in the narrow room that housed the compost toilet and a dry sink. He needed to shave today. Not that anyone would see him, but he didn't like the shaggy look. Smooth-faced and fresh-feeling, he closed the only door in the cabin before entering the kitchen. It was rudimentary – a plywood counter, open shelves above and below, a wash basin and an assortment of pots, pans, dishes and cups. No one used the propane stove in the winter since propane had a tendency to freeze and then explode when being warmed. He'd almost gotten good cooking on the wood stove since he'd been here.

After he was done cooking, he adjusted the stack damper to slow the fire for a nice long, even burn. The Temperature Dogs thermometer outside the window the table sat under climbed from -15 to 0 just while he prepared and ate breakfast. Most years, he'd be bored stuck here at the cabin and start hoping for a break in the cold, so he could ski to the roadhouse and let them know he was fine. This year he was enjoying his alone time too much. He could use the satellite phone to call Paula and forestall a family visitation. He'd probably do that tonight.

Dan tossed the last quarter of warm birch into the fire before he donned his outerwear and boots to do the outside chores, assuring maybe two hours of burn time. He'd shoveled the yard after the last storm about three weeks ago, so the sled outside the door slid easily across the snow as he dragged it to the woodshed. Beyond the yard, snow was four feet deep across untouched taiga. His breath fogged in great clouds as he crunched across the yard. He had enough seasoned wood to last until fall if he decided to stay, but he'd need to return to town by April 15 to sign the tax reports. There was a stand of fire-killed trees not far away that he really should harvest before then.

The valley fascinated him. A raven cawed far up the valley. More than half a mile away, he heard a semi headed to Central downshift for the hill. Odd how sounds carried so far in the northern cold. If the air was just right, he could hear the neighbor on the other side of the creek talking to his dog. He loved the quiet here and the physical labor needed to stay alive. It was well worth the effort ... for part of the year anyway.

He skidded the sled into the arctic entryway and began unloading wood into the storage rack. He paused to wipe snot off his cold nose before dragging the sled along the trail out to the road where he'd set up a snow harvesting field. You wanted clean snow that hadn't been walked in and that didn't have a lot of fallen pine needles. You still had to filter and treat it just to be sure, but if it was done right, it wasn't too gross. He packed eight buckets with snow, which when left to melt in the big metal tub next to the woodstove made just enough water to wash the day's dishes and make a pot of coffee. Four trips in all left him sweaty and overheated, with enough water to do some laundry and take a sponge bath.

He paused outside the door, wiping the back of his glove across his forehead. He ought to add more wood to the fire and change his undershirt and socks before continuing with work, but time was fleeting. The sun had already dropped below the crest of the mountains to the southwest. Dusk here was long, especially this time of year, but he didn't like trying to navigate the cache's ladder in low-light conditions. Without street lights and in the new moon, the yard would grow truly dark by 6 pm. He could already feel the temperature veering back toward cold, making him shiver as sweat dried on his body.

He ought to go in, warm up, cool down and dry off, but he wanted to get this last bit taken care of before the day was done. He started to climb the cache ladder, catching himself when his foot slid on one rung. During a warm spell last week, some of the snow from the roof had leaked onto the ladder. He kicked at the ice, but it didn't break. He climbed the rest of the way. Sitting in the little opening, he dropped a slab of bacon into the sled with a resounding boom. He followed that with butter and bread. His

An Investment Returns

fingers stung with contact frostbite as he slid the bolt closed. Halfway down, he remembered the steak and vegetables.

Yeah, he wanted the steak. The shadows were growing long from the west when he reversed directions. He dropped the steak down into the sled and started downwards. Moving too fast. He'd not shot the bolt and the ravens would get into the cache if he didn't close the door properly. He stepped up to the next rung, felt his foot slide and hastily grabbed for the ladder. Too late! His gloved fingers brushed the wood as he fell backward into a flash of white pain followed by darkness.

†††

The turnout at Moose Creek provided excellent parking for both SUV and trailers now that the DOT had plowed it out. Mallory supposed Justin Branaugh could wield that sort of power, though Scott had once said the DOT used the turnout as a turnaround for their snowplowing operations. Hard to know which was true and she probably oughtn't to be thinking snarky thoughts considering he'd let her get away with damaging his truck. The air higher in the mountains was warmer ... still crisp and clean, but Mallory wasn't worried about frostbiting fingers or toes while she unstrapped the old Kawasaki from the trailer. She'd cozied the end of the trailer right up to the berm the DOT had created, so she could just drive off the trailer without worrying about dumping the sled.

Mallory wondered if Webb had done all the work at improving the trail or if it were some State of Alaska initiative. It certainly seemed like a real road that had been encroached by trees over the last 30 years. Because of the historical significance of the Davidson Ditch, the Wolf Creek fire a decade ago had been held back, so there were still tall trees here. She kept her speed low so as to not be concerned with being whipped in the face with low branches. At the bottom of the first slope, the trail turned to cross the creek. She headed upstream toward the 48-inch rusted metal pipe that ran across the creek on wooden pilings. The Davidson Ditch was actually ditches in the hills but going over the creeks it was pipes somehow designed to give the water enough pressure to climb the next hill. It had been an integral part of the mining operations in the Chatanika Valley until the 1967

Flood had blown out the dam some 50 miles upstream and rendered the Ditch just an odd historical artifact.

The ice of the creek was a pure white-blue streaked here and there with rusty red as she skirted the edge on the old snow machine. She ducked low under the Ditch, feeling the weight of tons of steel above her. She wondered how long 100-year-old steel could hold up against the elements. The Ditch answered her question by making a twanging sound that overwhelmed the sound of the snow machine. She shivered despite her warm clothes.

The creek narrowed, and a big hump appeared from bank to bank. That was Webb's summer bridge. Mallory turned right to climb the bank and take his trail the rest of the way. She slowed as a moose cow and calf ran across the trail ahead of her, but they headed up the hill, so she didn't stop. It no longer surprised her when Webb came out onto his porch as she pulled across the creek. In the crisp Alaskan air, he could hear her preparing to get on the trail way up by the road, not to mention how loud the snow machine itself was. She was always amazed at how quiet it became when the machine was turned off. In this valley several hundred feet in elevation above the roadhouse, the snow sparkled like aquamarine mixed in sugar, the temperature somewhere between zero and freezing. She pushed back her hood and pulled down her balaclava.

"Just drag that sled into the shed here," the septuagenarian of the Other Moose Creek, Alaska, ordered. "I've got the kettle on. You want some tea?"

Webb had been doing this for long enough that he had a system worked out. The shed was attached to his cabin, so he could easily unload the sled over the next few days while not having to worry about wildlife getting to it. He provided another fold-a-sled for her to tow back with her. That had probably been the one David had brought supplies with last month. Mallory left her boots by the door and walked in stocking feet across Webb's pristine rubbed plywood floor to sit down by the fire. Two rockers waited there. Webb's wife would join him starting in March, but she preferred the easier winter life in town.

"Anything I need to know going on in the world out there?" he asked, handing her a mug of tea.

"Nothing major. No wars, famines or plagues. Well, a bunch

An Investment Returns

of people in the Lower 48 have the flu." She slipped a stack of envelopes out of her sweater. Callie, Webb's wife, wrote him every week, care of the roadhouse. He grinned and set them on the table to read later. She stripped to her indoor wear, leaving the gun on top of the bookcase in the living room. Everything else went by the wood stove to warm it through.

"I got a pot of grouse stew on. You hungry?" It was on the tip of her tongue to say "yes" because his biscuits were mouth-wateringly tender, but something made her hesitate. "Can't do pancakes in the morning. My hens are still confused and aren't laying."

The roadhouse used electric lights in the henhouse to convince the birds that the world was not ending, so they would lay eggs. Webb had said before that he didn't like generators. They made too much noise. Someone really needed to tell him about solar panels and wind mills.

"I think I'm going to head back after I finish my tea. The Winter Olympics are playing."

"Yup," Webb said. He must have been a tall spare man all of his life because he was still pretty tall and slender with no signs of a paunch. He still had a thick shock of white hair and greyish green eyes. If she'd said "yes" to supper and breakfast he'd have been just as nonplussed. She didn't think he cared whether he had company or not. "What event you like best?"

"Wow? Snowboarding – luge – slalom. Might be easier to ask me which I like least – ski jump. It's boring. It's just about distance, no speed, skill or endurance."

"Yup." Hard to tell if the old man was agreeing with her or just giving her permission to change the subject. Visiting Webb's cabin was an exercise in the art of silence. He gave you tea and sometimes you played backgammon or cribbage if you stayed overnight. Somehow it felt like the best visit in the world, but you might get away with saying fewer than 100 words in an evening.

Webb's cabin was stick-built with framing rather than logs, the bays insulated, and the inside sheathed in plywood. The lower floor had the kitchen on one side, the living room on the other of one large room with the wood stove in the middle. A bedroom was tucked in under the loft along with a water closet, which Mallory would use before she left. A door beside it led to the bunk room where the kids slept when they came out. Webb didn't try to heat that when he was here alone. Winter guests could sleep on a mattress in the loft. There were nice touches of blue and red throughout the cabin, signs of Callie's ministrations. Mallory pulled her thick brown braid over her shoulder and sipped the warm spiced tea. There was Labrador tea with the Lipton's.

"David told me you were thinking about going back to college next year."

"Maybe," she said. He wouldn't pursue that any further. He didn't really like to talk. He was just being polite. "By next fall, I'll have enough money to go back without needing loans."

"My boy's getting his Master's this year. Put himself through, no debt, sometimes working two jobs."

Mallory had known Webb and Callie had children, but this was the first time she'd ever heard him speak of them when they weren't there.

"You must be proud."

"Yup." He actually smiled. "Gonna have to go to town for that one." Silence ensued. A log in the Papa Bear stove popped loudly. Her cup was nearly empty.

"I suppose I should get going."

"If you want."

The water closet smelled of the evergreen boughs he'd hung on the wall. He used an old-fashioned bucket, the foam seat leaning against the wall under the dry sink shelf. He kept the place really neat, ready for Callie when she came out. Mallory had seen this week's laundry hanging in the loft. What it must take to do laundry in a dry cabin, she just couldn't imagine.

She thought of putting on all of her outerwear and starting back along the trail. It made staying for grouse stew and whatever would replace Webb's legendary sourdough pancakes seem very attractive, but again, she felt uncomfortable. It had never been like that before. She'd always felt welcome and the old man had always been polite, welcoming in a quiet sort of way, exactly as he was today. Maybe she was just worried about losing $20 to Scott. She pulled her chaps down over her boot tops and reached for her coat.

"It's been a nice visit," she said, sliding the gun back into its holster.

An Investment Returns

"Yup. Always enjoy it."

The sound of molars on wood caused her to look around as she threw a leg over the snow machine. Across the creek, right along her trail, that cow moose was stripping bark off a willow. Not far away, two yearling calves were imitating Mama.

"There's a trapper's trail, runs that way." Webb pointed up hill, north. "You can follow the trail markers. It'll take you almost to the Davidson Ditch where you'll hit the creek and that'll take you out."

"Sounds good. Thanks."

"You just be careful out there, girl." The hair on the back of her neck stood on end. Alaskans being independent individualists, it felt odd to hear a man express that kind of sentiment. Women won the Iditarod, Yukon Quest, and Open North American, competing nose to nose with men in those competitive dog races. Women weren't seen as weak or in need of protection. There was no other reason for his admonition to set her on edge.

Most of this land had been swept by two forest fires about a dozen years ago. Although there were probably a lot of small black spruce under the snow, mature spruce trees were sparse and what remained of the birch trees were mostly standing dead. She heard the Davidson Ditch cooling, the metal contracting with a loud pinging as the sun dropped behind the southern hills. The snow machine had a bit more get-up-and-go without hauling a load. The trail markers were frequent enough along the edge of Webb's property, but then she crossed a wide brushing line and they disappeared. It didn't really matter. She was headed south. West was up, the creek was east, and north was up valley. The creek was the easiest place to cross under the Davidson Ditch. That 90-mile long water pipeline made it very hard to get lost along the north side of Steese Highway.

The trail turned toward the creek and she followed because it was easier than trying to go through the deep woods. Ahead, a copse of trees had survived the fires, mostly birch and a few white spruce, probably grouped around a little rivulet of oozing ground water, barely enough to keep flowing, forming a crunchy layer of aufeis over the snow here. As the trail was keeping her downhill from that patch of forest, she continued. The world beyond her snow machine mask turned long-stretching shadows and silver sunlight glinting off blue snow. She stopped the machine to look uphill into the deep woods, shivering. It looked like a bear could be hiding in those trees. Yeah, too early for a bear, but she wouldn't be the first hapless traveler to surprise a spring bear looking to break its long winter's fast.

The paw prints running ahead of her snow machine could have been dogs. She knew there was a cabin between Webb's and the highway. She'd seen his inbound trail a few months ago and had seen no sign of an outbound trail today. She didn't remember seeing dog tracks.

"You're getting paranoid out here in the Big Lonely, girl."

She turned on the snow machine again and continued along the trail. When she saw the cabin, she thought about turning downhill toward the creek, to give the neighbor his privacy, but something made her slow. As dusk slid toward night, she should have been able to see smoke coming from the chimney. Maybe the neighbor had headed out. But wait ... she could see the shiver of transparent heat waves coming out of the chimney. The fire burned low, but not dead. The Ditch pinged again and then she heard a yip and a man's weak protest. She sped up over a snow berm and dropped into the yard around the cabin. The wolves all turned to look at her as the man on the ground waved a stick at them. She fumbled for the .357 in her coat, drew it and fired uphill into the hillside. The wolves scattered.

As the shot reverberated through the valley, she took in the setting. The neat cabin and yard, wood shed and cache, the man on the ground across the tongue of a plastic cargo sled, the blood on the snow near where his head now settled again. He looked at her standing over him with the gun still in her hand and his eyes rolled back in his head before closing.

He'd fallen from the cache, it seemed, but she'd seen him move his legs when he was trying to keep the wolves back, so she thought he hadn't fallen from very far. His breathing sounded labored. His cheeks were red with cold. Taking off her glove, she felt in his collar. He was getting cold – growing hypothermic. He needed warmth and soon. She didn't know if she could move him, but she had to.

She stomped into the cabin and grabbed wood from the warming stack beside the snow-melting pot. Wood stoves could be tricky things, but there was an Earth Stove in the employee quarters at the lodge, so she knew to open the air at the back

An Investment Returns

and the stack damper before opening the door. The fire had healthy coals. She threw newspaper and kindling in on top and while they were catching, she arranged a couple of quarters on top of the spruce boughs. Returning outside, she saw a wolf peeking over a berm on the side of the yard. An injured man was fair game to a pack of hungry wolves. She drove them off with shouts.

"Mister, you need to help me if you can," she said aloud, grabbing the man's coat with both hands and lifting him to sitting. He groaned in pain. She used his weight to roll his front half into the sled and then tugged and swore until she got his legs in as well. She slipped the harness over her shoulder and leaned into it. It didn't move. Her boots began to slip on the snow. She just wasn't big enough to move a man his size uphill to the door. She dropped the harness and unhitched the fold-a-sled from her snow machine to replace it with the man's sled. Her hands were getting cold, her left thumb starting to ache. She swung in a long loop, so she could pull up right outside the door and roll him out to drag him inside. She'd worry about the niceties of the thing once she got him to the warmth. Sweat stung her forehead and ice kissed her lips as she worked feverishly to get the sled into position to drag him into the cabin. Fortunately, there was no carpeting on the floor, so his clothes provided little friction as she dragged him in one heave after another across the floor. She pulled off her outerwear one item at a time until she was stripped to her Under Armor shirt and pants.

The fire was putting out a nimbus of heat as she began to undress him, fighting his long limbs to roll him out of his coat and snow pants and then his shirt. She then braced her legs and dragged him up onto the couch off the cold floor to where heat reigned.

Only once she had him on the sofa did she concern herself with his injuries – a bleeding lump on the back of his head and a purpling bruise on his left rib cage. The cabin had been fitted with a wind turbine and LED lights and as she ministered to him, she tried to remember where she'd seen him before. A lot of the back-country cabin folks dropped their vehicles at the roadhouse before setting out. It was easier to ski to the lodge than to try to start a vehicle that had been sitting for weeks. Webb had no intention of leaving until March when it warmed up, but maybe this guy had a vehicle at the lodge. Or, er ... wait a minute, now she knew.

†††

It hurt to breathe, and a truly bad steel drum band was playing on his head. A shiver ran through him, making the muscles across his left chest spasm in agony. Dan groaned and opened his eyes.

"Awake?" she asked, turning from the wood stove where she was cooking. He could smell beef, bacon and some sort of vegetable. He remembered that long dark braid and the way her blue jeans, now replaced with Under-Armor, skimmed her hips, but her name escaped him right now. He'd talked his father Justin into not making such a big deal out of the tiny dent in his truck. It had, after all, been Dan's truck that Justin had parked way too close to the roadhouse woodshed. He'd thought of her as a delicate young woman to his father's ravening beast. But what was she doing in his cabin in the middle of Moose Valley?

"I think you fell out of your cache," she told him, as if she could read his mind. "I was coming from Webb's place and you were lying unconscious across your sled with a half-dozen wolves checking you out."

Memory leaked back like molasses in January – missing the hand-hold, waking up with blood on his face and fearing he'd broken his back. The wolves ... the blaht-blaht sound of the snow machine ... the retort of a gunshot through the valley.

"You scared them away." His voice rasped like a cat's tongue, but he could feel his toes moving against the blankets she had piled on him. He could also feel that most of his clothes had been removed. Relief battled with embarrassment. "How'd I get inside?"

"I rolled you onto your sled and dragged you."

She said it very matter-of-factly, as if it were just an average day for her, but she was slender and not terribly tall, and he was muscular and at least a head taller than her. "You were hypothermic, so I needed to get you in somewhere warm. Your fire was just about dead – the cabin was cold, so I used body heat while it rebuilt."

He felt his cheeks warm with a blush. She crooked a smile at him.

An Investment Returns

"Mostly kidding on that part, but clothes insulate you from the heat as well as the cold."

Of course, he knew that, except when his head was being squeezed in a vise.

"I'm sorry. I forget your name."

"Mallory. I'll forgive it since you've probably got a concussion. Dan, right?"

So she remembered. He nodded.

"I think your ribs might be cracked, hopefully just bruised, not fractured."

He could breathe without stabbing pain. Cracked.

"Yeah, cracked I think. I've had those before. And my head?" He felt the bandage at the back of his head.

"It stopped bleeding on its own, so I don't think it needs stitches, but a loss of consciousness …."

"I would have needed a lot more stitches if those wolves had gotten to me. Thanks. I think I'd be dead if you hadn't come along."

"One good turn deserves another." They both smiled, remembering how they had met. It had been summer. She'd been wearing a blue tank top and sporting an awesome tan.

"I'm glad I didn't freak out over the truck. You might have just left me lying there if I had."

"Nah. Alaska karma would have bit me." She smiled. "I thought it was your dad's truck."

"He acted like it was, but it's mine. If it had been his, he would have pushed it until Paula fired you. I'm still glad you didn't hold a grudge."

Her blue eyes twinkled.

"I felt badly about it, because it was my responsibility."

"Justin shouldn't have parked there, and accidents happen. I figured if I didn't make a big deal out of it, you'd pay it forward to someone else."

She grinned.

"I have an Alaska story to tell now. Better than the ubiquitous bear story too."

Laughing hurt, so he wouldn't do that again. While he waited for the spasm to pass, he stared at his and her outerwear hanging on pegs behind the stove.

"So, I was starving … what with all the excitement … and you had steak and bacon in your sled, so I'm making dinner. I hope you don't mind."

"No. I'm hungry too." He tried to push up against the couch arm. His ribs crackled, making him wince with pain, but it didn't take his breath. They were cracked, not broken. He lifted the blankets to see a scarlet bruise. He was going to be in a lot of pain for a few days. She picked up a mug of coffee from the top of the wood stove and handed it to him wrapped in a dish towel. He accepted it gratefully. Even this morning's re-warmed coffee was welcome so long as it was hot. He felt the weight of the mug in his hands, pulling on his ribs. He saw she'd increased the stack of wood by the stove. She'd made vegetables and rice too. If his head hadn't been banging, he might have been embarrassed that she had gone through his cabinets.

"Wow, a complete meal. I got rescued by an angel."

"Well, you're providing the food, so maybe not that divine."

"Take the compliment. I'd be dead if you hadn't come along."

Their hands touched as she handed him the plate and their gazes met. Her dusky complexion hid blushes well, but the crinkle at the corner of her eyes was unmistakable. His cheeks were warmer than the wood stove could create. She got her own plate and took the chair across from the couch, pulling her rag-wool stockinged feet up beside her, so she could balance her plate on her knees.

"Will Paula be worried about you overnight?"

It hurt to cut the meat, but the medium rare steak tasted divine.

"Nah, she sort of gave me permission to indulge in Webb's pancakes in the morning. I'll need to sled out to the truck in the morning to radio them, let them know not to worry, because you can't be alone for a few days."

"There's a sat phone in the bedroom. I mean, if you plan on staying. I don't think I'm going to be up to hauling water and wood for a few days."

"Or weeks? I cracked a rib once too. They really slow your roll." He smiled rather than laughed. "I'll call them now, let them know I'll spend a few days, make sure you can stay on your own."

She set her plate on the floor and headed toward the bedroom. When she'd figured out how to turn on the LED light, she turned and smiled at him before disappearing around the wall to go to

An Investment Returns

the sat phone. Warmth spread through his body. It had seemed a small kindness not to make a big deal over the truck, but it turned into an investment that was now paying huge dividends.

THE KATYDID AND THE KATYDIDN'T
BY
GENESIS MICKEL

Two young Katydids once diverged on the street.
T'was late fall, and all had turned a blustery bleak.
Scant succor was found 'mongst the stems and the leaves,
Shriveled as they were with the wintery sleet.
Winds buffeted their leaf-shaped, green bodies,
Spurring them to cling with their spiked little feet.
All the other bugs were tucked underground,
With nobody 'round to give 'em crumbs or nice treats.

(Carl and Clarice knew not this thing called cold weather.
Oh, t'was not a thought for our young Katydid teens:
Summer babies they were who only knew days better!)

Their tummies did rumble, and with no more picnics,
The frost aboveground left our bugs in a fix.
So to live, one thought to take, the other to give.
And in dissent they parted to ply their next tricks.
Carl hopped one way and Clarice jumped the other,
Both to find Ant villages out well beyond the sticks.
There would be food, there would be beds, there would be
Winter passage for these two little derelicts.

(Carl and Clarice watched the Ants toil all the summer long,
Tidying homes, raising their young, hauling in grub,
Whilst these free spirits goofed 'n' played and sang a song.)

Katydid Carl crawled to a township most pleasing.
"For crying out loud, help me now - I'm near freezing!"
He banged on the door and was brought in by Guards.
For dramatic effect, Carl began sneezing.
"Sing, play and you can stay." "Nay! I'm no serf! In fact--
"You owe ME!" One guard snatched a bite he tried seizing,
Then tossed it back to him and told him to flee.
Carl turned 'bout and gave 'em a scowl most displeasing.

In indignation, he left that village nonplussed.
He fussed, "I play 'n sing, but not 'cause I must!"
At the next town, a worker answered with a sad little frown.
"Let me in and feed me!" the greedy one cussed.
The Ant conceded, "Our Queen decreed we help all in need..."
Past her he strutted. "Ants are quite dim," he spat with disgust.
Then smirking, he saw Ants bring lunch to bugs who lounged.
Carl ate, put up his feet, and played music for free in utopian trust.

Meanwhile, Sis' Clarice jumped along and sang a ditty.
Looking and searching, she found an Ant city.
The Katydid girl knocked and called out "Hello?"
Guards answered and presented her to their committee.
"I was caught unawares and surely will die."
They whispered while she waited with a smile oh, so pretty.
Nods all around and the leader then spoke:
"You may stay if you help. We don't give you pity."

"I will, I will!" the 'Did did cheer as gratitude flowed.
Two workers appeared to show their happy abode.
She saw Ladybug Nannies tend to Ant little weans.
A spider proudly showed her the sweaters she sewed.
She smiled at chubby bumblebees buzzing a warm breeze,
And beetles burrowing a new underground road.
Finding her niche, she spent the freeze busy and pleased.
They greeted the sun by the time springtime showed.

The Katydid and the Katydidn't

Ants are industrious, the story is told,
But consent and aid outpace being owed.
All are fed, all are bed, and everyone's talents lighten work loads.

(As for Carl, our Katy who didn't, how are things grooving?
The colony 'bout collapsed as springtime drew near.
He fled and finally learned he was nearly his own undoing!)

THE FAIRY MOTHERS
BY
DONNARAE MENARD

In a land far, far away and yet right here.
In a time long ago and still now.
Within a small bright spot of the purest golden sunshine,
Live the Fairy Mothers.
Each working gleefully all day, sending their children out to touch each living creature.
Caring not about race, creed, or color.
Caring nothing about the boundaries set by man or any race of animal that separate one from the other.
The Fairy Mothers entrust their beloved children to find the truth in the hearts of all.
And maybe to bring it forth like the first leaf of spring,
The tiny legs of tadpoles,
Or the promise in a mother's kiss.

Each Fairy Mother has a duty; a job, a place to be.
One the twinkle in a baby's eye; another the fleet of movement (winged or not); and so forth through all the joys of life.
And so, they are known by what they do best; Fairy Mother Twinkle and Fairy Mother Dash.
Among the Fairy Mothers is one known as Fairy Mother Shoe.
For every Fairy wears shoes; even though sometimes Fairy Magic makes them invisible.
The Mugtug Fairies; which of course are the fairies that allow little boys to find the dirtiest mud puddles, need a sturdy shoe that will allow them to slide exactly three feet and one third inch to a mud puddle two and one-half feet away.

The On-High Fairies, who light up the highest night skies, need to keep their toes warm and snug so they won't catch a chill.

The Night Dew fairies need a special shoe that will allow them to flit about the garden on a warm summer's eve, dancing, dancing, with a quick hop, skip, and a jump.

There are so many.

In every country; in every land; each special shoe for each special Fairy has its own magic.

When a Fairy wears out their shoes, they return to Fairy Mother Shoe to stand in line, waiting patiently for their turn to have their shoes repaired.

Each fairy knows Fairy Mother Shoe will be quick and loving.

At Fairy Mother's feet is a quilted hassock of rainbow colors.

There the fairy will sit eating a gingersnap cookie and telling of adventures they have had.

Fairy Mother Shoe rubs her hand over the fairy's head to see what kind of magic they need.

Then she takes one shoe at a time between her fingers, kneading, patting, and mixing with a small amount of magic from her sewing basket.

By the time the fairy's tales are done and their cookie eaten, their shoes are ready.

With a final pat, she sends them soaring away.

It has been this way since before time.

Now Fairy Mother Shoe has many, many children, as do all fairy Mothers.

Among her children is a tiny little sprite named Lorraine.

Lorraine is different than other fairies because where their legs are strong and supple, hers are thin and short.

Her feet are quick but round, a little crooked on the end of her bent little legs.

No one knows why, no one had an answer, but Fairy Mother Shoe loves her just the same.

So, Lorraine sits on her own hassock beside her mother, passing out gingersnap cookies, listening to the adventures of others.

She rarely says a word but sits quietly, remembering what everyone else has to say.

The Fairy Mothers

So, it went for years and years through time.

All the other fairies know Lorraine, quiet and gentle, and often they bring her small gifts from lands far away.

One day a rag-tag Mugtug sat on Fairy Mother Shoe's hassock.

His shoes were a mess.

Fairy Mother Shoe tsk-tsked him through her smile.

Lorraine peeked around her mother's knee as the Mugtug gobbled up his cookie.

A magic cookie, however, will last until Fairy Mother Shoe is finished.

Her little black eyes shone with delight as the Mugtug Azoey talked.

Azoey also watched Lorraine; he reached into his pocket bringing forth a shiny agate marble of yellow and green which he gave to her.

"Oooh" she said.

Then from his pocket he brought out a tattered piece of red kite string.

"Aaah" she said.

With his arm in his pocket up to the elbow he searched for something else.

What was this?

Oh yes, a miniature black piano that he had traded half a bologna sandwich for.

It only played three notes; plink, plank, plunk, but he gave this also to Lorraine.

Her eyes were wide, her mouth round, no sound came forth as she marveled at this unusual gift.

Ajoey laughed aloud.

Fairy Mother Shoe gave him an extra pat, an extra cookie then sent him on his way.

So, it went for years through time.

Lorraine would sit all day and plink, plank, plunk happily.

Though this pleased her mother, Fairy Mother Shoe still watched her child with great sorrow.

She did everything she could to help Lorraine but even her good heart and clever fingers were no match against how nature had molded the child.

Fairy Mother Shoe made several pairs of shoes for Lorraine, but none seemed to be able to give her the magic she would need to race off on fairy business.

Fairy Mother Shoe grew sadder and sadder; her work, though still perfect, became slower.

All the Fairy Mothers loved Fairy Mother Shoe.

They loved Lorraine also, but with all the magic they had they did not know how to right this wrong.

The line of fairies waiting to have their shoes repaired grew long.

Even though Fairy Mother Shoe still enjoyed the tales each fairy had to share, she smiled less.

Always beside Fairy Mother Shoe was Lorraine playing on her toy piano.

Twice a year a woodland Elf whose name was Brownwart would rise from the depths of the Great Forests to visit the fairies.

He would bring bags of acorns in the fall to be brewed into acorn soup against the winter chill.

The tender most Lily leaves in the spring to be spun into Fairy clothes.

With him he would bring his heavy leather apron for Fairy Mother Shoe to repair.

For holes are often left by snagging branches or other Elfen work.

He watched Lorraine plink, plank, plunk away on her piano while he waited.

He watched Fairy Mother Shoe.

When he left he had sadness in his heart for his friend, what could he do? What?

So, the winter settled down upon the land.

Brownwart stayed cozy in his burrow in the bottom of an old Beech tree stump.

He made lists of where he was going to have to build new nests for the squirrels the next summer.

Then there were the song birds, the deer, the mischievous baby skunks.

There was so much to do in the winter!

But he found time to sit before his tiny flicker of fire thinking

The Fairy Mothers

about Fairy Mother Shoe's smallest daughter.

He thought of her bright head and glittery smile showing above the tiny black piano.

The joy all who could hear her playing received.

Brownwart thought and thought for many days.

Then when he was sure no answer was there, an idea whispered in his ear.

It was late, and he was tired, so he shook his head as he closed his eyes.

But the next day the idea whispered again in his other ear!

"I have nothing to use for a project that grand," he said aloud.

Then he rose slowly to his feet. There in his pile of saved bits and pieces was a long curly piece of Golden Birch.

Brownwart held it in his hands, gently rubbing it across his cheek.

The strength of the inner wood tingled against him.

Yes, yes this would do fine.

So, winter passed.

Spring had come!

The fairies were buzzing happily through the air, with quick turns.

Speedy races they played.

Fairy Mother Shoe looked up at the line of little fairies before her and smiled.

There, patiently waiting his turn, was Brownwart, his sack of aprons over his shoulder and his arms full of Lily leaves.

When, finally, it was his turn, he put down his big sack.

"Walk with me, Mother?" he asked.

Fairy Mother Shoe and Brownwart wandered across the glen.

In one arm he carried Lorraine, in the other a smaller woven sack.

When at last he found a place in the sun, high over the glen, he sat Lorraine on a tall rock warmed by the sun.

"Long have I known you," he said to Fairy Mother Shoe. "Long have I seen your love abound to all. This is my gift to you."

From his sack, he withdrew a piano made of Golden Birch.

It was much larger than the small black toy. The keys seemed to pulsate with music waiting to burst forth.

The entire piano glowed with nature's power.

Fairy Mother gasped with surprise.

Lorraine clapped her hands in pleasure, giggling merrily.

Brownwart sat the small fairy on the bench, then lifted both piano and fairy high in the air.

Raven swooped down, lifting both higher, passing them to Hawk, who passed them on to the Great Eagle.

Eagle arced higher and higher into the sky until he reached that high place where Wind lived.

Wind eagerly took on the load of piano and fairy, holding them safe high above the ground.

Lorraine ran her fingers eagerly over the keys.

She did not care where she was, only that she could play.

She played the mournful cry of the whales, the swish of the wind, and the joy of all the earthbound.

Fairy Mother Shoe stood with her hand pressed on her heart, watching her smallest child soar higher until she was almost lost in the void that was sky turning into the darkness of space.

Even then Wind held her child, swirling her gently on his strong currents.

Then swoosh, like a racing comet, Lorraine's piano sped off with her fingers still playing the wonders of the world.

From that day forth, the Fairy child rode the wind.

Spinning around the earth every day, chasing the night, playing the hope of all people.

Fairy Mother Shoe sits, mending fairy shoes and smiling at the skies when her child passes.

The brightest of all the shooting stars.

A TALE OF TWO BOOTS

BY
JACKIE FERRIS

Charlie Tyler was eight and three-quarter years old. The three-quarter mark of his birth-year had been celebrated a day earlier with a candle-free cake and a dandelion and burdock toast surrounded by his five sisters and parents. Today, as a special treat, he was to visit the zoo.

Charlie was dressed in his best clothes, not the cosy hoodie and jeans he had hoped for - the blazer and slacks were his mother's choice. His gleaming leather shoes weren't the scuffed plastic trainers he would have preferred either, but they were the perfect accompaniment for his mobile - neither smart nor on-trend. Their outmoded style was the primary reason he spent every spare minute on his computer checking out the net where his friends were virtual, and he was invisible – unlike today.

Their double-decker bus journey to the zoo was in deference to his mother's bi-monthly urge to join the masses. It coincided with one of her wine-spritzer mornings that occurred shortly afterwards. They were occasions designated to deconstruct the lesser-spotted common people.

Invariably, the bus journey had added to his embarrassment. His mother had spotted a group of hoodies nestled in the back of the bus. To his horror, she had devoted the remainder of the journey to dissecting their appearance and comparing it with his, in spite of his best efforts to dissuade her. His cheeks were as red as his hair as he jumped off the bus.

Feeling like a Mars bar at a Weight Watcher's meeting, he

shuffled his way towards the zoo. A waddle of penguins, their chests puffed with self-importance, greeted them as they pushed their way through the turnstiles. Unable to resist they followed the birds to their unnatural habitat. Their carefully constructed concrete pool area spewed laughter as the bumptious penguins swaggered around it – even his mother was grinning. For once their genial mood continued as they checked out the lions and tigers and laughed with the chimpanzees over a mess of afternoon tea.

It was only as they made their way back to the bus that Charlie's mood began to dip – he couldn't stop replaying their journey there. Nightmare scenarios of a repeat mortification jarred through his mind – but as he spotted the boot lying on a smattering of grass that doubled as a dog loo, those thoughts vanished. He studied the boot; it was magnificent – the shoelace went all the way up its scuffed leather – it was the sort of thing his mother hated, and Charlie loved. He couldn't take his eyes off it as he ran towards it. He picked it up and dangled it in the air. 'Look mother, someone's lost it.'

She pulled a face. 'Throw it away; no doubt it belonged to some homeless druggie. Goodness knows how many germs you've picked up. Take a shower as soon as we get in.'

'It's not dirty, just used.' He looked at her slightly puzzled. 'Whoever owned the boot loved it; it's been everywhere.'

She sucked in air loudly. 'Charlie, no one can love a boot. Get rid of it and hurry up or we'll miss the bus.' She glared at her watch.

Charlie compared the boot to his sparkling leather shoes before turning to his mother who was staring into the distance with her nose in the air. Quickly, he pulled the lace from the boot and stuffed it into his blazer pocket. He smiled, delighted that there were only two elderly people occupying seats as he followed her onto the bus. Carefully, he wiped the steamy glass with a paper handkerchief, and then, holding the lace between his fingers, he contented himself with staring out of the window thinking about the boot. It was only when he felt his mother stand up that he hurriedly jumped up and followed her.

It was a long walk back to the house and the lace was burning a hole of excitement in his pocket. He imagined that it belonged to a tramp or possibly – and more excitingly – a hippy that had

A Tale of Two Boots

trekked around India and Thailand on the ubiquitous year out. His sisters, who were much older, had done it but, if anything, it had narrowed their outlook and swelled their arrogance - like his mother, they looked on him as a well-dressed cuddly toy. He grinned - the clandestine shoelace in his pocket proved that he could do something on his own. As he entered the house he ran up the stairs to his beloved computer hoping that his mother would approve. To be certain he yelled: 'I'll take a shower, Mum.'

He pulled his books out from his leather satchel – everyone else had rucksacks but his father had insisted on the satchel. He gave the books a casual glance then reverently drew out the shoelace from his pocket.

'Charlie, have you started your homework?' His mother's voice calling him from downstairs made him drop it.

'Yes, Mum.' He doused his hair under the tap and then opened his Math book and began to write a few equations into his exercise book – she would be up to check it shortly.

Twenty minutes later she pushed the door open with her foot. A small copper tray decked with a glass of milk and a banana was balanced on her hand. 'Eat it while I check your answers and then off to bed.' She placed it carefully on his bedside table. 'You've had an exciting weekend – too much stress isn't good for young boys.' She wagged her finger. 'No computer for you tonight, Charlie.'

Charlie nodded, trying not to stare at the shoelace lying on the carpet. Instead he offered her a smile as he handed her the exercise book. 'Perfect timing, I've just finished.'

She patted his head. 'Good boy, now drink your milk, and then lights out. I'll be up in twenty minutes; leave your tray outside so I won't disturb you.'

After she closed the door he waited a second and then he picked up the lace and stuffed it into his pyjama pocket before peeling the banana. He ate it in three bites and then drained the glass as he always did.

Dutifully, he climbed into bed and turned off the light. In the darkness he ran the shoelace through his fingers, picturing the boot crossing mountains and rivers and staring at old castles until his eyes were weighted with sleep.

The muffled noise of someone talking woke him with a start - was it his parents coming to bed? Beside him his luminous clock

Jackie Ferris

declared it was just after midnight – much too late for them.

He rubbed his eyes - a chink of moonlight had snuck through the half-drawn curtain in front of his bed casting a sliver of light onto the floor. Charlie threw off the duvet and leapt out of bed as he gasped – the boot; the one on the grass next to the dog poo - was draped in moonlight. Tiptoeing towards it, he breathed in deeply as he reached out his hand to touch it. A wave of silver swept over him as the moonbeam engulfed him. The room shimmered in silent light and then the noise erupted. He strained his ears trying to make sense of it.

'I've lost my other half.' The sad voice echoed around the room as Charlie stared at the boot, dumbfounded.

'Is that you?'

'Were you expecting someone else?' The boot dropped its tongue.

Charlie rubbed his eyes again. 'I must be dreaming; boots can't talk.'

'People think that all we do is squeak. You were different; you read me like a boot.'

'You sort of looked like you'd been around a bit.' Charlie swallowed hard, wondering if he'd been too impolite.

'I was lying there for ages, but no one noticed me. Have you any idea how that feels?'

Charlie's silence prompted him to continue. 'It's not important, what is, is locating my other boot. You have to help me find her.'

'Her? Your other boot?'

'We are a pair! Boots mate for life; my other half was lost somewhere in Turkey. It was hot, everyone was sweating. We were rounded up like cattle – a bit like a knacker's yard.'

'Knacker's yard?' Charlie hadn't heard the word but instinctively knew that his mother would not approve.

'The place you go before you die.'

'Like an old folks' home?'

'Funny – not l.o.l. - there were hundreds of people trying to get on a boat or anything that might float. Our village was a multiple-bombing site - there were no houses, only ruins. We'd tramped hundreds of miles - the sea was our only hope of escape. Since my creation I'd seen many difficult things but nothing like that scramble for life.' He pulled himself upright. 'I had a noble birth. I was created by a master craftsman in Imperial China during the time of the dragon.'

'Real dragons?'

'Yes, but don't confuse the meaning of real.'

'How could I? Real is real.' Charlie pinched his striped pyjama sleeve.

'Imagination is real.'

'But it doesn't really happen.'

'It happens somewhere.'

'But not here in the real world.'

'Reality depends on the observer.'

'This is crazy.' Charlie shook his head. 'I can't believe that I'm talking to you.'

'Talk is cheap.'

'That's not what I meant.'

'Irrelevant, do you want to hear my story or not?'

'I'm here, aren't I?'

'Then hear what I have to say. I don't look it but I'm a pretty old boot. When my last wearer put us on there were dragons.'

'You're that old?'

'I am but I didn't see these dragons in China; I was in Syria. It was a memory stream of my creation at the time of the dragons.'

'Were flames bursting from their mouths?'

'Not flames – their breath stinks, it comes out in waves of putridity.'

'Putridity?'

'It's a dragon word; it means rotten; waves of rottenness rippled from their mouths as they flew through the air powered by their scaly wings. They rode the thermals like prehistoric surfers. My first wearer had ordered his boots to be specially made for the crowning of a Chinese Emperor. The Emperor rode on the dragon's back.' The boot tapped his toe on the carpet. 'I don't remember anything after that until I came into the custody of the man who was fleeing from Syria.'

'Wow, that's at least two thousand years later.'

'It doesn't seem that long. I have wipe-outs.'

'Wipe-outs?'

'When the sole of my boot is cleaned I lose my memory. Everything that happened between China and Syria was lost. The rest of my memories are recent. My partner and I walked from Syria to Turkey. I can't describe the journey. The smell of loss and defeat suffocates everything but sometimes kindness shines through like the moonbeam that woke you.

We were waiting for the next dinghy when this young girl appeared through the crowd. She looked like she could slip through time she was so thin. She had one leg but no crutches or even a stick to help her walk. Her foot was blister-red and oozing sores. You could smell her from 100 metres away; it's probably why the crowd parted.

My wearer pulled off his linen shirt and ripped it into shreds. He used the cloth to bandage her foot once he'd cleaned it in the salty sea. Afterwards he took off his boot and gave it to her. The linen bandage had swelled her foot so it fit her perfectly.

She stared at the man and smiled. "My parents, and my two brothers and three sisters, were killed. I was at the bakers; I'd queued for five hours – I hated it but it saved my life. When I returned the stones that were once our home were their tombstones. Panic took over. I didn't notice the beam. It fell on my leg. I'm not sure how long I lay there, pinned to the ground. Blood poured from the gaping wound as the flies feasted on me. By the time I was spotted in the rubble the infection had ripped through my body. There were no antibiotics, so they cut off my leg. I spent two days in the makeshift hut they called a hospital." She sighed. "As I lay on a blood-stained mattress the words of my father echoed in my head – he used to whisper them in my ear before I went to sleep each night.

'Salah, our land is poisoned by people who seek power. Don't suffer my fate. I must die here in the land of my parents. The buildings can be replaced but our culture, our pride, will never be rebuilt. Don't let the legacy of the past chain you to its future; if you survive this war-without-meaning leave this place. Seek your fortune in another land where neighbour doesn't kill his neighbour and brother his sister.

"His words carried me as I taught myself to hop on one leg. It was hard, but crutches were more valuable than gold. I hit my head so many times in the first few weeks, but my father's words drove me on." She smiled up at the man. "So here I am, propelled by his wisdom."

The man stared at her for a long time before he spoke. "My

journey was about fear, yours is about people and a future you must fulfil. Your father would be proud, but your journey is only beginning. Once you have crossed the sea you must make a new life. The boot at least will help. I wish you luck."

He picked her up in his arms and carried her onto the dinghy. Her hair was blond and long like a fairy princess's. She was about your age.'

'My age! But she sounded so old.'

'Age rests on experience, Charlie, not numbers. Her eyes were as blue as the sea, except for the missing leg, she looked like she'd stepped out of a fable and was searching for her prince.'

Charlie thought about it before answering. 'She made a big impression on you so how did you lose her?'

'I didn't; as soon as we got into the dinghy the kind man tossed me overboard. My heart was heavy from the loss of my partner, not the water.'

'You have a heart?'

'And a soul.'

Charlie studied the sole poking from the boot. 'I get that; what I don't is how you got from the sea to here.'

'I hitched a ride on a turtle, it took me to Greece.'

'Greece is still a long way from here.'

'Tell me about it. I was picked up and put in a recycling truck because they thought I was plastic - they threw me out when they discovered I was leather. An old tramp tried to wear me, but he soon realised one boot was pretty useless. He tossed me onto the dog loo. I was hanging around for days until you spotted me.'

'But how did you get into my bedroom? You don't even know where I live.'

'The force of your imagination brought me here on a wave of illusion.'

'Illusion?'

'Magic; whatever you want to call it.' The boot stamped on the carpet again. 'The lace also had a pretty strong pull.'

Charlie felt the lace in his pyjama pocket.

'DNA, string, we are tied together by the fabric of life. Look, we've wasted too much time already. I need my partner. You have to help me find my right boot, Trekka, I'm her left, Trek. We all have a yin and yang.'

Charlie wondered if his parents had any side other than what the neighbours thought. 'Are you serious?'

'Why do you think I'm here?'

Charlie re-ran the news footage of the small dinghies that tried to make it across the Mediterranean —only a few of them did. 'It's a big sea, Trekka could be anywhere.'

'The dinghy was headed for Cyprus, not Greece; it's Aphrodite's island – the island of love; it has a heart.' He studied Charlie's blank expression and decided to continue. 'Cyprus is close to Turkey - they had a good chance of making it.'

'You can't be sure.'

'Boot intuition, we have a built-in tracking device. It's a kind of echo that sends sound waves. I hear Salah's footsteps; she's the girl I told you about. I hear her because my heart is attuned to my other half, Trekka.'

Charlie raised his eyebrows, yet it made a strange sort of sense. 'Go on.'

'There's a legend on Cyprus that relates to the Five Finger Mountains; Trekka is somewhere in the foothills of those mountains.'

'She might as well be on the moon. There's no way we can get there; we don't even have money.'

'We don't need money.'

'We can't get there without money; it's not like we have a magic carpet.' Charlie's eyes strayed to the carpet he was standing on.

'You don't need a magic carpet; you have me, the magic boot.'

Charlie laughed. 'If you could take us there, why didn't you go on your own?'

'A boot has no purpose without a human. You gave me a purpose.'

'Really?'

'Perhaps I was wrong. I can't stay here all night. Are you coming or not?'

'How?' Charlie swallowed hard regretting that he'd asked yet another question.

'This boot is big enough for both your feet. I know you still have the lace. Where is it?'

Charlie pulled it out of the pocket of his pyjamas and swung it in the air.

A Tale of Two Boots

'Good, then step in here with both feet and tie the lace tight around my boot.'

Charlie put his feet into the boot. It was hard to balance, and he felt a little foolish wearing his striped red-and-orange pyjamas.

'Ready?'

Charlie nodded.

'Close your eyes and imagine you're an owl flying through the night sky.'

Charlie shut his eyes - it was hard to visualize anything standing precariously in the boot but suddenly he felt a whoosh underneath him and the sting from the cold night air as it hit his face. He opened his eyes; beneath him he saw his house and the woods beyond it. They quickly disappeared as they soared into the clouds and they rode the cloud-waves. Charlie couldn't remember the last time he had so much fun.

Then suddenly the clouds parted to reveal the sea glistening in the moonlight below them. In the distance Charlie glimpsed land. 'Is that Cyprus?'

'We're about to find out.' The boot dunked as the land reared up in front of them. 'Brace yourself for landing – it was never my strong point.' They wobbled and then dipped. Charlie tried to roll as he hit the ground. When he came to a halt he was staring up at a mountain that looked like it had a big fist on top of it.

'What's that?'

'The Five Finger Mountains; I hope we don't meet the same fate as the luckless boy.'

A sliver of fear shot through Charlie. 'You didn't mention a boy.'

'According to legend a young villager fell in love with a local queen. To get rid of him she told him to fetch water from the Andreas monastery on the opposite side of the island. She promised that if he brought the water to her without spilling a drop she would marry him. It was – she knew – a hopeless task. Imagine her surprise when weeks later he turned up with the water. Horrified, she told him that she had no intention of marrying him because he had used witchcraft to bring the water to her.

Beyond angry the young peasant boy tipped the water onto the ground creating a huge puddle between them. The boy bent down and thrust his hands into the water. He gathered the black mud into his fist and threw it at the queen. She ducked but the mud flew through the air and landed on top of the mountain.

When the mud dried it formed the five fingers. The queen claimed it proved that the boy had been mesmerized by a witch and was under her power. She cast him out of her kingdom and the boy was forced to wander for the rest of his life.'

Charlie stared at the mountain and shuddered. 'That won't happen to us, will it?'

'Impossible; my other half wants me back – we belong together.'

'The young boy had similar thoughts and look what happened to him.' Charlie pointed towards the mountain. 'I never imagined that tonight I would end up in Cyprus. Life is full of surprises. We can't take anything for granted.'

'You're right; what's more, we don't have much time. The moon gives me powers but I'm nothing in the sunlight even with you wearing me. We have to hurry.'

Charlie looked around. 'Hurry – where? There's nothing here but mountains.'

'My other half is here; there are a lot of caves, they are in one of them. Pick me up so we can move faster.'

Charlie strung the boot over his shoulder as it barked orders in his ear. 'Do you see that cave on the right? It's about halfway up the mountain; my guess is they are there.'

Half an hour later they had almost reached the entrance to the cave. The darkness was scary. Charlie gulped and then ducked as a bat flew out.

'The ghosts have let it out.' The boot whispered in his ear. 'The ghosts of the spirits past are friendly – it's the ghosts of the future you need to worry about. We shouldn't waste any more time, let's go in.'

Charlie swallowed hard and then crept inside. At first, he saw only black but slowly his eyes became accustomed to the darkness. Towards the end of the cave some people were lying on the floor.

The boot nudged him on his chin. 'It's Trekka.' He wriggled out from Charlie's grasp and bounded towards the sleeping figures. Charlie counted about twelve people.

He watched the boot study each figure until finally it stopped in front of a one-legged girl; a boot that Charlie assumed was

A Tale of Two Boots

Trekka, was beside her. Trekka must have heard him because she woke up and smiled. 'You're back.'

'Home is where the heart is, Trekka.'

'Home is a luxury a boot can't afford.' She glanced at Salah. 'There's only one foot here, there's no room for two boots.'

'Trekka, your boot is too big; it's doing Salah's foot more damage now that she doesn't need the bandages.'

'Salah no longer wears me but that doesn't mean I don't have a role.'

'A boot that doesn't walk, what sort of role is that?'

'You can't know a person until they walk in your boots. I've learned many things, sadly most are bad. Have you any idea how many refugees come through here?'

'Too many.'

'Most are rounded up by the authorities and placed into camps. We don't want to be one of those numbers. No one will look for us here; the climb is too hard. Besides, they have too many refugees arriving every day to look for more.'

Trek nodded. 'We don't have to stay; you're right, we aren't refugees.'

Trekka tightened her laces, pulling her leather so that she gained a little height. 'I'm not going anywhere. I'm going to make a new life here where people are accepted for what they are.'

'You're not people. Besides, what can you do here in a cave?'

'There's so much to do; it's why I summoned you.' Trek's tongue lolled onto the ground.

'You summoned me?'

'We both did.' Salah used her hands to help her stand up and then moved towards the cave entrance. 'There's a war going on.'

'I know, I was in it.' Trek tugged on his lace.

'12 million people are displaced by a war begun with hope – you must remember the Arab Spring? Syria was its biggest casualty - it's now a place where countries fight for religious control.'

Charlie gazed at her in wonder as he moved towards the little group. 'You're the same age as me and yet you know so much.'

'War affected children more than any other age group. War is all we know. I'm almost 9 years old; I was one year old when it started. For years we lived underground during the day to protect ourselves from the shells. The cave reminds me of home. No child should have to go through what I've been through. Other countries don't care about us; people describe us as collateral damage. Do you even know what that is?'

Charlie shook his head. It was stuffed with his own issues about how his mother didn't let him have on-trend clothes and how his father made him take a satchel to school – it all seemed stupid now. 'I don't know what to say, I can't begin to imagine what you've been through.'

She smiled. 'You're no different to the rest but we are more than collateral damage. We're people with a future and we're going to prove it.'

'How? Charlie looked around the cave. 'There are only twelve children here.'

'We represent the millions who were displaced. Trekka summoned you because you can use the internet – it's a kind of modern day magic. You can do anything you want with it.'

'But I don't even know Trekka so how could she summon me?'

'She is far more intuitive than Trek. The lace that ties them together is invisible. When Trek was in your bedroom she could see how good you were on the computer using their invisible lace.'

'But I wasn't using the computer.'

'It doesn't matter, you also have an invisible lace. You use it on the computer to communicate with the world. It's part of you. Trust me, you can help us.'

'How?'

'Show the world that we count for something.'

'And boots, you can show boots too,' Trekka interrupted. 'A relative of mine was one of the boots used in the holocaust memorial – it represented the five or six million Jews that were killed during the Second World War. That memorial has an epic effect on people who visit it, even today.'

'Trekka's right, grown-ups won't do anything; all they care about is power. We must make it happen and you can help, Charlie.' Salah's bright blue eyes were somehow luminous in the darkness.

He swallowed hard; no one had ever believed that he was important – ideas were spilling through his head. 'I could upload something onto YouTube. I could photograph you all and then copy and paste, there would be millions of people. I have a software programme at home.' He stared at the ground, suddenly downcast. 'But I don't have a phone to take the pictures and I'm not at home to work the programme.'

Salah laughed. 'You wouldn't believe how many smart phones we pick up - no one is paying direct debits anymore. The internet doesn't work but we can still take photographs and Trek will get you home.'

Trek nodded and then peered at Trekka through a space where his lace hadn't gone through. 'Do you understand any of this internet stuff?'

'It doesn't matter, to understand a person's life you have to walk in their boots. If YouTube works, it will be the boots that people walk in.' Seeing disappointment cloud his leather she added: 'What is YouTube, anyway?'

'The new version of magic – it takes you to places without leaving your room. You no longer need a travelling boot. We're a bit outmoded. I processed the stuff about YouTube in Charlie's bedroom when I was waiting for him to wake up.'

'That was when I processed his computer skills. Whatever happens people will always need boots.'

'Yes, but not magic boots – the internet takes people to where they want to go by virtual reality.'

She pulled her tongue down as he continued. 'It's a place that's real but isn't - like us coming here tonight. The real world thinks it's impossible to use a boot to travel thousands of miles in a few minutes but we're here. Virtual reality makes things come to you; they are there but they aren't.'

'Illusion can work for us, too.'

'We aren't computer types.'

'Does it matter?' Trekka pulled the tongue further out of her boot. 'Trek, you of all boots should know the importance of illusion. You came here on the hopes of someone who wanted to be somewhere else - Charlie.'

'Hope is the limitation of life. We cannot live beyond what we hope for.'

Salah interrupted. 'But we can hope for a better life - we have that possibility. Take the photographs, we will all stand outside – Cyprus is the island of love, we must make the world love us and Charlie can do that.'

He smiled back but his eyes were sad. 'When I upload our

images, if people aren't moved by them, that's it. We cannot change the human condition.'

'Or the condition of the boot. I came here for my other half, not this.' Trek puffed out his tongue.

'Trek, you can't turn your back on this,' Trekka said, horrified.

'I came here to find you, not make war on the world.'

'The world has made war on itself and abused innocent people. We can show people what it's like to walk in someone else's boots.'

Salah snapped her fingers. 'That's perfect! We could make a video of someone from the UK stepping into my boots in Syria. Parents would understand if they thought it was one of their kids.'

Charlie grinned and then pulled a face. 'It's a great idea. We can use news footage, there's loads of it. I'll superimpose a young English girl and put them in your boots.'

Trek's laces lit up. 'We need two boots to do that.' He looked at Trekka who glanced outside. 'Dawn will be breaking shortly. Get everyone out of the cave; we need as many photographs as possible. Everyone, grab a camera.'

Soon they had enough photographs to fill a dinghy and they threw their mobiles at Charlie.

'Time to go, mate.' Trek's voice broke into his thoughts. 'We have to get back to your bedroom.'

'We need you for filming too, Trekka,' Charlie added, winking at Trek. 'You need two boots for walking.'

Trekka threw her partner a scornful look. 'Don't think I'm staying, Trek.'

†††

Charlie's bedroom was strangely unfamiliar as he flew into it with the two boots tied to his feet. As he headed over to the computer and turned it on, he realised he had changed, not the room.

'Keep up, Trek, and walk straight, tie those laces up,' Trekka niggled as Charlie watched the two boots through his video camera on top of the computer screen. It was difficult to get them to walk in unison. Finally, he stood up. 'Please, stop nagging each other. I have to fit someone into your boots. At the very least try to look like you are a pair.'

A Tale of Two Boots

Trek stopped. 'Sorry, Charlie, we're always like this, but we love each other really. Give it another go; it will be perfect next time, I promise.'

Charlie re-set the camera and then smiled. 'Got you, now all I have to do is find someone to fill your boots.'

'That won't be easy – these are big boots to fill.'

'Don't kid yourself, Trek, but stop talking. We need to get out of here. Salah is waiting.' Trekka turned on him.

'I need a shot of both of you stationary,' Charlie shouted at them. 'And then I have to do the video of the girl.'

Trekka stamped her boot. 'You haven't got long.'

Charlie pressed his keyboard. 'No pressure there then.'

An hour later he looked up and smiled. 'It's done.'

Trek glanced out of the window. 'There's still time to get back to Cyprus before dawn.'

'I could upload the images to Salah instead – it would be quicker.'

'Wouldn't it be better if we were all together? With two boots we'll get there twice as fast.'

Charlie didn't need much convincing – it wasn't every day you got to boot-cloud-surf to Cyprus.

'Sounds good to me, Trekka.'

'Okay, then open the window and put one foot in each boot.'

Charlie unfastened the window sash and then put his feet into the boots.

'Duck!' Trek shouted as they ran towards the window.

Charlie did, just in time. He couldn't help laughing as they soared into the air to ride the clouds. Soon he could see Cyprus glittering in the Mediterranean like Aphrodite's jewel. As they slowed down, Trekka put her boot cap up and Trek followed her as they both yelled: 'Braking, boots to manual; prepare for landing.'

Charlie got ready to roll as they landed at the foot of the mountain.

'We should be up there in a few minutes if we hurry. Unfasten us and tie us around your neck,' Trek barked instructions at Charlie.

Salah, who was pacing outside the cave, waved to them as they drew nearer. 'I thought you were never coming.'

'We did have to go to England and back,' Trek retorted, a little peeved.

'And there was also the little problem of the video and photo-pasting,' Charlie added.

'You could have uploaded them to me.'

'We wanted to see it together and we weren't that much longer than cyberspace,' Trek added for good measure.

'Then let's see it.' Salah ignored Trek's dig as Charlie scrambled for his mobile, realising that he was still in his pyjamas.

He held it out. 'Take a look.'

The video flickered into life on the mobile's screen.

A young girl was staring at the TV eating pizza with her family. They were arguing good naturedly about who should go through on X-Factor when suddenly she was transported into a landscape that looked as if it had been bulldozed several times. Buildings that were once houses were little more than rubble - through the wreckage a pair of boots stood out. The girl looked at the boots suddenly realising that she was bare-footed.

'Where am I?' she shrieked, peering through the smoke from the shells. 'Where's the TV?'

'There is no TV, you're in Aleppo, this was our home.' The man looked at her strangely. 'You don't recognise me, do you?'

She stared at him blankly.

'I'm your father — we have to go. Flying debris from one of the shells knocked you out. Put your boots on, Rajanga; we can take nothing but what we stand up in. It will have to do us for the months and years ahead.'

She tried to find something familiar, but her eyes were blinded by terror. Suddenly she saw something she recognised. 'What about my teddy?'

'We must leave everything behind. Put your boots on and hurry.'

She bent down and put the boots on to a backdrop of shells dropping and buildings crumbling. As she tied the laces she realised that the TV and the X-factor were a dream.

'What about Mummy?' She stared at the figure on what was left of a sofa.

'She's dead, Rajanga, we must leave her here.'

Rajanga remembered the debris dropping and her mother crying out just before she died. 'We can't leave her here.'

'If we stay we will die too. Your mother begged me to leave

but this was the land of our fathers. Now it is no man's land - our lives are hostages to oil and Middle East supremacy.

'The shells killed her but my reluctance to leave the killing arena cost her her life. I won't make the same mistake with you. We must walk thousands of miles through hard winters and scorching summers to lands where people don't want us, and communities will treat us with suspicion. We've done nothing wrong, but people will hate us for inflicting our sufferings on their lands.'

'Then why should we leave?'

'Because life is better than death and perhaps one day people will treat us as humans not aliens.'

'We can't even treat ourselves as humans. How can others treat us better than we treat ourselves? I was brought up among the shells and the snipers. I've never eaten food off a table because we were too afraid to sit down.'

He smiled. 'I'm glad you remember who you are but maybe it would be better if you didn't - the war is not your home and fear should not be your neighbour.' They both dropped to the ground as another shell struck a ruined building.

'Hurry, already our route may be blocked with snipers but at least we will have tried. You cannot fail if you don't try, Rajanga. We must think of that as we make our journey.'

'It was Mum's favourite saying.'

'I laughed at her then. I was wrong: to succeed you can't be afraid of failure. History will record that we were innocent victims. Sadly, history has a kinder face than the present. Come, child, we must go. Whatever awaits us is better than this.'

They watched the camera pan out to individuals and the words *12 million displaced people* appeared on the screen. Underneath it: *How many more will be displaced before the world listens? It could be you, it could be me, it just happens to be me -* was written.

A photograph of a pile of boots replaced the sub-titles. *This was a memorial to 5 or 6 million dead Jews. How dare we watch in silence again?*

Salah jumped up and down. 'It's brilliant, Charlie, you have learned so much. No one could have done this better.'

Charlie smiled, pleased. 'We should upload it onto YouTube immediately; we haven't a moment to lose.'

They nodded their agreement and ten minutes later they were laughing.

'It's even better than I imagined, just look at the hits.' Salah glanced at Charlie.

'You're a genius.'

'I only did what you told me to do,' Charlie answered, wishing that he wasn't in his pyjamas.

'I hate to break this up, but we can't stay here for much longer, we must get you home, young man.' Trek stamped his foot forcing them to look down.

'I can't go home now, this is just the beginning.'

'It will be the end if we don't get you home before sun up, the dawn is already breaking.'

'What difference does that make?'

'Night is a magical time, dawn sweeps it all away. We must get you back.' Trek was determined.

'The internet, we can talk on that,' Salah added but her words were already fading as Charlie was lifted into the night sky.

†††

'Charlie,' his mother's voice woke him with a start. He rubbed his eyes and then jumped out of bed but as he glanced around the room his heart dropped. There were no boots.

'Charlie, hurry up; you'll be late for school.'

Resisting the urge to cry, he ran to the bathroom trying to make sense of everything – had it really been a dream?

Five minutes later he staggered downstairs dressed in his school uniform, but his eyes were brimming with tears.

'Gosh you look shattered - didn't you sleep?'

'I must have been dreaming.'

'Then take some anti-histamines for your allergy. Your eyes are streaming.'

He pulled out his handkerchief and blew his nose hoping it would stop his tears.

'I'll get the car out and then we're off; you can't be late for school.'

Charlie gulped down his cereal and then ran back upstairs for his satchel. As he entered the bedroom his computer screen was flickering. He strode over to it and laughed. YouTube was streaming his video - it had 5 million hits, everyone was talking about it. He ran over to his pillow and put his hand in his pyjama pocket. The camera was still there.

As he went downstairs, the Prime Minister was on the TV. She was talking about his video and claiming that countries around the world had been shamed into action.

His mother pointed at the screen. 'It's about time they did something about that.'

'You can't fail if you don't try. No one should be afraid of failing. At least the video is shaming people into doing something.'

She looked at her son. 'Charlie, I'm taking your computer out of your room tonight. It's filling your brain with silly ideas. You need to do something worthwhile like read a book.'

He smiled. 'I might be better off with a pair of boots, mum. I'd like to try hiking.'

FROGS
BY
MARIE ANDERSON

Sighing, Harriet sat down on her tidy, twin-sized bed. She leaned back into soft pillows, stretched her legs, and logged on to her laptop. The latest Facebook-vistas of beaches, lake resorts, nightclubs, concerts—all showing her various girlfriends gallivanting with their various boyfriends—hurtled a frown between her eyes. Everyone having fun, hilarious fun, everyone but her.

She closed her laptop and slapped the cover, furious not at her friends but at herself.

She had no one, no special one, no boyfriend. Twenty-six years old and never been kissed. She was a princess without a prince. An *Insufficient*. Take the prince out of princess, and what was left? Two meaningless squiggles.

Was it her height that scared away a special someone? She was just under six feet, taller than all her friends, girls as well as the guys.

Was it her too-long nose? Aristocratic, her best friend assured her.

Her too-high forehead? A sign of intelligence, proclaimed her grandmother—who'd raised her after her parents' fatal car accident when Harriet was a toddler.

It certainly couldn't be the fault of her porcelain skin, her long pale-yellow hair, her round blue eyes (her best feature, Harriet believed), or her slim build (though one sarcastic frenemy called her Popsicle Stick.)

More likely, Harriet feared, she'd been *born* an *Insufficient*, a girl who lacked the stamina to keep up with people, a girl who liked the idea of people better than being with them, a girl who felt safer staying home with good books, good TV shows, and her good granny than she did pushing through the noisy, unpredictable, and confusing world.

Except when she saw how much delight everyone else took in being out and about with each other. How was it that she both wanted—and didn't want—that?

Harriet shook her head and sighed. From the parlor, came a soap opera's dramatic conversation and the soothing purr of her granny's snores.

Harriet cleared her throat—she'd woken that morning with laryngitis—and said aloud her granny's advice: "Walk time, Harriet. One foot in front of the other walks out the *bothers*."

She filled a cinch sack with a water bottle, apple, and six chocolate chip cookies (leaving six for her granny), laced up her walking shoes, and hurried to the parlor.

"Granny?"

Her grandmother, cocooned in her rocker under an afghan, opened her eyes and smiled at Harriet.

"Heading to work, sweetie? Can you bring back a buttercrust not sliced?"

"Bakery's closed for the week, Granny. Starting today."

"Oh yeah, that's right. Your boss and his brood are doin' Disney."

"Yup." *More people having fun together.*

"Sound like you got a frog in your throat, sweetie."

"Yup."

"Sound like you in one of your yup moods, sweetie."

"Yup. That's why I'm heading out for a walk, a long walk."

"Walkin' with anyone, sweetie?"

Harriet was ready to fib out a yes just to make her granny happy, but instead she stuck out her tongue and winked. "Just me and the frog in my throat, Granny."

"Aw," her granny said. "It's that kind of walk, huh? Well, I better let you hop to it then."

Harriet smiled. Her granny could always make her smile.

†††

Forty minutes of walking quiet suburban blocks brought Harriet to Bullfrog Pond, a big blue eye in the middle of sloping grass bordered by leafy trees. Though it was a pleasant Wednesday afternoon in the middle of summer, the little nature preserve was empty. *Everyone out having adventures with everyone,* Harriet thought. *Everyone but me.*

Three laps Harriet walked the gravel path circling the pond. Slowing, she grabbed the apple from her cinch sack and opened her mouth to take a bite, but instead of juicy apple a bug zoomed in. Fierce coughing brought her to her knees, lowered her head, squeezed shut her eyes. Something coughed out, sweet relief. She sank onto the soft grass, heart thumping, pain stitching her middle.

"God bless it all to hell," she said. "Gruesome."

Her heart settled. The pain left. "Hey, hey, hey!" She smiled. Her voice was back! Coughing out the bug had also coughed out the frog in her throat. "Silver lining in every cloud," she said, liking the restored smoothness of her voice.

She brought out her water and cookies, ate and sipped and watched sunlight and dragonflies dimple the pond water. She stretched out on the soft grass and closed her eyes.

†††

A cow's mooing woke her. She sat up. No cow in sight.

The sound came again, close, deep, and loud: "Jug-a-room, jug-a-room."

From the mud at the pond's edge, a nose poked up. Followed by humped golden eyes, an emerald head freckled with dark spots, a pulsing yellow throat.

"Hello, Bullfrog," Harriet said. "Aren't you a buff one!"

"Jug-a-room," mooed the bullfrog.

Harriet laughed. "Are you the frog I coughed out?" she joked.

The frog suddenly leaped, its mouth wide open, landed near her feet, shot out its long, sticky-looking tongue, and grabbed a yellow jacket that had been targeting Harriet's cookies.

"My hero!" Harriet said, clapping her hands.

"Kiss-a-me, kiss-a-me," croaked the frog. He bulged his golden eyes right at her.

"Oh, you expect a reward, do you, for saving my cookies from the yellow jacket?"

"Jug-a-room," mooed the frog.

Harriet kissed her fingertips, then blew the kiss from her fingers to the frog.

"Now if this were a fairy tale," Harriet said, "you'd turn into my prince."

"That can't happen just yet," said the frog.

Harriet blinked. She rubbed her ears, then her eyes. "Come again?"

"To achieve the transformation, you must answer two questions, correctly, of course," said the frog.

"Come again?" was all Harriet could manage to say.

"Pick a category: Language, Art, Science, Religion, Everything Else."

Hands shaking, Harriet lifted her water bottle and took a long swig. Water spilled down her chin. She set the bottle on the grass and took a deep breath.

Not Everything Else, Harriet thought. Way too scary. Not Science. She'd fainted dissecting a frog in high school bio, and struggled through chem and physics, the only C's to infect her otherwise healthy report cards. Not Art. She could draw a straight line and an almost perfect circle, but not much else. Not Religion. She only went to church every Sunday to make her grandmother happy.

"Language," she said to the frog.

"My favorite category, too!" exclaimed the frog. 'So. Here's question one. What's the shortest sentence in English?"

"I don't know!" Harriet heard herself wail.

"Nope," said the frog. "Try again."

"Try!" Harriet exclaimed.

"Close," the frog said, "but no cigar."

Suddenly frustrated with this crazy dream she was having—because she knew it was a dream, one of those crazy lucid dreams where people are conscious of the fact that they're dreaming while they're still asleep—Harriet flung out her arms and yelled, "Go! Just go!"

"Correct!" exclaimed the frog. "*Go* is the shortest sentence!"

For a moment, Harriet and the frog just stared at each other, the only sound wind whistling through the trees. "Well?" Harriet said. "I'm waiting. When do you turn into my prince?"

"That can't happen just yet," said the frog. "There's one more question."

Harriet sighed and nodded.

"But be sure to take your time before you answer. For question two, you get only one chance to get it right."

Harriet nodded. "Shoot," she said.

"What," asked the frog, "is the *longest* sentence?'"

Harriet took her time. The sky darkened, releasing a full moon, Venus, and the stronger stars from their daylight prison.

What a crazy cool dream I'm having, Harriet thought as she watched the frog watching her, occasionally launching his tongue to catch a fat bug. *Too bad I can't take Facebook pictures of my dreams. My dream life is way more adventurous than my real life.*

Life.

She gasped, sat straight up, the correct answer hitting her smack in her heart.

"Life!" she exclaimed. "The longest sentence is life!"

†††

Just before supper, Harriet's grandmother called Harriet's cell. Her granddaughter, she worried, had been gone too long for just a walk. She heard Harriet's phone warble and found it on Harriet's bed.

"Where are you, sweetie?" she asked aloud.

The day darkened, the 9 PM TV news ended, and Harriet's grandmother was lifting the landline to call 911 when she heard commotion outside her front door.

Sighing with relief, she hurried to the front door. "Sweetie!" she exclaimed as she flung open the door. "I was getting worried!"

But no one stood there. "Harriet?" She leaned out, propping open the door with her elbow. "Harriet?" she called again into the moonlit night.

A soft sound mooed at her feet. She looked down. Two fat, beautiful bullfrogs leaped past her into the house. The smaller one paused, turned, and bulged shockingly blue eyes at her.

"Harriet?" the grandmother whispered. The frog's wide mouth seemed to stretch into a smile. Then it flicked its tongue and winked.

THE BIG BAD ELEPHANT
BY
ANDREW BUNDY

The world was bright and new outside the hospital where the Big Bad Wolf sat chained to an oxygen tank.

It was spring, and the Enchanted Forest had just shaken off winter's chilly hold. Flowers were blooming, trees were dancing in a cool spring breeze, and Wolf's claws scratched at his wheelchair as he ached to huff and puff a cigarette.

Cigarettes were what got him into this mess in the first place.

"Mr. Wolf," said a nurse who hovered on her translucent wings somewhere around his right ear. "There's a phone call for you. It's the Order of Evil Fairy Tale Animals."

"It's probably about that Little Pigs lawsuit," Wolf coughed. "I should have eaten them when I had the chance."

He waited while a nurse who *wasn't* two inches tall and flying came over to wheel him to the phone.

"Big Bad, is that you?" asked the caller.

"Who else would it be, your grandma?" Wolf said.

"That's why I'm calling," Papa Bear said. "We need you to do a job."

"I'm kind of busy right now," the wolf said. He coughed and wheezed for a moment before wiping sticky spittle from his chops.

"You're familiar with the grievance filed by the old lady who lives deep in the forest?" Papa Bear asked.

"Which old lady? You know how many old ladies live in the Enchanted Forest? I think even Snow White is a grandmother now."

"Mrs. Opal Riding Hood," Bear said. "Well, anyway, her granddaughter, Red, is flittering through the forest as we speak. If we got her, we could use her as leverage against the old lady."

"So, you want me to get Little Red Riding Hood?" Wolf asked.

"If possible," Bear said.

"Well, it's not. Apparently, the Surgeon Magician was serious about his warnings on cigarettes, and I've huffed and puffed my way into lung cancer. Try one of the other Big Bads."

"All the other Big Bads are on assignment!" Papa Bear said. "I have a family to take care of and this creepy blond chick who doesn't understand the meaning of a restraining order..." He suddenly shouted to someone: "I see you out there!"

Wolf had to move the phone away from his ear.

A few seconds later, breathing deeply to calm himself, the bear said: "Anyway, you're our only hope."

"No, there's one more," Wolf said. He hung up the phone and then picked it back up and dialed a number.

"Big Bad?" Wolf asked. "This is Big Bad. I need your help."

"For a price," answered the Big Bad Elephant. "If you're in a hurry, I'd have to catch the red-eye, and you know they make me pay for four seats."

"Oh, the Order will pay," said the wolf. A smile spread across his face before he fell into another coughing fit.

†††

Little Red Riding Hood skipped through the forest, humming to music blasting in her earbuds. She wasn't so little anymore and the only red on her was her hood and cloak. The gloves, though missing fingers, had one or two red stripes mixed with the white and gray ones. The rest of her clothes were black. Her combat boots thundered on the ground as she skipped along. Her black fingernails absorbed the sun. She had a backpack slung over one shoulder with her name, "R3D," stitched across the top.

Mr. Rabbit poked out of his hole.

"Off to see your grandma, Red?" he asked.

She pulled her earbud out and looked down at the furry woodland creature.

"I'm sorry," she said as angry music spewed out of the

displaced earbud. "I missed that, Mr. Rabbit."

"You'll make yourself deaf, kiddo," Mr. Rabbit said. "Tell your grandmother I said hi. Oh, and be careful. The Big Bad Wolf may be out of the hospital by now."

The sun vanished behind a cloud and the magical orchestra playing in a tree behind Mr. Rabbit switched into a minor key.

"He can bite me," Red said. She turned her nose up.

"I think he plans on it."

"Don't worry about me, Mr. Rabbit," Red said as she brandished her pepper spray. "I can take care of myself."

The sun came back out and the magical orchestra resumed the happy tune it had abandoned earlier.

Ahead of Red, the Enchanted Forest danced in the breeze. Birds sang and flew in well-executed arcs until Red started skipping again. She distracted a robin that flew into a cardinal, causing a mid-air collision that ended in two unconscious birds and Mr. Rabbit getting a mouthful of feathers.

Red was deep into the forest before she noticed something was wrong. In the break between songs, she noticed that there were no woodland sounds around her. As she paused her music and removed her earbuds, she found that the orchestra was only playing a solitary violin.

Red reached into the tree and pulled out the tiny violinist, causing the music to end in a screech.

"What's going on?" Red demanded.

"Stalking music," said the tiny creature as he adjusted his tuxedo.

"I'm being stalked?" Red asked.

The little musician nodded. "May I continue?"

Red put the creature back into the tree and pocketed her earbuds. Cautiously, she made her way deeper into the Enchanted Forest. The music around her continued to play softly and in a minor key. Red spun around as the music swelled.

Her stalker was in plain sight, although he attempted to hide behind a bush that only covered his face.

"I can see your butt," she said.

The elephant rose out of the small bush.

"I didn't mean to startle you," he said.

"Are you on drugs? Your eyes are red," Red asked.

The elephant blinked and rubbed his eyes for a moment. One

of the tiny musicians came out of the tree, handed him some eye drops, and then retreated back to his instrument.

The elephant blinked at Red. "I caught a late flight to get here."

"Who are you?" Red asked.

"I'm...well...I'm an exchange woodland creature," the elephant said. "A squirrel is back home while I'm here now."

"I hope he doesn't get trampled," Red said.

"He picked the exchange," the elephant said. He rubbed his trunk for a moment. "I was really cramped in that plane." He pointed at his trunk. "I had to stow this in the overhead compartment!"

Red eyed the elephant up for a moment. She noticed that the orchestra had switched to a tuba while he was talking. Tubas rarely meant that the person across from you was anything more than a buffoon.

"Well, I'd invite you to walk with me, but I'm sure you'd slow me down," Red said. "I'll see you around."

Red turned, and the music suddenly swelled again. Red whirled around, and the elephant froze in an awkward pouncing posture.

"Are you trying to pounce on me?" Red asked.

The elephant stepped back and wrung his trunk in his hands. "Uh, no."

"I think you were," Red said. "That looked like a standard pounce."

The elephant got a leaf stuck on one of his tusks. He tried to pull it off. "It wasn't a standard pounce. It was a Leopard Type-II Pounce."

The elephant covered his mouth and gasped.

"Ah-HA!" Red said. "You *were* trying to pounce! And you're trained in the art of pouncing!"

"I was in better shape in Evil Animal School," the elephant said. "And we didn't have tiny orchestras."

The elephant kicked the tree and the whole orchestra fell out with a crash.

The woods were silent.

"All right, kid," the elephant said, rising to his full height. "We can do this the easy way or the hard way..."

Red sprayed him in the face with her pepper spray.

The Big Bad Elephant

Leaving the elephant rolling in the dead leaves of the forest floor, Red resumed her walk through the Enchanted Forest.

†††

Red stopped at a convenience store run by two gnomes and bought a hot dog for dinner. While she was eating, the elephant crawled in and asked for water.

"Are you okay?" Red asked.

"Out of shape," the elephant gasped. He greedily drank the water from the bottle.

"Look, if you're going to follow me through the woods, you might want to arrange another form of transportation." Red stepped onto his chest, over his belly, and back down on the other side. She left the convenience store.

"May I make a suggestion?" asked one of the gnomes as it perched on his chest.

"Sure," the elephant said. "Anything."

"There's a fairy flight service around the corner. You could hire them to flitter you a short distance."

The elephant gasped and gasped, and then asked for the number.

†††

Grandma sat on her front porch with an iced tea. She listened to the news complaining about the King's stance on the use of live newts in witches' brews. In the distance, her old ears picked up the strangest sound. It was like a lot of high-pitched screeching. Grandma stood up and looked out over her lawn. Suddenly, a giant shape exploded from the cover of the trees. The shape sagged in the middle and seemed to be held up by a hundred screaming fairies. The object fell like a rock to her lawn, and the fairies sprawled out on the grass like they were dead.

An elephant charged for her house.

"Oh, my!" Grandma said. Before she could respond, she was bound and gagged and slammed into her closet.

"I'll get you this time, my pretty," the elephant said with a laugh.

His cell phone rang.

"Hello?" he asked as he answered.

A nasally voice spoke. In the background, the elephant heard a small dog yipping. "This is Albert from the Magical Catch Phrase Patent Office. We just got word that you used a phrase similar to one used by one of our clients. Please desist or you will have to pay a fee."

"Oh, yeah?" the elephant said. "I'll get you and your little dog, too."

"That's another one of hers. You'll be hearing from one of our lawyers. Have an enchanted evening."

The elephant put away his cell phone and started digging through grandma's dresser.

He held up a thong. "Geez. What's a little old lady need *this* for?"

Finally, the elephant found a night shirt and a little sleeping cap. He only managed to get the shirt around his leg. The cap was speared by one of his tusks. The elephant decided on closing the blinds and hopping into grandma's bed.

The bed collapsed with a titanic crash.

"This better work," the elephant muttered.

The elephant settled in to wait for Red. The television had switched to the latest scandal. Sleeping Beauty was claiming that her latest affair happened while she was sleepwalking.

It wasn't long until the elephant heard Red at the front door.

†††

Red didn't think about the passed-out fairies on her grandmother's lawn until after she had opened the door.

"Grandma?" Red asked. Her boots thumped on the floor as she walked in.

"In here, my pretty."

A cell phone started to ring, and Red heard muffled swearing.

"Are you okay, Grandma?" Red asked as she made her way through her grandma's house.

"Just fine," came the reply. "Just a little summer cold."

Red was in her grandmother's room now. Grandma was on a demolished bed, wearing her nightgown on one of her enormous tusks.

"Grandma," Red said as she stepped closer, "what big eyes

you have."

"All the better to see you with."

"Grandma," Red said as she rummaged through her basket, "what big ears you have."

"I know," Grandma said. "As you get older, your ears keep growing. You won't look so pretty at my age, either, you know."

"Grandma," Red said as she was right beside the bed, "what big tusks you have."

"All the better to gore you with, my dear!" the elephant roared. He reared back and screamed, "Don't taze me, Red!"

It was too late. Red jammed her industrial-sized Taser right into the elephant's nose.

The elephant twitched and rolled away from Red. Suddenly, Grandma came bounding out of her closet with a baseball bat. She smacked the elephant on the top of the head while Red zapped him with her Taser.

"I've already called the woodsman next door – and he's such a sweet boy, honey, you should really go out with him," Grandma said.

"Not now, Grandma," Red said as she zapped the elephant again.

"I'm just saying that you're not getting any younger," Grandma said.

"I'm just not that into flannel," Red said.

"I surrender! I surrender!" the elephant wailed. He crawled toward the door.

Red ran ahead of him and stood in the doorway. "Not so fast, pal."

"Look, I'm just doing my job," the elephant said.

"You need a new line of work," Grandma said.

"Don't zap me again! I'm melting," the elephant moaned.

His cell phone rang again.

†††

Even though the sun was out, the Big Bad Wolf didn't think it was a beautiful day.

For one thing, the magical orchestra was playing ominous music. Then there was the news report about an elephant being rushed to the hospital after a savage beating in a failed home invasion.

"As you know," the young reporter on the news said, "elephants aren't built for stealth."

In his head, the wolf began to add up the legal costs for this latest debacle. The Order of Evil Fairy Tale Animals would have to file for bankruptcy.

"Maybe the King would consider a government bailout," said another patient. "Doesn't the government usually help bloated, evil organizations?"

The wolf coughed.

"Mr. Wolf," said the nurse by his ear. "It's the phone again. It's someone from the Law Offices of Frog, Toad, and Friends."

The wolf coughed. The pigs again.

"And there's a bear on another line."

The wolf reached into his pocket and pulled out a crumpled cigarette.

ARTIE THE MILLENNIAL
BY
ALEXANDRA FAYE CARCICH

Artie always knew he was special. Everything he believed about himself was validated by his foster brother Merrydin, called Merlin. Merlin came into the Fitzdrake family when Artie's parents realized their son had changed from a tax deduction to a tax burden.

Merlin talked like the old books that had been assigned in high school, or at least the impression Artie had from their summary online. Merlin insisted he was born of a demon, he had once known the future, and that Artie was fated for greatness. The latter detail allowed Artie to forgive the other oddities - including Merlin's insistence that he had been stuck in a tree for an undisclosed amount of time, aging backwards. He was a scrawny preteen just beginning his battle with acne, but he claimed he was the wizard advisor to the King of Camelot.

Artie's unwavering faith in himself had sustained him for twenty-three years, despite his circumstances. Most recently, his career as a professional gamer had stagnated. On his top day, his live stream collected five viewers: three were friends from high school, one was a troll, the other might have been his mom. Monetization was just around the corner, he claimed, while filling in the bubbles on a Stuffmart job application. At work he was the smartest employee at any given time, according to him, and quickly moved from cashiering to the electronics department, where he reigned supreme over speakers and USB cords. He liked the idea that greatness was owed him without hard work or sacrifice.

Artie had just finished a demoralizing shift at Stuffmart. He had been called into the manager's office, where he was reminded about protecting merchandise from teenagers on spring break. At home, Artie wanted to explore distant solar systems on his game console nonstop until he had to work again. Merlin said there was something important waiting for him at the mall, something life-changing. Merlin's speech went something like, "Dost thou not know that thy destiny, the sword, waiteth for thee in the hand of the fair maid in the mists of Avalon."

"I don't have Destiny 2 yet," said Artie with a shrug and led his brother to the car.

The Avalon Shopping Center had fallen on hard times. Between parking lot muggings, and the growth of internet shopping, few bothered to visit brick and mortar stores. Stores closed. The magical carousel rarely had staff to push the start button.

Merlin pulled his black hoodie up to shadow his face. He led Artie through the food court, past the strong-smelling nail salon, past the game store, down the central thoroughfare. Artie's heart gave a little leap and a fall when they left Round Table Gaming behind. He wondered where Merlin was headed and if he could ditch the kid and peruse the latest releases.

Natural sunlight shone through the glass ceiling. The aisle was lined with broadleaf trees with braided trunks.

"Twas not long ago that this very vessel was contained within trees such as these." Merlin stretched his fingers and reached up, wiggling them at the sky.

Artie put some space between them, so they would not be immediately associated.

At the center of the mall they passed a brass stag with painted gold collar, both challenging and inviting the visitors to look on the misty veil beyond. Ivy grew wild and flowed over its pot as they passed between planters of ferns. Parting the fronds, the boy and man stood before the fountain.

Near them, a woman sat on a bench. Her hair was a sleek purple-black. She pursed glossed lips, tilted her head, and raised an eyebrow. Held aloft, her bedazzled phone caught the perfect angle of face, tile, and water. A flash. The photo uploaded to MirrorLove.

#again #instamood #beautifulgirl #narcissist #day84

#whenwillthisbeover

Artie and Merlin had a whispered war. Across the fountain from them, a pack of teenagers tried to toss each other into the water, in lieu of petty change. Artie stepped toward the girl.

"Hi, I'm Artie." He offered his hand, which the girl of the fountain ignored. After hesitating he continued, "My *friend*," (he stressed the word friend in a way that made it clear Merlin was no friend) "says you have a, ah, sword, or something for me."

The girl looked at him appraisingly. "The costume shop is closed until Halloween."

Artie was embarrassed and retreated. There were more whispers, with much urging. He emerged reluctantly and went back to the girl, "Yeah. I know. It's just, you see, my *friend*, he says it's your *destiny* to give it to me."

"Oh," said the girl, "That. Well let's get it over with." She stood and lifted her hand, open palm over the water. The fountain hiccupped, and a spatter-like mist spread to its edges.

"Stay thy hand," said Merlin. "Thou hast not prescribed an honorable quest that this supplicant must complete before bestowing your bounty, your blessing, the noble sword Excalibur upon this yet unworthy vessel."

"Thanks a lot," said Artie.

The girl scrunched her nose and looked skeptically at the preteen. "Is this an audition? Like 'Oh Romeo'?"

"No, he just talks that way. He's older than he looks. It's complicated."

The phone vibrated on the bench. The girl turned her attention to the latest text: *Yo hotty, what u up to.* She smiled as she typed a response. Her nails, extending half an inch past her finger tip, were matte teal with sparkling stones on her ring finger and thumbnail.

Artie shifted uncomfortably. He did not usually talk to attractive women, unless they wanted to buy a phone from him. The girl of the fountain was mascaraed perfection. She was clearly not interested in him, and he wished he could slip away while she was not looking and pretend he had never spoken.

Merlin had no such holdups. He clapped his hands once, and the sound echoed through the hollow building. The girl's face scrunched as her screen went black. Merlin said, "Dost thou not wish to fulfill thy duty? Fate is a terrible master and shalt cause thee to linger here for all thy days until it has been executed."

"Okay!" She thrust her hand over the water and clawed at the air.

"Is there none who prizeth honor!" cried the boy.

Artie took out his cell phone, with a screen half the size of his face; he swiped at it a few times. "Hey, Merlin, there's wifi here." He passed the phone to the younger boy, who took it gleefully, and stabbed at it with focused aggression. "He loves Raging Dragons," Artie said to the girl.

The girl tapped the screen insistently before rebooting the phone. "Why don't you do whatever it is that kid wants you to do and lemme know when you're done. Pick some good deed or whatever."

"I already donated at the Almsgiving pot," said Artie. "Can I get you something from Ethical Grail? I'm stopping for coffee."

"A Latte Frappe with a double shot," she answered. "Thanks."

Artie and Merlin wandered directionless, pausing by Round Table Gaming where a Knight's Templar display filled the window. The poster displayed an authentically-armored knight side by side with a barely-covered female archer. Artie was unsure where he should go to find a quest and was less sure why he was bothering. Merlin was no help. His entire attention was now focused on the phone's screen. Occasionally he shouted an epitaph such as, "Curses upon thee, Green Sheep, until thy fourth and fifth generation!"

Artie pointed out possible quests to Merlin, who rejected each suggestion. The security guard had little to do and did not need help. The disobedient child was quickly caught. The lost teenager found the mall map. The man was in the process of mopping up his own coffee.

Finally, they reached the end of the mall, where a department store had been converted to a go-kart track and arcade. The arcade summoned them like a beacon. Nearby a girl screamed profanity into her cellphone. Her voice competed in level with the karts. She was shapeless in a plaid lumberjack shirt. Half her head was clipped short and the other half was the pastel colors of a unicorn's tail.

Merlin's attention flickered up from the phone. "Your esteemed ancestor always aided the fairest and most virtuous of maidens."

The girl flipped the bird at someone in the arcade.

Artie observed, "Well, she's not a ten, but she's kinda cute."

Merlin jabbed Artie with his elbow in a soft place. Artie swatted at Merlin's shoulder, but the shoulder had vanished. The girl was watching him skeptically.

"Can I help you . . . with something?" said Artie.

"Yeah," said the girl, "Those jerks won't give me my prize. I won the jackpot on Red Saxon and they're holding out!" She pointed at the poster advertising a gaming system in exchange for a certain number of tickets.

"Oh, uh, you want me to talk to them?"

"No, I'm gonna post this all over Reddit and Facebook and Tumblr and Twitter, leave a Yelp review, and start a petition so no one will play here again." Proudly, she invoked the power of every social network she engaged with and combined their collective weight to crush the arcade.

"Have you asked to speak to a manager?" Being a veteran of just this tactic from customers, Artie knew the power of summoning the overlord.

She gave him a look.

Artie looked over his shoulder at Merlin. "Does this count?"

Merlin nodded his head. "Go ye forth to do battle with Manager."

Artie led the procession back into the arcade, with his sincere insecurity. The girl followed, armed with cellphone and righteous indignation. Merlin lagged, distracted by the bright colors of the gaming machines. They marched to the desk, where the only attendant stood, exchanging tickets for packets of gum or stuffed dragons. Artie waited to be noticed for a few minutes. The girl's need for vindication pressed him to interrupt. "Excuse me, hey, when you have a minute, please, um, can I speak to the manager?" He said the magic words that summoned the sorcerer to grant all wishes.

The pockmarked, bespectacled, worker turned his glower on them. "I am the manager. What's the problem?" His physiognomy did not reflect his stubborn attitude. Where chin was weak and slipped back into his neck, his determination was strong.

Artie hopelessly looked at the girl who glared at the manager who glared back. There was clearly a history of animosity. Artie stammered over his explanation of the injustice done the girl by the game that gave a jackpot but not the necessary tickets.

"That guy already won the jackpot on Red Saxon today." The manager pointed to a middle-aged man, now at a colored spinning wheel, titled Witches Brew. "The game doesn't have more than one jackpot a day."

"My score was higher than his, the game is rigged in favor of white men."

"No," said the worker, "the points for a jackpot change from game to game. I told you already."

The two devolved to name calling, as Merlin tugged at Artie's sleeve. "What we now observe be a false cause, where nary an injustice is done."

Artie and Merlin slunk back through the arcade toward the exit, passing the 'Winner's Circle,' where a teenager pointed to photos of his likeness on the wall. Austin Pellnor was the name below the photo of the dashing, dark-haired victor.

"This is the champ." The victor, present in the flesh, thumped his chest. "The only champ at this track. No one can beat me."

Collected around him was a crowd of friends, challengers, and indifferent bystanders. Merlin began bouncing up on his toes.

"I won last week," said someone in the crowd. "You raced until my picture was taken down."

"You didn't race against me," Austin challenged.

"Yo," said Merlin, "my bro challenges you to single combat." He held up Artie's hand while he waved at the braggard. To Artie he said, "Never have I seen a more worthy quest. This be the quest thy very ancestor set upon before he won Excalibur."

The crowd parted around them. Artie was examined by all onlookers. He was unathletic, to put it mildly. His mother called it baby fat, but he never grew out of it. Every year, Artie's fair hair was growing thinner. He had considered shaving his head and growing a beard to look like a viking. But the sparse beard failed to make the strong masculine statement that the rest of his demeanor lacked. There he stood in the crowd of the curious and the ambivalent; all of his personal weakness exposed, on display for assessment. They did not care about his vision of himself, but whether he could justify Merlin's boasting.

Austin observed the competition. He smiled malevolently.

Merlin's grin for Artie went beyond his appearance to who he could be. Looking at his brother, Artie wanted to be the Arthur that was reflected in Merlin's eyes.

Artie lifted a limp hand to acknowledge the crowd. Sweat trickled down his brow. "Yeah, I'll race."

They shook hands. Austin Pellnor's grip was firm. Artie was not competitive by nature, even abstaining from competitive video games. In high school, he felt that sports were a primitive mating ritual where the fittest males performed feats of strength for the most attractive females. Those females never preferred Artie. Artie embraced the contemporary view that everyone deserved to win in life. Standing before a red go-kart, Artie felt that this race violated his values, and he knew he could not win.

Pellnor rode a black go-kart with a black helmet, covered in the dates of his victories. Artie's kart was in advance in the lineup at the gate. He hoped the advantage would be enough. The engine whirred; the go-kart jerked its driver as it sputtered to life. Then he was off.

The half-mile track twisted back and forth over itself. This race would consist of four laps, but whoever posted the best individual lap time won. Artie wanted to win. He zoomed ahead into the first right turn. With no sign of Pellnor, he thought he had a good chance. After the turn was a long straightaway where Pellnor passed him on the outside, cut in front, and transitioned through a left turn. For the first lap Artie struggled to find the balance between accelerating and breaking. With every bungled turn, sliding wide, or hitting the barrier of tires, Pellnor pulled farther ahead. In the second lap, Artie made progress after grasping the basics. The third lap, Artie closed with Pellnor.

After drafting in his wake, Artie passed Pellnor off the third turn. He was jubilant anticipating his victory, until the black kart passed him on the next straightaway. Artie zoomed up next to his opponent and was forced to brake and fall behind as they went into the next turn. Soon the competition was so fierce that the karts collided in a turn, stopping abruptly.

By the fourth lap the race had devolved to a vindictive game of bumper cars. Every time he smashed into the bumper of his rival, Artie was overcome with wicked glee as Merlin cheered from the sidelines.

Artie reached the finish line ahead of his rival, but it was all for naught. Austin Pellnor's best lap had been five whole seconds faster than Artie's best. The victor uncapped a silver marker and wrote the date on his helmet. Merlin thumped Artie on the back and did not understand at first that his racer had lost based on obscure win conditions.

"Twas a heroic joust! Thy great ancestor would smile upon such as this. All the fairest damsels would bestow their ribbons and roses upon thee."

Merlin's exuberant joy made Artie more unhappy than the actual results of the contest. "But I lost. As usual."

"As did your ancestor on a number of occasions. If you were not defeated, you would have no need of the sword Excalibur."

"Merlin, this is the twenty-first century! No one uses swords. I don't need a sword for anything. It won't get me a job with a company or a house or even a girlfriend, or . . . anything."

Abruptly the boy stopped walking and sat down on the floor. He propped his head in his hands, and his elbows on his knees. Artie nudged him with his toe, but the boy did not stand.

"Much has changed since I emerged from the tree. I used to see the future as if I had lived it already. Then the vixen stole my powers and imprisoned me in the wood. I prayed to all the gods that when I was released I might reunite with my liege. To what end? I do not now remember.

"But I remember the times of old. I remember the sword. Was midst arduous questing that thy ancestor did receive the sword unto his hands. It shone bright with its own light, as't were the sun that broke across the very lake, and t'was the sun that the king holdeth in his hand. T'was that very sword that gave him his kingdom."

Artie had always been told he was special, a unique snowflake in a snowstorm. He was special to this brother who saw so much in him. Again, Artie felt the stir of Merlin seeing him differently. He could become this Arthur. Maybe it would not be easy. But to see the confident pride return to Merlin's face it might be worth it. He sat down next to the boy and patted his knee. "Then let's go get the sword."

†††

"Where's my Latte?" asked the Girl of the Fountain. She had been reclined on the bench examining her nails. As soon as she spotted the boys she stood up and smiled eagerly at them.

"I'm sorry," said Artie, just remembering the coffee he had promised. "I've failed at all of the quests too. So I guess I'll see you tomorrow to try again." He turned to go.

"Wait." She caught his arm. "Why don't you get me that guy's phone number." She nodded toward the phone case booth, where a man of middle eastern descent sat, poking at his phone, waiting for a customer.

Artie's face was glowing red from the physical contact. He looked from the sales clerk, to Merlin, and back to the girl.

Blushing slightly, she explained, "While I've been sitting here every day I've seen him a lot."

"Matchmaking is not a quest," objected Merlin.

Artie went to the man and gestured to the girl of the fountain. The man glanced over. She was busily looking at her phone's black screen. Artie returned and handed over a receipt slip, with ten digits scrawled in pencil on the back. He shoved a plastic bag with a cellphone case into his pocket.

The girl stood. She stepped down the first step into the fountain. Water kissed the toes of her boot. She raised her hand over the pool, her open palm facing down. For a moment, the lights flickered, and the hum of electricity was silenced. Then a sword appeared in her hand. She held it gingerly, pointed at the floor, so the fountain water dripped onto the tile and not her designer jeans. Artie stepped forward, with some coaxing from Merlin, and received it.

The girl stepped away from the fountain. "What are you going to do with it, anyway?"

"I don't know," Artie answered. He looked at Merlin, who shrugged.

The girl next held her phone in front of Merlin. "Fix it."

Merlin snapped his fingers. One of the lights down the hall grew extra bright, then burst, showering glass onto the floor. The cell phone lit up and beeped with a storm of delayed messages. The girl turned absently away from the boys.

Sword in hand, Artie felt a new courage. "Hey," he said to the girl, "Can I have your number?"

"Nope."

"Okay, well, see ya."

She lifted her free hand in parting.

Leaving the mall, Artie felt strangely rewarded by the unusual day and its events. The race was not so bad. Neither was talking to the girls. Maybe there were other things he was missing out on. Maybe he could become good at them if he kept trying. Merlin was there beside him, swollen with smiles. Artie realized that his foster brother was proud of him.

PRINCE PERFECT
BY
KETURAH LAMB

My name is Prince Téleois and I am on a quest to find the most perfect bride. One who is beautiful, sweet, kind, confident, motherly. I have several imaginings of what she will look like and of the sort of character she will possess. But I am trying to not hold onto these thoughts too tightly — after all, it's hard to fit people into our molds of perfection.

I possess the qualities all princes should — honor, valor, strength, determination. While I know I am not perfect, I have high expectations of perfection in both others and myself.

That is why I expect this journey of mine to be long and hard.

The perfect princess will be hard to find. This I know without a doubt. At times it is a frustrating and sad thought. But I have not lost hope in my abilities.

I will find her.

Another thing of tremendous importance: my looks. I have been very blessed beyond many expectations of perfection. I am tall. My features are strong, defined. My body and muscles are hardened by work and exercise. My hair is black, and falls in wavy, thick locks just past my wide shoulders. And my eyes.

My eyes.

I could have a room full of mirrors just for admiring my eyes, to ponder the deep green colors. Such a beauty and depth that surely must reflect the whole of my exterior and even my soul.

I am leaving my kingdom with my father's blessing. But not before having gone through years of practice and training.

I am ready for my quest. I have trained my mind in thought and motive so that I understand myself and what I want. I have trained; my hand knows my sword as it does each finger. I know all I need to know, and my heart is excited, ready, anxious.

I have gathered up rumors from the kingdom — so many girls are in bondage. Most men are afraid to rescue them, but I, Prince Téleois, am not. I will rescue everyone, and in the end find one that is worthy of standing by my side.

Surely, there will be more than one. But who knows? As of yet I have not met one that is capable of living according to my standards.

I saddle my horse, and speak gently to my mount, "Elfrid, let us go!"

We trot out of the stables, down the narrow stone path. I'd like to imagine that dust flies behind me as we ride on, but the road is too clean — for once the servants have done an amazing job.

I see a woman outside of the gates. Skimpy, satin rags drape over her curvy figure, her hair is piled high. Her face is painted with bright colors. I want to ride by quickly and hide my disgust. She is a whore! She is not old, but neither is she young. Her whole appearance speaks of outward beauty. Perfect beauty — quite opposite than her soul, I am sure.

"Where are you going, my lord?" She steps into my path, not allowing me to pass her.

"To seek the hand of a maiden." I see no reason to hide the truth. Maybe even this truth will make her turn from the errors of her way — make her yearn to be a woman of virtue.

Her whole bearing is confident. She does not hide, cower, or act unsure even though I know she lives a dirty, immoral life. I cannot hate her, though, as I witness her honesty.

Fate has not been good to her. But she is above it somehow. Or acts so. She is not an ashamed woman. And for this I can't despise her.

"Ah," she says, as if knowing. "You go to rescue a princess. That should be no hardship on your part."

"I fear you are both correct and mistaken."

"Pardon?" She looks at me curiously. I can tell she is not accustomed with such intelligent conversation being reciprocated. Many do not require such from her.

"I don't only go to save a princess, but to find one worthy of saving."

Prince Perfect

At that she lets out a laugh. But not of the kind I would have imagined. It is not at all like the sound of a cackle of a witch, but beautiful even while it mocks me. "Prince, I am afraid you will find yourself sadly disappointed. There are none worthy. Never."

"What do you mean?" I am truly puzzled by her whole outburst and words.

"You will find something wrong with every princess, mark my words. But if you choose to know someone of themselves, aside from their faults, if you choose to work and put effort into her as you have yourself, only then may you find a satisfactory bride. I have no hope for you. Your arrogance is drowning me, it's so thick — you will never be able to love anyone past your high opinion of yourself."

I look at the woman condescendingly. How would she know? Just a whore, and of no consequence.

She sees my look and understands it. "You think I do not understand? Mark my words, in the end you will have none and settle for those like me. Or you will have opened eyes. I pray the latter but doubt my prayer will be heard as I am but a whore." She winks provocatively.

I can't help but squirm, but not from her flirtations. I nod my head, "Good day." I press my thighs into my horse's side.

I will not heed her words but find the princess I am looking for. Never will my tastes be lowered for such filth. Perfection is my goal, my destiny.

†††

I have to travel for three days to find Rapunzel's tower. I eat little and pray much. The woods are peaceful, and it gives me a sense of feeling close to my Maker. How wonderful the day is already — but the sight of the tower makes it all the more so.

The tower is tall. I hear an enchanting musical sound coming from up above. A girl's voice. This has to be the place.

Wind rushes around me from the tower as a cascade of hair is let down from the topmost window. Oh, but it is beautiful hair. Golden, shiny, thick, fascinating. It reaches to the ground — as long as the tower is tall. I wonder how all that hair can possibly fit up inside.

A small, old, and ugly woman climbs down the hair. Despite

the previous adjectives she is quite nimble, and it doesn't take her long to land. As soon as the old woman is on the ground the girl pulls her hair back up through the window. "Be good, my child. I will return in three days!"

I wait until she leaves, then walk up to the edge of the tower. "My fair maiden, I see you are trapped. I have come to rescue you."

The girl looks down. I can tell right away that she is taken with my looks. "Who are you?"

"I am Prince Téleois, and I am here to rescue you."

"Rescue me?" She sounds unsure.

"Yes, I mean to save you from that witch, and bring you into a life of freedom and happiness."

"Oh." She still does not appear to know whether to trust me or not. But I can tell she is deeply fascinated. I am not surprised. I have been told that my features are indeed quite unique and spellbinding.

I must say I am immediately worried at her hesitation. It does not seem natural or right that she should be content in her current situation. She should be more anxious to escape bondage and live as she is meant.

But I push this thought away, for I still have hope she may be the *one*.

Finally, her sweet voice replies, "I am told to let my hair down for no one unless they say certain words."

I am irked at this. Can't she see I am here to save her? Why would she be demanding such formality when I am offering her freedom from *this*? But I smile and ask, "Pray tell, what are these words?"

"Rapunzel, Rapunzel, let down your hair!" She sings the words.

"Is Rapunzel your name?"

"Yes," she answers.

"Well, then, my dear girl: Rapunzel, Rapunzel, let down your hair!"

Immediately all of her golden beauty falls from the sky.

I start climbing up at once, hoping my weight is no more than the old lady's and that I am not putting the girl in pain. She makes no sounds, and so I assume we both are good.

Once I am in I am able to look at the girl. She is stunning.

And seems scared of me.

Her hair still hangs out the window, but she does not care.

"Now, let's see... how shall we escape?" It suddenly occurs to me that two of us cannot go down her own hair.

"There are many sheets in the cupboard," she answers swiftly.

So, she knows strategy. Not just beautiful, but she has brains, too. I am pleased — until a thought comes to me.

"Why have you not escaped already? There is obviously a means for you to do so."

She is stunned at my question.

"Why would I have escaped? I would have had no one to go to, no place to go."

"But is not this witch keeping you captive?"

"Yes," she nods slowly. "But I cannot free myself. I have been waiting for my prince to come and take me away."

I am not pleased at all anymore. This girl is too content to be here. She has no motivation to leave on her own. That cannot be good.

I am not sure what to do next.

"Shall I get the sheets? I am quite good at tying knots, too."

"That would be... uh... fine. But I should warn you that once I have freed you, we shall be parting ways."

She stops walking toward the cupboard. "Why?"

"Because I do not feel I can rescue you when you are in such a predicament by choice."

She laughs as if confused. "I am not here by choice but have been remaining here until I was freed. You have come to free me, yes?"

"I came to help out a damsel in distress. You are not in distress as you could have escaped easily."

"And to where or to whom?" Tears are in the poor girl's eyes. She cannot understand even the simplest truths in my words. I feel a little mean for causing her tears — but what else am I to do?

"I am sorry. I'll let you exit on your own... if you don't mind I'll just climb down your hair."

She nods. I almost expect her to say more as I can see she still does not understand. I see a small bit of anger in her eyes — she wants to throw some sort of insult at me. This in itself verifies in my mind that she does not have a character of quality. Her undue frustration is selfish and wrong.

There is nothing more to say, and so I leave.

I must say, I am slightly disappointed. I was hoping to find *her* on the first try. But this is not to be so.

Maybe the next one will be my bride.

I can but hope. And shove the whore's words to the back of my mind. Far, far to the back.

†††

I pull my sword out of the dragon's throat, wiping the blade on the ground. Blood spurts from the fatal wound. He is not dead yet, but I do not need to worry about him anymore.

He is almost gone.

He was very easy to kill. From the stories I've heard, one would have thought it would have been a matter of life and death to kill this dragon. But he was embarrassingly small.

I walked right up to him and slid my sword between his scales into his lungs. That was it.

No fire.

No smoke.

No teeth or claws or body weight.

Just my sword inserted into his throat.

As the beast groans, I walk past it toward the castle. I half expect the girl of this castle to be waiting for me at the gates. But she is not.

Nor on the main floor. Or the second. Or the third.

Ah, well, she must be in the top tower — where it seems many damsels in distress like to abide. I wonder why she doesn't just come meet me. Or has she even seen I've killed the dragon that had been keeping her captive?

Never mind. Soon she will know. And be grateful.

I reach the tower door and open it slowly.

All at once, something — or someone — comes rushing toward me and falls at my feet. A young girl.

"You have saved me, my lord! I thank you so much and am yours forever."

I snicker at the display. I would very much like to see what she looks like. All I can see at this point is a pile of fancy material and ratty brown hair.

"I glance about the room and the first thing I see is a sword.
"You have a sword, miss?"

She looks up revealing big, bright eyes. They are not ugly. "Yes, it was my brother's. He gave it to me in case I would need it."

I step away from the girl to feel the sword. "It is a very fine sword. Why did you not kill the dragon yourself?"

The girl laughs, as if I'd told a joke.

"No, I'm serious. Why not just kill the thing if you had a way to do so?"

She looks at me, shocked, eyes wide. "I could never kill anything — I'd rather die first. And besides, the sword is too heavy for me."

I pick it up. It is a very light blade. Perfect for females. "How could you not kill the dragon? You'd rather waste your life away than kill a monster and be free?"

"I always knew someone would come to rescue me," she replies.

"And how did you always know this? And why would you expect someone *else* to kill the beast for you? Does that not seem a bit selfish, to want another to do something that is very much your duty, when you are fully capable?"

I realize my words must be a bit harsh, for now she is crying. And not soft tears, either.

"I'm sorry, Princess. I do not mean to hurt you. But can't you see the wrong of your thinking?"

She shrugs, refusing to answer.

I walk back to her and lay the sword at her side.

"Here. The dragon is dead. So, you will be safe to leave. But keep the sword with you in case of robbers or such. I'm sure you'll find once you try to pick it up it's quite light."

I start for the door.

"You aren't taking me with you?" She panics.

"No, why would I?" I reply, puzzled myself.

"Why else would you have killed the beast?"

"I do not see how that relates," I reply. "I did you a favor, and now I wish you a good life."

Before I have to witness more of her tears, I leave. Her crying and begging follow me as I leave the castle. I try to not let her tears get to me. But I do pity the girl. *Slightly*.

†††

I hope the third princess will be the one.

I am not really that upset about the first two. I know there are plenty of girls to rescue. And I am also sure that I have helped both of those previous girls open their eyes and see life differently. I have done good thus far, and selflessly so. Maybe I will yet be rewarded with the perfect bride.

This next girl really needs an awakening — she has been sleeping a hundred years, or so legend has it.

The *Sleeping Beauty*.

It has not been hard to reach this girl — a very smooth walk. I find her in a tower, of course.

I must say she is not really a beauty *anymore*. That part of her legendary name must only have been kept for poetic reasons. Her hair is dusty and holds no shine to it, which I guess makes sense considering she hasn't been able to wash it in a century.

I shudder as I look at her body. I can imagine that once upon a time she *was* a beauty. But now? Time has not been kind to her.

And though sleep has preserved her youth, it has not kept her form toned. She is not obese, true. But over this past century her skin has shrunk and is sagging about her body, making her look fat and very bloated.

I know what I have to do to wake her.

Her face is covered in a heavy layer of dirt. I take out my handkerchief and wipe her face clean. She really does not have special or amazing features. Out of all the princesses, she is by far the ugliest.

But no matter.

I will do what I came to do.

And her lips do not look terribly unappealing. Lips, after all, are lips... at first, I enjoy kissing her. Until I taste something... old food in her teeth? I nearly vomit right into her mouth.

I pull back, gagging.

Thankfully she wakes up right away, and I am able to contain my disgust.

"Hello!" She is too bright and happy for such an appearance.

Prince Perfect

She looks at me, then at herself. "Oh, my. What has happened to me?"

Tears come to her eyes.

"I look like an old woman," she whispers. "My skin... it's falling off?"

Her *breath*. It's still in my mouth.

I want to ask her if they brushed their teeth back in her day before lying down to sleep. But I keep my manners in place, and smile.

How am I to tell this girl I am not going to sweep her off her feet and carry her out of here? Especially after just having kissed her. Not that it was a great kiss...

"Where are you from? What is your name?" She is curious. The poor girl. I hope her curiosity for a new life will keep her from crying for too long. I am not too enthused about making a third girl cry.

"I'm from a kingdom just north of here. I am Prince Téleois."

"Oh, what a perfect name! I am -"

I cut her off, wanting to keep her hopes from mounting anymore. "I must say, Princess, that I need to go."

"Go?"

"Yes..." I know not what to say. Or more like, how to say what I must say.

"Are you saying you aren't taking me with you?" This girl at least catches on quickly. "But did you not wake me from my curse?"

"Yes."

"Why? Did you only come here for a kiss then? I must say that is very low down and cowardly."

I feel bad — she is not seeing this in the right perspective. "Oh, no! I came to save you... but I realize I do not think I could make you my queen."

She looks about the room, then down at herself once more.

"This dirt will wash off," she says at length, half-guessing my disgust. "And now that I am awake I will soon have my form returned with movement."

I am sure that all she says is true. But how am I to know what her health habits will really be like after this... for a hundred years!? How am I to know that a century of sleep has not made her lazy, even though at one time she may have not been so? No,

I can't... I am still queasy at the thought of kissing her. I can still feel and taste it all too much.

"I just don't think it's wise for us to be together. You have been out of life for a hundred years. You need time to learn about it more fully. I cannot marry anyone unless I am attracted to them. I can see that you once were beautiful and have the potential to be once more. But at this time... you cannot be my bride."

"But who better to help me learn to live in this new century and find life again but the one that woke me?" she asks pointedly.

"You don't need help..."

She laughs. "I'm not going to argue with you, Prince Téleois. It's obvious you have some high and selfish standards. And I'm not sure I want to win this argument."

Now I am shocked. And impressed. Fine words for sure. I grin. "I do have a question, Princess. But I do not wish to offend."

"Offend?" She laughs mockingly. "We are past that. Proceed."

"How did you manage to stay so... so... well, plump after 100 years?"

"I have been asleep for a hundred years? It didn't feel that long!" She laughs. "But to answer your question, I do not know. I was fit before I was cursed. But there had been a huge ball that day with a scrumptious feast. I suppose I was so inactive, that even a hundred years of not eating was not enough to counter the food from that day. But it won't take me long to lose it now that I'm awake."

"One other question of curiosity, but did you dream?" I have always wondered what sort of dreams one would have for such a long sleep.

"Oh, yes. Seemed to be about every sort of food... "

Ah. Now that has me doubly worried — and grateful that I turned her down. Dreaming about food when she already needs to take some time to refrain from it?

She laughs. "You do know I am playing with you? Why would I tell *you* of my dreams?"

I raise my head. There is no point in us talking further. "I really should be going,"

No tears shine in her eyes. Just something else... anger? This girl does not understand me either, but she has a completely different way of showing so. As if I am an idiot and unworthy of her tears. This I find both fascinating and frustrating — frustrating because she is unable to see I am correct.

I am curious to know more about her, and to hear what she may say — her word choices are intriguing. But I am short of time and need to find my bride.

Her uniqueness is lost to me as I begin my search once again.

†††

And so, I travel all over, rescuing and searching.

I find Cinderella. She is very sweet, loyal, and humble. But the girl has so many things wrong with her.

For instance, she does not have to live with her step-family, but still does. And she chooses to sleep among the ashes and animals. In that she is worse than the Sleeping Beauty.

Cinderella actually does not mind being dirty.

She tries to excuse her actions by claiming, "It is cold, and I cannot stand being cold. It is impossible to close my eyes in my attic room — it is so cold up there! So, I sleep by the ashes. I do what I have to, so I may sleep and be warm."

But I am neither pleased nor convinced. How can one so accustomed and accepting of dirt ever be a true princess?

I meet so many princesses. So many girls cursed, waiting for a prince to rescue them. So many supposed damsels in distress. But they are all the same.

All are too content. Most of them can do better or escape. Most choose not to, *waiting*.

I feel so bad as each girl cries. I am surprised by the occasional woman that acts haughty — as if *I am the one failing a test*. Many call me horrible names. I wish I could make them understand, and maybe even show them how to move on and enjoy perfect lives.

I know most of them won't. Most of them will continue on as they are, living lives waiting on a man to do what they are capable of doing.

As I travel, I occasionally hear stories about the girls I have rescued and what became of them. Rapunzel never seemed to stop crying.

In fact, I heard she led a traumatized couple of years, then was committed to a mental asylum.

The second princess went in another direction, completely. She at last learned to use her brother's sword. She is now a soldier and seems to be fighting to outrank every man.

Sleeping Beauty seems to be living a normal life. It didn't take her long to adjust after all. It would appear little affects her. She has started a home for girls. She is known for her practicality. And kindness. I must say I am very impressed with her.

Once I did go back to visit her. But she would hardly talk to me, as if I were the plague.

Cinderella is living a quiet life. Some say she is content. But I've mostly heard she is often sad.

Each of the princesses have led some odd, unique sort of life after I encountered them.

The little mermaid, even. For a while, it was said she hated all humans. Now it is only men. I do not understand why she limits herself so.

I am almost at my wit's end.

There are still more princesses. So many. But how many must I save to find my own beloved?

I remember the whore's words.

I am still determined to not return until I find my bride. I am frustrated as I witness so much imperfection. And even as I see each girl make drastic life changes I am convinced in my mind that I was right in what I decided concerning each girl. I do not feel responsible for their irrational behavior. If they had accepted my counsel, I would have helped each of them find perfection.

I keep looking.

I know there will be a girl out there, somewhere. I just know it.

And so, I am continuing on. I will keep searching until I have freed every woman in bondage.

I am Prince Téleois. I will have nothing less than that which is good and perfect in my eyes.

THE TURTLE AND THE RABBIT
BY
CAMERON METREJEAN

It was well known that the rabbit was the fastest animal in the forest while the turtle was the slowest. Tired of seeing the rabbit always come first, one day the turtle challenged him to a race. The rabbit, rather amused by the notion, accepted the challenge, but all the forest dwellers were bewildered.

"Are you crazy?" they said to the turtle. "You know he's the fastest around."

The turtle replied, "But HE knows it too, and that overconfidence will get to him eventually," for he knew how the story was said to go.

When the day of the race came, the fox agreed to be the judge of the race and laid out what the course was to be. It was a 2-mile path through the forest with all the rest of the forest animals waiting at the other end. The turtle and the rabbit stood at the starting line until the fox gave his signal to go. No sooner had the race begun when the rabbit dashed ahead leaving the turtle in his dust. But the turtle, undeterred, started his slow and steady plod to the end, confident that the rabbit would eventually take a break from his sprint.

Sure enough, a couple of hours into the race, the turtle passed the rabbit who was lying down in the shade of a tree taking what looked to be a very relaxing nap. Certain in his slow stride, the turtle kept up his steady pace, never stopping as he had seen the rabbit do. After hours of plodding along, the turtle saw the finish line just up ahead with all the animals waiting.

Cameron Metrejean

"Slow and steady," the turtle smiled to himself a bit smugly.

But just as the turtle was nearing the finish line, seemingly out of nowhere, the rabbit darted up from behind him and crossed the finish line first. The animals cheered, and the rabbit took his praise—and his prize.

The poor turtle stood aghast. "But how? I saw you sleeping down the road a while ago."

"I was, but I had deduced that I could spare the time," said the rabbit, pulling out his notepad showing his math. "You see, my top speed as a rabbit is around 30 miles per hour, whereas the average speed for a turtle such as yourself is .25 mph effectively meaning it would take me 4 minutes to run the path that would take you 8 hours to complete. Figuring this out last night, I scheduled a nice nap, dropped by to visit the wife and kids, and stopped by the pond where I like to just sit and think. And by setting aside a couple minutes of leeway, all this gave me just enough time to run back here to finish the race. I certainly wasn't going to waste those 8 hours waiting for you, but it would have been unsportsmanlike not to see you to the finish."

The turtle was lost in thought at that but eventually concluded that if you focus too much on another's overconfidence, you may very well not notice your own. Moreover, in a time of fanciful ideas and wishful thinking, it's best just to stick to the facts.

THE INN
BY
RONEL JANSE VAN VUUREN

Kelly stepped from the shadows, allowing humans and fae to see her. Her glamour made her look like a twenty-year-old mortal. Even her clothes screamed youth and foolishness. *Anything to look non-threatening. Everything she wasn't.*

She remembered the town from her younger days, back when horses were still the main source of transportation. A motorcycle screeched past. A few wolf whistles came from across the street. She paid them no heed.

'You really don't want to be in this town,' a young man dressed all in black with piercings over his face said from the shadow of a building.

'I don't scare easily.' She kept the boy's abyss-black gaze.

She'd done everything she could to find the cause of the disappearances. Everything she knew had failed her. There was one other alternative... Kelly breathed deeply. No. She had found the boy.

'Good luck,' the youth said and turned away.

'I need a guide...' she said before he left.

'Why?' he asked. She could smell that he was now suspicious of her.

'I'm looking for someone. Though I'm not sure how to find him...'

'We all live life in darkness, waiting for the sun of love that hardly ever shines.'

'He isn't even a reflection of the sun.'

'Then why do you seek him?'

Terror washed over her. She stepped into the shadow of the

building as two of the Wild Hunt raced past on their steeds. The boy stared after the invisible fae.

She watched the young half-deathfae, assessing his strength. The creature she was hunting reminded her of one she'd only encountered twice in the last millennium but involving other fae had never been his style. No. This was someone even worse than *him*.

'The one I seek kills mortals with impunity and curses fae with his misdeeds.'

The boy narrowed his eyes. Different emotions ran over his face. Kelly waited. She knew no deathfae, even a halfling, could allow anyone to encroach on their territory.

'I'll help you. But what will you do when you find him?'

'Neutralise the threat.'

'Life is always the cause of death.'

She nearly smiled. She liked the youth's infectious melodrama.

'Come with me, if you dare.'

Kelly followed the boy through the crowded streets where fae barely concealed their true natures; flickers of wings and light shining off scaly flesh made Kelly frown at their recklessness. She followed him through grimy alleys that snaked through the town into the true heart of Bremen: The Inn standing on the border between town and forest, humans and fae, one realm and another.

She tried not to cringe at the inevitability of her quarry hiding in the one place she'd rather not go.

'I believe he is here. Though *why* he would choose such a cliched hide-out...' The youth shrugged.

Kelly hid her grin. The building's glamour made it look like just another derelict building – at least to mortal eyes.

'Look again,' she told her companion.

When he gasped, she knew he could see the Inn for what it truly was: a stone castle from medieval Europe with towers to lock up princesses and all.

'You should use your gifts more often. Only the needy, the strong and deathfae can find this place.'

'How do you know?' he asked, glaring at her.

'Your heartbeat, the delicate features you try to hide beneath make-up and piercings, your smell...' She shrugged. 'Many

The Inn

things tell me your parentage,' she said before approaching the portcullis. She had avoided the Inn during her search for several reasons; none of them pleasant to examine.

A horned goblin barred her way, and another came hopping into the path, dragging a mace behind him.

'What's yer business?' the first goblin asked.

'Do not ask what you do not wish to hear,' she answered, using her most haughty voice learned from her high-fae mother.

'We meant no disrespect, your worshipness,' the other goblin said, bowing low enough that its long nose touched the ground.

They quickly scampered away, raised the portcullis and bowed as she passed them.

'What was that about?' her companion whispered as they crossed the paved bailey to the main door.

'They fear and hate the high fae in equal measure.'

'I don't get it.'

'You don't have to.'

Kelly decided it would be easier to *not* answer his questions. And safer. Especially for her secrets. Something about the smell of funeral lilies coming from the youth made her want to bare her soul. She clenched her jaw and watched the gargoyles skittering over the roof and along windows from the corner of her eye.

The entrance hall didn't permit them to enter the rest of the castle. So they went through the only door open to them. The great hall was filled with tables, low-hanging chandeliers and fae of every sort. It was a mix between a roadside tavern and a high society restaurant. There was no need to hide their true form here: the fae showed their horns, tusks, lion manes, pointy ears and *otherness* without fear.

Kelly tried very hard not to smell all the emotions in the room. Sometimes her heightened senses from her *other* parent were a problem. Not as much as the haughty indifference she'd inherited from her mother, though. She clenched her fists, digging her nails into her palms to focus...

A phouka sauntered up to them. She wore the outfit of a tavern wench from days gone by, not hiding her furry ears, tail or doe-like eyes contrasting with her humanlike form.

'You're new here. How can we help?'

Kelly grinned. Phoukas were fearless. Well, most of them

were. She looked away from the furry-eared faery cowering in the shadows.

'A light lunch.'

'Follow me.'

The phouka led them to an open table in the centre of the room. From there they could observe everyone without being obvious about it.

'Would you like some wine while you wait? We have, ah, several delicious varieties.'

'The house special, please,' Kelly ordered.

A slight widening of the eyes was the phouka's only slip in composure before she turned and left.

Kelly could still smell the faery's shock, fear and surprise. She had hoped that the house special would reveal something. But she hadn't thought it would show how deep the claws of the rogues dug.

When the wine arrived, she could smell the youth, vitality and sweetness of young mortals trapped within. Her stomach turned. There might not be as great a curse upon it as would have been if unicorns had been used in their place, but Kelly knew that a price would still be paid for drinking it.

'Don't,' she warned her companion when he reached for his goblet.

Quickly scanning the room with all her senses, she swapped their full goblets for identical empty ones. The laughing fae, slapping their hands with extra digits on their table, sharing some drunken joke, wouldn't notice the exchange.

'Why?' the boy whispered.

'Later.'

She didn't particularly feel like explaining the addictive nature of *that* wine to the youth. Or the pining away, until death, if denied for too long.

Something was very wrong at the Inn if curses were handed out to unwitting fae. And if the servers were too scared to warn anyone...

Their food arrived, and their empty goblets were removed by the silent phouka. Kelly looked at the innocuous offering of stew and bread. Sighing, she pushed her plate to her companion.

'Eat everything. I'll be back.'

He opened his mouth to argue and she glared at him. The

halfling shrugged and pulled her plate closer.

Kelly slipped from the table and made her way to the shadowed arch the servers disappeared into before emerging with food and drink.

The shadows caressed her and whispered things that she ignored. She was in no mood for their flattery. They quieted and hid her from the others as was their job. She made her way to the cellar: casks of wine and other types of aging alcohol lined the walls. She could smell berries, cloves, clover, oak and... She shivered. Three open casks stood on a dais. They've been recently opened and stirred.

Bile rose in her throat before she clamped down her emotions. Kelly was glad that she hadn't eaten. The smell of wasted youth, lost dreams and death was just too much. This was part of what had brought her to Bremen.

Soft sounds on the stone stairs make her hide between empty barrels in a corner. The shadows were still cloaking her, but one never knew when someone would accidentally bump into you. She could still see the dais from her position.

Eight goblins, uniform in look but each carrying a different weapon, followed a cloaked man into the room. Though she couldn't see his face, she could place his scent: The Dark Lands. He didn't belong in the mortal realm, not like the goblins and their greed. There was something familiar about his scent...

He stirred the contents of the open casks, breathed in the sweet smell of fermented youth and mortality, and then gestured something to his servants.

The goblins quickly grabbed nine empty barrels, making Kelly glad for her shadows keeping her hidden, a large sieve and several vats of wine. The contents of the already-open containers were divided among the empty barrels, the sieve catching the few pieces that hadn't liquefied. They topped the barrels off with wine – almost the same purple-red of the original casks – mixed the contents and sealed it. The goblins popped the remains the sieve had caught into their mouths like delicious morsels. Kelly gagged.

'Is that the last one?' the hooded man asked, looking at something outside of Kelly's range of vision. She felt cold.

'Yes, milord.'

'Then I'll have to go hunting. Make the necessary

arrangements.'

When they all left, Kelly still felt chilled. She leaned against the wall, empty barrels rising up both sides of her, and ran through the odds that it could be *him*. Exhaling softly, she stood up straight.

She knew *exactly* who she was up against. That voice... She shivered.

Fear? Anticipation? She wasn't sure which. She'd known that she was hunting something old and evil. She hadn't known it was *him*. The two times she'd encountered him, he was out to destroy the tentative peace between humans and fae. Off for a high fae to do, but she didn't have time to ask questions on either occasion: he'd stopped his games with the humans and moved on. Both times. But now... This time he was dooming fae with his game.

Quickly, she returned to her table and quietly observed the goblins sneaking around. They didn't speak to anyone except... The shift in the feelings of those around her derailed her train of thought. Laughter turned to sobs; fae hid beneath tables; those who could, fled the hall. She felt their presence acutely — part of her wanted to howl joyously... Her nails dug into her palms.

The Wild Hunt had arrived.

She took steadying breaths. Everyone in the great hall had started crying — either in fear or pain — as a result of the Wild Hunt's presence. It was a wonder fights hadn't broken out too. But if they entered the hall...

'Stay here,' she whispered to her companion.

Kelly pulled the shadows close and disappeared from sight. She knew she couldn't risk running into the Hunt. Too many questions would be asked. And... She shivered as a thrill of excitement ran through her.

With everyone distracted, she went down to the cellar again. She found herself in the buttery first, though. Gleaming containers filled with sauces, spices and sugar filled the shelves lining the stone walls. Bags of flour, apples and produce only found in Faerie covered the floor. And things too awful to mention filled the spaces between.

Kelly retreated from the room and found herself in the cellar. She opened the lone vat. Viscous red fluid filled it to the brim.

Using a ladle, she mixed through the purple-red goo and gelatinous bones. Unlike the vats from earlier, these remains were still liquefying.

Though her nose burned, she could still smell the approach of the young half-deathfae.

'Everything ends in death and decay.'

'What are you doing here?' Kelly hissed.

'I came to tell you that the Inn is emptying.'

'What?'

'The gargoyles announced that everyone should either go home or to their rooms – no snooping about.'

Kelly closed the barrel.

'Go to your room and stay there.'

'Why?'

'Because the Hunt will smell you no matter how you try to hide. I'd rather not have them know you're here.'

The boy glared at her, but wisely followed orders.

She allowed the shadows to surround her and guide her from the cellar to where the Wild Hunt was gathered. Lights flickered in and out of existence throughout the Inn; the hairs on her arms stood on end.

The Wild Hunt's steeds were all in the form of motorcycles. And the Hunt... they were dressed like the scariest of biker gangs.

In the moonlit bailey, Kelly kept to the shadows of the buildings. She watched as magical cooler boxes were filled with containers of milk and blood. She could smell that most of it was human.

What are you up to? she wondered as she watched the Hunt attach the cooler boxes to their motorcycles.

'We'll be back by morning,' the Gabriel said, his words more a threat than he probably knew.

The goblins and gargoyles scattered as the Hunt left with more growls and roars than actual motorcycles could make. Kelly's heart raced, her breath came too fast. She wanted to ride with the Hunt. She dug her nails into her palms and the pain brought back clarity and logic. She was there to hunt, not join a pack of wild things.

She breathed slowly. The one she'd hunted through centuries, encountered in Ireland at the height of his power and again in

Victorian England toying with humans, was the one responsible for the shift in power and magic in Bremen.

Gargoyles and goblins chattered excitedly. Kelly glared at them. It was one thing to hunt humans for sport, but he'd crossed a line when he started to harm unwitting fae and lead a weird cult.

She didn't have to wait too long for her quarry to step out of the Inn. He wore a guitar gig bag like a backpack. His clothes screamed rock band. With a wicked grin on his face and the acoustic guitar cradled in his arms, he looked deadly charming.

Kelly finally knew how he was seducing and capturing mortals. Yet, without hard evidence, she couldn't arrest the entire crew. Even the fae have their silly rules of law.

The magic imbued in her tablet made of shadows angled each camera in town to record his misdeeds.

She followed him from a safe distance, the shadows of her trade keeping her invisible from mortal and fae sight. Her Hunt heritage kept her immune to the fae music that lured young women from their homes.

Kelly stood frozen against a wall as the realisation swept over her: she was using magic she'd always despised and denied.

She didn't blink as her quarry opened his mouth impossibly wide to swallow the occasional young man whole.

Stories live in human folklore about him. Sometimes they got it right – the swallowing a victim whole, for example – but they never got his name or appearance right. They even believe him to be several different beings.

Perhaps seeing young women turned into light and sucked into his gig bag was to blame for the confusion.

But she knew the truth.

Long before she was even born he had terrorised mortals and fae. Humans wrote about him in the Dark Ages:

"It rained a shower of blood... Butter turned to lumps of gore and blood... The wolf was heard speaking with human voice, which was horrible to all."

Mactíre.

The Wolf.

He couldn't be allowed to do as he wished. Not again. And especially not the way he was going about his game this time.

It felt like her head would explode from inaction as mortal

The Inn

after mortal fell for his charms. *Talk about a wolf in sheep's clothing.* She grimaced at the awful wordplay.

Kelly left the town, knowing that the cameras would keep recording and her tablet would keep saving the data.

†††

In the dark early hours of morning, Mactíre entered the Inn with his guitar gig bag only slightly bulged. Kelly followed him down past the buttery, down past the cellar, down to the dark, dank dungeons.

A creature stepped out of the darkness to meet him in the strip of light filtering in from the grates above.

Kelly had known what to expect when she'd seen the gargoyles. Yet she'd never encountered a solo redcap before.

With her heightened vision she could see that he was at least a hand-length taller than the rest of his race. But what truly made him stand out – and what she was sure had him kicked out of any band of redcaps he tried to join – was his obvious troll features.

The Inn welcomed more halflings through its doors than any other place in the mortal realm. The thought sent shivers through her. Breathing slowly, she focused on what was before her.

She knew this creature kept out of the sun for fear of turning to stone. One could never be too careful with ones' heritage.

'They'll do nicely,' the redcap said, looking into the bag.

'Prepare them for tomorrow night.'

'What about the Hunt?'

'I'm sure the goblins can keep them busy in the forest.'

†††

She waited outside the stables. Night was slowly giving way to dawn. Part of her wanted to howl, telling her that the Wild Hunt was approaching. She was giving in to her heritage more and more as time passed on this mission. She wasn't sure what to make of it.

As they raced up to her, she could clearly see them through their respective glamours. She knew that if other fae could truly see them, they would grovel in fear.

The Hunt passed her, some looking at her with curiosity.

'Why do you wait for us?' asked a large man with writhing tattoos that crept up to his clean-shaven head. His biceps were big enough to make gym-loving mortals feel puny.

'I need to speak with you, Gabriel.'

She saw him narrow his eyes at her use of his anglicised name; his pack edged closer, obviously not liking her intrusion one bit. Being from the Council, she knew everything about everyone. It was her job. Keeping up appearances had become a chore.

He sniffed in her direction and she dropped the part of her glamour that could even fool the Wild Hunt. His eyes widened.

'Come inside. There are too many eyes out here.'

She followed him as he led his steed to a stall. In the comfort of their stable, the steeds changed form. Chimeras, cars, horses, dragons – whatever they fancied. Kelly grinned as the Gabriel's steed turned into a giant rabbit.

'You haven't come to join the Hunt.'

It wasn't a question, yet she felt like he expected an explanation. Her Hunt side instinctively wanted to obey the Gabriel, the leader.

'I came for answers.'

He watched her over the back of his giant rabbit steed. His narrowed eyes and the way he swallowed had her bite the inside of her cheek not to laugh.

'I don't think I know –'

'I know who my father is, Gabriel. Relax. I'm far too old to have left that question unanswered. No. I'm here about the Inn.'

He visibly relaxed. It made her wonder how many halflings the Wild Hunt had sired over the millennia. Especially females who came searching for answers from a Pack that's renowned for having the most vicious – and thus low in number – females.

'Have you been in the cellar, Gabriel?' Kelly asked.

'No. But I suspect it holds as many horrors as the buttery.' He filled a bowl with carrots and another with water.

Kelly swallowed. She'd seen the pixies drowned in honey, the chargrilled imps and other things she'd rather forget.

'Why do you allow it?'

He shrugged. 'This is Bremen. The town, the forest, even the

The Inn

desert beyond belongs to the Dark King. Disorder rules. Everyone who stops here for nourishment inevitably help to pay the Tithe.' He petted the giant rabbit's head.

'But if innocents are involved?'

'Then the Council will send someone to investigate. They're never wrong.'

She didn't like the way he was looking at her, like he could see right through her carefully-erected barriers.

'Part of you is Pack. That means you have excellent senses. And you are female... your instincts are flawless.'

He left her to marvel this on her own in the stable full of steeds.

†††

A strange clarity had settled over Kelly. It was midmorning when she finally left the stable, at ease with *both* sides of her heritage for the first time in her very long life. She found the phouka who had served her the previous day in the entrance hall.

'We need to talk.'

The phouka looked around like someone might save her then followed Kelly, resignation on her face.

Kelly led her out to the stables.

'You know everything that goes on here. Start talking.'

'I don't know what you mean.'

'Either tell me who is involved with the cellar, or I'll arrest every last creature in this Inn.'

'You're from the Council.'

The phouka drew Kelly closer to the stall of a sleeping steed. Its snores could cover a banshee's screech.

'All the goblins. They get lots of money out of it, the mercenaries. The troll who lives beneath the south bridge – he allows *him* to come and go as he pleases. And...' the phouka gulped. 'The cellar master.'

'Who?'

'He keeps to himself. I would too if my own kind had cast me out.'

Kelly watched the phouka nervously chew her cheek.

'Just be careful: the goblins fear him, and the gargoyles obey him.'

She knew then that the phouka was speaking of the redcap that hid in the shadows. She didn't need to ask about the high fae who did the actual killing. He'd been on her target list for as many centuries as she had been a Hunter.

Kelly waited on the stairs leading down to the parts of the Inn not meant for guests for the phouka and half-deathfae to join her.

They followed her in silence down to the dungeon. Sunlight flooded the path between the cells. There wasn't a lot of space for the redcap to hide down there. Nevertheless, she wasn't going to take chances.

Kelly opened the first cell. The frightened creatures cowered in the corner. She accessed the magic of the Hunt she had never used. Breathing deeply to steady herself, she used her power over emotion and made the girls get up and follow the phouka.

She opened the second cell and forced them to follow the boy in the same manner.

With the last cell, she bade them all to follow her.

Each time she used her magic, it became easier.

She didn't like toying with emotions, but it was the lesser of her magic and, she realised, very effective in situations like these. She understood, though, why her mother had always forbidden her to use the magic of the Hunt flowing in her blood.

Following the secret tunnel the shadows had shown her, Kelly was very aware of the ground pressing in from all sides. Suffocating in a tunnel like this was high on her list of nightmares.

The tunnel let them out in the warehouse district of Bremen. Judging by the sun's position, it was already noon. She led them into an abandoned building.

She pulled her tablet from the shadows and looked up the best way to alter their memories without damaging their minds.

Manipulating their emotions again, Kelly made the girls take hands to form a big circle. She chanted the simple incantation to make them forget and watched the magic work on the girls.

'You two will have to stay here and watch over them.'

'Why?' the phouka asked.

'Because it will take a while for the magic to work its way through them. It's best if they aren't interrupted by the uninformed.'

The phouka nodded and made herself comfortable against a wall.

Kelly walked to the young man watching the circle of young women.

'They're beautiful, aren't they?' she asked.

There was something about the beauty of fleeting youth that called to all fae.

'Very beautiful, yes,' the halfling agreed. 'Now,' he added in his morbid way.

'Will you keep them safe?'

'Yes.'

'Chances are, they'll be fine in a few hours. They won't remember their adventure with the fae.'

'Only birth and death give distinction to our lives. The dark road in between we travel unnoticed.'

'Enough! You are as close to immortal as any human can get: your life is extended beyond its natural limits by your fae parent. Your melodrama is cute, but you need to learn how to enjoy life. Eternity is a long time to be miserable. Even for a deathfae.'

When he rolled his eyes she was reminded, again, how young he was. She felt her years right then. She was exhausted. Even with all her centuries of experience, she had no idea how to deal with the power she now allowed to flow freely through her. Part of her wanted to punch the youth for his morbidity. Another part wanted to praise him for sticking to the order of things.

'I have work to do.'

She returned to the shadows, embraced them as they concealed her on her journey back to the Inn.

†††

It was time. Late afternoon light flooded the bailey. Kelly reached for the iron concealed in the shadows constant in her life. Her fingers grazed over the cool links and she yanked hard. It was time to announce her true nature by wielding a weapon only one of the Hunt could.

She was dressed in black leather, armoured in places, and with the seal of the Council emblazoned on her sleeve.

She was Pack and she was a Hunter for the Council.

She was a daughter of the Wild Hunt and of the cold high fae.

She held the shadows of the Dark Court and the merciless judgement of the Bright Court.

She was the worst nightmare of wrongdoers in Faerie.

The sun was setting. It had taken time to build up her strength after what she had done to save the innocents. But she was ready to make an end to Mactíre and his little scheme.

She dragged the chain behind her on the paving stones of the bailey. It was an awful, high-pitched sound that only hurt the ears of the fae. The Wild Hunt – and Kelly – were immune to it. A few fae fainted from the sound. But they weren't her quarry.

Goblins and gargoyles flooded the bailey. There were far more of them than she had anticipated. She couldn't believe that so many goblin clans had united in one cause. They were meant for disorder, not to follow one leader blindly.

They gathered around her. The cellar master and Mactíre joined them. Everyone the phouka had mentioned was there. She'd take care of the troll later.

She continued to drag her chain across the paving stones. It might hurt their ears, but it didn't incapacitate them. She didn't let it bother her. Kelly knew that it was magic that she had to practice. She grinned. She was a Hunter for the Council. She was part Pack. She was a powerful high fae. Goblins, gargoyles and redcaps didn't stand a chance against her.

Mactíre crossed his arms and leaned back against the castle wall. He grinned as he watched them.

It infuriated Kelly.

Forgetting her training, forgetting logic, she attacked the fae encircling her. Her chain whipped through the air and slashed through goblins and gargoyles alike. The iron burned them. Quickly she sent shadows to encase and capture them. Fury goaded her to continue to slash through her opponents. She could only see Mactíre's grin on all of their faces, his blue eyes mocking her.

'You're good, Hunter, but not good enough,' the lone redcap said and whistled. More gargoyles appeared from the castle.

Her chain was ripped from her by screeching gargoyles. She pulled two swords from the shadows swirling around her. She did her best to capture, not kill. Even with more goblins entering the fray, she could hold them and their feeble weapons off. She's a Hunter, a master of all weapons and fighting styles.

Yet... when a contingent of mountain trolls arrived with the darkness, she knew that she had miscalculated and that the phouka was sorely misinformed about Mactíre's allies.

She could fight better – but without restraint, she feared that she would kill and maim without thought. Kelly swallowed slowly as she watched her opponents.

Knowing that she's all that stood between Mactíre and his ilk running wild, devouring the mortal realm, she drew from the strength within she usually denied: her Wild Hunt heritage.

Allowing their emotions to touch her, she yanked on that part of them they kept hidden. Some dropped their weapons and cowered, others held their weapons and comrades close as they wept. But no-one ran. Mactíre laughed.

She side-stepped a troop of crying goblins, ducked down from a club wielded by a blubbering troll and disarmed a few gargoyles.

But their numbers were legion.

She wanted to punch Mactíre until he stopped laughing. He had evaded her, and the rest of the Council, for centuries. If not longer. She couldn't let him win. Not again.

'I thought Hunters were better strategists,' the redcap said. He knocked one of her swords away with brute force. It skittered over the paving stones. 'But it seems you're just like the rest of your kind: weak. High fae are all weak.' He spat in Mactíre's direction.

Kelly narrowed her eyes at him, caught his red cap from his head with her sword and laughed. His eyes widened as her laugh turned into a howl.

'You know nothing about me.'

She choked him on his own emotions – especially fear – before allowing the shadows to take him.

Even without the restraint of her high-fae side, she was clear-headed in the heat of battle. She understood, now, why Mactíre's game was different.

A battle cry from the gate made her look around. Ly Ergs stormed in. Unaffected by her earlier spell, the battle-hungry fae rushed through the weeping gargoyles, goblins and trolls. With red palms extended towards her, they ran blindly into the shadows.

Kelly reached out and her chain returned to her grasp. She

should've felt hopeless, yet a rush of excitement filled her.

The Wild Hunt was close.

'Aren't you afraid?' Mactíre asked as the Ly Ergs reached her.

'No. But you should be.'

She lashed out with her chain, burning the fae with its iron, catching them in shadows.

The Wild Hunt blasted through the gate on their steeds. Screams of terror filled the bailey.

'Sorry we're late,' the Gabriel said. 'Are you having problems?'

Kelly grinned. She stretched her neck from side to side and said: 'It's sweets, but with blood. So much better.'

The Wild Hunt all laughed. She knew they'd understand. They were Pack.

She slashed her way through trolls and Ly Ergs towards Mactíre. She could smell the fear coming from him. He tripped over a cowering gargoyle as he retreated. Kelly held her sword pointed at his heart. His hands clenched. He threw them up...

'I don't think so,' Kelly said, keeping a force-field between them. His magic sizzled ineffectually between them.

She blinked, and iron shackles formed on his hands and feet. The chain connecting them landed at her feet, like a leash to lead him.

She narrowed her eyes, trying to figure out what changed about him. He seemed... Ordinary. Weak. Resigned to his fate.

'Not bad,' the Gabriel said behind her.

'Not bad yourself. Mind locking this lot up in the shadow cages?'

'Sure.'

Two of the Hunt took Mactíre away.

'Where are you going?' the Gabriel asked.

'To round up the rest.'

'The troll under the bridge?'

She nodded.

'He's outside, turned to stone until someone releases him.'

'Good.'

'Uhm...' He led her to the side of the Pack and prisoners. 'Are we in trouble?'

'For your negligence?'

She watched him. 'No. The fae will always follow their dark natures. It's not your responsibility to keep them in line. But...'

The Inn

She watched Mactíre struggle against his bonds of shadow and iron, trying to scoot away from the angry redcap who'd controlled him and the others. 'You should know better than to allow one to take control of so many. You're old enough to know the signs, Gabriel.'

He nodded.

'I won't mention this to the Council.'

'But if *they* mention us...'

'The Council trusts my judgement. Just don't make me come and hunt for you, alright?'

The Gabriel grinned.

'Oh, there's a half-deathfae in town. I think he can do with a bit of guidance...'

He grimaced.

'Will you be alright transporting this lot on your own?' he asked.

'Of course. I'm a Hunter. And I'm Pack.'

He hugged her, briefly, before stepping back.

'You always have a home with us.'

'Thank you.' She felt at peace with herself.

Grinning, she pulled on the shadows and disappeared with her prisoners.

Mactíre howled in agony as they entered the cleansing mists between the realms.

She had finally put an end to the Big Bad Wolf.

SONIC SAM OF BOSTON
BY
BILLIE HOLLADAY SKELLEY

Boston, the capital and largest city in Massachusetts, has long been recognized for its world-renowned universities, museums, symphonies, and historical sites. This municipality also features several popular athletic, artistic, and recreational attractions. Known as "the birthplace of the American Revolution" and "Beantown," the city received a less desirable moniker in 2016. That year it was named "Rat City" because of its widespread rat infestation. Boston had a serious rodent problem, and it was quickly escalating into a crisis.

Rats seemed to be everywhere in the city. They were in alleys, sewers, parks, homes, and buildings. They especially loved the trash bins located behind Boston's popular restaurants because the flimsy, plastic bags used to hold garbage were no challenge for the hungry animals and their razor-sharp teeth.

These rodents could swim, climb, and dig. Their strong teeth were capable of gnawing through electrical wires, wood, cement, brick, and even soft metals. Their burrowing was eroding the foundations of homes and buildings. They were causing thousands of dollars in damage every day.

Even worse, the rats contaminated food supplies, inflicted painful bites, and carried several harmful diseases. With their remarkable reproductive capabilities, the number of rats plaguing the city was constantly increasing, and the creatures were contaminating Boston with their urine, feces, and parasites. It was clear the rodents were posing a significant health hazard for the city.

Boston's city leaders had fought the rat problem for decades with poisons, rodenticides, traps, bait boxes, and dry ice, but they had achieved little success. In 2016, the rat problem intensified so severely that everyone realized the problem was out of hand. Residents refused to live under such conditions any longer. They marched on City Hall and demanded Boston's city leaders do something about the problem.

Boston's mayor, a tall, proud man named Fillmore, understood their concern, but he was perplexed about what to do. He met privately with the town council, but the council members had no new suggestions or solutions to offer. They were frustrated and exasperated, but most of all, they knew they would not get reelected if they didn't do something. Unfortunately, they had no idea what to do. No one seemed to know how to fix the rodent problem.

Mayor Fillmore finally decided to have an open meeting to see if anyone in Boston had any new ideas on the issue or any new solutions for the problem. On the night of the scheduled meeting, Mayor Fillmore and the council members gathered in City Hall. They waited, but no one came. They continued to wait, hoping for someone to arrive who might suggest a solution for their rat problem.

Finally, as the city's leaders were about to leave, a young, short fellow, dressed all in black, entered City Hall. He had dark bushy hair, thick horn-rimmed glasses, and two gold earrings in each ear. He held a large metal box in front of him that was partially obscured by his long, black coat. On the top surface of the box, there were several lights, dials, switches, and buttons.

Mayor Fillmore studied the strange man closely. Despite his small stature and pleasant smile, he thought the fellow looked dangerous. All that black clothing had a gothic and sinister look. Behind those thick glasses, the fellow had huge, round eyes that kept darting around the room, moving from face to face, like an owl looking for prey. Plus, his eyes had a strange light in them. I bet he's on drugs, thought Mayor Fillmore—and then there was the matter of that box he held so tightly in front of him. It's probably some sort of electronic control panel, Mayor Fillmore thought, but then he grew more concerned. Does this fellow intend to set off some weapon? Is the box a bomb?

"What are you doing here?" demanded Mayor Fillmore. "This is a formal city meeting, and unruly visitors will be removed by security."

"I'm Sonic Sam, and I've come to neutralize your rat population."

Hearing this proclamation, the Mayor chuckled softly to himself, and several members of the town council grinned in disbelief.

"How can *you* solve our rat problem?" sneered Mayor Fillmore. "We are looking for serious people with serious solutions."

"I am serious," answered Sam. "I will use high frequency ultrasonic sound waves to create an acoustically hostile environment for the rats."

The Mayor laughed openly at this statement.

"You're going to play loud music for our rats?" he questioned sarcastically. Several members of the town council joined him in a round of hearty laughter.

"No," answered Sam, smiling. "The sound I will transmit cannot be heard by humans or regular pets. It will only affect the rats, and it will give them great auditory stress."

"Stress!" exclaimed Mayor Fillmore, laughing more heartily now and holding his sides. "We want to kill the bloody pests—not stress them out. We want them gone!"

"It wouldn't be right to kill so many creatures that are just trying to survive," answered Sam. "Rats have rights, too—just like your pet dog—but don't worry, my sound will remove the rats from the city. They will leave because the sound hurts their ears. They'll move to get away from it."

Mayor Fillmore thought for a minute and rubbed his chin. Could this fellow actually do something to rid them of the rats? He doubted it. This Sonic Sam most likely was a nut job, but no one else had come to the meeting and offered any ideas. This kid might be weird, but if they let him take a stab at the problem, at least it would look like they were doing something. All those voters would have to admit the city's leaders were *trying* to solve the rat problem. Still, he weighed the possibilities. This crazy fellow might blow up City Hall with his strange ideas and metal box. He continued to stroke his chin and consider the possibilities.

The truth was that "Sonic Sam" was really Samuel Bell.

"Sonic Sam" was just a nickname he had earned in graduate school when he was pursuing a doctoral degree in acoustical engineering. In fact, Sam Bell had three degrees—all from those renowned Boston universities that Mayor Fillmore was always talking about in his speeches. Sam had one in engineering, one in zoology, and one in law. He may have been short in stature, but Sam was long on brains and creativity.

Finally, Mayor Fillmore spoke.

"Fellow council members, since no one else has ventured forth to aid us in our hour of distress, perhaps we should allow Sam to try. At least our citizens would know we are trying to fix the problem."

The members of the town council understood the Mayor's thinking and nodded in agreement.

"What will you do, Sam ... lead all the rats into the Charles River and drown them?" asked Mayor Fillmore smiling.

"Mayor, that would be inhumane and useless. Rats can swim. Besides, if they were all in the river, they would contaminate the water. I'll lead them out of the city to No Man's Land—the uninhabited island off Martha's Vineyard. Researchers will be able to study and care for them there."

Mayor Fillmore considered this statement. If the kid actually could do what he said, it might work.

"What do you want in return for removing the rats?" asked Mayor Fillmore.

"All you have to do is sign this contract," said Sam, pulling a long piece of paper from beneath his black coat. "It says you will pay me a million dollars for removing the rats."

Mayor Fillmore took the document, glanced at the paper, and considered the offer and its conditions. A million dollars is nothing, he thought, if it actually works. If the rats were gone today, I'd pay that amount right now. No problem. It would be worth it. The odds are, however, this nerdy kid can accomplish nothing, so no payment would ever be necessary. What's the harm in allowing him to try? It will show the city's citizens we are trying to solve the rat problem, and it will give the news media something to focus on besides constantly reminding everyone of our lack of success in preventing the rat infestation.

"If my fellow council members have no objections," said Mayor Fillmore, "I'll sign your contract, and I promise you a million dollars if you successfully remove our rats."

When no one objected, Mayor Fillmore signed the contract.

"Wonderful," said Sam. "I will start tomorrow morning, and the rats will be gone by tomorrow evening."

The mayor and the council members laughed out loud at this statement. They thought Sam was boasting, misguided, and foolish. They felt he was describing the impossible.

The next day, however, Sam stood in the middle of Beacon Hill and turned on his machine. Not a sound was heard by anyone, but soon rats started emerging from the alleys, sewers, and buildings. Like a cowboy herding cattle, Sam rounded up the multitude of rodents into a herd and pushed them toward the coast. At the water's edge, he boarded a small boat, and continued to direct the swimming rodents toward the island known as No Man's Land. By nightfall, all the rats had been relocated. Not one rat remained in Boston!

Mayor Fillmore and the town council were shocked, but they happily celebrated the successful removal of the rodents. By the afternoon of the next day, they were complimenting each other on their decision to use Sam for the job. Several remarked how they knew he would be successful.

The citizens of Boston were overjoyed. They danced in the streets at their good fortune. Churches rang their steeple bells at the glad tidings. No longer "Rat City," Boston was a happy town.

When Sam arrived the next afternoon at City Hall, however, Mayor Fillmore and the council members regretted promising him a million dollars. They had neglected to have his contract approved by the city's legal advisors because they didn't think Sam's claims were achievable. Now, they had no monetary appropriations from the city to give to Sam.

Mayor Fillmore quickly decided to treat the whole thing as a misunderstanding. There was no real need now, he decided, to pay Sam anything. The rats were gone. They wouldn't be back. The problem was solved. Besides, a million dollars could be used to help the city in other ways. Surely Sam would appreciate that logic. A young fellow like him couldn't afford to seem greedy. Besides, Mayor Fillmore thought, what can Sam do about it if we don't pay? Let him take us to court. It'll take years, and everyone will have forgotten about the whole affair by then.

"Please give me my money," said Sam.

"Sam," said Mayor Fillmore, "you must realize we don't have that much money at our disposal. We can't just dispense an amount like that lightly. We are very grateful for your services, but you must be reasonable. To justify your effort, I will see that you get a thousand dollars by the end of the day."

"No, Mayor Fillmore. Our contract is legally binding. I drew it up myself. Furthermore, if you read the contract carefully, you will see that for every week you do not pay me, my reimbursement increases another million dollars." Sam pointed to a paragraph in the lower half of the document.

Mayor Fillmore grabbed the contract and read the section Sam had indicated. Instead of acknowledging Sam was correct, he got flustered and angry.

"Why, you ... you impudent whippersnapper! Who do you think you are? You hoodwinked us. You ... you are a greedy little nerd," cried the Mayor. "Why should we pay you now? After all, the rats are gone. They aren't our problem anymore."

"Keep your promise, Mayor Fillmore," said Sam, "or I will make sounds of a more negative nature."

"Are you threatening me, boy? You've gone too far. I think you should leave at once. Get out now before I call security!"

Sam left quietly, but his heart was filled with resentment and bitterness.

The next morning Sam stood at the very same spot in Beacon Hill where he had started the rat removal. Adjusting the dials, switches, and buttons on his metal box, he created an electromagnetic pulse generator. When he pushed the green button on the top right corner of the control panel, a transient electromagnetic disturbance was created. This pulse radiated over the city and disrupted certain electronic devices which he had carefully selected—mainly cell phones and televisions.

When Sam pushed the button, all the cell phones and televisions across Boston stopped working. None of those devices continued to function. Sam had been careful to set the pulse so that no emergency or essential equipment was disrupted, but any phone or television used for personal or recreational purposes was now defunct. In a matter of seconds, the phones and televisions in Boston became useless paperweights.

The residents of the city, especially the youth, quickly became upset and frustrated. They were more agitated now, with the loss of their electronics, than they had been with the rat infestation. At first, people were confused, but they soon became angry. How could they live without their phones and TVs?

Life in Boston was now terrible—much worse than when they just had a rat problem. A pall came over the whole town. Bostonians entered a deep depression. The sadness and gloom affected everyone. The city leaders knew they had to do something or soon Boston would have another nickname, "The Unhappy Town."

Mayor Fillmore, however, did not know what to do. None of the city's engineers had been successful in turning the phones and televisions back on, and he refused to ask Sonic Sam for help. He felt Sam had tricked him, and he didn't trust him. Weeks went by, and still Mayor Fillmore refused to pay Sam or ask him for help.

It was true, Mayor Fillmore had not read the legal document Sam had gotten him to sign, but the city's legal advisors were carefully reading it now. They pointed out to Mayor Fillmore the provision that stipulated, with any delay of payment, the amount due to Sam would increase by a million dollars for each week payment was delayed. Mayor Fillmore didn't care. He wasn't anyone's fool, and he refused to consider such a large payment. He thought if he just waited, the little gothic nerd would go away and forget the whole affair. He kept making excuses, and he refused to pay Sam.

Bostonians, however, grew tired of waiting. They were angry and distressed. The rats had made life unpleasant and difficult, but the absence of working phones and functioning televisions was intolerable. People across the city knew they had to do something to get Mayor Fillmore to act.

Consequently, many adults in Boston formed voluntary associations in an effort to persuade the Mayor to get Sonic Sam to turn their electronic devices back on. They felt Mayor Fillmore should keep his promise to Sam. These groups had various names such as "Restore Our Phones" and "Return Boston to the 21st Century." Boston's teens also formed voluntary organizations that were united in an effort to get their phones and televisions working again. These groups had somewhat more explicit names, such as "Fed Up with Fillmore" and "Move the

Mayor to No Man's Land."

Before long, the people of Boston were united in this effort. They held rallies, and they marched on City Hall. They demanded Mayor Fillmore meet with Sam and set things rights.

"Pay him anything he wants," they cried. "Just get our electronic devices back on."

Finally, Mayor Fillmore realized he would never get reelected if he did not settle this issue. He thought it over carefully and finally agreed to meet with Sam. He wasn't happy about the turn of events, but he couldn't see any other solution.

It had been three weeks since Sam had removed the rats, so an additional three million dollars were now due. Counting the original million-dollar payment, the city now owed Sam four million dollars!

Mayor Fillmore arranged a big ceremony in City Hall where all the media could record him solving the problem and setting things right. As reporters snapped pictures, he presented Sam with a four-million-dollar check. Then, everyone watched as Sam adjusted a few dials and switches on his metal box. Finally, he pushed a button and instantly everyone's phones started working again. Mayor Fillmore had one of the council members check that the televisions were back on, also, and when he was assured they were working again, he shook hands with Sam—in front of all the cameras.

The year had been a difficult one for Mayor Fillmore and for Boston, but some lessons were learned. The first lesson was that appearances can be deceiving. The second was that one should always respect the individual and his or her talents—no matter how different or unusual he or she may appear. The freedom of expression that comes with being an individual is paramount. The third lesson was to never underestimate the power of people coming together in pursuit of a common cause. Most of all, the Mayor and the citizens of Boston learned that a promise is a promise—and when made in good faith, it should be honored (especially when it is spelled out in legal terms in a binding contract).

To acknowledge the events and to remember these lessons, the citizens of Boston had a small plaque made. They placed the plaque on Joy Street in Beacon Hill. The simple inscription upon this plaque states: "Honor the promises you make."

THE RED SHOES
BY
CARA SCHULZ

The shoes were cursed.

Karen looked down at the red soles of her Christian Louboutins. They used to give her a feeling of power. Invincibility. A secret little rush. Now she only felt shame and a crushing remorse as she looked at her heels.

It all started with these damn shoes and would end with them, too.

In twenty more minutes she would be sentenced in court after confessing every misdeed. Twenty more minutes and she would be free in the only way a truly guilty person can be free.

Karen sighed, then looked up and nervously smiled at her attorney, Angela Gold, the only friend she had left.

"You can do this, Karen," Angela said to her while giving her hand a squeeze. "I'll be with you. I'll never leave your side."

Karen couldn't help but ask, "Even if...when...my sentence is carried out?"

"Even then."

Karen looked down at her carefully-prepared notes and tried to order her mind, yet every time she looked down at them she caught a flash of red. The shoes.

†††

She first saw them when she was considering running for State Representative. She was on her way to a meeting with Party officials, in fact. She had been wearing a properly conservative suit in charcoal gray. When she left the house, she thought her look was perfect. Somber, respectable. Yet as she walked by the window where those shoes were displayed, black with that flash of red at the sole and heel, she stopped dead.

Those were the shoes of a powerful woman. A woman who Gets Shit Done.

She was almost late to the meeting, she had stared at those shoes for so long. The meeting went as expected. Pleasantries exchanged, options explored, but the upshot was the Party was interested in running her on their ticket because of her reputation for incorruptibility and her years of volunteer work in her community. They needed a clean candidate who wouldn't damage the Party in a race she was expected to gracefully lose.

But her mind was only half on the meeting. The other half was on the shoes. A woman wearing those shoes wouldn't lose gracefully. She would kick electoral ass and shock everyone (except herself, of course) with a win. But the shoes cost a cool $800 and there was no way she could afford them.

The campaign kicked off in a very bland, perfunctory way. Everyone going through the motions. Her Treasurer, a woman everyone called Mom for her caring disposition, let her know when the donations started to come in. Mom may not have been the best Treasurer, but she loved Karen and doted on her. And she was a major donor, so there was that.

As the time for Karen's first big rally came closer, she daydreamed about cheering crowds and eager volunteers rushing to join her campaign team. She also dreamed about those shoes.

Looking for inspiration for her speech, she went to visit "her shoes," as she now thought about them. The sales ladies were getting used to her, standing outside, looking at the shoes. Sometimes for a few minutes, other times for far longer.

"I could get them. I could say it was a campaign expense and walk right out of there with them on my feet this very minute. Mom would be easy to fool with a slight alteration of the receipt. I would be standing on the stage at my rally and everyone would see me as a winner," Karen thought.

It was so tempting. All her life she had been a straight arrow. Dependable. Always thinking of others and never doing for herself.

A doormat.

A loser.

Muttering "not any more", she opened the door to the store and walked in.

†††

That was the start of a shocking rise. She did electrify the crowd at her first rally. As her red heels clicked across the stage, she knew exactly what to say. A deep breath at the microphone and then her words danced right into their hearts.

Volunteers flocked, donors opened their checkbooks, and news media covered it all. Karen traded favors with power brokers who sensed an electoral upset, telling herself it was for a greater good. After all, what good were intentions if you never got a chance to act on them? All while wearing her trademark shoes.

On election day, her supporters posted photos of themselves on social media, their fingers in a V for victory, stained red from the dye used to mark their prints on the ballot. Far from a graceful loss, it was a commanding victory.

A few years as a State Rep and her reputation changed. She was a woman who Got Shit Done. A powerful woman. A ruthless, driven politician who was amassing great personal wealth. She dined with the right people, accepted "favors" and "contributions" from the right kind of wrong people, and stopped thinking in terms of good and bad. Any time she had doubt as to what to do or hit a roadblock, she slipped on her red shoes and the path cleared before her. They were her lucky shoes.

Which is why she wore them when she became a Senator and danced in them at her Presidential Inauguration Ball. She wore them in the War Room when she greenlighted the bombing of a country which didn't fall in line with her country's demands - demands which also benefited her personally. She wore them when she sold a Supreme Court seat. Each step forward in her red heels was a step further from the person she was before.

Her days were never-ending tests of her endurance and at times she felt more like a prisoner than the most powerful woman in the free world.

With all the demands on her time, and the time spent with her new friends, she lost touch with the people she knew back in her old neighborhood. Not surprising and she rarely thought of them, anyway.

Yet there was one friend whom she had hoped would be more than a friend. The Karen of eleven years ago had been too timid to ask Angela on a date. So when Karen spotted Angela in a crowd at an airport meet-and-greet it was as if the old Karen with the big heart came to life again. Her mouth went dry. She shifted slightly and felt the soft leather of her Louboutins. No, this Karen didn't let chances slide by. This Karen seized them.

Karen altered her direction and came to stop directly in front of Angela.

"Well hello, lovely," Karen said warmly as she took Angela's hand to shake it.

Angela's eyes widened and then crinkled in a smile. "Hello yourself, big shot."

Karen had to move on to shake more hands, but she motioned a staffer to come closer. "That woman, there, in the gold-and-black suit, escort her onto my plane, please."

Karen gave a last wave to the crowd while standing at the top of the plane stairs and then ducked into the relatively dimmer light of the interior. Walking past the press pool, smiling and nodding hello, past the staffers, to the private area in the back.

Where a bemused Angela sat on a plush couch.

"Am I being kidnapped?" asked Angela.

Karen sat down next to her, looking steadily into her eyes, "Oh yes. Yes, you are."

†††

Life with Angela was one of passion. Passionate love, even more passionate disagreements. Arguments, you could even say. Increasing in duration and frequency.

The most frustrating thing was everything Angela said was something Karen had once believed in. The People didn't need a master. Using violence to achieve her goals, especially her private goals, was wrong. Not just wrong sometimes, but always wrong. Trading favors hurt others. Using regulations to bankrupt opponents' businesses and obscure criminal laws to jail those who spoke out about her made her a tyrant.

Angela was frustratingly naive, Karen reassured herself. After all, this was just how things were done. Angela was a smart woman, she would understand eventually. *She's an attorney, for God's sake, not a virgin saint!*

Karen was going over her sausage-making-is-ugly speech in her head as she walked into their bedroom. They had had another fight and Karen wanted to smooth things over and try yet again to explain how the real world worked. She stopped in mid-sentence as she realized Angela wasn't in the room. And neither were most of her things.

Except for the red dress Karen had bought her. It was the very first gift she had given to Angela and it was laying on the bed with a small, white card laying on top.

Karen,

If all you want is power, that is all you will have for the rest of your days.

Angela

That was it. That was all she wrote. Karen threw the note away and resolved to never look back even though she felt her heart dripping bright red blood with every beat.

Much as she used to constantly think about her red-soled shoes, Karen now found her thoughts coming back time and again to Angela's note. What did that mean "If all you want is power, that is all you will have?" I mean, what is so bad about wanting power? And why can't she have power and Angela?

Now, each time, when Karen went to make a decision or make another deal, she heard Angela's voice. Asking if what she was doing was hurting others. If using force was the right thing to do. Karen started questioning if the money which changed hands, the bribes, if she was honest, was to grease the wheels of government or to line her own pockets? And was either really the right thing to do?

Karen reread the books she and Angela used to share over a decade ago, when they would spend hours happily talking about their favorite quotes from Konklin or Rothbard or Hayek or Paterson.

When her cabinet or staff presented her with policy options she began asking if government action was really needed. If, perhaps, government should step back and let citizens come up with their own solutions? Perhaps use trade instead of troops in dealings with foreign nations?

Her powerful friends were angry. Her approval ratings

tanked. Her staff wondered if she had lost her mind. Her party wished she would snap out of whatever radical mid-life crisis was gripping her.

Karen just wanted out of the nightmare her life had become.

†††

"And that is why I will not seek my Party's nomination for re-election as your President."

There was more to her speech from the Oval Office, but none of it mattered. That one line said it all. Hopefully the person she most wanted to hear it was watching and would come back to her. She didn't want to steal, and kill, and imprison. She wanted a peaceful life with respect earned and given. She wanted to own herself again and wanted that for others, too. And she wanted Angela to want to be with her.

They could have a quiet life filled with every comfort. Karen was willing to put her funds to good use, helping others and pushing back against injustice. Working to repeal laws and regulations. A charitable foundation.

The day Karen left office, and put away her red shoes, came and went with no word from Angela. Karen felt herself falling into a deep depression.

Then a year went by, spent in a quiet house where Karen based her charity. She hoped Angela would hear about all the good things she was doing and come back. Still no word.

Finally, Karen called Angela's cell and left a message.

"I'm ready, you know. I'm ready to do what I need to do. What I should have done. I'm going to call the FBI and lay it all out. How corrupt our entire cesspool of government is and will always be. How it corrupts everyone it touches because that is the very nature of power. The million ways it harms everyone it tramples on. Every law I've broken and every person whom I broke it with. The deals. The bullshit about how it's for the children or for your safety when it's really about power or money or both. But I think I need a good attorney or a good friend. Someone to hold my hand. If that can be you, I'd be so thankful. If it can't, I understand. I love you."

†††

The Red Shoes

Angela's voice startled her out of the murky past. "Karen, it's time."

Yes, after a year of interviews with the FBI and the Department of Justice and non-stop media coverage, it was time. She had pled guilty and the country was wrapped up wondering if she was telling the truth or lying. Those also implicated, which was most everyone in Congress and most heads of corporations, were doing everything they could to discredit her and save themselves. Yes, it was time. Time for her sentencing.

Karen stood up, smoothed down her skirt, and walked calmly into the courtroom, her heels clicking. These shoes had one last trick to play. One last bit of magic. And then she'd be rid of them forever.

†††

"Your Honor, thank you for forgoing a sentence of death and granting me exile instead. I had come into this courtroom at peace with my decision to come forward and accept whatever consequences you thought appropriate. I also want to do something more.

"I want citizens to know, without a shred of doubt, just how bad their government truly is so they can decide if this is the path they wish to continue. Or if they want another path. One where the guiding principle is that all human interactions should be honest, voluntary, and mutually beneficial. Where there are no masters.

"I am guilty, but I am no more or less guilty than our entire system. I say this not to make light or excuse what I did, but so everyone understands how bad it really is.

"To that end, your Honor, I give the court my shoes. Concealed in them are micro-recorders. I have worn them from my first day in office to my last. Every deal I've made, every conversation I had, every law I broke is all there. I hope the court, and the people, find these shoes as powerful as I have."

And with that, Karen and Angela headed into exile, where they lived happily (in a mutually-beneficial, voluntary relationship) ever after.

GODIVA
BY
BLAKE JESSOP

Outside fences so high they might guard a castle, a young student dares to disagree with leaders gathered for the largest economic summit in her country's history. It's the first time she's ever done anything like this, and she's terrified.

Dressed all in black, she has her dreads tied up tight and her face hidden by a black paisley handkerchief. She folded it and tied it around her neck so that she could pull it up fast. Before leaving her dorm, she checked out the effect in the mirror and thought, *I make this look good.*

She stops caring how good it looks when a tear gas canister clatters by her feet. It happens so fast she can't imagine a time before it, like the hissing arc of the grenade cut her off from her previous life. One minute she's easing along, chanting some slogans. The next her black Chucks are squeaking on the metal top of the police cruiser she climbed to get away from the acrid gas.

She's a chemistry major, so she doesn't really understand economics until she has to calculate how long she can stay on top of a burning car until she has to get down there and breathe the cyanocarbons.

She chokes all the way out of the war zone with bile in her throat, tears streaming from her eyes and the snarl of dogs straining at her heels. She resolves to bring a gas mask next time.

†††

At a different time entirely, on an estate above the city of

Coventry, the loyal young Countess of Mercia dared to disagree with her husband. Though their lands were rich, her dowry glistening, and her future as secure as the moon and stars, she was upset.

Lately, upon the road to Caludon Castle, she had gazed from the windows of her carriage at the growing city. It was market day, and her husband's people had come from far and wide to sell their produce. She heard a yell.

"Tom, you cur! Why can't I sell my weaving?" a decrepit charwoman cried.

"Because you ain't paid the tax!" Tom yelled back. The Lady recognized him as one of her husband's tax collectors and bailiffs.

"What tax?" the woman begged.

"The heregeld," said the bailiff, rapping his halberd against the ground for emphasis. "And the window tax."

"I do not understand," the charwoman pleaded, "what does it matter how many windows I have? Don't you know my husband died fighting the Earl's wars? How can he tax me for new ones?"

"That's obvious," said the bailiff. "If your husband's dead the Earl will need more men, won't he?"

"I do not understand!" cried the charwoman again.

As her carriage clattered out of earshot, the Countess found that she did not understand either.

†††

"Sure, you can take my picture," the girl with the gasmask says. It's redundant, because the hip-looking guy with the old-school Nikon is already snapping away.

"Great," he says, bending back unnecessarily on his heels and cranking his 35mm antique. "So I want to do a long-form piece on this protest. Why are you out here?"

"I'm just a chemistry student," she admits. "I'm super anti-austerity, though."

"I bet the chemistry is coming in handy now, with all that gas. To be honest most people don't know what's wrong with the G8."

He obviously wants her to ask him about it, so she does. The explanation doesn't satisfy the chemist part of her at all, but one thing he says sticks with her.

"You got student loans, right? You pay taxes? Well, that's where the money comes from to pay those cops and buy that tear gas. That's pretty messed up, if you think about it."

She does, and it is. She hadn't thought of it that way. All she did was go home, stock up on bottled water, buy the mask, and try to get herself emotionally ready to face the riot cops. They look like terrifying bipedal insects, and just thinking about the wall of glossy riot shields freaks her out.

"Worker bees," she says. The photographer isn't listening.

"I'm Wendel," he says. "What's your name?"

"I'd rather not," the girl in the gasmask says. "I'm nobody special."

"That's cool, but I still want pictures — you've really got a look. Dreads and that mask. It'll really get the message across. Let me show you the Burger King we use to wash up."

†††

The Countess could not forget the charwoman.

Rather than go to and fro in her carriage with the drapes drawn, the Countess of Mercia rode the countryside on her own horse. Everywhere the avarice of her husband was to be seen. In hovels left unrepaired by men levied for war, in their unreaped crops and the faces of their wives, lined with worry and care.

The Countess knew little of these things, but her dowry had been rich, and her lands were huge. *What need they*, she asked her husband upon her return, *with all these taxes*?

"Godiva, my love," Earl Leofric said, "you do not understand wars and matters of state."

"Perhaps not," his lady replied, "but is minding the state of these lands not part of my duty as keeper of your household? Our people are weary and starving."

"You understand your duties as my wife very poorly," said her husband, starting to get cross. "You oughtn't to speak so plainly."

"But it pains my heart so, to see them suffer. Could you not reduce your taxes just a little?"

"I would no more do that," the Earl of Mercia cried, "than you would ride naked through the city of Coventry!"

At this utterance the Earl's advisors looked aghast. The matron almost fainted and had to be supported by two of her blushing maids. The Countess reddened, not for shame at the vulgar words, but at their implication. The bailiffs laughed along with the Earl. He had to quiet them when his wife raised her head to speak.

"Surely you jest, Leofric."

"Not at all!" her husband roared.

"Can I assume, then," said his wife, "that we have a bargain?"

The court went silent and none, not even the Earl, could like the look in Godiva's eyes.

†††

What the girl in the gasmask does when the motorcade arrives is put herself bodily in its way. Bodily *all the way*. She does it half naked, with a slogan daubed across her breasts in red body paint. She keeps the mask on, because tear gas is as inevitable as sunburn. She's ready for the gas, so she gets hit with a water cannon instead.

It feels like getting kicked by a horse. She's never been kicked by a horse, but this is probably what it feels like. That's what goes through her head as it bounces on the concrete. Her naked shoulder blades gather a collection of long red scrapes as her fellow marchers drag her to safety.

Later, with the headache finally dwindling, she starts thinking that showing her breasts isn't enough. In fact, it isn't really nudity at all. You can find a picture of a half-naked girl with tattoos and a gasmask on the internet without leaving your living room. Watching her bleed and squirm in real time is compelling, but five minutes from now, no one is going to care.

†††

Word spread quickly in Coventry, though only a few shopkeepers and the Jewish moneylender could read the proclamations. In a hasty meeting, old differences were thrown aside in favor of a more theological question: *is it acceptable to humiliate an angel?*

The men shouted and disagreed. They drank and ruminated. They came to a decision, for Lady Godiva had begun to take on the air of something more than a Countess. Each man spread the word in his quarter — *it must be a market day like no other.*

When the day came, the Lady dressed in a robe of fine mink and smooth linen. On her feet were the tiny slippers she wore only in her private rooms. Her maid combed her luxuriant brown hair with special care, crying quietly for the humiliation the day promised. Imaging the leering crowd, she was barely able to hold the brush.

Godiva's horse, saddled and bridled, was held by a blushing stable boy. The white stallion was her favorite, tall and swift, and had a fine mane almost as long as hers. He looked particularly handsome with Leofric's golden coat of arms upon his flowing red caparison.

Godiva took the reins and the stable boy rushed back to his work. The Countess mounted carefully, keeping the robe drawn tightly around her shoulders. Looking at the open gate and the long road down the hill to the city, she hesitated. She glanced up at her husband's window. From the tower Leofric looked down at her, full of anger and amazement. She let the robe slip, showing him her graceful back, and rode toward Coventry.

†††

In the tents after a day of violence, Wendel photographs her. He thinks one day people will look at his portraits the way they look at paintings. At the Pre-Raphaelites or maybe John Collier.

Wendel did get some good shots during the day. There's nothing quite like a German Shepherd rearing against its leash in black-and-white. He takes his pictures in monochrome because it makes things look stark, marking an easy division between dark and light. Now he's shooting the girl in the gasmask just as she came off the line; topless and bruised, with her back looking like it has been scourged. He takes his pictures and flicks his long hair out of the way at intervals. He lets a cigarette dangle out of the side of his mouth like Robert Mapplethorpe.

The girl in the gasmask has mostly figured out he's missing the point. She's been thinking about the reasons she's still here and turning him on is not one of them. The last shot he takes is the best, though he doesn't know it. The bruises have risen. She stops posing and just stands, arms loose by her sides, breathing. The slogan has been scoured into illegibility by the water cannon. The mask covers her face and makes her an anonymous human body, beaten, tired, trying to decide how much more it can take.

When the shoot is done she puts her top back on and winces when the dirty cotton touches the long scrapes. Somebody has a small portable TV droning in the background. *What, after all* the commentator says, *are these people protesting? They don't know anything about international finance. They have no idea how Wall Street works. In the sixties, at least we knew what the issues were!*

She wonders if the commentator knows that's the entire point. That she doesn't have a clue what's going on. That the system is designed so that she never will. She wonders if she's going to have the courage to come back tomorrow, and as she does she takes off the mask.

†††

Lady Godiva shivered in the morning chill of market day. She had tried to prepare herself for whatever might come. Made peace with her nudity, with baring herself to the throng. *What matters my humiliation under their stares,* she thought, *if it sets them free?*

She still rode with her head bowed. Just because she was resolved, she realized, did not mean it wouldn't hurt. When Lady Godiva reached the square, however, she witnessed a miracle.

The town was so quiet the rustle of the ribbon that tied her hair could be heard whispering to the damp and fragrant earth when she let down her hair. All around her the town had bolted its doors and shuttered its windows. None looked. None dared. They loved her too much. Worn wooden slats covered her with a veil of respect better than the finest silk.

As Lady Godiva rode through the market, as empty as though there were plague, she caught a glimmer in the corner of her eye.

Had someone dared to look? The Countess felt a stab of humiliation, then began to wonder; w*hy feel shame at all? My body is young and fair. Why feel chagrin for my choices, which were noble and decent, even if I am not?*

She approached the solitary figure by the well. He gazed up at her with unashamed, lecherous glee. Tom, the tax collector.

Of course, it would be him. *Were there any justice,* she thought, *God would strike this man blind.*

Lady Godiva's face was a mask of tears and discontent. Her eyes met those of the peeping Tom and the heavens did nothing. Shifting her smooth white legs in the saddle, she leant over and lashed the reins across his eyes.

†††

The clatter of tear gas canisters against concrete has the premonitory clang of a church bell being rung to drive away the damned. When the time comes to really bear down, to clear the barricades and end the riots, the cops come like marauders raiding a village at dawn.

If they had every wondered who the girl in the gasmask was, they know now. She's at the center of a line of messed-up looking people with their arms linked. The water cannon cannot move them, just rattle the living chain. Their eyes squint against the smoke.

In the middle of it all she stands without her mask. Her face as bare as a child's under the glare of her persecutors. *This,* she decides, *is the only kind of nakedness that matters.* All around the girl and the water and the dogs, images burn themselves into film and eyes and memories.

Water crashes over the protestors. Gas fills their eyes. The girl stands at their center. Her eyes are a vibrant and electric blue, narrowed now in rage.

†††

Still as naked as she was during her ride, as she was when she was born, Lady Godiva entered Leofric's great hall. Every pair of eyes turned from her as they would from the brightest summer sun. It is as though all shame had been burned away from her like dew at the break of dawn.

With an effort worthy of a hero, Leofric raised his eyes to hers.

"Will you finally cover yourself?" he asked.

"Will you keep your word?" Godiva replied.

The Earl gazed in mute surrender at his Countess, her eyes the glacial blue of meltwater in spring, narrowed now in rage.

VISION IN ACTION
BY
G.R. LYONS

"There's nothing I can do for you, Red."

Henry 'Red' Stark dropped the heavy basket of laundry and tried to catch his breath as his youngest brother walked out of the room. Wiping the sweat from his brow, he shoved his red hair out of his eyes. He needed a haircut again, but there just wasn't enough time in the day.

He turned to his three other brothers, watching them play a game of cards at the dining table, the breakfast dishes still not cleared. Apparently Red would have to do that, too.

"Guys?" he asked.

His second brother shook his head. "Sorry, Red. Got plans today."

Red groaned. "We're supposed to be doing this together." They knew perfectly well the farm was failing, and the only reliable income they currently had came from the laundry services they provided for the folks in town. With their father on his death bed, it was up to Red and his brothers to keep the farm going, but he was the only one who ever wound up doing any of the work.

"Sorry, Red." His third brother tossed down his cards, shoved his chair back, and left.

The last brother followed a moment later, leaving Red alone in the messy dining room, a basket of laundry at his feet. It was just one of many that he had to wash by hand, hang out to dry, sort, fold, and deliver that day.

Assuming the horses had been fed.

Assuming the wagon was in repair.

Assuming he had the strength and the time to do it all on top of the household chores and caring for his ailing father.

But if no one was going to help him, he'd just have to do it himself.

Red sighed, hefted the basket that seemed to weigh almost as much as he did, and headed for the washroom just off the kitchen. He worked all day, skipping lunch to get it all done. He scrubbed until his hands ached, and once every load was hanging outside, he tackled the household chores, cleaning the messes in the kitchen and dining room that his brothers had left from both breakfast and lunch. Red checked on their father, gave the man his medicine and his meals, then spent the afternoon folding, sorting, and delivering the various loads to his customers, collecting money—and new loads to wash—as he went.

At the end of the day, he collapsed into bed, knowing he'd have to do it all over again tomorrow. But at least the bills would be paid.

As Red drifted off to sleep, he couldn't help thinking there had to be a better way.

†††

Red jumped out of bed early the next morning, his mind buzzing with an idea that had suddenly come to him. He tried to blink the sleep from his eyes while his body protested every inch of distance he put between himself and his bed, but he couldn't stop.

He'd studied to be an engineer, after all, before he'd had to quit school to take over the farm when his father fell ill. Surely, those lessons could help him now.

Red found a blank sheet of paper and started sketching out ideas, his hand unable to keep up with the figures and images in his mind. When he heard his brothers rise and clomp downstairs, Red snatched up his drawing and took it with him, sketching away and running calculations while he put on the coffee and started cooking the eggs.

His younger brothers all towered over him as they clamored for a place in the kitchen, fighting over coffee mugs and who's turn it was to bake the bread. Red wound up doing it all, of course. He wasn't sure if it was because he was the oldest—and therefore expected to be the most responsible—or because he was the smallest—and therefore easy to bully around; either way, he charged in and got it all done, ignoring the urge to snap back when his brothers refused to help.

"What's Henry doodling now?" one asked.

Red snatched the drawing away and started to stuff it into his pocket as he carried a platter of eggs and toast to the table, then changed his mind. If they all chipped in, he could start building his design right away. In the long run, it would save them time, so they could work on other things. Maybe even get the farm back up to its former glory.

"It's a machine to wash clothes," Red said, getting excited as he spread the drawing on the table. "If you guy can get me these things..." He rattled off some supplies he would need, writing himself notes as he went and adding things to the list as they occurred to him.

"Sorry, Red," one of his brothers said, shaking his head. "I don't have time."

Red looked at the others.

"Me neither."

"Not me."

The last also said no.

Red sighed. "Fine. I'll do it myself."

He rolled up the drawing, snatched up a piece of bread, and left the room to start on that day's orders. Once again, he scrubbed and hung, folded and delivered. He spotted his brothers either playing cards or wandering off to town for lunch, spending the hard-earned money Red had made for the farm the day before.

But he collected a few coins again that night when he made his deliveries, used them to pay their suppliers on his way back, then went home to make dinner for his brothers before ducking into the barn.

He lost track of time as he tinkered and fussed and tried to make his idea a reality. With barely any progress made, he finally had to drag himself to bed, knowing he'd be useless the next day if he didn't get to sleep soon.

The next morning, he got up and did it all over again. And the next day. And the next. Every night, he'd sneak away to have an hour alone, going over his design and trying to bring it to life, but there was only so much he could do on his own. The motor came together, but the body of the machine was physically beyond him. He needed someone stronger to lift and assemble all the pieces.

So he asked his brothers.

"Nope, sorry, Red," the biggest of them said. "Can't help you."

"Not me."

"Me neither."

Red sighed. "Fine." He shook his head, trying to work out the problem. "I guess I'll figure it out myself."

†††

Red trudged out to the barn after dinner, just as he'd done every night for weeks. He covered a yawn, then rubbed his eyes and shook his head, trying to keep himself awake. It was all he could do to keep up with the orders and the chores, but his invention was finally coming together, and he knew he'd never get to sleep if he didn't make at least some progress on it that night.

Using the new pulley system that he'd designed and installed in the barn, Red lifted the heavy pieces that would make up the body of the machine and maneuvered them into place. He got as much assembled as he could, then finally called it a night. The next day, he assembled a bit more, and continued for an hour each night after that until the whole thing was finally complete.

All that remained was to run a final test.

Red plugged in the machine, threw in some of his own clothes, added some cleaning agents, and turned it on.

The motor fired up, and the machine came to life.

Red threw his arms up in triumph. He'd done it! Granted, the whole thing was cobbled together from scraps, found objects, and reclaimed mechanical and electronic parts, but he'd done it.

When the machine finished its cycle, Red pulled out the damp clothes and inspected them. All the dirt stains were gone.

"Ha!" Red shouted with glee. It worked!

He went to bed with a smile on his face and got up the next morning with more energy than he'd felt in months. Even his brothers' impatient demands for food couldn't get him down. Red made breakfast, then left his brothers to their own devices as he hauled that day's laundry orders out to the barn.

Red tossed in the first load and let the machine run, then went back to the house and cleaned up the mess in the kitchen. He darted back out to the barn, pulled out the clothes to hang, and tossed in the next. While that load ran, Red got his father's medications and meals prepared. And while the third load ran, he found time to weed and till the kitchen garden for the first time in years. Maybe they could at least get that growing again rather than having to run to the market for vegetables and herbs.

By the time the last load had been hung up to dry, Red had all the household chores done as well.

He looked at the clock. *Good gods.* He still had half a day left, yet his *To-Do* list was complete.

The same thing happened the next day. All the laundry orders and chores were done by lunch, leaving Red all afternoon with nothing pressing to do.

Definitely time to start getting the farm back in shape.

"Hey, guys," he called to his brothers as he brought lunch to the table. "What do you say we get the south field turned? It's the right time of year for planting."

The second oldest brother shook his head. "Sorry, Red. Can't help you."

"Me neither," another said.

The other two said the same.

Red sighed. "Fine. I'll do it myself."

†††

Red finished planting the south field, then raced back to the barn to gather that day's orders. Making sure everything was properly folded and sorted, he loaded it all up in the wagon and hauled it all back to town, delivering the orders and collecting coins along the way.

And many of his customers were paying more, now. He hadn't asked them to do so, but they'd noticed that their clothes and linens were coming back cleaner than ever and offered him tips in thanks. Red smiled, feeling the weight of all those coins in the purse tied to his belt. Slowly but surely, the farm was coming back together, and he was using some of that extra money to improve his machine, buying better parts and redesigning the whole thing so that it was quieter, more thorough, and faster.

When he returned home and got the horses taken care of, he noticed a strange man idling about near the barn. Red frowned. He kept the barn doors locked so no one could get in and steal any of their equipment—including his washing machine—but the sight of a stranger on his property still made him uneasy.

Where were his brothers? Why weren't they keeping an eye on things?

"Can I help you?" Red called.

The man brightened and strode over, extending a hand. "Hello. My name is George Westin."

"Mr. Westin," Red said, shaking the man's hand. "I'm Red– I mean, Henry Stark. What can I do for you?"

Clutching his hat in his hands, Mr. Westin asked, "I was wondering if I could buy one of your machines."

Red frowned, puzzled. Almost all of his farm equipment was in disrepair. Hardly worth selling. Though, he had come across other farmers in the past who were willing to buy anything and fix it up, when they were desperate. Besides, he was going to need all that equipment once he got it up and running. There was nothing he could spare.

"I'm sorry," he said, "but I'm going to need the tractor as soon as it's running again, and the–"

"Oh, no," Mr. Westin interrupted him, shaking his head. "I apologize. I should have been more specific. I'm not here for farm equipment." He paused, then said, "I was hoping to buy one of your washing contraptions."

Red blinked. "I beg your pardon?"

"I heard you had developed some sort of machine to wash clothes, and I was hoping to buy one, to install for my wife."

Red stared at the man, thoughts and plans spiraling out of control in his mind even as he shook his head. "I only have the one."

"Oh." Mr. Westin's smile faded. "Shame. I heard about your machine from three towns away, and everyone's eager to have one."

Red glanced at the barn, a smile slowly taking over his face as plans and possibilities bombarded his thoughts, demanding his attention. Could he build more of them? Sell them? It would eliminate his own laundry service there at the farm, but if there really was a demand for such things, he could build more of the machines and go around selling them. If he could make them smaller, better, and cheaper, he could probably even travel around and sell them in other towns and make money that way rather than doing the laundry services himself. For all he knew, there was need of the machine across the whole of the land.

The possibilities were endless.

Red considered the coins in his purse, then looked at his visitor.

"Tell you what," he said, and saw Mr. Westin perk up. "I'll build you a machine. It might take a few weeks, but I can do it." He paused, mentally calculating the cost of the materials he was going to need and the time to assemble it. "It'll cost you about five hundred."

The man didn't even blink. "If it gets the job done and frees up more of my wife's day so she can spend more time with the grandkids, it'll be worth it." Beaming, the man shot out a hand again, and Red shook it. "You have a deal, Mr. Stark."

Grinning from ear to ear, Red bid his visitor a good night, then raced into the house. All his brothers were there, gathered around the dining table, and started clamoring for dinner the moment Red set foot inside.

"Guys, wait, listen," Red said, bracing his hands on the table and looking at each face in turn. "We've got a huge profit opportunity." He went on to outline his conversation with Mr. Westin, and his proposal to build another washing machine, asking for their help to do it so they could get it done faster. With all hands involved, he could have the thing built in days instead of weeks, and maybe even have more time to spread the word and seek out other orders. The faster they could build it, the better their profit, which would mean more money to pour back into the farm and the development of more machines.

"Nope, sorry, Red," his youngest brother said. "Can't help you."

"Don't got the time," the next said.

"Me neither," said the third.

Red sighed. "Alright, fine. I'll do it myself."

✝✝✝

Red stared at the check in his hand. He'd sold his first machine, and word had already spread. More people wanted them. He had no idea how he'd find the time to build them all, but if it was going to mean collecting that much money in one go, he'd just have to make it happen.

He kept asking his brothers for help, but they kept throwing excuses at him. So Red kept working, handling all the laundry orders and the household chores as well as continuing to build his machines.

Red sold another. Then another. It wasn't long before his laundry orders stopped altogether, but Red wasn't too worried. Orders for machines kept coming in, and the more he built them, the faster he got at it, saving himself time and cost and thus improving his profits. The saved time and increased income meant he could turn the profits right back into further improving his designs, as well as his manufacturing process.

Pretty soon, Red was completely out of space. His little barn couldn't handle the kind of output he was going to need to complete all the orders coming in. And that didn't even touch on the problem of having to travel farther and farther to deliver the machines to his customers.

It was time to expand.

"Guys, I need your help," he said to his brothers one morning.

"Now what?" one brother grumbled.

"I found a building the next town over," Red explained. "It'll be perfect for assembling the machines, but I can't do that and keep the farm going at the same time. I'll need you guys to either take over farm operations or come to the new factory to help me out."

One brother shook his head. "Sorry, Red. I don't have time."

"Me neither," another complained.

"Nor me," another said.

Red sighed. "Fine. I'll figure it out–"

A strangled cry sounded from upstairs. Red sprinted up to his father's bedroom, his brothers right on his heels. They all tumbled into the room and came to a stop, staring at the bed, the lone figure absolutely still.

Their father was gone.

Red felt tears spring to his eyes, not only for his father but for himself. Now it was all truly on his shoulders. He'd have to carry the family. Somehow.

They buried their father, but the old man was no sooner in the ground than Red was back to work.

"What's wrong with you?" his youngest brother asked. "Dad's dead, and you're *working*?"

"You should be grieving with us," another complained.

Red stared at them, dumbfounded. Yes, he was grieving his father—it was all he could do to drag himself out of bed in the morning, feeling the old man's absence—but that didn't mean they could just give up and stop living. There was still work to be done.

And who else was going to do it but him?

"We can't let this stuff go," Red insisted. "How are we going to eat and pay the bills if we don't get the chores and orders done?"

Another brother waved a careless hand. "You always find a way."

Red stared at him for a moment, then shook his head and walked away. He went to his bedroom, packed his few clothes, and left the house. He stopped by his father's grave, the mound of dirt still fresh, and let a few tears fall.

"I'm sorry, Father. I have to go."

He got no response, of course, but he almost thought he heard one anyway, a whisper of sound on the warm breeze that caressed his cheek. Red sniffed, gave a nod, and turned away.

Loading up his completed machines and parts into the wagon, he left the farm behind and headed off to the next town. His brothers would have to make the farm work without him. Red couldn't do it all on his own anymore.

He reached the next town, struck a deal to buy the factory, and set up shop. For several weeks, Red hardly ate, having invested all his money in buying the building, paying for utilities, setting up business licenses, and installing equipment. It got even worse when his brothers tracked him down and demanded the horses and wagon back, though Red doubted they'd actually put either to good use.

He slept right on the factory floor. A makeshift shower in one corner and a tiny kitchen in another served his needs well enough. Red spent every waking hour building his machines, trying to keep up with his orders, which kept coming in faster now that he had an established storefront of sorts.

Red tried one more time to ask his brothers for help, but again they refused.

"Fine," Red sighed, a grim look on his face. "I'll do it on my own."

†††

Red grinned as he looked down at his factory floor from the catwalk above it. His new assembly line was up and running, his workers buzzing about, getting pieces assembled. Despite his early struggles, the orders just kept coming in, spanning farther and farther out until he was shipping washing machines to other cities and counties, hundreds of miles away. With the increase in sales and the profits he made, he kept turning the money right back into the business, improving his methods and designs until he was able to make the machines lighter, cheaper, and better.

He still slept in the factory, but at least he had his own room, now. A little bit of privacy for sleeping, washing, and eating, but close enough that he could still work each day, right there to take care of any issues and assist in all aspects of design, assembly, and delivery.

"Hey, Red!" his shop foreman called.

Red waved at him and waited for the man to join him up on the catwalk.

"I just heard a rumor," the man said, "that someone else is trying to get in on the business. They're designing a machine in competition with ours."

Red grinned and shrugged.

"Aren't you worried?" his foreman asked, looking flabbergasted.

Red shook his head. "If this guy can build a better machine, he deserves to put us out of business." He paused, then added, "It's just more incentive for us to keep on top of things. We'll keep improving our designs and keep trying to find ways to build them cheaper without sacrificing quality." Red looked at the foreman. "Competition is an incentive, not something to be feared."

"If you say so, boss."

Red gave a sharp nod, and they went back to work.

†††

Red grinned as he signed the mortgage documents for his new house. His machines had been so successful that he'd been able to lower the price on them little by little each year while still making a profit. He employed dozens of people, providing a livelihood for all those families, as well as improving the lives of all his customers by providing them with a machine that would save them time and labor.

Once he had the keys to his new house, he went right back to the factory and jumped into work, keeping tabs on all the operations and solving small issues as they arose.

In between monitoring operations, he was also spending time in his R&D office. They were working on a matching machine that could dry clothes, saving families the time to hang everything and the space required to do so.

In the midst of it all, four large men walked through the front door, distracting him. Red blinked. His brothers. He hadn't so much as heard from them in years.

"Hey, guys," he greeted them, stepping away from the assembly line so they could speak.

The brothers looked around in awe, and the youngest said, "We need help, Red."

"Yeah, sure," Red said. "What's going on? How's the farm?"

Another brother grimaced. "The farm's all washed up. No crops. All the equipment got repossessed."

Red grimaced, a pang in his chest as he realized his father's legacy had come to an end. "I'm so sorry."

The third brother looked at him imploringly. "Can you give us some money? We're about to lose the house, and we don't have anywhere else to go."

Red stared at them. They wanted him to just give them some money? After all those years that he did all the work without their help?

"Tell you what," he suggested, "I'm constantly expanding operations here, and could always use more workers. What if I hire you guys to work the assembly line, and that way you can have steady employment and a regular paycheck? I'm sure that, all together, you guys could easily afford a house in this area."

His brothers all shook their heads, the youngest one scoffing.

"You want us to *work*?"

Red blinked. "Yeah…"

"Come on, Red," another brother said. "You're doing so well. Surely you can spare some money."

Red stared at them again. "You don't want to work?"

All three shook their heads.

"You want me to just give you some money, for nothing?"

"Well…yeah," one brother said, as though it should be obvious.

"In that case…" Red shrugged. "There's nothing I can do for you."

For more information about how to support the Agorist Writers' Workshop or contributing authors, please visit:

www.agoristwritersworkshop.com

ABOUT THE CONTRIBUTORS

Jon Garett is co-creator of *The Adventures of Seamus Tripp* and author of *Willy Wise's Garden*. He is a founding member of the Agorist Writers' Workshop and partner in Very Good Books.

He lives and writes in Minnesota with his inspirations: three cats and his wife. He spends his non-writing time hiking and camping and hoping that through his literary enterprises he can entertain and inform a new audience about the world of voluntarism.

A lover of the convergence between art and the written word, **Genesis Mickel** is co-creator of the Agorist Writers' Workshop. She hopes the project inspires and sparks a thousand flames of liberty in an audience ready for a new, yet timeless, message of freedom. Her first loves include her talented muse of a husband and the sunshine of her life - her young daughter, as well as enjoying backyard forays into nature, birdwatching, and hobby farming, presently including several chickens, several thousand honeybees, and plenty of dreams to do more.

Matthew Lewis is a thoughtful artist who aspires to excellence and embodying beauty in everything he makes. He loves tea, airships, the idea of turtles, red pandas, and all things beautiful. He can be consulted at elyonai7@gmail.com. View his other work at lefein.artstation.com

Karen Ovér is currently living and writing in New York City, after fifteen years in Austin, Texas. Her work has appeared in Collective Fallout, Sweater Weather, Sci Phi Journal, and is available at Amazon.com and
balletsandbogeys.weebly.com/golemwerks

When not in the midst of negotiating with the cat for desk space, she can sometimes be found clinging to a ballet barre, attempting to realign the vertebrae sent in all directions by hours of maniacal word processing.

Allen Baird PhD is a writer, trainer and speaker from Northern Ireland. Along with his wife Dawn, he runs Sensei, a communications consultancy. Allen's first published book was a work of faction called The First Jedi. He's currently looking to collaborate with an American publisher on The Adventures of Alice the Entrepreneur, a series of short stories for children promoting a free market and the spirit of independence. Allen's Twitter name is @thesensei.

Lynne Lumsden Green has twin bachelor degrees in both Science and the Arts, giving her the balance between rationality and creativity. She spent fifteen years as the Science Queen for HarperCollins Voyager Online. These days, she captains the Writing Race for the Australian Writers Marketplace on Facebook. You can find her blog at:
https://cogpunksteamscribe.wordpress.com/

Robina Rader has taught high school French and English, and spent twenty years as a reference librarian. She is now focusing on creative writing. She lives in State College, Pennsylvania.

N.B. Williams writes about fact, fantasy, and the realms between. A journalist and content writer by day, she moonlights as an author of twisted tales designed to make people question her mental health, which they do. Often. In between penning novels and churning out short stories, she wrangles bees in the Texas Hill Country and cares for a growing number of pets, all of whom consider her work too scary to read. She's currently working on a novel about Viking vampires and is toying with the idea of getting out of her pajamas one day soon. Maybe...

Keturah Lamb is a young woman learning how to both live in and embrace God's reality. The written and verbal words help this process. She likes to call herself a realistic idealist. She has many passions in life, the first being her ideas concerning friendship {love}, the second being laughter {smile}. She resides in Montana, cleaning houses as her mind dances through story plots.

Motivated by his lifelong love of reading, **John M. Olsen** writes about ordinary people doing extraordinary things and hopes to entertain and inspire others. His father's library started him on this journey as a teenager, and he now owns and expands that library to pass his passion on to the next generation of avid readers.

He loves to create things, whether writing novels or short stories or working in his secret lair equipped with dangerous power tools. In all cases, he applies engineering principles and processes to the task at hand, often in unpredictable ways. He usually prefers "Renaissance Man" to "Mad Scientist" as a goal and aesthetic.

Catulle Mendès (1841-1909), a French writer of Portuguese descent, was allied with Parnassian poets who advocated restraint and technical perfection in writing, using fantastic tales to criticize bourgeois values. Mendès wrote prolifically, producing among other works a number of original and reworked fairy tales aimed at a Decadent adult readership. 'Les Larmes sur l'épée' ('Tears on the Sword') was first published in 1885.

Patricia Worth has translated stories from the 19th and 21st centuries, including George Sand's *Spiridion,* published by SUNY Press in 2015. Shorter translations, including other Catulle Mendès stories, have been published in Australian, New Caledonian and US literary journals, among them *Southerly Journal, Sillages d'Océanie 2014, The Brooklyn Rail* and *Peacock Journal.*

Justine Johnston Hemmestad is a writer and a Master's Degree student in Literature through NAU. She is the mother of seven children and author of several books and short stories (including an essay in *Chicken Soup for the Soul: Recovering from Traumatic Brain Injuries,* all available on Amazon.

Christa Conklin is the home educator of her two children. She graduated cum laude from Rutgers College, studied in France, received her Master's Degree from Monmouth University, and once took first place in a solo women's kayak river race.

She worked for the New York Philharmonic and Young Audiences New Jersey and is currently an instrumental instructor at a music school in her hometown.

Christa Conklin's short story, *Moontail,* was published in *The*

Clarion Call Vol. 3: Unbound. She is represented by Golden Wheat Literary. Her debut novel, *Tranquility*, is being released this fall by Elk Lake Publishing, Inc.

Jakob Morris is a starving artist working out how exactly to make money out of writing words, while also working on a comic book rendition of *Necromancer*.

Skian McGuire is a 60-year-old blue collar guy in Western Massachusetts.

Christine Cassello was born in Chicago, IL on February 14, 1946. She still lives in the neighborhood she grew up in, at the border of South Shore and South Chicago. She has written since early childhood. THE HUNTER AND THE DEER is her first eBook. It is a collection of stories told in rhyme. Her second book THE SALTY PRINCE contains more story poems. She also has an eBook picture book TYLER AND THE ATOMIC COLD.

Justin Fowler has one foot set in the future, and one in the distant past, what with his avid thirst for ancient history and his associate's degree in web design and digital multimedia, and all. A voluntaryist with Anabaptist leanings who advocates for the abolition of the state, he believes that the march of freedom down through the eons comes through the vein of seeing the innocence of the victim of history as revealed by Yeshua Mashiach. He is co-founder of Altar & Throne, a Christian libertarian site, and The Wondering Pilgrims, a Youtube broadcast with open-ended theological and philosophical dialogue. Also, he'll do up your website if you exchange something valuable in return, at www.justinfowlerdesign.com.

Lela Markham is an Alaska-based novelist of speculative fiction and blogger of radical ideas. When she's not wearing out keyboards, she's having adventures under the midnight sun somewhere just south of the Arctic Circle.

DonnaRae Menard is a resident of Vermont and New Hampshire who spends her days looking for new places to hide the bodies of her victims for her mystery novels. She's the nosy lady on the street asking 'what is this'? She enjoys the outdoors, reading, sewing, and good coffee.

Jackie Ferris is a woman of many reincarnations. Currently a writer but by trade a PhD in psychiatry. She has developed numerous community health projects around Europe and also written many mental health articles and teaching manuals.

More recently she has published short stories and hopefully will have her first novel coming out next year.

Jackie's first passion is writing but she loves history and travelling and mostly enjoys watching the past unfurl hidden mysteries and the future reveal paths we never expected to take.

Marie Anderson lives near Chicago. After completing two years at The University of Chicago Law School, she escaped without a law degree, married, raised three children, and worked in schools and offices. Her stories (39) have appeared in 25 publications, including *LampLight* and *Brain Child*. She heads her library's writing critique group, now in its 10th year. She has two books available, "What Good Moms Do and Other Stories," a collection of some of her previously published stories, and "The Wrong Coat," a themed multi-author anthology which she edited. In her daily life, she strives for tidiness, timeliness, and simplicity.

Andrew Bundy is an English teacher in Western Pennsylvania. He has been published in Suspense Magazine along with various local news outlets. He is also the primary writer for a regional theater group and has ghost-written doctoral dissertations and created marketing materials for several organizations.

Alexandra Faye Carcich is a long-time hobby writer with a passion for myth retellings. Her obsession with authenticity has led her through the Black Forest, to plague stricken London, and on Napoleon's invasion of Jaffa. Her writing inspirations are Peter Beagel, Neil Gaiman, Maggie Stiefvater, Fydor Dostoyevsky, and Samuel Clemens. Recently her writing was featured in Timeless Tales Magazine, Ariel Chart, and Enchanted Conversations. When she is not writing, Alexandra works at a bakery, and shares her baking experiments with her husband and siblings. She enjoys gardening, painting, and teaching the Argentine Tango on occasion.

Cameron Metrejean is a Louisiana native who has been writing since he was 13. Starting off with poetry, Cameron eventually went on to writing short stories, scripts, plays, as well as a trilogy of Fanfiction stories under the name Joe 'Po' Navark. In 2014 he graduated from Northwestern State University where he majored in Theatre having performed in shows such as *Hairspray* and *Westside Story*. When not acting in local films and stage shows Cameron spends his time writing film critiques. Armed with Asperger Syndrome and a love for movies, Cameron enjoys giving his own thoughts and ruminations on cinema and other mediums. Cameron lives in Lafayette, Louisiana.

Ronel Janse van Vuuren is the author of New Adult, Young Adult and children's fiction filled with mythology and folklore. Her dark fantasy stories can be read for free on Wattpad and on her blog *Ronel the Mythmaker*. She won *Fiction Writer of the Year 2016* for her Afrikaans stories on INK: Skryf in Afrikaans. Her published works can be viewed on Goodreads.

Ronel can be found tweeting about writing and other things that interest her, arguing with her characters, researching folklore for her newest story or playing with her Rottweilers when she's not actually writing.

All of her books are available for purchase on Amazon.

Billie Holladay Skelley, a retired cardiovascular and thoracic surgery clinical nurse specialist, earned her bachelor's and master's degrees at the University of Wisconsin-Madison. A mother of four and grandmother of two, she lives in Missouri with her husband and two cats. Crossing several different genres, her writing has appeared in various journals, magazines, and anthologies in print and online—ranging from the *American Journal of Nursing* and *Harvard Magazine* to the *Haiku Journal* and the *American Aviation Historical Society Journal*. An award-winning author, she also has written books for children and teens. Billie spends her non-writing time reading, gardening, and traveling. Connect with Billie at www.bhskelley.com.

Cara Schulz lives in the Minneapolis area with her husband and tyrannical cat, Mabel. She enjoys camping, red wine, and rainy afternoons.

Blake Jessop is a Canadian author of speculative fiction with a master's degree in creative writing from the University of Adelaide. He makes his bones as a writer, lecturer, poet and bouncer. Check out more of his work on Amazon.com or follow him on twitter @everydayjisei.

G.R. Lyons is the author of several fantasy/sci-fi/paranormal and m/m romance novels set in his fictional world of the Shifting Isles. While daylighting as office manager for the family auto repair business, G.R. Lyons can often be found working on one of multiple manuscripts or desperately trying to keep up with the TBR pile.

If you enjoyed **FairyTale Riot,** you can find more stories of freedom and voluntary action in **The Clarion Call, Vol 3: Unbound**, such as:

TALONFIRE AND THE TAX AVADER
BY
BOB MILLER

This is a true story. I know 'cause I'm telling it.

Here in the People's Quingdom of Bern everybody's an equal, from the Twisted Horn Unicorns to the Flatulant Fairies in the Farthing Woods to the Dire Wolves crossing the borders. It's a perfect place except for one thing: we got problems.

When there's a problem, that's when I fly into action.

The name's Talonfire.

I'm a Griffin for hire.

It was the second Whigday in the month of Fructidor. I was at the Vet's office, a small barn with a handful of stalls. It was all Doc Mann could afford, but it was all right. He was subsidized by the Quingdom. (For those of you in Mushroom Meadows, a Quingdom is run by *either* a Queen or King. So it's "Quing." We don't discriminate gender here.)

The doc was about to give me my booster shot when there came a knock on the door. Peg, the receptionist, went to answer it. The door busted open on its own. Peg squealed—for what else would a pig do if someone busted into their barn?

A gorilla and a chicken stood outside in the drizzle, sharing an umbrella. "It's all right, ma'am," the gorilla said. "We're from the Department of Revenue Enhancement." They flashed their signet rings to prove it.

"What do you want?" Peg asked, still a little shaken. But it was all right, they were from the government. The gorilla was male and the chicken was female. They weren't the same species so they were properly diversified.

"We're looking for Talonfire. We want to see him, please," the chicken clucked.

Peg gave an oink. "In a minute. Doctor Mann is busy with him."

She gave everyone ear plugs. Everyone but me, that is. She knew what was going to happen.

"Let's get it over with," I said to the doc. I squeezed my eyes and bit my beak. Then came a jab hotter than dragonfire. "Ee-yaaaaahhhh-ha-haaaaaaaaaa!" My screech probably carried all the way to Mushroom Meadows. Blasted chemicals, roasting my innards. But the government said I needed them for my own good. That's what you get when you're an endangered species.

"You'll be fine now," Mann said.

"Says you. My butt's sore as all get-out."

Doc Mann laughed at this. Yeah. Ha-ha. Chuckle.

So I trotted over to the gorilla and the chicken, who were warming themselves by the heater, and I asked, "How'd you know I was here?"

"It is our business to know," the gorilla grunted.

"The Right to Be Nosy and Blame the Previous Administration Act," the chicken said.

Yeah, I knew that. The Quingdom of Bern knows all about privacy, all hail to them.

"So what's the problem?"

"We have a 401. Condition Red," the chicken said.

"A 401? That's pretty serious," I said, which made me ask, "Why can't you handle it? Why do you need me?" Not that I was complaining. I needed the cash.

(You people in Mushroom Meadows be patient. I'll tell you what a 401 is in a little bit.)

"Mr. Talonfire, the 401 is in Ohn Santone," the chicken said plainly.

Ohn Santone. That explained it.

"Pretty dangerous place. You must think I'm expendable," I said.

The gorilla sounded like he had culture. "We know your reputation. You know how to deal with lupin carnivorans."

"Wolves, you mean?"

The chicken popped her eyes wide. "No, no-no-no-no," she clucked, flapping her wings. "They are lupin carnivorans. That's what they're calling themselves now."

"So what? A rose by any other name is still a rose."

"I'd advise you to be more sensitive, Mr. Talonfire. You don't want to be an unmutual phobic deplorable, now, do you?"

"Perish the thought," I said, rubbing the spot where the needle went in. "They can call themselves whatever they like." I didn't argue. I'm the client and I'll do what I'm told. Besides, I didn't want to be an unmutual phobic deplorable.

"Good," Chicken clucked. "Now, I trust we can count on your help?" She made it sound more like a demand than a request.

"Sure, as long as you pay my usual fee. I'll also need a signet ring and a lupin carnivoran relief bundle." I was already conjuring up my strategy.

"Agreed," Chicken said. I gave her a clay invoice pad and she scratched her signature on it, while Gorilla slipped a signet ring on my claw, a perfect fit.

"Doc, you got any Eau de Appetite Number 5 on you?" I asked.

Doc checked his shelves, lined with boxes and bottles and jars filled with liquids and pills and all kinds of concoctions. A fully-stocked Vet. We've been friends for years, and he keeps me healthy. Good ol' Doc Mann. If you get chomped on or mauled, drop by his office in Compton Corners. He's a good one to patch you up.

He gave me a can of Eau de Appetite which I stuffed in my satchel. "Thanks, Doc. Put it on my bill."

Chicken showed me a clay tab with the address:

298 N. BeHappy St., Ohn Santone, Biscane Prov

I memorized it easy. We Griffins have total recall.

Then I said my goodbyes and took off for the Bern Nourishment Distribution Center over on Fairness Lane. Kind of lousy weather to fly in. Overcast sky, drizzle, cold breeze. Typical fall day in these parts. I can handle it, of course. My feathers are waterproof and my mane is quilted warm. I'm an all-weather Griff.

I arrived at the Distribution Center. There was a long line of people standing in the drizzle, waiting to get their allotments. No problem for me. I flew over them and my signet ring got me in. In a land of equals, some can be more equal than others. Besides, this was an emergency.

So I did the paperwork routine, grabbed the relief package and winged my way over to Ohn Santone, a good 20-minute flight 'cause it was in the province next door.

Yes, I deliver packages, anywhere. I'll do whatever it takes to fill my belly, pay the Vet, tithe to church and pay my taxes. So the next time you need air mail special delivery, hire me. Go Griffin.

The sky was clear by the time I got to Ohn Santone. Humans used to live there. Actually, some still do. What happened was the Quingdom of Bern, in its infinite wisdom, declared it to be a haven for wolves—I mean, the lupin carnivorans. When the lupin carnivorans outnumbered the humans, they imposed their own rules. Nothing the humans could do about it. The carnivorans were a government-protected species. Anyone who didn't like it, left. Now the lupin carnivorans are running the place.

But in the Quingdom of Bern, even the lupin carnivorans have to pay tax.

One fellow had problems with that. It's why we now had a Code 401 situation going on.

OK, you people from Mushroom Meadows, here's what happened next.

I zeroed in on 298 N. BeHappy St. (We Griffins are good at zeroing in on things). As I expected, the place was surrounded by lupins, some carrying signs that read, "Lupin lives count." They were yipping and howling at two horses at the doorstep of a one-story home, one a black stallion, the other a white mare. They were cops, judging from the silver badges on their pointed hats. They assumed martial arts postures, hooves ready to chop. They had no guns, of course. This was a weapons-free zone.

A good thing I came along and just in time. I gave a loud whistle, which caught the attention of the lupins. I dangled the benefits package above their heads. Their noses sniffed and their tongues hung down and they wagged their tails. They knew what it was: Nom noms. Food.

I backflapped to a couple blocks away, the lupin pack

following along. I dropped the bundle. It hit the street and the meat went flying. The scene turned into a frenzy of gnashing teeth and wiggling tails.

Back I flew to the house, where the cops dropped to all four hooves and did a happy prance.

"That should keep 'em busy for a few minutes," I chirped as I landed on all fours and folded my wings. "You all right?"

"Yes, thanks to you," the stallion said, and his mare partner nodded vigorously.

"Talonfire, Griffin for Hire. Been deputized to help out." I flashed my signet ring to show I was legit. "I understand we're in a 401."

"That's right. He doesn't want to pay his taxes," the stallion said.

Cue dramatic music.

"He's barricaded himself and he's armed," the mare said.

I cocked my head. "I thought this was a no-weapons zone."

"It is. Since when do criminals follow the law?" The stallion snorted.

"Right. So how is he armed?"

"With his breath. He's a HuffenPuffer," the mare said. "Name's HuffenPuff."

"Oh, so he's a wolf," I said.

"Nay," Stallion said. "A lupin carnivoran."

"Oh. Right. Sorry. Don't want to be an unmutual phobic deplorable."

"We'll overlook it this time."

"So you want me to bust him out of there, is that it?"

"Nay!" said the stallion. "You try and he'll huff and puff and blow the house up. The fallout would contaminate the whole town and we'd have to evacuate everyone."

"That's right. The walls have asbestos. It would pollute the air," the mare said. "The Environmental Defense Agency would be furious."

"And it would lower Hizzer Majesty's approval rating," the stallion said. "We can't let that happen. Our jobs are on the line."

"Then what are we supposed to do? Sweet-talk him out of it?"

"That *is* government policy," Stallion said....

Continued in The Clarion Call, Vol 3: Unbound

Made in the USA
Middletown, DE
13 April 2019